Praise for Tasmina Perry

*'Gripping from the off: sexy, scandalous brilliance, this book is a genuine must-read *****'* – Heat

'Takes you to the most glamorous corners of the globe while keeping you on the edge of your seat' – Glamour

'A gripping, pacy read with a few dark twists I did not see coming. The perfect end-of-summer novel' – Daily Mail

'Well-drawn characters and a twisty plot make this page-turner a must-read' – Good Housekeeping

'Excellent . . . A dark and devious thriller but with all the glamour you'd expect from Tasmina' – Red

'A book to cancel plans for – we were completely gripped' – Closer

About The Author

Tasmina Perry is a *Sunday Times* bestselling novelist. Her books have been translated into twenty languages and have sold over two million copies worldwide.

A former lawyer and award-winning magazine journalist, she has edited several national titles including InStyle UK and More.

She also writes psychological thrillers under the pseudonym JL Butler. JL Butler's debut thriller 'Mine' has been optioned by Sony Pictures for development with Original Film.

Tasmina is the founder of Sunflower & Co, a female-focused media company. The team plots escapist stories and creates content from their boathouse office by the River Thames.

This edition published by Sunflower & Co 2022

ISBN 978-1-911297-34-5

* * *

www.tasminaperry.com

facebook.com/officialtasminaperry

instagram.com/tasminaperry

If you'd like to be kept up to date on all the new releases from Tasmina Perry, why not join my VIP Book Club for news on books, giveaways, events and other book recommendations.
www.tasminaperry.com/joinbookclub

The Last Supper

A Lara Stone Mystery

Tasmina Perry

Prologue

He came out of the forest roaring in pain and anger. His beard and shirt were spattered with blood, his hair white with snow. Wiping a frozen hand across his mouth, he spat, the red streak immediately erased by the swirling storm.

'Why can't they leave me *alone*?' he bellowed into the wind. Eyes always watching him, hands clawing at him, dragging him down like wolves on an elk. 'Not any more,' he said through his teeth. Not after tonight.

Staggering up onto the path, he turned in a circle, trying to get his bearings. Over the past six years, Viggo Widlund had walked every inch of these woods: hunting, tracking and foraging, until he felt he knew every grain on every tree, but this storm was brutal. It had come from nowhere, the sub-zero wind coming straight across the lake, carrying the snow in blinding gusts, spinning him around until he didn't know which way was up. This had been his forest, his home, but now he feared he was lost.

No, there: to his left, the glowing outline of the Lodge, then just as quickly it was gone, like a curtain dropping on a stage. He wavered for a second, tempted by the warmth of the kitchen where right now there must be a party revving up: Stuart's champagne, Michel's eau de vie, there'd be war chants and singing. That was the tradition on the last night of the season, one earth-shaking blow-out to send the staff flying back to their homes for the festivities.

But first he had somewhere else to be. Viggo bent against the wind, head down, skin stinging as he pushed on, eyes barely slits. *Where is it?* Had he taken the wrong path? Suddenly anxious, he felt in his pocket, big hand clutching at the smooth stone he kept there, stroking it between thumb and finger. Viggo had similar pebbles in every pocket, soothed by their gentle, unchanging shape.

And then he saw it, humped against the dark wall of the forest, the frosted windows lit from within. The root cellar was little more than a cave, a room dug into the earth with only a brick façade to mark the entrance. He tramped up to the single door and dragged it open, almost falling inside.

'Hello?' he called, eyes screwed against the sudden light of a lantern. And a silhouette, familiar and stark.

'You came.'

Viggo wiped his nose and unzipped his parka.

'You didn't give me much choice, did you?'

'We needed to talk...properly.'

He shook his head, droplets falling in the orange glow.

'It's over,' he said. 'I thought I made that clear.'

The figure moved closer, sending jagged shadows skittering across the walls.

'It's over when I say it's over.'

And behind them, the door slammed shut.

Chapter 1

'Is that it?' said Lara, her breath fogging the aeroplane window.

'Well, I hope it's still Sweden,' said Alex from the seat beside her. 'Otherwise we've taken a considerable detour.'

Lara peered down. There was snow in every direction, as far as the glittering horizon. They had spent most of the 90-minute flight north from Stockholm with a frozen ocean beneath them, only a rash of sagging trees and the occasional dark scar of a high peak to break up the endless sheet of white. There were lakes and rivers down there, but in December, they were invisible, only due to reappear with the spring thaw in March at the earliest. Just one of the many fascinating facts about northern Sweden Alex had read out from the in-flight magazine he'd found in the seat-back pouch. Lara leant closer to the window and saw a tiny clutch of flat buildings as the plane dipped its wings and angled in that direction. Kiruna airport, she assumed. It wasn't much, but at least it was civilisation. She was beginning to think they were flying off the edge of the world, like sailors voyaging beyond the limits of the map. *Here be monsters.*

'I think I can see the terminal building,' said Lara, leaning closer. Although it was lunchtime, dark was already gathering outside, a soft, grey twilight that reminded Lara that in this part of the world, the winter days were so short they barely had any light at all. 'But where's the runway?'

'Anywhere there are no trees,' said Alex with a hint of amusement in his voice.

Lara wasn't sure why she was so jumpy. She was an experienced traveller, having spent the last decade as chief investigative reporter on London's respected broadsheet, the *Chronicle*. Lara Stone had flown into warzones, jungles and narco-controlled villages, but she couldn't remember ever landing anywhere without an actual runway. Just then, there was a jolt, and Lara's hand flew out and grasped Alex's fingers.

'It's fine,' he smiled. Alex was unflappable, solid. Handsome. Very handsome, in fact. She let go, annoyed at herself for noticing. Still, nothing seemed to faze Alex Ford. As Deputy Editor of the *Chronicle*, glacial calm was part of the job description. Bombings, scandals, royal babies, his newsroom was in a perpetual state of crisis, and Alex was always there, the steady hand on the tiller, steering the paper through the dark waters of world events. For a long time, Lara had been right there with him because she had loved that high-octane lifestyle too– excitement, action, hitting the ground running – but six months ago, something had changed. Her best friend Sandrine had been murdered, and when Lara had investigated Sandrine's death, she had almost lost her life too. Shaken and disenchanted, Lara had handed her notice in at the *Chronicle* and taken a freelance role, which was just as intense and demanding. The only difference was that she usually did the work in her pyjamas. Had Lara been keeping busy to stave off her pain? Perhaps. But she had some experience with grief, and she didn't believe you could avoid it. You had to push through the middle.

Lara jerked back in her seat as the plane touched down. She let out a long breath and uncurled her fingers from the seat arms as the passengers stood up and started grabbing their bags. That was one advantage of being 150 kilometres inside the Arctic Circle: the flight wasn't busy, plus the plane could taxi right up to the terminal. She watched people shrugging into giant padded parkas with fur-trimmed hoods, a reminder that all that snow out there was real. For the past hour, the pine and spruce passing below had just seemed set-dressing, a 3D Christmas card scene. Now they were going to have to walk into it – minus 15, or so the weather forecast had said that morning.

There was no air bridge, just a flight of stairs that led to the tarmac, and as the plane door opened, the frigid air hit Lara with a shock.

'It's parky, isn't it?' said Alex, his breath coming out in a cloud as they walked across to the terminal. He zipped up his coat – bulky, utilitarian – trust him to have the right kit. Before climbing the ladder to deputy of the *Chronicle*, Alex had been a dashing foreign correspondent, tearing through shell craters in the back of a jeep. Even now, the passport he was handing over to the bored-looking Swedish woman on security was filled with exotic stamps and visas. Back in the mists of time, Lara had sometimes joined Alex on those crazy jaunts, but not for a long time. Relationships, work, life, it all got in the way, didn't it?

She watched Alex smile at the security officer, who seemed to be sitting up straighter and taking her time looking him over. 'Business or pleasure?' she asked.

'Pleasure,' smiled Alex, pushing his dark hair from his eyes.

Oh please, thought Lara.

'We're off to Kluven,' said Alex. 'Last supper of the season.'

'Ah, Viggo Widlund, our famous chef,' said the guard, her interest in Alex moving up another notch. Kluven was one of the most exclusive gourmand destinations in Europe, and Viggo Widlund was an almost mythical figure in the foodie world, plus there were only twelve seats at the communal table. You had to be wealthy or connected to eat at Kluven, usually both.

'Enjoy your meal,' she said, slowly handing back his passport. 'I hear it's delicious.'

As they walked out into the tiny arrivals hall, Lara glanced over to her friend.

'I hear it's delicious,' said Lara teasingly. 'I think she wanted to eat *you*.'

Alex slung his overnight bag over his shoulder.

'Do you think?' he said, clearly pleased. 'I just thought she was being friendly.'

'Check your passport; she's probably written her phone number inside.'

Dragging her wheelie case, Lara walked out of the airport into the snow, hissing at the cold. The 'Welcome to Kiruna' sign on the outside wall was half-obscured by a stark beam of wind-blown snow. Across the road, beyond a chain-link fence, were a team of barking, snapping husky dogs strapped to an actual sledge, like an Arctic taxi rank. Maybe they *had* slipped off the edge of the map.

'Miss Stone?' A middle-aged man walked across wearing a green Barbour-style coat with the three-pronged fork of the Kluven logo stitched on the breast. 'I'm Johan; I'll be taking you the rest of the way to the estate. May I carry your bags?'

Lara handed over the case while Alex held up a leather

hold-all barely big enough to carry a Chihuahua. Johan was doing to best not to look surprised, but Alex noticed it.

'I travel light,' he smiled.

They both did. Packing one-upmanship was something of a sport among journos, and the game was 'who could travel the lightest?' Lara had pared down her essentials to a laptop, a multi-use scarf, an uncrushable silk dress in case she was invited to drinks at the embassy (this had rarely happened), a universal plug adaptor and some dental floss, which could double as a washing line over the bath. It sounded light, but for most 'serious' hacks, Lara's baggage was the equivalent of packing a mule train. She'd once met a gorgeous French writer in Sudan who had nothing but a toothbrush poking out of the top pocket of his elegantly-crumpled jacket. *Ah, whatever happened to Jean-Claude?*

Johan opened the back of a pristine forest green Land Rover and carefully placed their bags inside. Another advantage of the tiny airport: the car was parked right by the entrance.

'Are we the only guests?' asked Lara as Johan held open the rear door. There was only one flight in and out of Kiruna that day.

'The other arrivals have requested a private transfer,' said Johan. She glanced at Alex and knew he was thinking the same thing: the only people who demanded private limos were generally famous and definitely rich. Things were already getting interesting.

Lara clambered inside the car. She had been in Land Rovers many times before – her Uncle Nicholas, chairman of the *Chronicle's* holding company AMG, had a considerable estate in Oxfordshire where two dented Defenders were used to transport them around the grounds. But the Kluven car was unlike any Land Rover she had seen before.

Highly customised with sheepskin seats, overlaid with cashmere rugs and a drinks dispenser that contained a whiskey decanter and Kluven branded thermos flasks. Lara had winced at the cost when she had booked the trip almost twelve months earlier, but now she was starting to see where the money was going.

'Make yourselves at home,' said Johan, turning in his seat. 'Viggo's hot chocolate is in the flasks, and it's about an hour's drive to the estate.'

'An hour?'

'We're remote, but that's what makes it so special.'

They turned onto a two-lane highway with grey snow heaped at the sides, and dark ruts cut into the roadway. It didn't look as if it had been cleared for a while. As they drove, Johan told them a little about the area. The world's largest iron ore mine was close by, where some of the accommodation and living space was buried underground too.

'The miners live underground? Really?'

'Some do,' said Johan. 'Anything above ground would get buried in snow, so they built the place into a hillside with tunnels connecting the dwellings. The workers stay all winter.'

Lara stared out of the window, looking between the trees, imagining living here in the coldest months, imagining being lost in the forest, wolves surrounding her. Dark, cold, alone. Facing the darkness. She shivered, reminding herself that this was supposed to be fun, but it was hard not to feel the heavy weight of guilt. She was supposed to have come on this trip with Sandrine, a lifelong foodie, for whom visiting Kluven had been a long-standing dream. After Sandrine's murder, Lara had thrown herself into work so entirely that she had almost forgotten about the trip until two weeks ago when it had been too late to cancel. Alex had come round to her houseboat one night after work, and at some point during their second bottle of wine, she'd invited him to Kluven. *Twin room,* she'd said pointedly, not entirely expecting him to accept. Alex hardly ever went on holiday; hardly ever left the *Chronicle* office if the truth be told. But he'd said yes, noting that Sandrine would have wanted Lara to experience Kluven, even if she could not.

'You okay? Said Alex, handing her a hot chocolate. It was as if he had read her mind. Then again, Alex had also been Sandrine's friend, so this had to be a bittersweet thing for him too.

'Sure, just taking it all in.'

Lara fell into silence as she watched the Swedish north roll past. The sky bruised and glowered over frozen lakes and trackless forest; presumably, the only things moving out there would be owls and polar bears. Or did polar bears live on the ice floes? Alex would know; he'd probably be able to tell you the Latin name. *Biggus Bearus.* Lara smiled to herself, then turned back into Alex's conversation with the driver about the Winter Solstice, which was almost upon them. She listened to Johan explain the concept of polar nights when the sun never rises above the horizon, but how the sky was still streaked with pink, grey or gold, due to the reflection of the sun.

'So what can we expect tonight, Johan?' said Lara, trying to get into the mood. The hot chocolate, which tasted just like a fresh cinnamon roll straight out of the oven, had perked her up a little.

'Is it true there are thirty courses?' she asked.

'Twenty, thirty. It depends. Viggo makes his choices on the day. He has even been known to change his mind over what to serve halfway through a course. But you can guarantee it will be an experience to remember.'

'And the guests? How many are coming?'

'Twelve, as always, one table. You all eat together; it's a Viking tradition.'

Lara smiled cynically. She doubted it had much to do with Norse traditions and a lot to do with marketing. She wasn't as well versed about Kluven as Sandrine had been. Still, she knew that Viggo Widlund, Kluven's patron chef, was a mainstay of the lifestyle magazines and their interviews generally portrayed him as the archetypical chef – macho, explosive, half-mad – with all the kitchen tropes dialled up by the notion that Viggo was a Viking chief stomping through the woods hunting elk with nothing but a spear. Lara wondered how much of it was true and how much was slick marketing. *It doesn't matter*, she told herself. *Relax, enjoy yourself.* Both she and Alex suffered from the same affliction; they couldn't turn off because they saw stories everywhere.

'And we're here,' said Johan, as the car turned into a set of wide iron gates. Dense trees flanked the drive, their branches sagging with the snow. In the thin strip overhead, the pink and grey light was turning to a deep, rich blue.

'This estate started as a hunting lodge for one of the Swedish royal family,' said Johan, continuing his commentary. 'By the 1960s, it had become the estate of a reclusive aristocrat named Magnus Polson who'd spend months up here hunting elk and fishing for salmon. After his death, the house fell into ruin until Martin Svenson bought it fifteen years ago. As you'll see, the Svensons have quite transformed the place.'

'Does Martin live here full time?'

Alex used the owner's first name like they were old friends. Lara wouldn't put it past him – Alex's Rolodex was the size of a Fiat 500.

'Martin and his wife Anna lived in the lodge, but when they decided to launch a restaurant here, they had a new house built on the grounds. You should take a look; it's really something.'

At that moment, the main building appeared in the darkness, the windows glowing orange. Alex gave a low whistle. 'That's something too.'

Lara could see the royal influence; Kluven was like a rustic palace, a low, wide Alpine barn made from brick and wood with elaborate balconies, but it was immediately apparent it had been modernised. The front doors were all glass, and the steps looked like black granite. Nature may rule the forest outside, thought Lara, but on the Kluven Estate, someone was carefully tweaking the design.

'The restaurant and bar are in the lodge,' said Johan, slowing the car until she could hear the snow crunching under the wheels. 'Over there is the thermal spa. The guest cabins are to the right. I believe you are in Loganberry. It's very quiet.'

Lara got the implication but didn't think it was worth correcting. At least Johan had the good grace not to wink. He pulled up at the side of the building and took the bags inside as Alex followed. Lara stood for a moment on the steps, turning to face the indigo sky. She had expected a rash of stars, but they were hidden by a cushion of cloud. It was so calm, so quiet that Lara found herself holding her breath. She could hear nothing, not even a breath of wind, everything muted by the snow. Just then, she caught the distant shuffle of footsteps. Turning, she watched a man walking along the path – but it wasn't just any man. Craggy, striking, with long hair and a beard, he was the epitome of a Viking warrior.

'Viggo,' Lara whispered, smiling. The chef seemed to be walking with purpose, maybe heading off to pillage a monastery or something equally Norse.

As Viggo turned his head towards her, she quickly took

a step back into the foyer, instinct telling her that the chef didn't want to be seen. And it was only then that Lara saw that he had a knife in his hand.

Chapter 2

Viggo Widlund stalked up the path, his footfall barely making a sound. The ground staff used a snow-blower to keep all walkways free of anything as inconvenient as leaves or moss – God forbid a snowflake should settle on the flags. Here within the estate's grounds, it was as if Martin and Anna Svenson felt they could keep the true nature of the land at arm's length. It was one of the many things that had been annoying him lately: every tree branch trimmed, every pebble in its place. Kluven was turning into Disneyland. But some things couldn't be tamed – as his so-called partner was about to find out.

He walked on towards the house, swishing the knife through the air. It had caught his eye just as he was turning to leave the kitchen, and he had grabbed it on impulse. It wasn't an expensive knife. Some chefs were exacting about their equipment, insisting on Japanese Kyoto knives, hand-forged or folded Damascus steel; whatever was seen as 'the best' among the blade nerds, but Viggo saw everything he used in the kitchen for what it was: a tool. Look after them, keep them clean and sharp; they all did pretty much the same thing. They cut, they sliced, they crushed. A knife with a plastic handle chopped garlic the same as one with a handle made from a narwhal tusk.

But the knife in Viggo's hand was different: it was gold or had been gold-coloured at one time. Years of hard use and dishwashing had left it a vague yellow, but this particular blade had kept its symbolic value. It was the knife Martin Svenson had presented to Viggo the day Kluven opened. 'The best for the best,' Martin had grinned: Viggo could still picture his face as he said it. He suspected Martin had picked up the knife on a whim in Stockholm, but he was also pretty sure that Martin had meant what he said that day. Back then, they had been on this adventure together, both believing in what they wanted to achieve, both pushing in the same direction: making Kluven one of the most talked-about restaurants in the world. But that had been a long time ago. Viggo looked down at the faded gold, remembering how touched he'd been by the gesture. It seemed fitting that he should have the conversation he was about to have with the knife in hand.

Viggo turned the corner of the path, the Big House – Martin's house – appearing between the trees.

The Svensons' home still had the power to stop him in his tracks. A modernist shard, located just behind the main Kluven compound, Viggo always thought it looked like a Bond villain's lair, especially on days like today when it was lit from inside, golden from the floor to ceiling. To his surprise, Viggo felt a flutter of emotion in his belly. It wasn't nerves. Growing up in Malmo, Viggo had thought he might become an actor, and this knot of anticipation felt the same as when he had been about to step on his tiny school stage.

He increased his pace. Better to get this over with.

For a moment, he thought of Martin, sitting in his book-lined library, handling his empire from the computer atop a desk that had once belonged to the King of Sweden. Martin was a strategist. You didn't get to be the CEO of a conglomerate that spanned telecoms, timber and manufacturing without being a ruthless planner. Still, even the greatest generals could be wrong-footed, especially when they lost touch with the men on the ground. Either way, it didn't matter. Viggo had made his decision, and there wasn't a damn thing Martin Svenson could do about it.

An eagle flew overhead, its squawk filling the space between the forest and sky. Viggo inhaled sharply to savour it all: wood, smoke, pine, nature, the magnificence of the Kluven estate. However he was feeling today, this spot, this gap in the woods, had been a fitting setting for the things he had created here. A place at one with the land and yet its own glorious entity; Kluven was special, always had been even before Anna Svenson had got her hands on it. And the thought struck him with a peculiar sadness, that this might be the last time he walked this way. *Nothing lasts forever, does it?*

Viggo ascended the steps in front of the house and pushed through the wide oak door. It was hardly ever locked; why would it be? They were fifty miles from anywhere, and even in the unlikely event that a kitchen porter or God forbid, a guest, decided to snatch one of Martin's Picassos – he had three if you counted the pencil sketch in the downstairs bathroom – where would they go? Ride a reindeer to Norway?

The door closed behind him with a gentle hiss, and Viggo looked up at the high atrium of glass and steel, the hard lines softened by the use of light wood and stone. That was Anna's doing, of course. Martin's wife was the yin to Martin's yang, a creative with an excellent eye for design and in Kluven she had taken the concept of 'Scandi chic' to new heights. The house was sumptuous, a riot of cedarwood, glass and stone from a nearby quarry, almost a living thing in neutral colours both tasteful and rich. All the right notes were being played here. Or perhaps Viggo was more aware of it all today, now that it was all coming to an end.

He stopped in the hallway, catching sight of himself in the long mirror above the fireplace, barking out a laugh at the reflection staring back at him. *Look at you,* he thought, *a crazy man holding a knife.* It was still something of a surprise to see his reflection, even now. Craggy, deep lines on his face, wild hair and a beard. When he had first met Martin Svenson, Viggo's hair had been short, and he'd rarely even had a five o'clock shadow. But in those first frantic months launching Kluven, he'd let it grow, too busy to make it to the barbers in Kiruna. When a local journalist had come to interview them – the billionaire and the maverick dreaming of culinary greatness in the wilds of Swedish Lapland – he'd taken the beard at face value, calling Viggo 'the Viking chef'. Martin had immediately seen the possibilities of the brand. If in the public's mind Viggo was a lunatic in the woods, a magician, an alchemist who could conjure mouth-watering delicacies from the forest floor, then let then think it.

'Martin!' he shouted. 'Anna?'

He waited, hearing padding footsteps from the floor above.

'Viggo, what are you doing here?'

Martin Svenson walked down the wide stairs. Polished wood, open risers, maximum impact. Martin was not a particularly handsome man, but he was still impressive, especially for a sixty-something, tall and chiselled, his silver hair coiffed and unmoving.

'Are you planning to chop something?' said Martin with a half-smile.

'That's up to you,' said Viggo. He flipped the knife over, holding the handle towards Martin.

'What's this?'

'My knife.'

His partner hesitated, looking down at the knife, then up at Viggo. Martin Svenson was many things, but dumb he was not and right now, he was sharp enough to sense something was afoot.

'You want me to take it?'

When Viggo didn't reply, Martin shrugged and took the knife.

'Do you remember giving me that?' asked Viggo.

'Wait, is this the actual knife I gave you back when....'

Viggo nodded, suddenly enjoying the theatre of it.

Martin's face remained impassive. 'I didn't think you were the sentimental type, Viggo.'

'I still use it,' shrugged Viggo. 'Keeps a good edge. Did, anyway.'

Martin nodded, then walked through to the kitchen. Anna's design touch was evident here too. It was as if she had created it in deliberate opposition to the working kitchen in the lodge. Viggo's sterile workplace was all scrubbed white tile and stainless steel, whereas this space was sumptuous: stained oak cabinets, grey marble countertops, gold fittings. Martin carefully placed the knife on a walnut chopping board, then opened the fridge, pulling out a bottle of wine. 'Drink?' he said affably, but Viggo could tell he was covering up his discomfort. Martin didn't like being off-balance, out of control, but he would have to get used to it.

'It's over, Martin,' said Viggo, seeing no point stringing it out.

Martin kept his eyes on the glass, concentrating as he poured. 'Over?' he said, looking up. 'What's over?'

'All this,' said Viggo, gesturing with a hand. 'Kluven, the restaurant. Me.'

'Of course,' said Martin, not missing a beat. 'Tonight is the last night of the season. Take a break, recharge; we'll come back....'

'No, Martin, tonight is the last supper,' said Viggo. 'And I mean ever. After tonight's service, I am leaving Kluven, and I won't be back.'

'You're leaving?'

He said it with such composure that Viggo drew himself up to his full height and gave a tight nod. The older man put the glass down, meeting Viggo's eye directly for the first time.

'What's this all about, Viggo?'

Viggo took a moment to admire Martin's cool. Viggo was arguably the only member of staff the business could not do without, and yet Martin took it all in his stride. Not a gasp or a single raised eyebrow.

'Have you had a better offer?' he asked cooly. 'Is it Klaus Pregan at the Peninsula because I can match him if it is.'

'It's not Klaus Pregan or anyone else,' said Viggo, trying to hide his surprise. It was true that rival restauranteur Klaus had tried to poach Viggo from Kluven about a year earlier, but he'd had no idea Martin had that intel. 'I'm not going to another restaurant,' he said. 'And no, I'm not setting up a rival operation. It's typical that you would think that, Martin.'

Martin frowned.

'Then... why?'

Viggo tried to compose himself, preparing to deliver the speech he had spent the last few days composing and honing in his head.

'Martin, I am an artist. And an artist needs to keep constantly challenged. For months now, I've felt stale, bored. Kluven is no longer my passion.'

'Even if we can improve your financial compensation?'

It was just like Martin Svenson to make it all about cash. He might be good at making money, but that was where his creativity ended.

'Kluven was never about the money,' said Viggo with irritation. 'Not for me.'

It was true. When Martin Svenson had first approached him over five years ago and offered him the chance to launch a new dining concept, money had been relatively low down the list of Viggo's reasons for accepting the position.

'Well, what about another site?' said Martin. 'Somewhere nearer to Stockholm? Maybe even in the city itself. I could get one of my property team to start looking.'

Viggo had expected this. Martin had never understood Viggo's urge to narrow the distance between the land and the dining table. For him, it had just been a slogan, not a philosophy, and now that the supermarkets had so bastardised the 'farm fresh' thing, Kluven's raison d'etre had lost its meaning.

'No more sites, no more restaurants, Martin,' said Viggo firmly. 'My decision is made.'

Martin gave a soft, patronising snort.

'Really, Viggo?' he said sceptically. 'So this is it? You're just ending it, with one day's notice.'

'Martin, the new season doesn't start for another two months.'

'But reservations open on Monday, Viggo – you know that. After all this time, you could have had the courtesy to give us more than 24 hours' notice.'

When Viggo didn't respond, Martin's mouth curled in distaste.

'I made you, Viggo,' he said, his voice lowering and acquiring a touch of menace. 'I backed you, I opened my home to you, and this is how you repay me?' He shook his head in disbelief.

'Don't pretend you did me any favours, Martin,' Viggo replied. 'You loved every minute of this. The status, the glory. How many of your precious business deals were oiled over my food?'

Martin's eyes flared with anger, then Viggo saw him rein it in, taking a deep breath. Martin could be ruthless; he'd seen it plenty of times, but only when there was a strategic need. Business always came first.

'Maybe I'll move Petra up,' he said.

Viggo felt himself tense: that was a sucker punch.

'No,' he said. 'Not her.'

To think that there might be someone who could carry the flag and continue the myth was one thing, but Petra? That was an insult.

'She's been with us since the beginning,' pressed Martin.

'No.'

'She's worked side-by-side with you; she knows the recipes inside out...'

'I said NO!' Viggo snatched up the knife and slammed it, point down into the chopping board. It stood there, vibrating gently. Viggo looked up, and Martin's eyes were wide. He guessed Martin was thinking about the cost of a new board, rather than the violence, but Viggo was glad he'd finally got a genuine reaction from him.

'We have an agreement, Martin,' he said, a hint of warning in his voice. 'There is no Kluven without me.'

Martin recovered himself, raising his chin.

'I suspect my lawyers will say otherwise.'

'Lawyers,' he replied. 'Is that a threat?'

'Not a threat. Simply a matter of fact. I run a business here, Viggo. You might think of it as some sort of poetic crusade, but the reality is that we put food on plates and backsides on seats in the dining room. If you propose getting in the way of that, then I'll do whatever is necessary.'

'And so will I,' said Viggo, imagining Kluven reduced to some cut-price version of what it once was. 'You know what our contract says. Let's not make this bloody.'

He turned to leave, but Martin called after him.

'You're going to leave this all behind? The house, the kitchen, the fame? For what, Viggo? What do you want?'

Viggo turned back and spread his arms.

'Freedom,' he said simply. 'Freedom from all this.'

The other man put down his glass and shook his head slowly.

'Fine, you've made up your mind. But know this Viggo: they're not going to be happy.'

'Who?' said Viggo. 'Who's not going to be happy?'

'Everyone,' said Martin, looking over at the knife still sticking up from the kitchen side.

'Everyone's going to hate you, Viggo.'

Chapter 3

'Nice room,' said Alex, looking around their cabin with hands on his hips.

Lara rolled her eyes. 'Don't get too carried away, Mr Vegas.'

Alex tried not to react. Somehow he kept putting his foot in it with Lara. He had been going for understatement – the cabin was gorgeous, the Ralph-Lauren-does-Apres-Ski from the reception area had been carried through to the guest accommodation. Cream upholstery over fluffy sheepskin rugs lit in spreading pools of soft yellow from elegant lamps on artfully distressed furniture. It was perfect in every way, apart from the beds. They looked lovely too, with crisp linens and what looked like a polar bear fleece thrown across the foot, but it was the plural – 'beds' – which made Alex feel awkward. Not from a romantic point of view. He'd known Lara for years, from their very first day at journalism college, and while there had once been a crackle of electricity between them, right now they were firmly in the 'friend zone'. No, the difficulty was the ghost in the room: Sandrine. This twin room hadn't been booked with Alex in mind; Lara had meant this to be a girl's trip, hence the single beds. Which made him a substitute, an inadequate replacement – and he wasn't exactly sure how to play it. Was this the point where they were supposed to crack open the Prosecco?

Lara threw herself on the bed nearest the bathroom, landing on her back.

'I could get used to this,' she said, spreading her arms out like a duvet snow angel.

'Well, don't get too used to it; we've got to get back down for the drinks reception at seven.'

Lara groaned and pulled the pillow over her face.

'So bossy,' she muttered.

Smiling, Alex walked over to the window. From here, he could see across to the dining room, the lights sending a golden glow out onto the snow. The whole place was wonderful, like a visit to Santa's workshop for grown-ups. He wasn't sure how the Swedes celebrated Christmas – wasn't St. Nicholas Norwegian? – but there were plenty of concessions towards the Western European tradition: wreaths and tasteful lights strung in the trees, but then for all Alex knew, they could be there all year round.

'Fancy a quick sauna then?'

He regretted saying it as soon as the words came out of his mouth. Saunas were hot, sweaty, intimate, probably not the vibe they were after on a platonic trip.

Thankfully Lara waved a distracted hand. 'You go; I think I'll just have a snooze before dinner.'

Alex pushed his disappointment away. He had wanted this trip to be a chance to reconnect with Lara. Sandrine's death had brought them much closer together, but still, he didn't see her enough since Lara had left the *Chronicle*'s investigations team to take a more flexible 'editor-at-large' position. He missed having her in the office. Plus, he wanted Lara to have fun, something she desperately needed; perhaps he should just drag her to the sauna. But by the time Alex had changed into his swimming shorts and a Kluven robe, Lara was gently snoring.

Alex smiled affectionately and reached across, pulling a blanket over her. Lara stirred slightly, then fell back into her breathing. At the door, Alex stopped and looked down at his flimsy slippers. They weren't going to cut it in the snow, and neither was his robe. Alex pulled on his boots, then zipped his parka over the robe. It was tight, but it was better than freezing. He clumped out down the path, head down, trying to ignore the icy wind nipping at his bare legs.

'Nice boots.'

He looked up and saw a staff member smiling back at him. The guest manager – Kat, was it? – they'd met briefly at check-in. She was mid-thirties and pretty; he'd noticed that much.

'I wasn't sure the resort flip-flops were up to the weather.'

'The paths are heated,' said Kat. 'You'd have been fine with the slippers.'

'Now you tell me.'

Kat smiled; did Alex detect a flirtatious twinkle? It was hard to tell from inside her furry hood. Not that he was interested, however attractive she was. Since his almost-fiance Alicia had cheated on him a few months before, Alex had sworn off women. That was the plan, anyway.

'I'm Kat Mikaelsson. Guest Relations manager,' she said, handing him her business card. 'I assume you're heading for the thermal spa?' said Kat.

'If that's where the sauna is, yes.'

'It is, I'll show you. Would you like a tour of the resort on the way?'

It was freezing, but Alex's dad had always drilled into him the importance of being curious about the world. Terry

Ford owned a newsagent in the Lake District and would often say to his young son, 'I may only sell the papers, but I get to hear about the news before everyone else.' It was an approach that Alex had taken to its logical conclusion when choosing a career: be the one who writes the news.

'Sure, a tour would be good,' he said, stamping his feet. 'But we'd better get moving, or I'm going to lose some toes.'

She twirled a gloved finger in the air before pointing back the way she'd come.

'So what do you think so far?'

'The first person Lara saw was Viggo himself, and he was holding a knife. It was quite the welcome.'

'Ah, that does sound like Viggo,' said Kat, unfazed. 'If you get up early, I mean really early, you might catch him in the woods with an axe.'

Alex detected the ring of a well-honed soundbite. The *Chronicle* had done several pieces on the Viking Chef since Kluven had become the hot foodie destination. Viggo was a brand, and he played the role to the hilt. Alex didn't blame him. Myth-building wasn't exclusive to chefs; everyone did it to some extent, picking the stories that cast you in a positive light. Alex himself told exciting stories about his time as a foreign correspondent, dodging tracer fire and having dinner with spies at the embassy. Still, he tended to edit out all the time he'd spent sitting in stuffy halls listening to dull press conferences. The same was true of his time as Deputy Editor of the *Chronicle*. You gave people what they wanted. Everyone loved his story about getting stuck in a lift with Madonna, but no one wanted to hear that it had been the longest three minutes of his life.

'Everything all right with your cabin?' asked Kat as they walked.

'Everything's perfect. It's like a movie set.'

'They are pretty special, aren't they? Of course,

everyone focuses on Viggo's cooking, but I think Anna is equally important to Kluven's success.'

'Anna?'

'Anna Svenson, Martin Svenson's wife. They own Kluven. Anna's an extraordinary designer; she completely re-designed the complex, re-purposing the old buildings with sustainable wood, locally quarried stone and bespoke textiles. You come for the food, but you stay for the luxury.'

Alex didn't like to admit he wasn't here for the food, didn't even really enjoy high-end restaurants. As a senior member of the *Chronicle*'s executive team, he went to many expensive gourmet places, but honestly, he was happier with a fish finger sandwich. Luxury hotels, on the other hand, were addictive. Kat was right about that. The best hotels appealed to all the senses, sight, touch, taste, but most of all, they appealed to your sense of self. For one night, you could be whoever you wanted, you could step into another world – and Kluven certainly had that dialled up to ten.

Kat pointed out the staff accommodation in the former stables block and the smokery where the meat and fish were cured. She explained that most of the fish was caught locally, although a small amount of seafood, mahogany clams, mackerel and char, was brought in from Tromsø. Beef, pork and reindeer came from nearby farms; Elk, deer and moose were hunted in the forest, where abundant wildlife, including the occasional bear, roamed.

'And what are those?' asked Alex, pointing to a series of low log cabins that disappeared into the ground, just the door and a slice of gabled roof peeking out like a hobbit house.

'Storage barns. The building on the far right is the root cellar. We try and use mainly local products, and as you can imagine, that gets difficult in the winter months, so we store as much as we can during the summer: tomatoes, asparagus, rhubarb, carrots, berries – six months' worth of quality fruit and vegetables on hand.'

'Won't they freeze?'

'Don't be fooled by the logs on the outside; they're temperature and humidity-controlled. They keep food from freezing in the winter and keeps it nice and fresh in the summer.'

'Can we look?'

Kat shook her head.

'Sorry, only Viggo and the General Manager Theo have a key. Viggo is very exacting about his ingredients.'

Now that sounded like the truth. You didn't get multiple Michelin stars without paying attention to how plump your berries were.

'Voila, the thermal spa,' said Kat as they turned off the path to a low-slung barn. Alex was glad to step inside the sliding glass doors. Here too, the spa's rustic facade belied a slick interior with honey-coloured stone walls and elegantly-carved furniture. There was the gentle tinkling of running water coming from somewhere, and the air smelled of pine.

'You must try the crystal room and the ice bath,' said Kat.

'Ice bath?' he shivered. 'I think I might be cold enough.'

'Don't knock an ice bath; they're really good for you; they improve circulation, increase your energy levels, deepen your sleep. I have one every day.'

Definitely flirtation that time, thought Alex, unzipping his parka. 'Well, you'll have plenty of time for all that now,' he said. 'This is the last night of the season, isn't it? Time for a lovely long sabbatical in the Caribbean.'

'No chance of that,' said Kat, a look of real anger crossing her face. Catching herself, Kat forced a smile.

'It's one of our busiest times,' she said. 'Viggo and his

team work on recipe development. As for management, reservations for next year open on Monday, and it's always a bun fight. I can't tell you the lengths people will go to to get a table.'

Alex felt his journalistic instincts prickle.

The primary reason for the trip was to support Lara, but Alex had journalism in his blood; he was fascinated with how things worked and what made people tick. To Alex, the news was not just a series of events one after the other; his perspective was that world history was created by emotions: jealousy, anger, love and despair. That was where you found the news; in people's secret motivations.

'What sort of lengths? Bribes?' he asked, but Kat seemed to clam up.

'Go on,' he said, flirting himself now. 'You can tell me.'

He felt slightly ridiculous trying to be charming in his robe and his big brown boots, but he had a feeling this was going to be worth it. Kat hesitated, then lowered her voice.

'Once a representative for a Saudi prince called up Viggo personally – no idea how he found his number – and offered him a racehorse if he would make an extra place at the table that night.'

'A racehorse?' said Alex sceptically. 'That's it?'

'Apparently, one racehorse made $15 million in stud fees alone last year.'

'Nice work if you can get it. So did Viggo get the horse?' asked Alex, picturing the chef riding it across Kluven grounds, his beard waving in the wind. Kat shook her head.

'There was nowhere to land the prince's private jet close by, so his security detail decided against it. But it does show you the value people put on dining at Kluven.'

Alex saw an opening.

'So who's coming tonight?' he asked casually. 'Any royalty?'

Kat smiled.

'Don't worry; I'll seat you next to someone nice.'

'I'd prefer interesting or famous,' said Alex, turning up the charm a notch. 'Any big names?

Kat gave a playful shake of the head.

'Come on. Just a hint?'

The guest manager relented. 'There is a doctor and his partner. Dr Green's a plastic surgeon from New York. His partner is a psychotherapist of some note, I believe. They arrived yesterday actually but chose to eat tonight.'

The plastic surgeon sounded promising, especially one from the Big Apple. Alex could imagine his client base would be a who's who, but it was doubtful that the doc would name names. Alex waited, hoping Kat would fill the gap.

'...And we've got a couple celebrating their 50th wedding anniversary,' she said. 'They're coming from Tromsø because they've been on a cruise.'

Alex tried not to pull a face. He hoped the couple were having a lovely holiday, but it wasn't the celeb-fest he was hoping for.

'Two friends of Mr and Mrs Svenson are also dining with us tonight. Oh, and there's another chef.'

Alex perked up at that, immediately imagining the story: a deadly rivalry, duelling chefs, knives drawn. Clearly, it showed on his face because Kat gave a soft smile.

'No, that's a regular thing,' she said. 'We often get other chefs coming to see how it's done. It's a bit like Tracey Emin checking out Damien Hirst's new exhibition. Professional curiosity, I suppose.'

Alex held up his fingers, making a show of counting.

'So with myself and Lara, that's ten....'

Kat laughed. 'Okay,' she said, lowering her voice. 'There is one guest you might be interested in. I suppose there's no harm in telling you now, as you'll be meeting him very soon.'

She paused for effect.

'Justin Blake.'

Alex took a step back. He hadn't been expecting a real celebrity, much less one he wanted to meet.

'The singer? From Joystick?'

She nodded, pleased at his reaction. Alex supposed a genuine A-list rock star reflected well on the restaurant. Well, Justin Blake had been A-list at one time. Justin's star had peaked about five years previously when his band Joystick had been selling out stadiums and pouring out the hits. Alex was a genuine fan, having seen them at an edgy Berlin club a stone's throw from Checkpoint Charlie in their early days. The band had since split up, and Justin had disappeared from the public eye, although he had recently resurfaced as part of The Velvetines, a so-called supergroup formed with a couple of lesser-known LA-based rockers. Alex remembered a flurry of excitable press releases about them, but he didn't recall the charts being set ablaze by the music.

'Doesn't Justin go out with that supermodel?'

'Emily Francis,' said Kat. 'I believe she will also be here.'

Things were looking up. A Justin Blake exclusive for the weekend edition would be dynamite, and the model would give a dash of glamour. He leant forward and gave Kat a blast of his lop-sided grin.

'And who is Justin sitting next to at the meal?'

'His girlfriend, of course. It's communal, but we do keep groups together. Some people enjoy mixing more than others.'

'Presumably, there's a space on Justin's other side?'

'I suppose I could swap things around a little if you ask nicely.'

'How nice would I have to be? I forgot to pack a racehorse.'

Kat laughed. 'On that note, I think I'll leave you to your ice bath,' she said, handing him a fluffy white towel.

She was giving him the brush off, but Alex noted that she still threw a smile over her shoulder as she walked through the glass doors.

Chapter 4

Theo Mikaelsson stood in the doorway of the empty dining room, not moving, just standing there, hands on hips, taking it all in. People thought of the kitchen as the heart of Kluven, and of course, in the human body, the heart was vital. It was blood, energy, oxygen, passion. But it wasn't everything. As general manager of the estate, Theo had to consider every part of the floorplan. The wet rooms in the guest cabins needed to be smear-free, the massive log fire in the bar raked and stoked, even the staff quarters needed to be kept at an optimum temperature. As he liked to tell them at his morning motivational meetings, a happy staff was an efficient staff.

Viggo would disagree with that, of course. Screaming, cursing and crashing pots seemed to be the norm in the kitchen. But Theo didn't work for Viggo. He worked for Martin and Anna Svenson, and most of all, Theo worked for the guests. That was why Theo considered the dining room the true heart of the resort because this was where the guests came to experience Kluven's legendary cuisine. The dining room was the stage, the auditorium, where they came to give a standing ovation. Without Theo arranging the supply trucks bringing in fresh linen, perfectly ironed, or shining plates, there would be nothing to eat off, nothing to sleep on. God was in the detail.

Theo slid back a panel, adjusted the lights – soft and warm – then turned the music up a notch. Sami folk music, or rather the modern version, filled the air. But no one came to Kluven for an authentic traditional Swedish experience; the music was just background to the chink and click of hand-crafted cutlery, the ting of fine wine poured into an elegant glass. It all looked effortless, but the whole thing was an oiled machine. Theo had always thought of Kluven's dining room as the upper deck of the Titanic. Society ladies gliding around in beaded ball gowns, a string quartet playing gently in the background, while Theo stood back steering the ship, the engine room pumping away reliably underneath. And this particular ship was unsinkable. They could fill this dining room ten times every night and still have clients queuing back to the Baltic.

Theo walked over to the long farmhouse table in the centre of the room and moved an artisan brass dessert fork half an inch to the left. Precision was everything, especially tonight, the last service of the season. Nothing could go wrong, and nothing would.

Except for the near-disastrous breakdown of the walk-in freezer in a rare heatwave in August, it had been a smooth season. Only one staff member had quit the kitchen over the summer: Karl, the kitchen hand and only then because he had secured a commis chef position back in his native Germany. He'd been replaced by an eager young man named Josh who had the right disposition for working in Viggo's kitchen: obedience and adoration. Theo supposed it was the equivalent of being a fine art student who found himself cleaning Picasso's brushes.

'No, no, no,' he muttered, leaning across to the centrepiece in the middle of the table. An arrangement of local spruce and wild berries, it was perfectly judged, with the possible exception of the strips of silver birch poking from the top like lizard tongues. That detail had been annoying him ever since Mrs Svenson had the arrangement in place. She created them herself, of course, foraging the foliage from the nearby woods and most of the time, her work was exquisite, but in Theo's opinion, the bark was too much.

'Improving my masterpiece?' said a voice behind him.

Recognising Anna Svenson's voice, Theo flinched, practically jumping away from the arrangement.

Anna was a beautiful woman with fine blonde hair that fell to her shoulders and she had a dancer's posture, upright and regal. Her skin was so pale that sometimes Theo thought she looked like a ghost.

'I was just seeing how it might look if I....'

He stopped as Anna stepped forward and took the long piece of bark from his hand.

'Yes, perhaps you're right. It might look better without,' she said, standing back to take in the table as a whole. She smiled at him, and Theo felt relief in every cell.

'Remind me to show you the crockery I have in mind for next season,' she continued, standing back to admire the tablescape. 'A ceramicist I know in Uppsala has offered to make a bespoke range for Kluven. Her work is sensational.'

Theo paused, aware that a window of opportunity had presented itself.

'Have you given any thought to the other development ideas we talked about?'

For a long time, Theo had felt it was time to take Kluven up to the next level. The restaurant and high-end cabins were fine, but Theo knew they needed to offer more. Husky safaris, fishing for salmon and trout, perhaps a glass igloo for viewing the Northern lights. Nothing tacky, all sustainable and crucially, all of it giving employment to local people. Theo had pitched his expansion plans to Anna a few weeks earlier, and she had made all the right noises, but he had been waiting for an answer.

'Martin's agreed to it in principle,' said Anna, then gave a pained smile. 'But Viggo might take some persuading. You know how he sees the kitchen as the only important part of Kluven.'

He sees himself as the only important part of Kluven, thought Theo, but held his tongue: the politics between the leading players at the resort were delicate, and he had no desire to step on toes. All he cared about was seeing his grand plan come to fruition.

'We'll talk him round, don't worry,' said Anna with more confidence. 'You just have to press the right buttons with Viggo. The only thing he'll be immovable on is the number of guests, however. He's always been clear that the numbers can't get too large.'

Too large. Theo almost laughed out loud. There was no other top-flight restaurant in the world that capped its diners at twelve because having so few covers just didn't make economic sense. With a 4:1 staff to guest ratio, profit margins at Kluven were low, which would become even slimmer if they made the improvements Theo was about to propose.

'Well, on the subject of numbers, we should discuss the staffing,' he said.

Anna raised a brow. 'Why? Is there a problem?'

'The long hours are punishing, particularly for the kitchen team. No one ever gets a proper break.'

He didn't need to mention that it was having an effect all the way to the top.

'How many more people do you think we need?'

Theo took a breath.

'Double, potentially. If we can make the improvements we've discussed.'

'Double?' repeated Anna with some surprise. 'Well, we'd need more staff accommodation.'

Theo could have hugged her: at the very least, she was taking it seriously.

'What about the Dutch barn on the west of the lake?' said Theo.

'It's a possibility,' said Anna thoughtfully. 'A little far from the Lodge though? Getting there late at night might be dangerous.'

Theo had anticipated the objection.

'There's already a path which goes down to the boathouse. We can extend that as soon as the snow thaws.'

Anna gave him an approving smile.

'I should have known you'd think of everything.'

Theo waved away the compliment, but Anna touched his arm.

'No, Theo, I mean it. I don't know what we'd do without you.'

Blushing, he opened his mouth to say something, but Anna was already moving away.

'You do remember our friends Kenneth and Serena are dining here tonight?' she said, looking back over her shoulder. 'Look after them,' she smiled.

Theo wasn't sure why he was so flustered as he returned to his office. Things were looking up, Martin and Anna were considering his plans, and Sunday was a day off, a breathing space before booking opened for the new season. The tech guys had assured him the server could take it, but every year there were more and more people who wanted to come to Kluven, the limited places making it all the more exclusive and elusive. Perhaps that was it? Nerves?

Or perhaps it was the gathering weather. That was one

thing that wasn't looking good. It hadn't snowed since Monday but apparently there was a big dump due that night. Thank goodness the guests had all arrived, although by the look of it, getting them out again tomorrow could be problematic.

As Theo clicked on his computer to call up the weather forecast, he caught sight of the framed picture standing on his desk: Theo as a younger man, barely out of his teens, his father standing at his side, one hand proudly on his only son's shoulder. Theo loved that picture and looked at it every day. Gelt Mikaelsson had been the doctor in Skellstad, the nearest town to Kluven and had been utterly committed to the notion of service.

'Remember why we do this,' he used to say. The community, especially one as isolated and fragile as Skellstad, had to pull together, or they would all perish together. 'We do it for each other.'

It was a noble aim, and since his father's death a year earlier, it was one that drove Theo harder every single day. He had returned home to Northern Sweden because of his father's ill-health, but now Theo was beginning to see that he was here for an even bigger mission. The growth of Kluven had proven vital to this part of rural Sweden. Not only did it provide jobs and income for local suppliers and small businesses, but for decades the young people of Skellstad would head for Stockholm or Oslo and never come back. Kluven had made this part of the world famous. Even if you didn't work on the complex, there was still a reason to stay. There was pride here again, something to boast about for the first time in generations. That was why it was vital to build, to expand as soon as possible.

Theo put down the photo as he heard a 'tap-tap-tap' behind him – boot-heels against the wooden floor. Theo didn't need to turn to know his wife Kat was walking into the office.

'What were you talking to Anna about?'

She made it sound like an accusation and the hands on the hips added to the effect. His wife had been in a terrible mood ever since he'd vetoed her idea to go to Antigua for a couple of weeks after they wrapped up after the season. It just wasn't possible – the cabins were due for a refresh, and the pool in the thermal spa needed re-lining. A holiday was fine for the rest of the staff, but someone had to take responsibility. And without Theo, the whole thing would unravel.

'Anna and I talked about my expansion ideas,' said Theo, still facing his desk. 'Anna likes them. The husky expeditions are certainly something we can start in February when we re-open.'

'Has anyone asked Viggo yet?' said Kat. The sour note in her voice made him turn.

'Anna's going to broach it, yes.'

Kat snorted. 'Good luck with that.'

A silence grew between them.

'And where have you've been?' said Theo.

'Showing a guest round. Alex Ford. I googled him. It turns out he's the Deputy Editor of the *Chronicle* in London, that paper which interviewed Viggo a few months ago?'

Theo remembered it. The interview had been generally complementary, and they'd done a nice side feature on Kluven's thermal suites. Alex Ford was obviously a contact worth cultivating: one of Kat's skills.

'How was he?'

Kat pulled a face.

'Pestering me to sit him next to Justin Blake.'

A pest. It was something that management had to deal with regularly. Many famous people had visited the resort over the years, and they were often surprised to find that Kluven's communal table policy applied to everyone, even them. The forced togetherness was often a good leveller. It did mean that a well-off plumber from Peckham could be sitting next to a television personality and sometimes people became starstruck, expecting autographs or selfies. Worse still, there were the professional networkers. The previous year, an A-list actor had stormed out in the middle of the scallops course when a film producer had badgered him to appear in his new project.

'I'll deal with it, don't worry,' said Kat. Theo shrugged: he knew she would. Doing her job was one thing he could trust her on. Kat walked towards the window and folded her arms across her chest as she looked up to the sky.

'By the way, I'm going to Stockholm on Wednesday.'

Theo frowned.

'Stockholm? Why?'

'Christmas shopping. See friends, to have a change of scenery. Why not?'

'You could have asked me.'

She swivelled to glare at him.

'I need your permission now, do I?'

'I didn't mean that. I could have come with you.'

She shook her head.

'You couldn't, though, could you? You have three suppliers' meetings.'

Theo wasn't surprised she knew. Kat had access to everyone's diaries; as head of guest management, she often needed to contact them at short notice. But Theo also suspected she was making a point about how busy he was – and how he was neglecting her.

'Look, I know you're disappointed about Antigua, but my friend Freddie has just started at Sugar Beach. He might be able to get us a discounted rate. We'll go next year.'

Kat's mouth twisted. 'Sure we will,' she said. 'This year, it's the staff cabins, next year, you'll be turning Kluven into an Arctic safari park. There's always an excuse.'

Theo didn't blame her for feeling frustrated. It was true he was busy year-round, but that was the price of being committed to your work. When they had met, Theo had been Assistant General Manager of The Shelby in London, and Kat had been a supervisor in the Foyer restaurant overseeing afternoon teas. When he first floated the idea of moving to Kluven, Kat had been all for it. As newlyweds, she had said it sounded like the perfect adventure. Kat had never been to Scandinavia before, and besides, for Kat, Kluven was a step up professionally. But the cold, dark Swedish winters could be hard on anyone, especially someone who wasn't used to it. He walked over and ran a hand down her arm.

'Come on, Kat, we're both just a little burnt out.'

'It's more than that, Theo,' she began, but

cut off immediately when there was a rap on the office door, and Martin Svenson stepped into the room, followed by Viggo. Both of them? Theo couldn't remember seeing Martin and Viggo in the same room this season, let alone in here in his office.

'Is everything OK?'

Martin glanced at Viggo and pursed his lips. The chef looked truculent, uncomfortable.

'We have some news,' said Martin.

'Bad news?' said Kat. She had always been street-smart, intuitive, and it seemed her assessment was correct because Martin nodded.

'I wanted to tell you two first; then we need to gather the staff: we have a rather, well, disappointing announcement to make.'

Theo looked back and forth between the two men, a sinking feeling in his stomach.

'Viggo is leaving us,' said Martin bluntly.

'You're leaving Kluven?' asked Theo, turning to Viggo. 'Where are you going?'

Viggo shrugged. It was a slight, vague movement at odds with his huge frame. Everything about Viggo Widlund was larger than life; subtle didn't suit him.

'We have done great things here, you and I,' said Viggo. He looked at Martin, but Theo noticed his eyes flitting across to Kat. 'But I am an artist, and an artist must keep developing his art.'

Theo felt as though a weight were pressing on his chest. This had to be a bad dream he'd wake up from. He was *leaving*?

'So will Petra be stepping up?' asked Kat. Her voice was cool, pragmatic—another one of her skills.

Theo noticed Viggo's eyes narrow.

'No. As of tomorrow, Kluven will close,' said Martin. 'Tonight will be the last supper.'

Theo could not believe what he was hearing. Sure, restaurants closed all the time. Poor management, cash-flow problems, fall-outs between owner and executive chef. But not Kluven. Kluven was one of the finest, most popular restaurants in the world.

'But why?' said Theo, hating the whine in his voice. 'When reservations open on Monday, the lines will be burning up. Kluven is the hottest ticket in the business.'

'I never wanted this to go on forever,' said Viggo, as if he was explaining something simple to a child. 'Sure, Kluven was special, but now I must move on, find new challenges. It is time for me to seek other battles, to find inspiration in other lands.'

Theo felt his anger rise. Viggo was a pompous idiot; he

always had been. Theo had never met a top chef who didn't have a huge ego, but Viggo's was off the scale. He forced himself to think.

'Viggo, there is still so much to do here,' he said, trying to appeal to his vanity. 'How can you deny all those people who have never tasted your creations?'

'They, like me, need to try something new.'

Theo could feel his blood boiling now. How dare Viggo tell him that it was time to try something new. Theo had barely started doing what he wanted to achieve at Kluven. They couldn't stop now.

'But what about the staff? What about all the suppliers in the local villages?'

'Things grow,' said Viggo casually. 'Things die. It's the way of things. It is *nature*.'

Theo's hands squeezed into fists, and he could feel the heat in his face; clearly, it showed as Martin stepped forward between them.

'We should go and tell the rest of the staff,' he said quickly. 'Kat, could you gather the waiting staff? Get everyone into the kitchen so we can make the announcement. We need to get this out of the way as soon as possible; reassure them as much as we can.'

'What shall we do about the guests?' asked Kat.

'We don't tell them anything,' said Martin with resolution in his voice. 'Not tonight. I need to speak to the PR agency first and get a strategy in place for the public announcement.'

At least Theo could agree with that. The fewer people who knew about this, the better, and stalling the news would buy him some time, although God knew what he could do.

Martin and Viggo shuffled out, followed by Kat, leaving Theo standing there alone.

The Titanic, he thought bitterly. Viggo was the iceberg. Selfish, arrogant, riddled with a twisted belief that the whole universe revolved around him. That's why Theo had always disliked Viggo, the fake Viking warrior. A Viking! He almost laughed out loud at the notion. Real tribal chiefs looked after their people; they didn't abandon them.

Well, Theo wasn't going to do that. He looked over at the photo still sitting on his desk. He wasn't going to let this happen. He couldn't.

Chapter 5

Petra had known something was wrong the second Martin Svenson had walked into the kitchen. Kluven's owner *never* came into the kitchen during service. And then, when Viggo walked in behind him looking so defiant, so smug, she knew that her world was about to be shattered. And so it was.

Kluven was closing. Viggo was leaving, off on some voyage of discovery, if they were to believe his ludicrous speech about 'artistry' and 'personal growth' or whatever he'd said. *Bullshit, utter bullshit,* she thought, her shock slowly turning to anger as Martin and Viggo left the kitchen.

What made it worse was that only this morning, Petra and Viggo had spoken at length, discussing recipes for the new season, talked about themes and flavours. Which, given the announcement, meant he'd lied straight to her face.

She looked down at the chopping board, at the onion she was holding in her hand, not entirely sure when she had picked it up. She was numb, on autopilot, because nothing made any sense anymore.

Petra picked up her knife, put it down, then picked it up

again. It was as if she could feel the cogs spinning in her head but couldn't get them to engage.

She and Viggo were partners, for God's sake. Petra Summers and Viggo Widlund: the Kluven creative team. It was like one half of a comedy double-act telling the world he was retiring without consulting his straight man. From that first day he strode into the kitchen at La Ferme Mougins, the famed Provence restaurant where Petra had been working as a commis chef, she had felt a connection. But when a studio in her apartment block had become available that same week and Viggo had moved in, Petra truly felt that destiny had brought them together.

When they weren't working, they hung out outside their building, drinking pastis, smoking cigarettes, and talking about work. Even though Viggo was just a chef de tournant back then, only a few rungs above dishwasher in the rigid hierarchy of the kitchen, Petra had known there was something special about him. He was larger than life and twice as loud; he was handsome, charismatic, and utterly convinced of his nascent greatness, whispering about his plans to revolutionise the culinary world. It was crazy, overblown, impossible, but young people were like that, weren't they?

And Petra had gone along with him every step of the way. As colleagues, flatmates, co-conspirators. Soulmates.

She closed her eyes, squeezed, then opened them. And then her hands began to move. Petra chopped the onion one way, then the other, creating uniform pieces that would melt in the pan. She took another onion, then another, blade and fingers moving with speed and precision. Slice, slice, slice, cool and smooth. From the outside, Petra looked entirely like a woman in control. Inside, however, Petra was screaming. In her mind, this was Viggo she was slicing, cutting him into smaller and smaller chunks. Because Viggo had betrayed her. *Again.*

Again and again and again.

Wasn't that supposed to be the definition of madness? Doing the same thing over and over and expecting a different outcome each time? How often had Petra trusted Viggo, and how many times had he stabbed her in the back?

Let me count the ways.

She winced, taking a second to register that the pain was coming from a cut on her finger.

'Dammit,' she said, pressing a towel against it to stem the bleeding. 'Stupid.'

'Chef?'

She looked up to see the pale face of Josh, the kitchen hand.

'You need a Band-Aid?' he said, holding one out.

'Thank you,' she said, a little embarrassed. She was supposed to be the expert, infallible.

'I'm always doing that,' he said, his voice flat. Petra looked at him; Josh looked as crestfallen as she felt. So did every other staff member in the kitchen, but Josh seemed particularly upset. Josh had only been with them a few months, but he was hard-working and disciplined a perfectionist – and he hero-worshipped Viggo. From the start, Petra had seen a little of herself in Josh. Even when she was small, she had liked her pencils sharpened in a particular way, wanted them to be perfectly lined up along her desk. Worried, her mother had taken her to a doctor, and there had been muted conversations about obsessive-compulsive disorder, medication suggested. But Petra had refused. Why shouldn't things be just so? Why shouldn't they be how she wanted?

Nodding to Josh, she crossed to the sink, running her finger under the tap, watching the blood swirl around the stainless steel, then disappear down the drain, an irresistible force pulling part of her down into the darkness. She held onto the edges of the basin, fighting the urge to sob, concentrating on the sharp pain of her wound.

'Hey.'

She turned to see Stuart, the Boucher. Scottish, red-faced, Stuart was a teddy bear of a man, the kitchen's meat expert, an artist with a blade who had that rare innate ability to know precisely when a steak was perfectly done. Like Petra, Stuart had been at Kluven from the beginning, hand-picked at her recommendation from an Edinburgh restaurant noted for its offal. They'd been through a lot together, so it was no surprise when Stuart opened his arms and pulled Petra into a hug. She held on tight, her face pressed hard into the shoulder of his whites.

'Did you know about this?' he murmured in his rich, Scottish baritone.

Petra felt her cheeks flush with embarrassment.

'I had no idea,' she said honestly. 'I'm still hoping you're going to wake me up and tell me it's a nightmare.'

'I can't believe they would do this to us,' said Stuart, releasing her. 'Whose decision do you think it was? Viggo? Martin? Or was it both of them?'

Petra shook her head, suddenly feeling weary.

'It doesn't matter, does it? It's happening.'

'And we have no bloody say in the matter?' growled Stuart. 'Viggo playing God without any thought for us. We slave away in Arctic conditions, six days a week, for what? A month's severance pay?'

Stuart was venting his fury, but if anything, Stuart had been as close to Viggo as Petra, going off on hunting expeditions together, staying up late in Viggo's cabin drinking vodka and setting the world to rights.

'Stu, good chefs will always be in demand. We'll find

something else,' she said, trying to put a brave face on it for her friend.

'But...' he shook his head, the hurt plain in his eyes. 'I like it here.'

Petra nodded as a wave of emotion swelled in her chest. There were certainly downsides to working at Kluven; conditions were harsh – brutal hours, brutal weather – but there was nothing like it when things were good—finishing a long shift and sitting outside the Stables drinking warm wine under a midnight sun—fishing for brown trout in the clear streams or swimming in the lake. And then there was the food and the unshakeable knowledge that they had done something special, had created something remarkable. Together.

'Where's he gone?' said Stuart disturbing her thoughts. 'Where is Viggo when we need him? Nowhere – again.'

That much was true. Viggo had been spending less and less time in the kitchen recently, always with an excuse: he was doing a phone interview with a journalist in LA or locked in meetings with Martin. Some nights he would make only the most fleeting appearances at the lodge. Petra felt conflicted by his disappearances. Sure, the energy was always higher when Viggo was at his station – the stakes seemed higher somehow – but as his number two, Petra was put in the driving seat in Viggo's absence. She loved those nights, running the kitchen with a cool efficiency that was in stark contrast to Viggo's fire and brimstone.

'You need to say something to them,' said Stuart with encouragement. 'Rally the troops; they're looking to you.'

Petra took a peek around the corner, back towards the kitchen. The staff were still gathered in a tight knot, muttering in a low hum. They looked pissed-off, surly. Indeed, no one looked as if they wished Viggo well on his new poetic journey. The whole staff looked mutinous like they might just disappear into the night. Petra looked at Stuart and gave a tight nod. She owed it to her colleagues; she owed it to the guests. She owed it to herself.

'All right,' she said, walking across, her voice raised. 'Let's get this thing moving, shall we? Mr Svenson said it's the last service – but we knew that already didn't we? Winter is here, and we're all heading to Barbados tomorrow, right?'

There was a ripple of laughter, and she felt a little of the tension ease.

'But before we hit the beach, we have tonight's guests to cook for. This might be the last supper but let's show them how good we can be, yes? Make this our best ever, okay?'

'Yes, chef!' they shouted, turning back to their stations. Petra let out a slow breath. If there was a positive in all this mess, it was right here: a kitchen she could be proud of, a team she had built and trained and nurtured. If it was over, it was a terrible waste, but at the same time, they were still game, still willing to see it through. She watched them bend to their tasks: frying, paring, blanching, assembling the recipes like they were putting together a complicated artwork. Which, she supposed, they were.

Petra glanced at her watch. 6.30. They were preparing all afternoon, but right now was when the kitchen kicked up a gear.

'Anton, don't let the beans oversteam,' she called out now. 'Remember, they'll keep cooking on the plate.'

'Yes, chef.'

Petra's style was quiet, authoritative, a swan gliding on the surface. Viggo was a shouter, a swearer, flames and fury, a devil when roused. *The devil you made a pact with,* said a voice in her head. But it wasn't the time to be dwelling on that now.

'Ten minutes everyone,' she called. She bent over the

dainty egg cups, carefully spooning truffle broth over thin slices of Elk belly, the first pre-course, an amuse-bouche, a flash of what was to come.

'Petra,' said Stuart, nudging her arm.

She looked up.

'He's back.'

And he was: Viggo was there, wearing full chef's whites, head held high, strutting into the kitchen as if nothing had ever happened. He walked straight over to the tray Petra had been working on.

'No,' he said. 'No, no.'

He snapped his fingers and crossed to a side table, picking up a small bowl. Carefully, Viggo dropped a single sliced chive on top of the broth. 'Now it is perfect.'

You shit, thought Petra, looking at him in disbelief. Undermining her, asserting his superiority, all surface, all show. Claiming her work for himself. Petra hadn't honestly expected to see Viggo in the kitchen after the announcement, but of course, that would be like Elton John announcing his final concert and failing to walk out into the spotlight. Tonight was his big night; he wasn't going to miss this for the world. Taking a deep breath, Petra walked across and touched his spotless sleeve.

'Viggo, could I have a word?'

She needed to know what was going on.

He barely looked up. 'What is it?' he said with irritation.

What is it? What the hell did he think?

'In private.'

'No time for chit-chat, Petra,' he said dismissively. He turned to Stuart. 'This beef is overdone! Are you trying to poison my guests?'

His guests, thought Petra pressing her lips together. No

one else mattered, only Viggo. Petra watched him, wide-eyed.

'Do it again,' he said to Stuart, his face growing red. 'This is crap.'

Stuart shot Petra a look and turned away. Sympathy, resignation. Anger, too – on his final night, Viggo was still scoring points, still trying to win every game. *Yeah? Well, two can play that way,* thought Petra.

She placed her spoon down on the counter and slipped down the back corridor, away from the heat and the noise. Her head was pulsing, her hands tight fists, she had to get away. She pushed open the kitchen door walked out into the snow, heading down the path towards the meat locker, not noticing the sharp wind or the falling flakes. At least inside the locker, it would be cool and quiet; at least there she could be alone, everyone else back in the kitchen, working hard to hit their marks. For a moment, Petra felt the tug of guilt. Running the kitchen was a delicate thing, like a juggler, keeping all those balls in the air. Without Petra there keeping the whole thing moving, it was possible – no, likely – that the whole thing would quickly come apart. Well, let Viggo do it; let him actually be in charge for once. And if everything went out late and cold, he could take the blame. For once, Viggo could be what he pretended to be.

'Let him see how it feels.'

Reaching the meat locker, Petra fumbled with the handle, pushing it open and stepping inside the old building. She waited until the door had closed, sealing her off from the weather, from the chaos, from the world.

Let's see how he does without me, she thought, throwing her head back and finally letting herself scream.

Chapter 6

Lara walked out of the bedroom and struck a pose in the doorway.

'What do you think?' she smiled. 'Does this say Viking queen?'

She was wearing a long black velvet dress, her hair piled up in a careless fashion that had actually taken twenty minutes and a lot of swearing.

'Wow,' said Alex. 'You look... nice.'

'Nice?' said Lara feeling a pang of disappointment. Most of the time, she gave little thought to her looks but passing through Heathrow, she had suddenly realised that the little silk slip she had packed might be too flimsy for a Michelin-starred restaurant in the Arctic Circle. So she had left Alex in a coffee shop and dashed around various high-end boutiques trying not to look at the prices.

'This cost me a fortune. I was hoping for "stunning" at the very least.'

She said it as a joke, but she was trying to settle her nerves. It wasn't just the awkwardness of sharing a cabin with Alex – they'd bunked up on holiday many times before, but those were in the days before he was her boss.

Why she really felt on edge was the nagging sense of guilt that she couldn't quite shake.

This should have been Sandrine's trip. Sandrine should have been feeling giddy at the thought of trying one of the most innovative menus in the world. Sandrine should have been dressing up, ready to have fun. But her friend was dead, and she was still alive. Alive and having fun with Alex Ford, and it didn't sit well.

'It *is* stunning, Lar. You are stunning,' said Alex after a moment. 'You look like... old school Hollywood glamour,' he said. 'Like Carole Lombard – the classic femme fatale.'

The light was low but she was sure that he was blushing. 'Yeah? Well Carole Lombard never wore heels like this,' she said, bending to lace up the practical but chunky boots she'd brought to deal with the snow. She had some gold ballet flats in her clutch, but even so, it wasn't quite Sophia Loren.

'I think you can carry it off,' smiled Alex, slipping on his suit jacket and parka. 'You always can. Now if I could add one more accessory?'

She looked up and he held out his arm in a crook. 'Me.'

Lara laughed gratefully. She needed a good night. Lately it felt like she was wading through snow, weighed down by all the baggage of the previous year. She glanced across to her friend, noting that Alex didn't look too bad himself in a sharp grey suit and crisp white shirt. Only pausing to wonder how he had crammed that outfit into his tiny bag, Lara allowed him to lead her out of their cabin and along the short path towards the main building. Dark clouds crowded above the inky treeline, but Lara could still see the black sky between, the stars bright like pinholes in a projection screen.

'Do you think everyone's going to be talking about

different types of caviar?' asked Alex as they made their way towards the lodge.

'I'm not sure they'll be serving caviar. Everything is locally sourced apparently, and the best caviar comes from the Caspian Sea.'

'So what are we going to eat?' Alex looked genuinely worried.

'Well,' said Lara, suppressing a smile. 'I heard the other week that Viggo came into the dining room, sawed a dead cow's shin in half, scooped out the bone marrow and served it up in espresso cups.'

It wasn't quite true, but she was enjoying the effect it had on Alex.

'Jesus. Is this a restaurant or an immersive horror experience?'

Lara laughed.

'Well, if it's awful,' said Alex lowering his tone, 'I'll break into his root cellar, nick a couple of potatoes and we can bake them on the fire pit.

'You're such a food philistine,' she smiled, although she really didn't mean it. Sandrine might have been the gourmand in their circle of friends but Alex was no slouch in that department either. Lara remembered the time she had gone out to visit Alex in Hong Kong when he'd been seconded to the *South China Post* for six months. He'd said no to Lara's offer of paying for dinner at the Peninsula and instead, had taken her on a tour of street food stalls in Kowloon, singling out one particular vendor who made the most amazing ramen. A few years later, that noodle shop was one of the first street food outlets to win a Michelin star. Alex always did have great taste.

They turned a corner, coming out of the trees and the low shape of Kluven's lodge appeared before them, windows glowing like a ship's lantern.

'Pretty special, isn't it?' said Lara, her voice low.

'It is. If I forget to tell you later, I had a really good time.'

Lara turned and grinned at him affectionately.

'Are you quoting *Pretty Woman* at me, Alex Ford?'

'Don't sound so surprised. I'm very in touch with my feminine side.'

She nudged into him. 'You're an old hack who has slept his way ruthlessly around London.'

'I do believe you've just insulted me twice in one sentence,' he said with mock offence. 'I didn't know you were so good with words, Stone. Maybe you should be a writer.'

Alex pulled open the side door and she stepped into the building, the warmth enveloping her like a hug. Lara gave her coat to a waitress who directed them towards the '*vardagsrum*' a homely space adjacent to the dining room. There was a crackling fireplace dominating one side with an inevitable set of moose antlers spreading above, and it was filled with comfortable-looking but stylish sofas. The whole place smelt of spices and vanilla and she could hear the light murmur of conversation: it looked as though most of the guests were already there, crowded around a small bar at the far end of the room.

She noticed that Alex seemed to be scanning the faces carefully.

'Who are you looking for?' she asked.

'Justin,' said Alex distractedly.

'Justin who?'

'Justin Blake,' said Alex keeping his voice low. 'From Joystick. He's one of the guests tonight.'

Lara looked at him quizzically.

'Tell me you've heard of Joystick,' he said, glancing back.

'Of course I've heard of Joystick. Justin Blake goes out with that supermodel, right?'

'So you do read the showbiz page?' he teased.

'I'm a shareholder in the company. I read every page.' said Lara, raising her chin. 'How do you know so much about the guest list.'

'I asked Kat, the guest manager. It would have been rude not to.'

Kat, of course, thought Lara. The very attractive blonde who had greeted them when they had first arrived at Kluven. She wasn't surprised that Alex had already managed to get the inside scoop on the guests – being ahead of the news was what he did – but she was intrigued about how Alex had managed to have this conversation with Kat. He was a fast worker.

She was struck by another thought.

'Wait a minute,' said Lara. 'You're not going to try and interview Justin Blake are you?'

'I might see if he's open to it.'

'Alex we're supposed to be on holiday,' she said with a warning tone.

'But Justin Blake is in the next cabin.'

'Exactly. And he's on holiday too. So let's forget about him and let's eat some meat.'

But Alex didn't seem to be listening, raising a hand in greeting as – Lara's heart sank – Kat the Guest Manager was walking across carrying a tray of small glasses.

'Mead?' asked Kat. Lara could smell it even before she lifted it to her lips. Honey and spices, a tiny bit medicinal. It ran down her throat, filling her with a glow.

'Viggo brews it out in one of the sheds on the grounds,' said Kat. 'He has to keep it separate because it's been known to explode.' Lara looked at her as she spoke. It sounded like one of those pre-prepared anecdotes tour guides use, but it was delivered in a disinterested monotone. Odd.

'Is it safe to drink?' asked Alex.

'What? Oh, sure,' said Kat. Her eyes kept flitting back towards the door, as if she was expecting someone to walk through.

'Shall I introduce you to some of your fellow guests?'

She didn't wait for an answer and she lead them over to a couple in their sixties. She had cropped grey hair, with a sequinned top and a warm smile and he was wearing a loud green jacket and a red tie that matched his cheeks. Lara liked them immediately.

'Lara Stone, Alex Ford, may I introduce Connie and Graham Edwards?' said Kat quickly. 'Connie and Graham are celebrating their golden wedding anniversary.'

'Isn't golden fifty years? Surely not,' said Alex as Kat slipped away. 'You'd have been a baby.'

Connie giggled dutifully, her sequins shimmering as she flashed a knowing look at Lara. 'He's a charmer this one, isn't he?'

Graham nudged his wife as Kat disappeared to dispense more mead.

'She seems to have cheered up.'

'What do you mean?' asked Alex.

'Connie saw her crying just before.'

'Crying?' said Lara.

'Down the corridor near the offices. She was trying to hide it but she was definitely upset,' said the woman, her eyes twinkling with mischief. 'I hope everything's alright with our food.'

Graham looked over at his wife with undisguised affection. 'Nothing slips by Connie. She knows people.'

Lara nodded: she didn't doubt it. At first glance Connie seemed a normal housewife with a taste for dressing up: her bangles jangled as she waved her arms and her ear-rings were huge, but there was something sharp underneath all that. Lara definitely wouldn't want to play cards against Connie Edwards.

'So what about the other guests?' she asked. 'Have you met any of them yet?'

Connie nodded to a couple standing by the window. 'That's Miles, he's a chef. Not very friendly. Wife's very quiet.'

'And what about over there?'

Lara looked towards a tall, thin man in a light grey jacket. He was looking intensely at a strikingly handsome younger man almost as if he were studying him.

'That's Doctor Green and his partner Coulson. And it's *Doctor* Green,' emphasised Connie. 'He likes you to know he's a doctor.'

'A plastic surgeon, actually,' added Graham.

'Coulson is a psychotherapist or a psycho-something. I never know the difference.'

Lara suppressed a smile, enjoying the Edwards' rundown of the Kluven crowd. She also liked how they were obviously having the time of their lives just being here. Journalists were often invited along to restaurants, galleries and premieres and it was easy to lose sight of how much of a privilege it was. Then again, Alex seemed to be enjoying himself with the Edwards, sharing his inside information about there being a rock star in their midst.

Looking around, Lara caught the eye of the man Connie had described as a chef: Miles something? Leaving Alex enthusing about Joystick, Lara excused herself and walked across.

The man had cropped black hair cut short and neat and Lara immediately noticed his manicured nails holding his glass.

'Hello, I'm Lara,' she said, beginning to offer her hand when the man jerked his head forward in a curt bow.

'I am Miles Namato. This is my partner, Nami.'

Nami was beautiful, wearing a red silk dress. She gave a shy 'hello', her eyes hidden behind a long fringe of rail-straight hair.

'Have you come far?'

'Tokyo.'

'That is far,' grinned Lara. 'Still, if Kluven reviews are anything to go by, it will be worth it.'

'We shall see,' said Miles with a brief smile.

'I believe you're also a chef.'

'I am.'

'I can't wait to see what we're eating tonight. I love the idea that each supper is unique here. Very original.'

Lara saw the man's elegant fingers tighten on the glass.

'"Mitt Val", said the man through tight lips. 'That's what Widlund calls it. In Swedish it means "Chef's choice", but it is *not* a new idea.'

He chopped a hand in the air to emphasise the point and his wife took a step forward, as if to head him off.

'The concept is borrowed from the ritual of *omakase* in Japanese cooking,' she said quietly. 'Guests leave themselves in the hands of the chef and receive a meal which is seasonal, elegant, artistic and uses the finest ingredients available.'

Miles' dark eyes met Lara's.

'Few formal dining experiences are as revered as *omakase*,' he said. 'It is all about trust. The chef trusts the customer to respect his decisions, the customer trusts the chef to create something... astonishing.'

'And you don't think that happens at Kluven?' asked Lara. She never got an answer; someone was clapping their hands for attention. A tall man in his sixties was standing by the door. Perfectly styled hair topped expensive casual wear and Lara spotted a gold Rolex peeking out from his sleeve.

'Ladies and gentlemen, I am Martin Svenson, I own the estate. I wanted to come to speak to you personally because something rather... unusual has occurred,' he said. 'Perhaps I'd better hand you over to Viggo to explain.'

A hush fell over the room as the great man stepped out, like a magician appearing onstage. Lara had seen the chef at a distance, but now he looked much bigger, more wild with his unkempt hair and grey-flecked beard.

'Hello, I am Viggo,' he said, his voice deep and strong. 'I will be your host tonight on this very special evening.'

Lara felt a thrill. It was hard not to be swept up in the drama of it all. The guests exchanged looks.

'You all knew it was to be the last supper of the season,' said Viggo. 'But no one knew that tonight would be the last Kluven supper... ever.'

There was a collective gasp. Viggo nodded to acknowledge their shock.

'Indeed, after tonight, I will be leaving Kluven as chef, so this evening's meal will be my finale and I have something wonderful planned for you.'

Lara nudged Alex. This was big news. He gave her a quick nod.

'But rest assured, tonight will be the pinnacle of the culinary arts,' continued Viggo. 'This will be a night you will speak about in hushed voices. Tonight will be my greatest gift to the world.'

Lara watched Martin Svenson shoot Viggo a look. Viggo shrugged and exited as quickly as he had come. For a moment, the room was hushed, then became alive with excited energy. Connie and Graham were obviously thrilled: what a story to take back to Manchester! Coulson and Doctor Green seemed similarly to be revelling in the drama, loudly speculating about what was happening 'backstage'. Only Miles Namato had a different expression: anger, which seemed strange. When they had been talking, there had seemed to be some resentment there towards Viggo for taking undue credit, but surely if Miles had disliked Viggo, he would be pleased he was retiring? As she watched, Miles' partner gently took her husband's hand and meeting his eye, squeezed his fingers. An intimate moment, but what did it mean?

'Told you,' said Connie leaning over. 'No wonder Kat was crying before. She must have got the news early.'

Alex tapped Lara's arm discreetly and nodded towards Martin Svenson, who was talking to a well-heeled couple in their fifties.

'We should go over,' said Alex.

'Alex, we're not here to work,' she sighed, knowing he had sensed an exclusive. Even so, Lara couldn't deny she was intrigued. Kluven was one of the world's most sought-after restaurants, so why close it down so suddenly? And Connie had been correct, Kat *had* seemed flustered and upset. Was it just the shock or something else?

'Come on Lar, this is huge,' said Alex, reading her expression. She laughed.

'It's not exactly Watergate.'

'In the food world, it *is*.'

Alex moved towards Svenson's group and reluctantly, Lara followed him.

'Mr Svenson, I'm Alex Ford,' he said, offering his hand. 'We knew tonight was going to be special, but I had no idea it would be so dramatic!'

Svenson didn't smile. 'Well, rest assured this isn't the end of the Kluven story.'

'So you're going to replace Viggo?'

Martin glanced at his companions with a tight look.

'Tonight is about celebrating Kluven in the here and now, we won't be sharing our future plans just yet.'

Alex looked at Svenson's companions. 'And are you involved with Kluven too?'

'Sorry, Kenneth Roscoe,' said the man, his hand thrust out in front of him, confidence exuding from every pore. 'My wife, Serena.'

He was early sixties at a guess, portly and dressed head to toe in Savile Row. His wife was more understated, but still the Roscoes seemed to float on their good fortune.

'I work with Martin, but I'm not involved with the restaurant,' said Kenneth. 'We've been meaning to come since it opened. As chance would have it, it looks like we sneaked in under the wire.'

Lara caught the look of irritation on Svenson's face. So Martin Svenson hadn't known about Viggo leaving either. Alex was right: there was definitely something going on under the surface here. Before she could ask any more questions, a blond-haired man in a three-piece suit stepped over. Younger than Svenson, he wore rimless glasses, which for some reason always made Lara suspicious.

'Mr Ford, Ms Stone?' he said, gently steering them to one side. 'Theo Mikaelsson, general manager of Kluven. Could I have a word?'

Lara could see Alex hesitate. He had Svenson on the hook and needed just another minute to reel him in, find out what the real story was. But he didn't have much choice – he followed Theo to one side.

'I understand that you are members of the press?' said Theo crisply.

'That's right,' they both said at the same time.

'I'm a great admirer of your newspaper,' said Theo. 'But you understand that we are in a delicate situation here. Viggo's departure needs to be managed very carefully and I would like to ask you both to keep quiet about the news for the time being.'

Alex and Lara exchanged a look.

'I appreciate your position, Mr. Mikaelsson,' said Alex. 'But Viggo himself has just made a public announcement.'

'He shouldn't have done that,' said Theo, without emotion. He was doing a good job of being professional and diplomatic, but Lara could tell he was annoyed.

'Please understand that people's jobs are on the line here,' he said, 'Livelihoods. The local village of Skellstad relies on the resort...'

'Of course,' said Lara, squeezing Alex's fingers. 'We'll keep quiet about it if that's what you want. No one will hear it from us.'

Relief crossed Theo's face. 'Thank you. We appreciate it. Now all that remains is for you to get ready for the night of your lives.' He clicked his fingers to summon a waitress who handed them each a glass of champagne. Alex waited until Theo had left before turning to Lara.

'What are you doing?' he said. 'We could get an exclusive here.'

Lara smiled. 'Not everything is a story,' she said. 'Didn't you tell me that?'

She saw him begin to object and she put a calming hand on his arm.

'We're on holiday, remember? Here to relax?'

'I get that, but....'

'And note that I only said, "No one will hear it from us." Two dozen waiters, drivers and washer-uppers will be on social media right now, freaking out, posting CVs. The world will know soon enough, then you can leap in with your exclusive about the shadowy goings-on behind the scenes.'

Alex grinned.

'Cunning.'

Lara lifted her glass, gracefully acknowledging the compliment.

'Now let's go and have this "night of our lives", shall we?'

Chapter 7

Kat had let Alex down. The guest manager had promised to sit him next to Justin Blake, but despite Coulson and Dr. Green's presence, there was still a boy-girl set-up, so Alex was next to Justin's girlfriend Emily. It was no hardship, obviously, given she was a supermodel, but his attempts to lean across and include the rock star in their conversation were being thwarted by Connie who it seemed was now best friends with Justin. Between the sudden bursts of laughter, he gleaned that Connie was telling Justin a story about how her washing machine had flooded the kitchen. Made a change from people asking him about Bono, he supposed.

Alex glanced across the table towards Lara who seemed similarly absorbed talking to Martin Svenson's friend Kenneth Roscoe. He hoped she was pumping him for information about the Kluven crisis.

'So why did you choose Kluven?' said Alex, turning his attention back to Emily. 'Are you a fan of meat?'

He inwardly winced; not exactly Oscar Wilde, was it?

'I'm from Texas,' said Emily. 'We have 3lb steaks out there.'

Alex glanced down at her willowy figure. He wasn't convinced she'd ever had steak, let alone one that size, but let it slide.

'No, Justin met Viggo at a Joystick after-show party – turns out Viggo's a fan – and they kept in touch,' continued Emily. 'When they had a cancellation we got a call.'

Alex looked over at Justin. He and Viggo were friends? That was interesting.

'Well, it was good timing after the dramatic announcement.'

Emily nodded. 'I was talking to Justin and he totally gets where Viggo's coming from: sometimes you just want to do something else, change the direction of your life, you know?'

Alex nodded. He'd spent a lot of time thinking about it lately. There was no denying that his career in newspapers had stalled, but at the same time, he couldn't bring himself to move sideways into digital media because newsprint was Alex's first love.

'My last boyfriend said the same. He was a drummer. He's a bioartist now.'

Alex had no idea what a bioartist was but didn't want to show his ignorance.

'You dated a lot of rock stars then?'

Another clanger. As a newspaper editor, Alex heard all the rumours, knew the inside track on everything and he could think of at least three musicians Emily had been romantically linked to. Happily, Emily laughed.

'Guilty,' she smiled. 'Pretty much every boyfriend I've ever had has been a musician. I'm a cliché aren't I?'

'Not if you love music,' he said.

Emily nodded thoughtfully.

'Actually I think I love music more than musicians most of the time. Music has always been my escape, my happy place. I adore that immediate connection music gives you.'

She tapped her chest. 'How it hits you there, you know?'

Alex nodded. Music had been a big part of his life growing up too, his record collection connecting him to something bigger and more exciting than the sleepy Lake District town he called home. Occasionally he'd make the long journey to the Manchester Apollo or the Duchess of York in Leeds and rush for the last train back to Kendal. On a couple of particularly daring nights out, in the summer after his GCSEs, he'd stayed out all night: but he did it because of the music. The funny thing was, he hardly listened to anything anymore.

'Alright, apart from Joystick,' he said, 'Who's your top three all-time artists?'

'Easy,' said Emily. 'Bowie, The Cure, Nick Drake.'

Alex nodded his appreciation.

'The poetic stuff, eh? Favourite Joystick song?'

'Die for You.'

'Really?' Justin Blake's biggest song was famously written about the breakdown of his relationship with his ex, actress Claire Hammond. Emily shrugged.

'It's a great song, whoever it's about. And on tour, he dedicates "Die For You" to me – well, every night I'm in the audience, anyway. But then he'll probably do that with whoever replaces me too.'

Alex looked at her.

'That's never going to happen,' he said. Alex genuinely couldn't imagine anyone dumping Emily Francis. She was beautiful obviously, but she was also smart, warm and fun. Why would anyone pass that over?

The model gave a soft snort. 'I'd love to agree with you, but you never know, do you? Justin's been going through some things lately.' She lowered her voice. 'He's in this new band, The Velvetines. Things aren't going as well with them as he hoped. I think it's put him on a bit of a downer. I was hoping coming here might be good for him.'

'Sometimes you just need a change of scenery,' said Alex. It sounded sympathetic – hell, it *was* sympathetic.

Alex wanted Emily and Justin to have a great time at Kluven but he also wanted to know more about their relationship. Across the table, Lara flashed him a look, which he knew was a warning sign to give Emily some space. That not everything was copy.

Alex couldn't help feeling guilty under his friend's watchful gaze. He hadn't told Emily he was a journalist and he suspected she might not be so open with him if she knew.

'So who's that you're with?' asked Emily, nodding towards Lara. 'Your wife?'

'No, no,' he laughed shaking his head.

'I see. Not yet,' said Emily knowingly.

'Lara's one of my best mates from college, we work together. And we go on trips together sometimes too.'

'Kluven is a pretty romantic place for a mini-break.'

'Actually I'm a stand-in, back up for someone else. We have a twin room.'

Emily put a hand on Alex's arm and whispered.

'I hear the beds push together pretty easily.'

'Stop it,' grinned Alex. 'You sound as bad as my dad. He's always saying, 'What about you and Lara?''

He could hear Terry Ford's voice saying it now. Terry adored Lara, always had, so had his mum, God rest her soul.

'Well I agree with your dad,' said Emily. 'Your friend's hot. Is she a model?'

'No, Lara's not a model. And yes, empirically, I can see

that she is very attractive. But we're just friends. I don't want to spoil that.'

Emily's eyes twinkled mischievously. 'The classic excuse of the commitment-phobe.'

Alex began to object, but Emily just grinned and excused herself to 'go to the bathroom'. Alex was glad of the break – he definitely wanted to change the subject. Alex certainly didn't like to consider himself a commitment-phobe. The previous month he'd had a one-night stand with an American executive he'd met at a tech conference in Edinburgh, and yes, he'd been glad when she'd flown back to New York the next day. But he'd almost popped the question to Alicia, his last girlfriend and had gone so far as to accept his mum's engagement ring from his father. Even though the proposal hadn't happened, Alex knew he wanted to have a wife and family one day, probably one day soon. But he was just mindful that this was the most important decision he would make in his life. Already the divorces were beginning to happen in his circle of friends and each mention of a separation was a stark reminder that even if you did find that person who you thought was right for you, that was just the beginning of the story, not the end.

Across the table, Lara was deep in conversation again with Kenneth Roscoe. He wondered if the older man was asking Lara the same thing as Emily had. Were they a couple? Alex couldn't deny that he sometimes imagined himself being with Lara, being together. In the cabin he had definitely had un-platonic thoughts when Lara had stepped out of the bathroom in that dress. But Lara was still Lara, his best friend. He didn't want to jeopardise that, however great she looked in black velvet.

'Ahem.'

Alex had been so deep in thought, he hadn't noticed a server standing at his elbow.

'Oh, sorry. I was miles away,' he said as the girl gently set a new plate in front of him.

'Here we have a butterflied ptarmigan from the estate,' she announced. 'Roasted over cherrywood with a preserved white heart cherry compote.'

This was the fifth course – there had been a braised carrot with beetroot, anchovies in a little cup, some sort of fancy grape with what could have been Peperami but was probably something much more sophisticated and...oh, he'd lost track already. Alex had a taste and groaned with pleasure. The juicy gaminess of the bird was elevated, lifted by the burst of sweetness from the cherries, undercut by a hint of something else; balsamic, perhaps? Alex hadn't really understood the idea of juxtaposing flavours until tonight – if he was honest, he hadn't really understood the fuss about high-end restaurants, but on both counts, this meal had been a revelation.

'You like the cherries?'

Alex looked to his right. Nami, the partner of 'the Rival Chef' Mile as Alex now thought of him.

'I do, it's delicious. So is this what's it like being married to a chef?' asked Alex, failing to keep the envy from his voice. 'Do you get to eat this stuff all the time?'

'No, not really. Miles hardly ever cooks at home.'

'So what do you eat?'

'Lucky Charms.'

Alex let out a surprised laugh. 'The breakfast cereal with the little marshmallows in?'

Nami nodded.

'Seriously. That was a treat when I was a little girl. And I guess it's like living with a concert pianist and wanting to listen to Bruno Mars when you get home.'

'So does Miles have his own restaurant?'

'He's head chef at the IHG in Tokyo.'

'Impressive.'

Now Nami looked surprised.

'You know it?'

'I do. I lived in Shinjuku for a few months. I'm a journalist and when I was a young reporter, I worked for our Tokyo bureau.'

'A foreign correspondent. How glamorous.'

'Not really, there's a lot of press conferences and a lot of hanging about in hotel lobbies, but occasionally we got taken out for a smart dinner and the IHG was always one of my favourites. How long have you been in Tokyo? Both your accents – they are American, aren't they?'

'We've been in Tokyo five years now, but yes, we were both brought up in Washington State. My parents are from Kyoto but we moved to Portland when I was five. They knew Miles' dad who is also from Japan.'

'So you're family friends who fell in love.'

'Something like that,' she smiled.

Alex took a sip of his wine.

'Is this a research trip?'

Nami nodded, more wary this time. Perhaps Alex shouldn't have confessed to being a writer.

'I think Miles' gameplan is to have somewhere like this; his own place. He's been following Viggo's career very closely over the past few years.'

'Is he a fan?'

Nami pulled a face.

'Not so much.'

Alex looked up from his cherries.

'Oh? Why not?'

The woman tapped the tines of her fork against her plate, as if thinking over what to say.

'Miles is a perfectionist when it comes to food. Not just the sourcing and the preparation, but the philosophy behind it too.' She laughed, trying to make light of it. 'Miles takes food very seriously.'

'And Viggo...?'

Nami shook her head tightly.

'Not so serious. That's what Miles thinks, anyway.'

Alex gestured towards his plate.

'Forgive me, but Viggo's food does seem very good.'

'Oh it is. Very good. But Miles, well...' She glanced over her shoulder. 'He has suspicions.'

'Of what?'

Nami looked towards her husband, then around the room. She dropped her voice to a whisper.

'He thinks that Viggo lies.'

'Lies?' Alex asked, picking a cherry stone from his dessert and raising it to his mouth. Like a snake, Nami's hand shot out to stop him.

'What's wrong?'

'The cherry stones. They're toxic,' she said, her expression serious. 'There's a compound inside the stones which breaks down into hydrogen cyanide.'

Alex dropped the stone onto his plate with a 'tink'.

'You have to be careful,' said Nami, meeting Alex's gaze. 'Not everything in the kitchen is good for you. And some things can be deadly.'

Chapter 8

'The honeycomb looks perfect,' said Petra, touching Michel Garnier's shoulder. Kluven's chocolatier was a quiet Frenchman whose speciality was making the tiny truffles stuffed with home-made duck-egg liqueur that they served at the restaurant every night with coffee. It was one of Kluven's signatures, one of those 'you haven't really eaten until you've eaten...' headlines the style magazines were so fond of. But tonight Michael had added something new. In consultation with Petra, he had created Kluven's own version of cinder toffee using honey from the hives in their summer meadows, dipped in chocolate, then hardened in copper pans left out in the snow.

'Try one,' he said, handing her a tiny dark square with a pair of miniature tongs. Although the chefs were tasting all the time in the Kluven kitchen – to check the temperature of a sauce or the seasoning in a jus, Viggo had decreed it was forbidden to actually consume food.

Petra glanced over at Viggo, who was busy salting the wheat crackers for the final cheese course and she felt an unusual surge of rebellion.

'Sure,' she said, popping the toffee into her mouth,

savouring both the deep caramel taste of the dark chocolate as well as the thrill of the forbidden.

She ran her tongue across her teeth, then exhaled. No more time to relax. The service was entering its final stretch: it was time for Petra to make a move.

'Can you watch my station?' she asked in a low voice.

Michel looked at her from under his thick black brows.

'Sure, is everything okay?'

'Everything's fine Michel. There's just something I need to do.'

Michel looked bemused. As executive sous chef, Petra did some of the preparation – she particularly enjoyed crafting the amuse bouches between courses – but largely it was an overseeing role, making sure that everything ran smoothly, checking that each dish, for each guest, was executed with perfection. She saw it as her responsibility to see it through from beginning to end and that meant being first to arrive and last to leave. While she felt a twinge of guilt over stepping out, Petra already knew that tonight had been a triumph. If Viggo's departure had stunned everyone, it hadn't shown in their work.

'Don't worry cherie,' said Michel, squeezing Petra's arm. 'You go.'

Stepping outside, she winced at the cold despite her Arctic-grade parka. She'd never got used to the temperatures at Kluven, not really. Petra didn't miss England all that much but she missed the certainties of the seasons and she missed the mild winters, and they *were* mild, however much her friends back home grumbled about the occasional snow day. Petra couldn't really complain: most of the day she was unbearably hot anyway, hunched over a stove or wincing at a rolling cloud of dry air as she opened an oven, but the sudden brutal changes were still a shock. She was just stepping out along the path when Petra realised she was not alone.

'Josh,' she said. The lad was throwing bulging black bags into the industrial sized bins. 'Shouldn't you have your coat on?'

'Chef,' he nodded, seeming slightly embarrassed. 'I only came out for a minute.'

'Josh, you know how quickly you can get frostbite...'

She stopped herself: Josh probably didn't know. This was his first winter at Kluven and it was only in the past couple of weeks that the weather that had turned so intensely cold.

'You'd better get back inside,' she said, wanting to get moving herself, but Josh hesitated, his face as pale as the moon.

'Can we not persuade him to stay?' he asked.

Petra let out a long breath. She supposed there was some consolation in knowing she wasn't the only one feeling bereft.

'I don't know, Josh. But I'm going to do everything I can to keep Kluven open.'

'But what if you can't?'

Petra heard the hurt in his voice, and took a moment to consider how Josh was feeling at that moment. The kitchen hand was nineteen, the same age she had been when she'd left the UK to learn how to cook. Looking back, Petra could still remember the aching loneliness, wanting someone – anyone – to tell you it was going to be alright when things felt anything but.

'You're from Stockholm, right?'

He nodded.

'I have a few contacts in the city. If Kluven closes – and it's a big if – then I can definitely make a few calls for you. We'll find you something else, okay?'

'Thank you so much.'

He blushed at her from under his fringe, cow eyes practically shooting love hearts in her direction, before turning and rushing back through the back door. Petra shouldn't have been surprised at his reaction: there weren't many women in any kitchen, even less so this far north.

But she felt her determination grow as she turned up the path towards the Svensons' house. If Viggo wouldn't talk to her – and he had barely exchanged a word with her since the announcement – then perhaps Martin Svenson would. Certainly Kluven's billionaire owner should be able to shed some light on it: he had not seemed at all happy when he and Viggo had made the announcement. And why would he be happy? Martin was a businessman and Kluven made money. Nothing like enough to fuel his private jet, she imagined, but it was a strong brand and the status and prestige attached to owning one of the world's great restaurants must carry its own weight in Svenson's high-flying world. That, surely, was something worth holding onto.

The path ahead of Petra was lit with tasteful downlights, but still it felt like darkness surrounded her, the banks of snow either side turning blue then black beyond the reach of the lights until it felt as if she were suspended in space. When she had first come to Kluven, Petra had known very little about Sweden beyond Abba and Ikea, so she had put some effort into reading up about her new home. She had particularly been fascinated by the Nordic myth of Bilfröst, a shimmering path that ran between Midgard, which was the human world and Asgard, home of the Gods. Here in the frozen north, where diamond teeth dripped from the eaves of houses, it was easy to imagine being tantalisingly close to another realm – and just by stepping off the path, you might find yourself in a Scandinavian version of Narnia. *More likely you'd just get snow in your boots,* thought Petra, pushing onwards.

She could see the lights from the Svenson house now – oblongs of gold, dancing in the darkness as she walked. And what was that? Petra narrowed her eyes: a silhouette moving across the wide porch of the house like a shadow puppet. As Petra got closer, the soft black outline sharpened like a photograph in developing fluid. Now she could see the figure was Anna Svenson.

Usually Mrs Svenson was the friendlier half of Kluven's owners, but right now Petra could see her expression was stony. Anna Svenson never looked anything other than utterly composed, but tonight she didn't look her usual self. Only to be expected of course, thought Petra. Even with the cushion of a healthy investment portfolio, it can't have been a good day for the Svenson family.

'Petra,' said Anna as she climbed the steps. She didn't look pleased to see her. 'Shouldn't you still be in the kitchen?'

'Viggo's there. I'm not needed for the moment.'

There was a short silence.

'I need to speak to Martin.'

Another pause. Petra took the opportunity to look more closely at Anna; her eyes were red. With a sudden realisation, Petra guessed she had walked into a domestic.

'It's not a good time,' said Anna, as if to confirm it.

Petra knew that this was where she should take the hint and go back to the lodge, but she couldn't, not now. There was no turning back for her.

'It's important, Anna,' she said. 'I just need a few minutes, that's all.'

She could hear the pleading in her own voice, the desperation, and presumably so could Anna.

'Petra. We're all just a bit emotional,' she said. 'It's been a shock.'

The old Petra would have made her excuses and sloped off. But not this time. She'd be willing to bet that no press release had been sent out. There was still time to stop it all from happening.

'I can fix this, Anna,' she said. 'It doesn't have to be over. I've just worked so hard for this.'

'We all have,' said Anna with feeling. 'But Viggo is a law unto himself. You know that better than anyone. I suppose we should be grateful we had him for so long.'

'Just a few minutes,' said Petra nodding towards the house. 'Please.'

Anna paused, then gave a mirthless, resigned sigh and pushed open the door.

'Go on. Go through,' she said as Petra stepped past her, feeling the rush of nerves she always got going into the main house. In the five years she had worked at Kluven, Petra had only visited the Svensons' a handful of times, mostly before Kluven had even opened, when she, Viggo, Theo and Kat were the only members of staff and they'd have meetings in Anna's dreamy kitchen over very good red wine. These days she only came for the End of Season drinks which the Svensons traditionally threw the night after closure.

Anna disappeared, gliding elegantly up the wide staircase without saying another word, leaving Petra alone in the huge atrium dominated by a tall Nordic pine, tastefully twinkling in silver and white. It was an elaborate display given the Svensons generally left Kluven after closing to return to their main home in Stockholm for *Juldagen* and *Annandag Jul,* the Swedish Christmas. Petra, however, stayed. She wasn't close to her family and had become distant from her friends back in the UK, having been out of the country for so long.

Despite her loneliness, she loved the festive season at Kluven. On Christmas Eve, she would creep around the back of the main house and put her face up against the French doors to peer inside, imagining herself curled up on the vast sofa with Viggo, the whole place smelling of gingerbread and spices, their bodies warm from the crackling fire. But that had never happened. And now, it seemed, it never would.

'Petra.'

Martin Svenson was standing in his office doorway holding a book, a surprised look on his face.

'Anna let me in,' she explained. 'I need to speak to you.'

'Perhaps we can set aside some time tomorrow...'

'But I'm here now. This won't take long, I promise.'

Martin rubbed one temple with the heel of his hand, as if that was exactly the last thing needed.

'Very well. Come through.'

Martin's office was even more impressive than the hall.

There was a half-full tumbler of whisky on the desk, ice-cubes glistening from the soft lights from the fire, popping in the hearth. Three walls had book-filled cases, many of the books old, many leather bound. The other main feature of the room was a polished grand piano, its top covered with framed photographs, the majority of them Martin and Anna in various glamourous locales; skiing, on a Nile cruise, relaxing under a beach umbrella. It was hard not to be intimidated by the smell of wealth in the room, but Petra was determined to push on.

'I'm sorry for bothering you, I realise it's a difficult time,' she said. 'But I knew you'd be awake as your friends are still eating.'

'I hope you put on a good show for them,' said Martin, lifting the tumbler to taking a sip. 'I've known Kenneth and

Serena for what feels like forever, but can you believe this is the first time they've ever come to Kluven?'

Petra gave a curt nod: she had no patience for small talk.

'I have a solution, Martin,' she said, cutting straight to the chase. She had spent hours at her station planning this discussion. She had considered using the word 'proposal', but decided that 'solution' was more powerful, much harder to turn down. Who wouldn't want a solution to this mess?

'Go on,' he said, gesturing with his glass. Petra paused a beat, then raised her chin.

'Promote me to executive chef of Kluven.'

The words seemed to shimmer in the air. *Executive chef.* Petra had dreamt the words, of course, but she had never spoken them aloud before.

'Viggo has resigned,' she continued in a rush. 'And from what he's said so far, it seems his mind is made up, but that doesn't have to mean the end of Kluven.'

Petra wasn't naturally pushy, but she had spent enough time around Viggo to know that people responded to confidence.

'Kluven isn't just about Viggo Widlund,' she continued. 'It's about astonishing food and an unrivalled dining experience. You know I run the kitchen and the team, you know how good I am and I think you know I can make Kluven an even better restaurant than it is. And obviously...'

Martin held up a hand, stopping her mid flow.

'Yes, I know all of those things, Petra. I listen to the staff, I know they respect you. More than that: they admire you and I know in a kitchen that's no small thing.'

He paused for a moment.

'But Kluven is different.'

'Why?'

She heard the tremor in her voice but she wasn't going

to back down now. Martin tapped his lips with one finger as if he was considering how to make a diplomatic point.

'For you, it's all about the food, what goes on the plate, the flavours and textures, yes? But that's not necessarily why people come here.'

'The food is the star, Martin,' said Petra, feeling defensive – protective.

'Perhaps,' nodded Martin. 'But do you think Kluven would be quite so popular, quite so special if it was in Stockholm?'

Petra was going to object, but had to admit it was a good point.

'But it's a combination of things,' she said. 'Eating the food in such an extraordinary place adds to the experience, which is why it must be allowed to continue. People want to come – open the bookings on Monday and see.'

Martin was shaking his head.

'The guests come here to see Viggo, to see the mad Viking stomping through the snow, chopping up the meat with an axe and cooking it on a bonfire. And perhaps you're right Petra, that's not the full story, but it's the sell, the public perception of the experience. They come here for the circus, for the highwire act.'

'The Viking thing is a novelty,' she sniffed. 'If you want theatre then we can let Stuart play his bagpipes.'

Martin let out an unexpected laugh.

'Listen Petra, I do know how good you are...'

But of course he didn't. Martin Svenson had no idea how good she was, no one did. No one knew the truth about Kluven, not even the man who had spent years bankrolling it. Only Petra knew – and Viggo. For one wavering second, Petra thought about telling him, bringing the whole lie crashing to the ground. But Martin was still talking.

'The problem is I have an agreement with Viggo.'

'You're partners. I know that. But partners can be bought out, no contract is that watertight.'

Petra knew all about this; she had been brought up on legalese and the nitty-gritty of the law. Her father had been senior partner at a law firm in Bath and until the age of 19, Petra had done everything she could to please him. Work hard at school, learn to ride and sail. Even the law degree she had begun at Newcastle had been a nod to her father's ambitions. And then Petra had taken a job in a local restaurant over the summer and found the thing she truly loved, the thing she was truly best at. Food. The buzz of the dining room, the fervour in the kitchen, the smells and the sounds. There was no way she was going back to dusty books and contracts. Her father had practically disowned her, but Petra couldn't turn back; she had found her own shimmering path to another realm, the down-lit path that lead her to Kluven and finally, right now to this spot. Petra watched as Martin steepled his fingers together, gathering his thoughts.

'Kluven was a joint venture between myself and Viggo,' he said. 'The agreement was always that if one of us wanted out, then the arrangement would end. And as you heard earlier, Viggo doesn't want to stay at Kluven, which means that Kluven must, sadly, come to an end.'

Martin said the words with finality, but Petra wasn't giving up that easily.

'Any decent lawyer could get around that – and I'm fairly sure your lawyers are better than decent.'

'You know, for a while earlier today, I almost called them,' nodded Martin. 'But perhaps Viggo is right. Perhaps it is time to end all this.'

Petra held up her hands in appeal. It felt as if her whole life was slipping through her fingers.

'But why, Martin? This is only our fifth season, we've

hardly begun. I know that Theo has worked up some expansion plans for the restaurant, we can get so much bigger, better. And I'm the chef to take Kluven to the next stage. I *am*.'

Martin's face showed regret, defeat. He looked like a man who had had enough.

'Petra – we're done here. We built something fabulous, but now the time has come to end it.'

He didn't say it unkindly, but to Petra it was like a body blow.

'Martin, I can't, I just...'

Martin put up a hand.

'Petra, no.'

He walked over to the window and looked out into the dark.

'More and more these days, my life is elsewhere,' he said, almost to himself. 'I have offices in Stockholm, London, Paris. Places I need to visit, teams I need to meet. And it's that business, Petra, which pays for all this. You know, I always thought I wanted a restaurant, but the truth is, I got confused between enjoying food and wine and being part of the hospitality business. One is pleasurable, the other is a tough, tough trade.'

'So what?' Said Petra fiercely. 'So what if it's hard? Remember when we started, sitting in your kitchen making plans? You loved all that, Martin, I saw it in your eyes. So maybe the business of it has become repetitive, so hand it over to Theo. Appoint a passionate new chef who'll rekindle your love for Kluven...'

'Stop!'

Petra looked at him, mouth open.

'That's enough, Petra.' There was a hardness to his voice now. 'This is my estate, my business. I will decide what to do with it.'

Martin's eyes glinted with emotion.

'We're all upset. It's a difficult time, but right now I need you in the kitchen, making sure the guests have a night they will remember for ever, making Kluven's greatest ever supper. That's all.'

'So this is it?'

'Of course there will be a generous settlement....'

Petra didn't listen to the rest. She turned and walked out of the house, fighting the tears. Why would no one listen? What would it take to get someone to pay attention to her? And then she knew: she turned and walked out into the snow.

Chapter 9

The applause rang around the dining room. 'Bravo!' came a shout from the end of the table.

'Maestro!'

'The best ever, Viggo – magnificent!'

Viggo stood at dining room door and bowed, taking the praise in his stride, graciously accepting the handshakes and backslaps, those earnest muttered compliments from the star-struck guests. It was all part of the show of course, and for a long, long time, this had been his favourite part of the evening, the curtain call when he could drink it all in.

But over the last year – longer, if he was truthful – it had begun to grate. More and more he had felt like a performing seal, the big finale of the circus. If he had done a backflip or a card trick, they would have clapped more. Tonight though, Viggo was acutely aware that this was his final bow. The last time ever. And yes, he felt the glow, a hint of what had once been there. People loved him, or at least, they loved what he could do for them, how he could make them feel – rich, happy, sated – and he supposed there was something beautiful in that. He brought pleasure to the people who came here.

'Thank you friends, thank you,' he said, steepling his hands and bowing. 'I am glad I could share all this with you on this golden night. Now – adieu!'

He backed out of the dining room, applause following him all the way, until he was in the corridor alone. Leaning back against the wall, he took a moment to breathe.

So that's it, he thought, putting both hands over his face. *The end.*

'Thank Christ for that,' he whispered.

The kitchen door was to his left. He could feel the heat still radiating from there, could hear the raised voices and laughter, the energy of the night still bouncing around looking for somewhere to go. Tradition dictated that at this point, the chef would go back into the kitchen and make a rousing speech to the team; another season gone, the best team ever, you were all incredible, but next year is going to be legendary, all that rubbish. Champagne would pop, vodka would pour, there would be toasting and Norse war chants.

But not now. Not tonight.

Viggo untied his apron and pulled it off, looking down at it bunched in his hands. He should hang it up on its hook, shouldn't he? Maybe hand it to one of the other chefs, a symbolic passing of the torch.

Viggo almost laughed at that. *Yeah, maybe I should give it to the boy Josh.* At least he seemed passionate about all this.

Carelessly, Viggo threw the apron on a side table, one of Anna's achingly tasteful pieces flown in from some chateau in the Loire. Let her tidy it up: she could frame it or drop it in the trash. Viggo realised he didn't care what happened next; there was something liberating in that, a chink of light, a whisper that he might actually get past this.

Suddenly Viggo had an urge for a cigarette. He hadn't

smoked for a long, long time, but he needed something to relax him. Over the years, he'd received many gifts from grateful guests – cigars, fine wines, and more telephone numbers and promises of sexual favours than he could remember. He thought of the Montecristo No. 4 he'd been given over the summer, then pushed through the outside door, heading for his cabin.

A series of paths spun off from the Kluven lodge. One went to the Svensons' home, another to the staff accommodation. One went to the spa, and the storage barns, another to the guest cabins. Viggo took the track towards the forest. His living quarters were on the fringe of the *skog*, the boreal woodland, away from both the guests and the rest of the staff who lived in the converted stable block. Viggo's cabin had always suited his image: slightly aloof, slightly mysterious, set to one side. Growing up in the city of Malmo, he had never imagined himself living in somewhere so remote and isolated, but he had come to genuinely love the silence, the feeling of being at one with nature, the frozen earth and that grey dome above. Now he knew he would miss it.

He wouldn't miss the intense cold though, he thought as he thrust his hands in his pockets, head down through the growing wind. He might be Swedish, but that didn't make him fond of snow and ice. Heavy cloud cover meant that the night-time temperatures were not quite as low as they could be at this time of year, but still, he felt cold to the bone. Soon though, soon he would be warm.

'Viggo.'

A voice carried across the breeze, soft and muffled by the shroud of snow. He looked to his left.

It was Petra, *Damn.* She was the last person he wanted to speak to. He'd felt her eyes boring into him all night in the kitchen, and yes, he had tried to avoid her – what was the point now? – but clearly she had other ideas.

'Viggo!' she called again.

Petra was coming from the direction of the Svenson house, following the connecting paths until she was right there in front of him. Viggo inhaled sharply and stopped. Perhaps he should just face this head-on and get it over and done with.

'Are you going into hiding now?' said Petra, her breath clouding in front of her.

'No, just going to my cabin to get something. I'll be back in the kitchen in ten minutes.'

'Like hell you will be,' she said. Obviously she was spoiling for a fight, but this wasn't the time or place. Too damn cold.

'Look, why don't we walk together?'

'Oh, so now you'll talk to me. Couldn't bring yourself to face me earlier, could you?'

'Petra, it's not that,' said Viggo wearily. 'We had a job to do, a supper to prepare.'

'And then what? You'd just disappear?'

'Look, let's go to my cabin.'

'What, you want to pour me a drink, sweet-talk me like the old days? Make more promises?'

Viggo clenched his jaw. *Promises?* She was really annoying him now. Of course Viggo had known from the start that Petra was in love with him, but there had never been anything on his side, no spark or connection. Not really. Her devotion and her earnestness were sometimes quite sweet and yes, there had been moments when he had wondered... But now Viggo realised she was just like everyone else: needy and insecure. He was glad he was leaving Kluven – and all the baggage – far behind him. He took a deep breath.

'Look Petra, I can see why you're upset, and perhaps I should have told you privately about my plans to leave. But

I only made my mind up in the past few days and besides, I didn't want people to start gossiping and unsettle the team.'

'You think I'd have gone around telling everyone you were going to resign?'

'Petra, no. But...'

'But what? I thought we told each other everything, Viggo. I thought we could trust each other. I thought we respected each other.'

'We do.'

'Like hell you do' she spat. 'You use me. I can see that now, as clear as day,' she said with a hard little laugh.

Viggo felt his hand clench around the phone in his pocket.

'Look Petra, I do care about you. I care about the whole team and I want this to be as painless as possible for everyone. But I can't change how I feel. My time here is done.'

'You *care* about me?' she said, mocking his words. 'Right. Martin told me about your bullshit arrangement, how you want to close the whole thing down, without a care for any of us. You've pulled the rug out from under us all, Viggo. Especially me.'

He rubbed a hand over his face. He should have known that it would come to this.

'It's not that I don't care, Petra. I just don't want to see Kluven become a poor copy of what it once was. Closing it down is about protecting its memory.'

She scowled at him. Viggo had always considered Petra to be quite sharp – hadn't she almost been a lawyer? – but she clearly wasn't getting it.

'Because Kluven wouldn't be Kluven without me.' He said simply.

'And what about me? You think Kluven couldn't continue with me in kitchen? You arrogant bastard.'

He sighed.

'Look, when people pay $500 to see the Rolling Stones, they want to see Mick, not the support band.'

'Support band?' she hissed, stepping forward, stabbing her finger towards his face. 'Is that how you think of me? After everything I've done for you?'

Her cheeks were pink now, pushing her face close to his.

'Petra, don't.'

'I made you, Viggo Widlund and I'm going to tell the whole world how and why.'

He tried to keep his voice calm but he didn't feel it. The creeping anxiety, the black dog skittering at the edge of his vision.

'Don't do that, Petra.'

'Why not?' she sneered. 'You know it's true.'

Her eyes were wild, like a horse about to kick. He backed away, feeling his anxiety rising.

'Petra, you need to calm down.'

'Calm down? You have ruined my life!'

'Let's go back to my cabin and talk all this through.'

'I don't want to talk,' she said, her voice rising. 'I want Kluven, Viggo. I want what's MINE!'

Viggo stepped back, palms out.

'And this is exactly why you could never run a kitchen.'

With a guttural cry, Petra sprang towards him, hands clawing at his face.

'Christ, Petra!' He caught her wrists, fending her off, pushing her back into the snow. She fell onto her backside with a shout.

Swearing under his breath, Viggo pressed his palm to his stinging cheek and when he pulled it away, even in the low light he could see blood.

'You silly little bitch,' he spat. Petra was still lying there on her back, like a beetle. Like she'd given up.

He snorted and headed back to the cabin.

'Viggo,' Petra moaned from behind, but he didn't turn. He was just focused on getting back to his cabin, getting inside.

'Viggo!' she screamed and her voice was like the howl of an animal.

Finally inside, Viggo slammed his cabin door shut, pressing his back against it, his whole body shaking.

He didn't turn on any lights. He just dropped his jacket to the floor and staggered to his armchair by the wood-burning stove. He closed his eyes, sucking in air, just concentrating on breathing. In, out. In, out.

It wasn't working and he felt the panic rise. Reaching out to the table next to him, Viggo grabbed one of the river stones he'd left there. Squeezing it between fingers and thumb, he stroked the smooth surface of the pebble. *Be calm like the lake, still like the water.* He rubbed the stone until it was warm and his hand had stopped trembling.

Viggo couldn't exactly pinpoint when he started feeling anxious, but the kitchen was where he noticed it first. Things that had once been mere annoyances made him boil with rage: a sauce that had curdled, an egg that had cracked. He'd feel jumpy, like a humming wire, his fists tight. He'd want to flee, run out of the kitchen and never come back. Even at home in his cabin, Viggo had found it difficult to relax. At one time, going outside, chopping wood, hunting or fishing would soothe him, bring him back from the edge. But not anymore. Simple things like losing the top of his tube of toothpaste brought on waves of panic.

And then a few weeks earlier, Viggo had simply not been able to get out of bed. It was as if the black cloud he'd felt hanging over him had descended, a huge hand pressing down on him, pinning him to the mattress.

He'd lay there motionless for hours, terrified he was

going to suffocate. Finally, summoning every last ounce of strength he had, Viggo had crawled to the door, then staggered out in his pyjamas, his parka and his boots. One foot in front of the other, just walking through the snow. If anyone had seen him – it had been a Sunday, the only day of the week Kluven didn't host guests – then no one had stopped him.

When Viggo felt he could walk no more, he discovered that his feet had led him to his friend Kjell's farm. Kjell supplied Kluven with reindeer milk and Viggo had taken shelter in a small stone bothy on the edge of his land. Making a small fire outside, Kjell had come to see where the smoke was coming from. Mercifully, Kjell hadn't asked Viggo why he was there, he'd just brought him blankets and food. And the words Viggo most needed to hear.

'Stay as long as you want.'

Viggo had stayed there for three days, just sleeping and breathing and sitting by the fire. Thinking about what was happening to him only made things worse and so he collected stones from a nearby river's edge where the ice was broken, picking pebbles out, selecting and rejecting them, searching for the smoothest he could find. Later, by the fire, Viggo found comfort with those stones, polished by water and time, so hard yet so soft against his fingers.

On Kjell's third visit, Viggo was finally able to talk.

'I never want to feel like that again,' he said.

'Then make sure you don't,' said Kjell and put out the fire.

Standing up now, replacing the stone on its small pile, Viggo walked to his empty desk and took the cigar from the drawer. He'd been saving it for a special occasion and now felt as good a time as any. The end of one chapter in his life and the beginning of another. He clipped the end of the cigar and lit it, rolling the tobacco back and forth across the flame. Coughing at the first hit of smoke, Viggo slid open the door that led onto the balcony at the back of the cabin.

The snow seemed to be easing off now, the clouds just sliding apart enough to reveal a hint of moon. He leaned against the rail, feeling some of the tension release as he breathed out the woody smoke. He really did have to get away from here.

Viggo knew that sometime soon, probably when he was launching his next venture, a journalist would ask him, 'why did you close down Kluven?' Viggo already had his answer prepared. 'I shuttered the restaurant because I knew I had achieved everything I'd wanted to', he'd say. 'I needed new challenges', 'I had to find beauty somewhere else.'

And part of that was true. Even at school, Viggo had never really been able to concentrate on one thing for too long. His teachers had said he showed academic promise and his sports teachers saw natural flair, but commitment had always been his problem. Too hungry for the next thing. Until he and Martin had founded Kluven.

Then Viggo knew he had found this place, a laboratory of innovation and creativity 100 miles inside the Arctic Circle. And for so long it had worked for him; launching the restaurant, seeing the spiralling success, feeling the adulation that for once he felt he deserved, it drove him harder and harder, always wanting more. Viggo had heard rumours of Theo's plans for the Kluven complex of course, and although he didn't think it was the way to go, he certainly loved the idea of expanding his personal empire. After all, Gordon Ramsay had a string of starred restaurants, a successful media career and a homeware range while keeping his reputation as a top chef. Viggo knew he was going to the same.

Until that morning. The morning he couldn't get out of bed, the morning of his breakdown. That was the real reason why he was leaving Kluven, why he had decided he had to go the moment he'd left Kjell's bothy. He was leaving because he was frightened of what would happen if he stayed. And yes, he was frightened of what *she* would say, of what she would do.

Viggo pulled on the cigar, listening to the crackle, his eyes drifting into the dark of the forest. He was feeling a little better now, although he could have done without the showdown with Petra. His sous chef had a point, of course. He should have told her about his plans to leave Kluven before Martin made the announcement to the whole staff, but he hadn't – because he was afraid. He was afraid that Petra might talk him into staying.

After all, it was Petra who had persuaded him to move to the frozen north in the first place. When Martin Svenson had originally made the offer, Viggo had laughed. He had no intention of leaving the beauty and the haze of Provence; he'd left Sweden to escape the harsh winters, vowing never to go back. But Petra, his then-colleague at La Ferme Mougins, had bullied and cajoled, insisted it was a wonderful opportunity, the chance to have an unforgettable adventure; that the prospect of co-owning a top restaurant was too good to miss and certainly worth the cold winters.

Viggo blew a smoke ring and gave a bitter smile. Yes, he was grateful for Petra's belief in him, but that didn't mean he owed her anything. Sure, they had come here as a team and there was no doubt Petra had shown him the path to glory, but would she have created all this without him? Not a chance. This was Viggo's edifice, built by sheer force of personality. Even so, it had been foolish to whip her up like that. Angry and resentful, Petra was dangerous. Dangerous because she knew too much. And she wasn't the only one. Viggo desperately wanted to put Kluven behind him but would they let him?

A noise in the forest made him start, dropping his cigar.

'Damn.'

He ducked down to grab it, peering out through the bars of the balcony. Trees and darkness and snow. That was all he could see. Of course, all kinds of creatures lived in the forest. Lynx, moose, fox, even the odd bear and wolf; sometimes he would see amber eyes peering back at him between the trunks. But was it just animals? For a few months now, Viggo had started having the unsettling feeling that he was being watched. It had started in the summer when the panic attacks were happening with more regularity, and at first he had put it down to general anxiety: seeing things that weren't there. But lately, he wasn't at all sure it was just his imagination. He'd find footprints outside his door very early in the morning and he'd hear noises: scratching on a window, or the soft 'crump' of snow dislodged. Rising now, Viggo backed into the cabin, locking the door behind him.

Had he seen something? Had he imagined the noise? Or was it Petra sneaking up on him? He wouldn't put it past her.

BANGBANGBANG!

Viggo actually jumped in the air, whirling around to face the front door, just as he saw the handle turn. And then a voice.

'I think it's about time we had a proper talk, don't you?'

Chapter 10

Justin should have felt terrible – he *did* feel terrible – but right now, it didn't matter. Right now his limbs felt as though he had sandpaper instead joints, frayed wire instead of bones and his eyeballs felt far too big in his head. But none of it mattered, because of what was clenched in his fist. Barely as big as one of those weird white cherries they'd served at dinner, it was a jewel beyond price: this was the cure.

He held it up to the light, pinched between thumb and forefinger, and a smile flicked across Justin's face. No, it was more than that: what he held in the palm of his hand was *salvation*. And as long as you knew it was coming, everything felt fine. The cramps, the headache, the guilt, it all slid off your back when you knew sunshine was just around the corner.

He looked across the cabin, all soft furs and golden light. Emily had loved it when they'd walked in, she had jabbered on about how they should do a Scandi make-over on their place in LA, but Justin had been scanning it for hiding places.

His smile faded, pierced by guilt. Drugs and rock'n'roll

– it was a such a cliché. If he was honest, that was what made him feel the worst. He'd met plenty of kids in bands who'd bought into the romance of Keef, Sid and Kurt. Die young, leave a good-looking legend. But Justin had got into this for the music, because that was the thing he loved most in the world.

Had loved most in the world. Because the drug didn't let anyone or anything come before her. Not music, not Emily, not anything.

Clenching his fist once more, he headed back outside.

He'd left Emily in the dining room, telling her he had an upset stomach. She'd let him go just as he knew she would. Who was going to accuse one of the world's greatest chefs of giving them food poisoning? Plus by the end of the meal, Justin probably *had* looked dreadful. On TV, every junkie had waxy skin, sunken eyes and a bad case of the sweats. Check, check and check. No wonder Emily had bought his story about a bad scallop. But still, she would be back any moment and if she caught him, he'd be screwed.

Their cabin was the furthest away from the lodge – Emily had apparently asked for Kluven's most private guest cabin, and for that he was grateful. Justin followed a track into the forest, letting the moon lead the way until he turned a corner and saw another cabin, its windows all lit up. Panicking, Justin stepped off the path and into the trees.

Then it went dark, very, very quickly, the thick branches blocking out any light from the cabin or the sky. Justin used the torch on his phone to locate somewhere he could sit, a quiet dry corner where he would not be disturbed, but not so deep into the forest that it would be dangerous. Kat the manager had told them about the wildlife you could find in this part of the world, and Justin had no wish to meet any of it.

He crawled under a low branch and found a patch of

soft dry pine needles, sitting cross-legged under the sagging arms of the tree.

Justin felt in his pocket and pulled out the ball, holding it between pursed lips as he unfolded a sheet of silver foil taken from the inside of a chocolate bar he'd found in the mini-bar. As he expertly set about preparing the hit, Justin thought about how he'd got here. After all, Justin Blake was the least likely druggie; ask anyone. Joystick was a soft-rock middle-class wet dream – likeable and melodic. The cooler end of the music press said they lacked edge, were too earnest and bland, but Justin had never cared. It meant they had broad appeal and as Justin could bang out hit after hit – crowd-pleasers with big choruses and soaring orchestral tunes, selling out stadiums and ringing up album sales in a time when no one bought albums any more.

And even though the music industry was full of drugs, Justin managed to spend almost a decade in Joystick without taking any of them. But then the band split and he hooked up with The Velvetines, he started hanging out with a different crowd for whom taking drugs was commonplace, every day. His descent into addiction had been fast and now Justin couldn't imagine his life without it.

He flicked his lighter and the rush, when it came, was sweet. As it hit his bloodstream all the aches just... floated away. Exhaling the smoke in a grateful, happy hiss, Justin leant back against the trunk of the tree and moaned.

That was when he heard voices coming from the cabin. Loud voices. He could hear what they were saying but he didn't care. Whatever it was, it didn't matter. Nothing mattered, except that he was at peace. The buzzing in his body and his mind had stilled and he looked up at the branches overhead, their criss-cross pattern suddenly fascinating to him. He felt good, sure, but it was the release from the need, a blissful relief. Like a rattling air con unit that had kept you awake all night, suddenly shutting off.

'Justin.'

At first he thought the voice was coming from the forest. Then he wondered if it was his dead father, calling him from beyond the grave. Brian Blake had been a dentist, a committed church goer, an enthusiastic mandolin player and a thoroughly decent man. Brian had introduced his son to the guitar at the age of twelve and quickly discovering that Justin was a natural, did everything he could to nurture his talent, paying for new instruments, music lessons and sheet music, ferrying him to orchestra practice and chamber choir concerts without ever grumbling.

If he had ever been disappointed that Justin had dropped out of his music degree for life on the road with Joystick, the band he'd begun in Freshers' week, Brian Blake never said.

'Just make the right choices, son,' he'd said to him and put £2,000 in his bank account so Justin could buy a fourth-hand transit van. Brian had died six months after Joystick signed their debut record deal; the first time they had played Wembley Stadium, Justin had dedicated their biggest hit to his father, knowing that he would be looking down on him feeling proud.

'Justin.'

Lately, he'd been thinking a lot about his father. He'd be glad that Justin was writing music again. But the fact that he was taking drugs daily would devastate him.

'Justin,' said the voice. And now a shadow was loomed over him.

Justin felt two hands on his shoulders and tried to focus. In a rush Justin returned to the present moment. The needles sticking into his back, the cold and wet in his shoes.

And a deep voice speaking from above, a *real* voice. Viggo Widlund was standing a few paces away, holding a lantern.

'What is this shit, Justin?' said the chef looking down at the silver foil he'd dropped.

'It's nothing. I just came out here for some air.'

'Like hell you did,' growled Viggo.

Justin didn't know Viggo all that well – they'd met at Joystick's Stockholm show and kept in sporadic touch – but he knew him well enough to know that he could be intimidating and now that legendary temper seemed to be directed at him.

'I could *smell* it, Justin,' he said pointing back towards the path. Now Justin could smell Viggo's breath too – smoky and sour as if he was about to exhale fire. Images and ideas were swirling in his head. He wasn't entirely sure what was real and what was the drug rushing through his bloodstream.

'Smell? What smell?' he said doubtfully. 'Look, I was just having a smoke.'

Before he could do anything, the chef darted forward, gripping Justin by the front of his jacket and thrusting a hand into Justin's pocket.

'Hey! What are you doing...?'

Then Viggo was holding up the little bundle. His *stuff*.

'How dare you come here,' hissed Viggo. 'To my place, at my invitation and take this shit outside my house?'

'Viggo, it's nothing.'

'Is it Justin?' said the chef. 'Let's see, shall we?'

And with that, Viggo turned and made to throw Justin's drugs into the trees.

'NO!' Justin yelled, leaping up and grabbing Viggo. Struggling with him, he prised Viggo's fingers apart, snatching the package back.

'You don't need it, Justin,' cried the chef, 'Let it go'.

Screaming a profanity, Justin flung a punch. Justin was not particularly strong or a very adept fighter, but the power of his roundhouse caught Viggo by surprise. Grunting, the chef fell forward into Justin's chest, then reeled backwards against the trunk of a tree, a shower of snow falling over them both.

'I'm sorry, I'm sorry,' said Justin, holding up a hand, terrified the Viking chef would launch a counter-attack. But Viggo didn't move except to wipe a trickle of blood from his nose.

'You're better than this,' he said, sitting down on the ground.

'Am I?' asked Justin. The coolness of Viggo's words had taken him by surprise and he looked down at the forest floor carpet in shame.

'Yes Justin,' said Viggo. 'You're gifted. You have the power to move people, to change the way they feel with a chord or a chorus – that's incredible. But taking this shit... you're going to throw it all away.'

Justin felt his back stiffen. He knew the drugs weren't good for him, but even so, Justin was writing great new material. Some of it was the best stuff he'd ever made.

'Don't tell me how to live my life, Viggo,' he said defensively.

'I'm not telling you, I'm *asking* you how you want to live your life,' Viggo replied.

'I am living the life I want to live,' he bit back.

He'd spoken to Viggo on the phone a few weeks earlier, telling the chef about his life in LA, how much time he had been spending in the studio, his plans for the future. And now this arrogant know-all Swede was questioning him, moralising like he was better than Justin Blake, the pop star.

'What would you know about it?' he sneered.

'Oh, I know Justin, I know,' said Viggo wearily. 'I've been exactly where you are now.'

Justin, frowned, wondered if he was hearing things again, wondered if this whole conversation was in his head. Viggo was the polar opposite of him. Tall, strong, always in control. How could Viggo Widlund know what heroin smelled like?

'I always liked the sensory experiences,' said Viggo almost to himself. 'Perhaps that was why I became a chef. But it took me a while to get here. First I immersed myself: sex, drink, drugs. I fought with it, like giants thundering behind the mountains. Then I got past it.'

'Got past it? Got past what?'

'I got out of Malmo, away from the bad crowd I was in with. I went to Australia to clean up. I was twenty-two years old and I decided to start my life all over again. Got a job in a restaurant, discovered I could cook. If there's such a thing as an addictive personality, I channelled it all into my cooking.'

'Oh,' said Justin. 'I never knew.'

'And now you do,' he said. 'And now you can see that it's possible to just walk away from it.'

Viggo stretched out a big hand towards Justin.

'Give it to me,' he said.

Justin hesitated, and closed his eyes. Instead of seeing the strung-out mess he'd become, he suddenly imagined himself back on stage, back in the Joystick glory days high on life and the energy of the crowd, with his dad in the wings, clapping and beaming with pride. He took a deep breath and when he opened his eyes again, he handed the stash to Viggo.

'Thank you,' said Viggo simply.

Justin heard a noise, the faint chirp of an incoming text.

Viggo put his hand in his pocket, pulled out a phone and glanced at it.

'I must go,' he said, putting the drugs and the phone back in the top pocket of his jacket.

'And you should go back to your cabin, it's too cold out here. Go back to your life, Justin, go back to Emily.'

He stood up, leaving his lantern under the tree. 'And spend the rest of your life thanking me.'

Viggo turned, ducked under a branch and was swallowed by the darkness.

Chapter 11

The bar at Kluven wasn't really a bar, more an extension of the dining room. There was a copper wood-burner to match the hammered copper bar where Alex was sitting knee-to-knee with Lara, sipping warm gluhwein – or whatever its Swedish name was. It was good though; spiced mulled wine with a citrusy kick. No surprise that everything was delicious here, even the nuts in a little bowl on the counter were light and crisp with a sweet caramel shell. In fact, Alex had enjoyed the supper far more than he had expected. Yes, there had been theatre – the juniper smoked salmon that had been de-boned at the table, the trout sashimi sliced and prepared in front of him, but for once, Alex had managed to put his cynicism to one side and allowed himself to be transported on a journey of taste and sensation. Each course had been more delicious than the one before it; the elk carpaccio, the mackerel and pickled carrot, rib of beef cooked on hot coals and wild duck served with forest fresh mushrooms, which were rich and complex – even to Alex's untrained tastebuds. Oh, and the cloudberry panna cotta made from creamy reindeer milk was so soft and delicate, it had been like a sweet cloud that just swam across his tongue.

The other diners in the bar were obviously feeling a similar level of wellbeing, having repaired to this cosy nook covered with fluffy white sheepskins to discuss the meal like sports pundits discussing the action after the final whistle. Only Miles the chef, Justin and Emily were missing; Justin had left before the end of the meal, Emily had gone to find him and Miles had just disappeared. Martin Svenson's friends Kenneth and Serena had also melted away. At dinner he'd overheard Kenneth mention trying out the hot tub, so perhaps he had gone to the spa. Alex was also keen to try it, but after thirty courses he wasn't sure it was the time.

'So do you think this is the end of Kluven?' asked Lara, her eyes shining in the low light.

'Could well be,' said Doctor Green. 'I can't imagine many people trekking out this far for just another chef.'

'It's so successful, why do you think he did it?' said Connie taking a thoughtful sip of brandy.

Coulson shrugged.

'I wonder if it's that review in *The Times* the other week?' he said.

'Which review?' asked Lara.

'They ran a piece about some new place out in Montana. Said they were doing what Kluven does only much better.'

Doctor Green shook his head. ''Well I'd like to see anyone top that,' he said nodding towards the dining room. Alex murmured his agreement.

'But no one likes to feel as if they are on the slide,' said Coulson, lowering his voice. 'Especially not elite performers. It's sometimes hard for laymen like us to understand that mindset, but for people running at that level, it's number one or it's nowhere.'

Alex didn't need a psychology degree to see the sense in Coulson's argument. Although Alex had enjoyed the meal immensely – he finally felt he understood how people could make the comparison between cooking and art – the truth was, you could get great food everywhere nowadays. Even bars in London sold things with jus and foam on top. It wasn't the same, obviously, but over the past decade, cooking standards had definitely risen. Viggo might well be the best, and after tonight, Alex was willing to agree, but if you could get something almost as good in your nearest city, then who was going to fly to Lapland?

'Well at least we got to try it,' said Connie, sipping her liqueur. 'Shame Miles isn't here. I wanted to ask him as a fellow professional what he thought of the meal.'

'He's a chef?' said Coulson with surprise. 'Ah, that might explain it. He was sitting opposite me and he seemed to scowl every time his server announced a new course.'

Alex had felt the same way: there was definitely some sort of rivalry going on there, even if Miles' other half Nami refused to be drawn on what the man's so-called 'lies' might have been. Alex had tried to push her on it, but all he could glean was that Miles believed Viggo lacked authenticity somehow. Perhaps all chefs felt that way about their contemporaries.

'I'm glad we made the journey, aren't you?' said Connie turning to Graham. 'That trout was the best thing I've tasted since that meal we had in Tierra del Fuego.'

'You've been down there?' said Coulson.

'We like to get out and about, don't we Con?' said Graham. Coulson turned to Dr. Green.

'We've always wanted to go there, haven't we Patrick?'

Dr Green murmured his assent, but he didn't look too happy that Connie and Graham had beaten him to it.

'Maybe knock off a few more boob jobs, eh love?' said Connie.

Alex tried to hide a smile; the Manchester couple had a disarming way of pricking pretence. Lara laughed first, then Coulson and even Patrick's icy demeanour cracked as he let out a reluctant smile. Perhaps the night hadn't gone the way the Kluven management had envisioned, but one thing had certainly worked: the communal table had brought them all together.

'Everyone happy?'

They all turned to the cheery trill of Kat, but Alex wasn't sure the guest manager shared their levity. The smile seemed fixed, thin lips over gritted teeth.

'Well, I think I may have something to make you all even happier, if you'd like to follow me outside,' she said.

'What's going on?' asked Connie.

'The aurora borealis,' said Kat gesturing towards the door.

Connie clapped her hands together.

'Ooh! The Northern Lights!'

'I thought the cloud cover was too thick?' Said Dr Green.

'The clouds have just parted above the lake,' said Kat over her shoulder as she led them to a pair of French doors. 'But there's a band of snow moving in, so we should hurry.'

Quickly, the guests gathered their coats and hats, but the temperature was brutal when they stepped outside; minus twenty, maybe lower.

'Wow,' said Lara, her face turned upwards. Alex followed her gaze and suddenly the cold didn't seem so important any more: ribbons of gentle green light were waving across the dark sky.

Similarly entranced, the group slowly split off into their own little groups, heads tilted back, falling into an awestruck silence.

'Have you ever seen them before?' Lara whispered to Alex. It was the same atmosphere as in a big cathedral: you felt you should talk in hushed voices.

'No, never,' he said, 'I've been to Russia, Norway, Alaska and wherever I went I always seemed to just miss them. But this...Oh, this was worth waiting for.'

The light fanned out across the dark dome overhead. Fluid in movement, it shape-shifted in the sky, dipping in and out of a range of colour, from emerald and jade fading to pale lilac and back again.

With each change, Lara let out a little gasp of wonder. Alex turned and grinned at her.

'It's incredible, isn't it?' she breathed. Alex nodded. Without thinking, he reached out and took Lara's hand. They stood there like that, for a long time, just the two of them lost in their own private show.

'Sandrine would have liked this,' said Lara after a while; her voice was soft, wistful.

'Yeah, Sandrine really knew how to enjoy life,' said Alex.

'Do you?' said Lara, dropping his hand. Had he said something to upset her? He wondered. To Alex it felt like a rejection, or was he reading too much into it? Either way, that was the moment the clouds chose to draw together and the colour winked out to a collective groan.

'Can we do this every year?' said Lara, pulling the hood of her parka up.

'Thirty courses with a Northern Lights chaser? I'm up for that every weekend.'

'Right up until the moment you get another girl-friend,' she said. Was that the issue with Lara? She was expecting him to disappear any moment into domestic bliss?

'That won't stop me,' he said, but Lara didn't look convinced.

'I hardly saw you when you were with Alicia,' she said more seriously.

Alex wanted to deny it, but it was true. He shrugged.

'Alicia was jealous of you,' he said.

They'd never really discussed it, but it was easier to talk honestly standing in the dark, surrounded by nothing, feeling as if they were somehow detached from the real world. Lara looked up at Alex, her dark eyes searching his. 'Jealous of me? Why?'

She was probably fishing for a compliment, but over the years they had side-stepped too many conversations like this.

'Insecurity, I suppose,' said Alex frankly. 'You can't blame someone for finding it hard when their partner's best friend is so clever and beautiful.'

Something told Alex that he'd said enough – or too much perhaps – so he just let the words drift away on the rising wind.

'Come on, let's go back in,' said Lara. 'The weather's starting to turn. We should try one of the brandies. Possibly all of them.'

They didn't talk for the rest of the way back to the bar, the only sound their footsteps, dampened by the falling snow.

'I'll see you in there,' said Alex as they approached the lodge. 'I'm just going to poke my head into the kitchen.'

'What for?'

He raised an eyebrow.

'To see if Viggo is there.'

'I thought you wanted to collar Justin Blake.'

'He can wait until breakfast.'

Alex was only half-joking, but he'd realised the clock was ticking and he had to prioritise. According to the schedule in their rooms, there would be breakfast tomorrow morning, then time for a short sauna or an ice bath, then it was straight back to the airport. If Alex knew anything about rock stars, it was that they liked to sleep late, but he was going to have to take his chances with Justin; tonight, Alex needed to push for an interview with Viggo. The chef's work was literally done and Alex sensed he wouldn't get another chance after tonight.

'Alex, remember what we said to Martin Svenson,' she said with disapproval.

'Sure, but it's different if Viggo decides to give me a world exclusive face-to-face,' said Alex, trying to make light of it. When Lara didn't laugh, he turned to face her. He needed her to understand.

'I know you think I work too hard, and that I never switch off,' he said. 'But if you've seen the *Chronicle*'s latest circulation figures you'll know why I'm pushing this.'

'I have seen the figures,' she replied. Alex shouldn't have been surprised. Lara's late father had bequeathed Lara his shares in the Avery Media Group, the *Chronicle*'s parent company and while she didn't attend board meetings or get involved with the nitty-gritty of running the company, it made sense that she would keep on top of the latest sales reports. They didn't make for happy reading. Newspapers were suffering badly as readers turned to the internet for their news and advertisers were following in droves.

'The *Chronicle* needs stories, Lar,' said Alex. 'We need headlines. And right here, tonight, there's about half a dozen of them, the biggest of which is the Viking Chef closing the most infamous restaurant in the world.'

Lara gave him a reluctant smile.

'Fine. You go. Save the value of my shareholding – it's what any true friend would do.'

Alex held up a hand. 'I'll be five minutes. Get me some more of that mead ready. Never been a fan of brandy.'

'Lightweight,' she smiled, heading back towards the bar.

Alex went the other way, following his nose towards the kitchens, hidden behind double doors across from the dining room. As he began thinking of his opening line, something like 'not many people would be brave enough to walk away from a global success' – flattery was always a winner – the doors swung open and a waitress stepped into the corridor holding a drink.

'Oh, hello,' said the young woman, looking down at her glass with embarrassment. Presumably their end-of-season celebration wasn't supposed to be seen by the guests. 'Can I help?'

'I was looking for Viggo actually,' said Alex, peering over her shoulder as the doors swung back and forth, a tantalising glimpse of the hidden behind-the-scenes of Kluven. 'He said he'd give me a phone number – we have a mutual friend I've lost touch with.' Total nonsense, but Alex was used to thinking on his feet.

'Viggo's not here,' said the girl. 'He's gone to his cabin, I think.'

'The one on the edge of the forest?'

Kat had pointed out the path which led to Viggo's cabin on their tour earlier. The girl nodded and stumbled on towards the ladies.

'So far, so good,' Alex muttered to himself as he crossed back to the outside door. Getting Viggo in private would be the ideal scenario – assuming he was alone, of course - but just as Alex was reaching for the door, it swung inwards and Kat stepped into the lodge. She pushed her hood back, which was glistening with snowflakes.

'Oh Alex,' she said, stomping her boots on the mat. 'Everything okay?

'Sure, I was just going out to look at the snow. I imagine it's old news to you, but I still get excited about it.'

It was more quick thinking: he wasn't about to tell her what he was really up to. Theo had already asked them not to go near the story and Alex imagined the Kluven management team were right now in crisis talks deciding how to deal with it all.

'Well, I wouldn't stay outside long,' she said. 'It looks like it's really going to come down. I'd go back to the bar if I were you.'

All the flirtation had gone from her voice, with just a hint of warning. Warning about spreading the Viggo story or about frostbite? Alex supposed they were equally unwelcome to Kat. He stepped out into the cold and immediately saw that she was right: those gentle flakes were now fat and wet and piling up where they fell. He couldn't imagine the ground staff would be coming out to clear the paths tonight, so he needed to move fast before everything was buried.

'Right, Viggo, where are you?' he said, striking out towards the path Kat had pointed out. He glanced at his watch as he picked up his pace. The wind was pushing the snow straight towards him, billowing inside his hood, stinging his face.

'What am I doing?' he muttered through clenched teeth.

As Lara kept pointing out, he was supposed to be on holiday. Did he want his abiding memory of the trip to be a missing toe? And for what exactly? A story that Darius, his temperamental editor might very well just dismiss.

To his left, Alex saw the storage barns silhouetted against the dark forest behind. His eyes narrowed: there was a light coming from the one furthest from the path – the root cellar. What had Kat said about it? That Viggo and Theo were the only ones with a key, which meant there was a 50/50 chance Viggo was inside. Plus it was much closer than Viggo's cabin and would at least be a respite from the wind. As he walked, Alex wrinkled up his face and blew out his cheeks; he remembered reading that's what Shackleton and Scott did to prevent frostbite. He was finding it harder to walk now; visibility was non-existent and the heated paths couldn't cope with the huge dump of snow. *This weekend was supposed to be fun,* he thought.

What he'd said to Kat only minutes ago was true: Alex loved the snow. In adult life, snow was mostly an irritation, the cause of traffic snarl-ups and cancelled trains, but back in his cherished childhood, snow had been a magical thing. It had meant school might be closed, sometimes for days on end, which would be then be filled with sledging at the near-legendary Setter Dog, a pub which just happened to have a field behind it of the correct gradient for thrilling rides on toboggan, tea-tray or even sliding on fertiliser bags. In hindsight, there were a hundred suitable slopes – it was the Lake District after all – but Alex's friends got dropped off at that particular place so their dads could watch through the back windows of the pub, pint in hand.

When did life stop being so simple? Alex knew it was a cliched question, but there was a certain truth to it. Just being happy to see snow, to catch it on your tongue. Making a snow angel or sticking a carrot nose on a snowman. In adult life, everything had weight and meaning. Sometimes you just wanted to wang a snowball at a stop sign.

Alex's numbing legs felt heavy now, but still he kept moving, wondering what Viggo was doing in the root cellar at such a late hour, imagining the culinary maverick liberating small batch berries from their hiding place. Maybe he planned to take them with him.

By the time Alex reached the root cellar it had almost disappeared beneath a drift. All he could see was an arch of wood and a giant door with small windows: it was the glass which had been glowing at him like soft amber eyes.

Alex pushed the door open, hoping he was right, that Viggo would be here. Much better than doorstepping the man at his cabin and much better for the story, too.

He ducked into the low room, pulling off his hood. The light was dim and the air felt earthy and musty, but it was better than being out there in the snow.

'Hello?' he called, just as the wind caught the door, rocking it back on its hinges. Surprised, Alex took a step back sideways and stumbled over a log lying on the floor.

He frowned. Why would there be a log in the root cellar? Pulling his phone from his pocket, Alex thumbed on the flashlight, directing it towards the floor.

'Oh. Shit.'

It wasn't a log. It was a leg, its toes pointing to the ceiling. Slowly Alex angled the light up the body to its neck, beard, face. Viggo's face.

Swinging the light back down: a dark damp circle on his neck. Blood.

'Viggo?'

Alex quickly knelt, looking closer. The chef's eyes were open, pupils fixed and dilated, that line remembered from a thousand hospital TV dramas. Alex tentatively touched the neck, feeling for a pulse, but he was fairly sure he wouldn't find one. Viggo Widlund – the Viking Chef – was dead.

Now *that* was a headline.

Chapter 12

Lara glanced at her watch, only half listening to the voices in the bar.

'Oh, Greenland was so beautiful, wasn't it Graham?' said Connie in the background. 'And when we were cruising through the icebergs, it was like we were surrounded by giant sculptures, wasn't it? So calm.'

'So bloody cold too.'

Lara smiled politely at Graham and turned towards the window, where the snowflakes now looked as big as eggs. Where *was* Alex? Connie and Graham were the only guests left in the bar; after a quick drink, everyone else had wisely sloped off to their cabins. After all, Kluven was an achingly romantic destination and anyone with any sense would be snuggling up under bearskins instead of listening to Connie and Graham gushing about their recent Arctic cruise.

'Looking for your man?' asked Connie, following Lara's gaze.

'He should be back by now,' said Lara, still staring out into the Arctic darkness. 'I'm worried he's frozen to death.'

Worried, but also irritated. Because it was much more likely that Alex had talked his way into Justin Blake's cabin and was at this moment quizzing him about the B-side of some obscure Japanese import. But there *was* still the slim chance Alex might be in trouble. He had gone out there looking for a story, but *Promising editor found frozen to death* was probably not the one he wanted.

'Are you sure he's not just waiting for you in the hot tub?' asked Connie mischievously and Lara almost laughed. Almost. Not that she blamed people for jumping to conclusions about her and Alex.

Earlier that week, at her annual Christmas lunch with her boarding school roommate Suzanne, Lara had confided in her friend that she was thinking about freezing her eggs.

'But what about Alex?' Suzanne had replied, wide-eyed, as if she didn't really believe that Lara was single.

When Lara had explained again that they were just friends, Suzanne's response had been a single wink and the words, 'Have a bottle of glog in Kluven and see what happens.'

And here in the Arctic, sharing a cabin with Alex, Lara did have to ask herself some serious questions too. Such as why it seemed more practical to turn to cryopresevation than consider becoming Mrs Ford. Sometimes she would see Alex out of the corner of her eye, and she'd feel the fuzzy rush of desire, until she realised who it was. She certainly hadn't liked seeing the security official flirt with him at Kiruna airport, but that had been nothing compared to the shock and panic she had felt in the summer when an engagement ring had dropped out of Alex's pocket, and he'd admitted that he was thinking of proposing to his girlfriend Alicia. When Alex and Alicia had split up a short time later, Lara hadn't even bothered to make sympathetic noises. At the time, she'd told herself it was because Alicia was bad news and that Alex deserved better. But now she wasn't so sure.

He was lovely, no question, but Alex was *Alex*, her closest friend. He was also the closest thing Lara had to family, the one person she could always rely on. When Lara's parents had died when she was just eleven years old, she had been sent to live with her uncle Nicholas and her Aunt Olivia on their huge country estate in Oxfordshire, but she had never felt part of their family unit there, not really. And since she had lost her best friend Sandrine, Alex was all she had: Lara was terrified of losing him too.

'There's terrible reception here,' she said, holding up her phone. The message she'd just sent Alex was just spinning around going nowhere.

'Try out at the front entrance,' said Connie. 'I managed to get two bars there earlier on.'

Lara nodded her thanks and jumped up.

'Remember when we were like that?' she heard Graham say as she strode off.

'Hey! *I* still am,' replied Connie.

The moment Lara walked into the foyer, her phone lit up and began to ring. Her shoulders sagged with relief when the number came up as Alex.

'At last!' she said. 'I've been worried sick...'

But Alex cut her off.

'Lar, quickly. Something's happened.'

She caught his urgent tone immediately.

'What? Tell me.'

There was a moment's pause.

'It's Viggo. Viggo Widlund. He's dead.'

'Dead?' she hissed, looking around to make sure they weren't overheard. 'Are you sure?'

'I'm pretty sure. He's been stabbed. There's a lot of blood and he doesn't seem to be breathing.'

Blood... Instantly Lara felt herself go cold all over, transported back to that horrible night standing next to her friend Sandrine's body. *Not again,* she thought. This can't be happening again.

'Lar, you need to find Martin Svenson or the general manager, what's his name – Theo?' said Alex. 'Dr Green too, in case it's not too late.'

Not too late. Lara closed her eyes, trying to get the image of Sandrine lying on a gurney from her mind. *Get a grip. Get a bloody grip.*

'Okay,' she said. 'Where are you?'

'In the root cellar, by the storage barns. Be quick.'

'Okay, I'm on it,' she said, switching the phone off and looking around. Priorities: they needed medical help. First the emergency services, then Doc Green. She turned and ran down the corridor. 'Mr Mikaelsson?' she shouted. 'Theo Mikaelsson?'

A door to her right opened and the manager looked out.

His glasses were half way down his nose. He was wearing one of the beige Kluven parkas.

'Miss Stone.' He said, with surprise.

'You need to get to the root cellar, Theo,' she said. 'Something has happened to Viggo. He's been stabbed.'

'Stabbed? Are you sure?'

'Alex is there with him. Just go.'

He blinked at her, then nodded.

'And call the emergency services before you go,' she called, backing down the passage, not convinced that anything, not even an air ambulance, would be able to get to Kluven in this weather. 'I'm going to find Doctor Green. I'll meet you there.'

At the back door, she grabbed her own parka from the hook by the door, pulling it on as she ran out into the biting cold, snowflakes falling down her neck. She pulled up the hood and ran as fast as the rising drifts would allow, eyes narrowed against the stinging cold. She knew that Coulson and Patrick were in the next cabin to theirs and she slid to a halt and banged hard on the door. It opened a sliver and Coulson peeked suspiciously out.

'Lara?'

'I need to speak to Patrick,' she panted. 'Quickly.'

Coulson looked bemused. 'He's on the back porch with a Scotch.' He clearly saw something in Lara's expression because he suddenly turned and bellowed his partner's name. The doctor came running out, still wearing his coat.

'Viggo is injured,' said Lara. 'Maybe dead. You need to come quickly.'

Dr. Green hesitated and looked at Coulson.

'Dead?'

'Well he certainly will be if you don't come quickly. This way.'

Patrick fumbled with the zip on his parka and followed her up the path. The wind lashed at them as Lara shouted out to the doctor what Alex had told her.

'Lara, I'm a plastic surgeon, not a paramedic,' Patrick called back.

'Maybe, but you'll be a hell of a lot more use than me.'

The downlights along the paths were still shining, but the way was becoming indistinct as they swished through the snow. The cold squeezed her lungs and her eyes were watering, but she powered on.

'There!' she shouted, pointing. Lara hadn't been to the root cellar, but on the fringe of the forest she saw the outline of the open door and the grey shape of Theo waving and beckoning her in.

Stepping into the cellar was like someone had turned off the weather, suddenly dead calm and cool, although warmer than outside.

She couldn't see Alex but the general manager was bent over Viggo's body which was lying prostrate on the concrete floor. A white cloth was bunched up in Theo's hands. Even in the low light, Lara could see that it was covered in blood.

Dr. Green crouched down and felt Viggo's neck, then reached for the pulse point on the chef's wrist. After a few moments listening close to Viggo's mouth, he looked up shaking his head with a grim expression.

'He's gone.'

He clambered to his feet and hung his head – sadness, respect, perhaps even regret that he'd not been able to do anything to help. There was a scuffle at the door.

Lara turned and saw Alex and Kat, who pushed past her to get inside.

Her eyes flew wide and she let out a low moan, raising a trembling hand to her lips. 'No,' she hissed. 'No, no, no...'

'Alright,' said Dr. Green, spreading his hands as if to herd them away. 'That's enough. Everybody should leave.'

Outside, Lara went to over to Alex. He had a smear of blood down his beige parka. His face was drained of any colour.

'Where have you been?'

'Theo sent me to get Kat.'

She glanced across to the general manager who was talking to Patrick Green.

'You okay?' she said gently.

He nodded.

'What happened?'

It was a moment before he spoke.

'I went to look for Viggo. I saw the light of the root cellar on. Kat told me he keeps the key to it, so I figured he'd be there.'

His voice trailed off. 'He was just lying on the floor, Lar. I grabbed a cloth. Tried to stem the blood. But it was too late.'

His voice cracked with despair.

Lara knew this wasn't Alex's first dead body. He'd been to war zones, seen bodies in graves covered in lime; he'd once told her about seeing – and smelling – twisted limbs sticking from the black skeleton of a burned-out truck in Syria.

She took his hand, ice cold in her palm, and squeezed it. For a moment she thought of the scene half an hour earlier; Alex taking her own hand as they watched the Northern Lights together. Now it seemed so long ago she could barely even remember why she'd let go.

'Where the bloody hell is Martin?' muttered Theo, although she could barely hear him through the wind.

Another moment and she could see Kluven's owner march down the path towards them, his face only barely visible through the circle of fur on the hood of his parka.

'What's happened?' he said, squinting towards Theo and shielding his face from the falling snowflakes.

Theo led him into the root cellar and then Lara heard him retch.

She turned to Patrick Green.

'What do you think happened?'

He gave a shrug, although she could barely tell he was moving in his thick parka.

'I'm not sure,' he said. 'At a guess, a knife wound to the chest. It looks like it's gone through the heart or there's been a penetration of the aorta or vena cava. Ruptures of that nature are generally fatal.'

'A knife wound?' said Alex.

Patrick nodded, the loop of fur around his hood bobbing up and down.

'I'm speculating but it's the likeliest cause.'

Martin Svenson came out wiping his mouth with the back of his glove. Theo followed and closed and locked the flapping door.

'Everyone. Back to the lodge,' he ordered.

Patrick Green needed no further encouragement and disappeared back to the main part of the complex. After an awkward pat on the shoulder from her husband, Kat Mikaelsson followed him.

Lara and Alex hung back. The fir tree next to the root cellar gave some protection from the swirling snow. Theo and Martin were having a hissed conversation in Swedish. The only word Lara could make out was a name: 'Magnus'. Finally Martin turned to Lara to acknowledge her presence.

'Please. Everyone should return to their cabins,' he said in brisk English.

'Have you called the police?' said Lara, ignoring the command. While Lara imagined the local residents were much more used to extreme weather conditions than back in the UK, she still didn't see how the police or any other emergency service could travel on roads that had to be all but impassable in this storm.

'Don't worry. I'm sure they'll be here soon,' said Martin.

'Which will be too late,' said Alex.

Martin Svenson shook his head.

'Sadly it's already too late, Mr. Ford.'

Lara glanced over at Alex. She knew they were both thinking the same thing.

'Mr Svenson,' she said. 'Your head chef has been killed, murdered and the longer it is before the police get here, the more likely it is that evidence will be lost or contaminated.'

'Murdered?' said Martin with more bluster. 'Now let's not jump to any conclusions.'

Lara nodded.

'That's just the point. We need to gather as much data as possible so we can form a conclusion. For any evidence to be useful, it has to be collected as soon as possible after the crime. Alex and I are experienced reporters. We can help.'

A thin, cynical smile passed across Martin's face.

'In my experience, reporters want the story, not to help the police.'

'We're not helping the police, Martin,' said Alex. 'We are helping you find out who killed Viggo.'

Martin shook his head.

'I understand that this is news for you, but Viggo was our *friend* and as you can imagine, the staff are going to be upset and frightened enough when they hear about it without some lurid story about murder all over your paper's website. I think you have a responsibility to keep this quiet until we've spoken to the police, found out what has happened and released a statement.'

'Keep it quiet?' said Alex cynically. 'How long do you think it will take to hit Twitter once the staff hear about it? With us at least you know the facts will be facts, not rumour and speculation.'

Lara nodded silently in agreement. It was a bugbear of modern journalists that they couldn't break the news anymore. Whether it was a protest, a bomb or a hurricane, they all made it to social media in the time it took someone to snap off a picture and add a hashtag.

'I am simply asking for your cooperation,' said Martin. 'Work with me now and we can come to some agreement with your press coverage.'

'That's exactly what we're proposing,' said Alex. 'We'll talk to the staff and the guests, get the facts straight, in a calm and measured way. If you leave it to social media, any wild story could take hold. We can control it.'

Martin snorted.

'Mr Ford, I can't have you charging around the complex playing Nancy Drew. I'm no law enforcement officer but there are procedures, protocols you need to follow. Breach that and we'll all end up in serious trouble.'

Lara gestured towards the wind-driven snow rattling Kluven's front doors.

'I've seen the forecast, Mr Svenson. The storm will last until morning at least. Are you suggesting we leave a murderer roaming around until then?'

Martin gave her a stern look.

'Miss Stone, I am not asking now. Return to your cabin. If a bear has got into the compound, you'll be safe there.'

'A *bear*?'

Svenson raised his chin defiantly.

'Theo and I have discussed the matter and we believe there is a possibility that Viggo was killed by a wild animal.'

Alex took a step towards Martin.

'I was there, Svenson,' he said, his voice low. 'I was in that root cellar alone with the man you call your friend. He was killed by an animal alright, but the human kind.'

'Miss Stone. Mr Ford. Back to your cabins...'

Lara could see the anger in Alex's eyes and she moved between the two men, turning Alex away.

'Come on Alex, let's go.'

'Thank you,' said Martin Svenson, his lips tight.

Martin and Theo lingered behind, as Alex and Lara walked quickly back to the main part of the complex. They stayed silent, their hands thrust in their pockets. They had to walk past the lodge to get back to their cabin. Kat was on the porch, banging her boots on a mat to dislodge the snow. She looked as if she was about to go inside but hung back as if she wanted to speak to them.

'Are you okay?' Kat had to raise her voice. The sound didn't carry well in the snow that was getting thicker and thicker.

Alex nodded.

'Come inside,' she instructed.

Lara was glad to get into the warmth. She looked at her

hands, which were mottled and pink. As she pulled off her hood, snowflakes fell to the ground dissolving on the parquet, leaving glittering droplets on the wood like a ribbon of tears, catching the light.

'There's brandy in your cabin but you should help yourself to whatever you want from in there,' she said

'Even the Macallan 65?'

He said it as a lame joke, and Kat raised a smile.

Lara was glad that the oppressive mood had been lightened.

'As I said, whatever you want.'

They followed Kat behind the bar, which was empty.

Dozens of bottles of amber liquid lined up against the illuminated mirrored wall. Kat took one of them and poured a large measure into three crystal tumblers.

'Brandy – it's supposed to be good for the nerves, isn't it?' she said, handing one to Lara. 'Theo's dad was a doctor and he swore by it. Although that might have been because he couldn't always get the right drugs out here.'

In the distance, they could still hear the sound of pots of pans clanging, the kitchen staff still cleaning up.

'They don't know?' asked Alex.

Kat shook her head.

'I'm not telling them. Theo and Martin can deal with it. In the meantime, I say let them enjoy a few more minutes of normality.'

Lara perched on the bar stool and took a slug of brandy. Lara didn't really like spirits, but she knocked it back anyway. She curled her lip as it burnt its way down, but at least she didn't feel cold to the bone any more. Back when Lara's father had worked at the *Chronicle*, Fleet Street still had a heavy drinking culture, but that had largely died out by the time she had got there; the modern media was far too fast-moving for a post-lunch doze at your desk. It had been slightly different for Alex who had spent his formative years in Beirut and Kandahar, where priming a contact over a bottle of Johnnie Walker was considered standard operating procedure. Alex didn't drink much either, but he still seemed able to knock it back without much ill effect. He leant on the bar, swilling the dark liquid around in his glass.

'Who would want Viggo dead?' he asked, almost to himself.

'I don't think bears are discriminate when they're hungry,' said Kat, with an ironic laugh.

'Did Theo and Martin mention the bear to you too?' asked Alex. 'Is that going to be the Kluven party line?'

'Why couldn't it be a bear that killed Viggo?' said Kat with a hint of sarcasm. 'Bears do attack humans. The last owner of the estate – Magnus Polson – was killed by a bear twenty years ago. It happens.'

Magnus. Theo had mentioned him back at the root cellar. Johan their driver had also mentioned him on the way back from the airport.

'As we say in the press, once is an accident, twice is a story,' said Alex, looking back at her over the rim of his glass.

'Anyway, I don't know who wanted Viggo dead,' said Kat, raising her glass unsteadily. 'You should ask Petra.'

'Who's Petra?'

'Viggo's sous chef. The lady with the red hair. She knew him best, came here with Viggo at the start. If anyone knows Viggo's little secrets it would be her.'

Secrets? Thought Lara, but before she could ask more, Kat knocked the drink back and banged the glass down on the bar. It was a tough, macho gesture, like something you'd see in spaghetti westerns. It seemed to jar with Kat's show-pony prettiness.

'Martin and Theo will be looking for me. I should go,' she said. 'Finish your drink, but then you should probably get back to your cabin unless you want to get snowed in here. Johan can work miracles with the snow-blower, but it's one filthy night out there.'

Alex waited until she had gone before he spoke.

'What was all that about?' he said. 'Viggo's little secrets?'

Lara didn't reply. She was just trying to process everything that had just happened. The night had certainly taken an unusual turn.

'She gave you the good stuff too?' said a voice above the crackle of the fire.

They both turned towards a wing-back chair by the fire, facing away from them. Exchanging a look, they walked around. Dr. Patrick Green was sitting with a glass in one hand and a bottle in the other.

'So that's where the Macallan went,' said Alex. 'There was a gap on the shelf.'

'You know this whisky can go for twenty thousand dollars a bottle?' he said, pouring a measure.

'Then I hope you can taste the peat,' said Alex.

He leaned against the table opposite Patrick.

'So you didn't fancy going back to your cabin either?' said Patrick, resting his tumbler on the arm of the chair. 'Don't blame you. I mean, in medical school, you dissect dead bodies and as an intern you have to deal with road accidents, heart attacks, those kind of things. But that?' He shook his head, his eyes focused on the glowing embers of the fire. 'That's the first time I've seen someone who's been murdered.'

He looked up at Lara, his eyes damp in the firelight.

'I didn't like it much: some doctor, huh?'

'I think you're allowed to be shocked and upset about seeing something like that,' replied Lara sympathetically.

'That's kind, but that's not it. I'm a surgeon, you see. I

make incisions almost every day of my professional life. I see blood...' He trailed off. 'Do you know how difficult it is to get though fat and muscle? Viggo's wound was deep, lethal. It had power behind it.'

He took a drink, spilling a little down his chin.

'Someone here, someone within these walls did that to Viggo. They were angry, full of rage.'

'So you think the killer knew him?' asked Alex.

Dr. Green shrugged. 'You're asking the wrong man, I do nose jobs and tummy tucks. Maybe Coulson might have some insight into it, he's the head-shrinker.'

He looked down at his hands, then rubbed them both on his trouser legs.

'But do you want to know my professional opinion?'

Lara nodded.

'I think we're snowed in with a psycho.'

Chapter 13

Theo held a cup of tea out to Petra. She looked at it blankly, then shook her head. She couldn't function, couldn't think. Petra had heard of stunned silence, but she had always thought it was just a figure of speech. No more: from the moment Theo had walked in and told her that Viggo was dead, Petra had felt like a boxer on the ropes. Reeling, hurt, barely staying on her feet. It just didn't compute. Viggo was dead. *Dead.*

Only five minutes ago, Petra had been in the bathroom brushing her teeth when she'd heard Theo knock.

Five minutes ago. Before the world had changed. She could still taste the mint.

'We're all devastated,' Theo was saying. 'But I know you were particularly close, Petra. Rest assured, first thing in the morning, I will be contacting a psychologist, a friend of my father's, and we will be offering counselling sessions to the entire staff.'

'I don't need counselling,' she said. 'I just want...'

What did she want?

'To be left alone.'

Kluven's general manager looked around her small

room as if he didn't think that was a good idea. It was one of the biggest in the staff accommodation block, a corner studio with a door that led out onto a grassy slope – but it was all relative. There was a shower room, desk, a tiny two-seater sofa and, for some reason, a double bed, which only made the place feel more claustrophobic. Petra sat on the edge of it now, her bathrobe wrapped tightly around her as Theo perched awkwardly on the sofa.

'It's just tragic,' he said, shaking his head.

'Why are you so sure it was a bear?' said Petra. She said it casually, but she watched Theo carefully, gauging his reaction.

Theo sat forward a little. 'Between you and me, we're not entirely sure what it was. But one of the guests – Dr. Green – looked at the body, and he thought Viggo had suffered a blow.'

'A blow?'

'Clawed. Attacked. We don't know. What I do know is there have always been predators in the area. Remember Magnus Polson, the previous owner? Killed by a bear. My uncle used to trap lynx too, they can be vicious. Anyway, the police will be able to give a better idea about what happened.'

Petra sat up straight, eyes wide. 'The police are coming? But if it was just an animal, surely they don't need to come out all this way?'

Theo's face clouded with his own concern, as if Petra was losing her faculties – which, she acknowledged, could be true.

'Violent deaths are always investigated Petra,' he said gently. 'They might even bring a forensic team.'

Theo suddenly looked irritated by the thought. 'All I hope is that they're quick. This is all difficult enough as it is.'

Petra pressed a fist against her lips, trying to stifle a sob.

'Petra, you mustn't blame yourself,' he said, tapping her knee.

'Blame myself?' she tried to sound calm but her heart was thudding. What was he implying? Had he seen her argument with Viggo on the path to his cabin? She had been sure they were alone: *sure* of it.

'Oh,' said Theo, as if he suddenly realised he might have made a mistake. 'It's just I spoke to Michel in the kitchen. He said you left the kitchen and Viggo disappeared a few minutes after you'd left. Michel thought Viggo might have gone looking for you?'

Petra looked at him warily. There was a definitely a change of tone in Theo's voice. A questioning lilt, like he was fishing for information. Petra was beginning to get frightened now. Clearly people were already talking, even people like Michel who she thought were loyal to her. There was a tiny part of Petra that was still a lawyer and she knew she had to be cautious.

'I don't know why Viggo left the kitchen,' she said. 'I went to see Martin at the Svenson house and then came back here.'

'I see,' said Theo, seemingly satisfied by her answer. Or perhaps he hadn't been fishing after all. Clearing his throat, he touched her arm awkwardly and then stood up.

'I'm really sorry to have brought such bad news Petra, but we'll all get through this together, okay?'

She nodded stiffly.

'Now I'd better be going – lots to do, as you can imagine. Will you be okay?'

Petra tried to speak, but the words seemed to catch in her throat. She could only nod. Apparently happy he'd done enough, Theo bustled out and closed the door behind him.

Finally alone, Petra covered her face with both hands

and tried to inhale deeply. Her palms were clammy, her breath seemed unable to reach her lungs.

Petra stumbled blindly into the bathroom, leaning over the narrow sink, not sure if she was going to be sick. She ran the water, splashing it over her face, reaching for the soap and scrubbing her already pink hands. With a force of will, Petra forced herself to look up into the mirror.

'Don't blame yourself.' That's what Theo had said. But she should, shouldn't she? After all, she *had* wanted Viggo gone. Tonight when it had become patently, painfully obvious that Viggo had no intention of handing her the reins of Kluven, she had hated him so much that she'd wished him dead.

Dead.

But now Viggo was gone, Petra knew she'd had it wrong, upside down. She hadn't wanted him gone – no, she had wanted Viggo Widlund to suffer, to be exposed as the lying cheat that he was. She had wanted Martin to recognise her superior talent, then hand her the head chef's apron. Then Petra would win star after star, her accolades built on skill, not theatre. That would be her revenge, served rare and bloody. And she wanted Viggo to see it and feel it, every last excruciating paper cut. But it was too late now, wasn't it? Because Viggo was gone.

She looked into the mirror, watched her face crease and fall, a loud sob hiccupping out.

Now that Viggo was dead, Petra realised that she just wanted to hear the sound of his voice, to see his strong silhouette striding through the snow. She wanted him to call her name, tell her she mattered. She wanted things to be as they were. Because the truth was, she loved him still, just as she always had.

'Don't blame yourself,' she whispered, as tears ran down

her face, dropping from her chin into the soapy water. So easy to say, so hard to do.

She hung her head, looking down at her wrinkled hands, clinging to the chipped edge of the sink.

Squeezing her eyes closed, she could see his pale face in the dark, the look of surprise on his face as she launched at him.

Clawed. Attacked. Theo's words came to her in a rush.

Suddenly Petra felt unclean – and vulnerable. Did she have Viggo's skin under her fingernails? Did she literally have his blood on her hands? She yanked open the bathroom cabinet, sending dental floss, vitamins and face cream clattering onto the floor.

'Where are they?' she whispered. 'Where?' She finally grabbed a pair of narrow scissors from a small nylon make-up bag and started clipping off her nails as close as she could. Would that be enough? She had already scrubbed her hands red. Petra looked down at the tiny crescents of nail lying on the porcelain. Was that really all that was left of Viggo? A few tiny pin-pricks of DNA clinging to a discarded nail? 'Oh mighty Caesar,' she whispered, then she turned on the tap, watching them swirl away.

Chapter 14

'It's out,' said Alex, holding up his phone.

'What is? The story?' said Lara, jumping up to read the snippet on Alex's screen. They'd only been back in the cabin a few minutes; Lara was still holding her glass of brandy from the bar. There was only one line:

Viggo Widlund, the Viking Chef is dead. The food world mourns.

'Who posted it?" asked Lara, leaning closer.

'Anonymous account,' said Alex. 'Probably someone on the compound.'

'The food world mourns. Do you think that's sarcastic? Someone who didn't like him?'

'That probably covers most of the staff, after putting them all out of a job,' said Alex. 'No, whoever posted this did it for the social currency. It's anonymous but they want the thrill of getting the news out first.'

Lara raised an eyebrow.

'Since when were you such an expert on the psychology behind social media?'

He looked up and smiled.

'We had a course on it last month. The *Chronicle* top brass clearly think it's time us old hacks got dragged kicking and screaming into the 21st century.'

'So are you going to call the news desk?'

Alex glanced at his watch. 'No. Not yet'. It was gone midnight and although technically, there was still time for the story to make the last edition of the morning papers, Alex knew they wouldn't hold the presses for anything other than a breaking major world news event.

'What we really want is for the Mail Online to pick up the story overnight, and then we're off the hook with Martin Svenson.'

Lara smiled. 'Richard Morgan would be proud of you.'

Alex smiled, glad that Lara had remembered that particular moment from their college days. Richard Morgan, a Fleet Street legend, had given a guest lecture at City, explaining that a good editor not only knew what stories to run, but when to print them. Most of the time, the 'get there first' approach in news journalism was the gold standard, as a great scoop could add hundreds of thousands of sales to a day's tally. But sometimes it was better to wait. 'First mover's advantage isn't always the best play' was Morgan's quote and Alex hadn't forgotten the advice. In this case, Alex knew he needed to keep Martin Svenson onside because real journalism was built on trust. If your sources trusted you, they would talk. If your readers trusted you, they would believe what you wrote was true. And here in Kluven, they desperately needed freedom of movement. They couldn't find out anything if Svenson kept them locked up in their cabin.

Lara took her phone out of her bag.

'I just need to make a call,' she said.

'Who to?'

'Stella.'

Stella Harris was a talented young reporter and friend to them both. She'd been part of Lara's investigations team at the *Chronicle* and had been instrumental in identifying the players behind Sandrine's murder a few months previously. Stella was back at the *Chronicle* full time now and no one was better at forensic data crunching and research. Alex made the mental calculation. Midnight in Kiruna meant 11pm in London.

'Won't she be in bed?'

Lara glanced up and raised her brow.

'Stella's 24 years old and it's a Friday night. Besides, as I'm a world class investigator, I've deduced that Stella is out with her mate Maisie at the pub.'

Alex bent closer and read the caption on Stella's social media post. 'With Maisie at The Shakespeare.'

Alex was about to say something, when Lara held up a finger and put the phone to her ear.

'Stella. It's Lara. Yes, I'm still in Sweden. Look, I wondered if you could help me with a few things...'

* * *

Lara went into the bedroom to make the rest of the call. When she came out she was wearing a heavy knit black jumper, leggings and boots. Her hair, which had been so intricately tied up for the meal, was back into a simple ponytail. She looked ready for business.

'Stella is going home to make a start on the staff and guest profiles,' she said. 'I'm going to find Petra the sous chef for a woman-to-woman chat. According to the forecast, this storm is in for the night. There's no way the police are getting here tonight so we should get busy before they come.'

'Fancy a brisk walk into the *skog* first?' said Alex, watching her slip on her coat and gloves. 'I hear Viggo's cabin is just over there in the woods. '

'Hmm, good thinking.'

Alex could see Lara grasped his point straight away: when the police arrived, they would immediately tape off Viggo's cabin, so if Alex and Lara were going to take a look at it, they needed to make it a priority.

Lara waited on the cabin's porch while Alex locked the door behind them, then turned to face the swirling snow. He felt as if he was waist high in a cold pool, preparing himself to submerge his shoulders.

'So what did you mean. Before,' said Alex as they set off.

'About what?'

He thrust his hands and the cabin key into his pockets.

'I said Sandrine knew how to enjoy life and you said, "Do you?"'

Lara shrugged.

'I was just pointing out that you work too hard.'

'Says she.'

'At least I've gone freelance. When was the last time you left London, Alex?'

He thought for a moment.

'Corsica in June.'

'That was for Sandrine's funeral. And only for a day, as I recall.'

Alex immediately felt a needle of guilt. He had flown in and out of Ajaccio within 24 hours, attending the service in a small Catholic church. Darius had only sanctioned his absence from the office once he'd heard it was for Sandrine's funeral, and only then because he'd seen the opportunity for a piece about the service and wake; given the *Chronicle* had exposed Sandrine's murderer, his editor had suggested it would be a strong follow-up piece and would 'tie the story up nicely'. It was the closest Alex had ever come to hitting his boss.

'This is what I do, Lar,' said Alex defensively. 'This is my life.'

It *was* his life, his career, but not for the first time, Alex asked himself why he did it. Why go charging towards trouble when most sane people would run in the opposite direction? Viggo Widlund had been attacked and killed only steps away and the person who'd done it was almost certainly still in the Kluven complex. Why were they out in a storm looking for clues when they should be inside a warm cabin with the door locked? His friend and mentor Max Devlin, a foreign correspondent who had worked in Saigon during the Tet Offensive had once summed it up: 'reporters like us, Alex,' he'd said, 'We would rather risk death than risk getting scooped.'

Alex couldn't deny he loved the thrill of getting to the frontline first, getting that big splashy headline ahead of the rest of the press pack, but he didn't feel bulletproof like Max. He could still remember the day he decided to give up bureau work and move back to a desk job. He'd been outside Kandahar, driving at top speed to get back to the Green Zone before curfew, when they had driven through a minefield. Alex had been blissfully unaware of the danger until the next day when he heard that a US convoy had been blown to pieces in the exact same spot. It had shaken Alex badly. Within the week, he'd contacted the *Chronicle* to sound out the move back to London, telling himself he was getting too long in the tooth for field work, but the truth was, he'd been frightened.

'Viggo's cabin is just behind that treeline,' he said, looking up to point towards the jagged stand of pines.

The snow was getting thick now. The wind had dropped a little, but the golfball-sized flakes were still falling with a dizzying, strobe-like intensity.

Alex considered himself fit, but it was hard work ploughing through the snow, like running through surf.

Finally they reached Viggo's cabin and he collapsed on the porch step. He looked up but Lara didn't even seem out of breath.

'How did you know this place was here?' said Lara wiping snow from her face.

'When you were having a nap, Kat gave me the grand tour.'

'I bet she did.'

Was there a hint of jealousy in her voice? Right now, it felt too frivolous to even think about. Alex tried Viggo's door which opened with just a gentle push.

'Not locked?'

'It's not that unusual,' said Alex. 'We always used to leave the back door open at my mum and dad's house, and that was the Lake District, not some remote farm in Lapland.'

'You probably wouldn't leave it unlocked for several hours though. Was he expecting to come back quickly?'

Alex frowned.

'And what was Viggo doing in the root cellar so late anyway?'

'He was leaving,' said Lara. 'Maybe he wanted to collect something valuable from there. Like truffles.'

'You think someone killed him for a truffle?'

'People have been killed for less.'

They stepped carefully inside. Viggo's cabin was not dissimilar to their own, but without the soft rugs and cushions; and it was much darker, the lamps turned downward, more shadows, more unseen corners.

'You search this side of the cabin,' said Lara. 'I'll take the other. Don't take off your gloves, obviously.'

'But be quick,' said Alex. Now he was actually here, he realised how bad it would look if they were caught. After all, Alex was the one who'd found the body, the one who had the chef's blood on his coat. He was in enough trouble as it was.

Lara glanced across, obviously thinking the same thing.

'Take photos. Lots of them,' she said. 'If someone comes, at least we can look over them later.'

Alex nodded. He had no problem deferring to Lara Stone when it came to investigations. Alex's specialist area was reporting from war zones, a job which required a rare set of skills: calm, diplomacy and a certain degree of ruthlessness, but it was not the sort of dogged investigative work at which Lara excelled. She just saw things in a different way.

'He's very neat, I'll give him that,' said Alex, opening a drawer full of neatly rolled gloves.

'A man after your own heart,' said Lara.

He ignored the jibe. As deputy at the *Chronicle*, Alex wore sharp suits and yes, his freshly laundered shirts were lined up on hangars in his custom-built wardrobe, but he hoped Lara remembered that he'd never been happier than bouncing around in the back of a dusty jeep wearing scuffed jump boots and a ratty Joystick T-shirt.

Alex crossed to the coffee table.

'Look at this,' said Alex as Lara came back into the room. A fat cigar on a plate, ash fanning out onto the white china. 'It's only a quarter burnt down. If he smoked it tonight, he didn't get round to finishing it. Perhaps he was disturbed.'

Lara looked at him with mock admiration. 'With a mind like that, you should be an investigative journalist.'

Alex smiled, 'Nah, no money in it.'

He stood still to take stock. It was strangely minimalist, like a mock-up of an Alpine cabin in a furniture showroom.

'Not much to go off is there?'

'I think he's been reading Marie Kondo. What are these do you think?' asked Lara, holding up something round and black. 'There's a few of them by his armchair.' Alex stepped over. Lara was holding a small stone, smooth and polished by the sea, exactly like the pebbles that Alex had loved collecting in a bucket on beach holidays as a child.

'Odd. There's a pile in the bedroom too.'

Lara nodded. 'The only other thing I found was under a pile of papers on his desk. A contract between Martin Svenson and Viggo.'

She held up her phone. 'I took a picture, we can read it later, but it seems significant that he had that out just before he was killed.'

Killed. Suddenly Alex became very aware of the reason for their visit here. The man who had lived here was now lying on the cold bare earth. He shivered.

'We should go.'

Seeming to pick up on his mood, Lara gave a brief nod and, zipping up their coats, they left Viggo's cabin just as they had found it – not even an extra fingerprint for the police to ponder over, should they ever get here. And that was the biggest mystery here, thought Alex as they stepped back into the stinging snow. Why wasn't there more to see? Viggo Widlund had been The Viking Chef, a huge personality, brimming with life, and yet his cabin was empty. No quirks, no souvenirs, no hint of any personality – and Alex was left with the feeling that something was badly askew here. The Viggo everyone saw on the TV or in the restaurant was a very different man from the one they had glimpsed in his cabin – that was only to be expected he supposed – but the neat, careful private Viggo they'd seen in his home didn't fit with the man they'd briefly met in Kluven's dining room either. That Viggo had been passionate, poetic, clearly yearning for a new creative adventure. And yet there had been no sign of that in the cabin. Hardly any books, no art on the walls, certainly no maps – and, now he thought about it, no suitcase. If Viggo had been planning his escape, why hadn't he packed?

Who are you, Viggo? Thought Alex. *And where were you going?*

Chapter 15

Lara rapped on the French door again, then moved to the window.

'Petra? Are you there?'

It had been an educated guess to come to the staff accommodation block, a converted stables on the fringe of the main complex. Everyone at Kluven had been dispatched back to their living quarters and Lara could see various silhouettes at the glowing windows. She'd debated just walking in through the front door, but when she'd seen a red-headed woman in the window of one of the downstairs units, she'd gone and tapped at the glass.

No one seemed to be answering; she could hardly blame them under the circumstances, but it meant Lara was quickly turning into a snowman out here – and if anything, the storm was getting worse.

She knocked on the glass again.

'Petra? Please, I need to talk to you.'

And I need to get the feeling back into my fingers before they drop off, she thought.

Finally she saw a face appear at the window.

'Who is that?' asked a muffled voice.

Lara had never met Petra before, but the face matched the photo of the sous chef on the Kluven website. And she had to admire the woman's moxie, confronting the person standing in the dark, knocking on her window at midnight.

'My name is Lara Stone. I'm a guest here. I really need to speak to you.'

'What about?'

'Could I come in to explain?'

'Explain there,' replied Petra, her voice tight.

Lara nodded, unfazed.

It wasn't her first time standing outside someone's house asking questions. She'd spent the first two years of her career doorstepping bereaved families and scandal-plagued politicians, and it never got any easier.

'I'm a writer, an investigative journalist actually,' she said. 'I'm here on holiday but I want to help find out what happened to Viggo.'

'Isn't that a job for the police?' said Petra.

'Of course – but look behind me,' said Lara gesturing to the swirling snow. 'No one's going to get here before morning. '

Lara saw the woman considering it.

'Can I come in?' Lara pressed, stamping her feet to emphasise the fact she was freezing. 'Kat Mikaelsson suggested we speak.'

Petra grunted. With that one dismissive noise, Lara learned a great deal. First, Petra didn't think much of Theo's wife and second, that Kat's position in the Kluven heirarchy was lower than she had believed.

After a brief moment, there was a scraping noise as the French door opened and a wedge of yellow light shone out into the night. Lara stepped inside gratefully, but tried to keep her distance from Petra who had already retreated to the other side of the room, little more than a bedsit. She imagined that the horses had been more comfortable.

Petra looked anxious, on edge. Her face was blotchy. Her eyes were pink and teary. She motioned with her hand. Lara noticed it was trembling.

'I should go and get one of the other chefs. He's just next door.'

Lara knew what she was really saying. That help was just a few metres away.

'If you like,' said Lara. 'But I only wanted a very quick talk. Just for a couple of minutes. Kat said you knew Viggo best....'

'Is this some hatchet job for your newspaper?' Petra interrupted.

'No,' said Lara calmly. 'I've just worked in the business long enough to know that evidence deteriorates really quickly. I don't know what happened to Viggo; no one does yet, but I think we all want to find out, and given the police won't be here until tomorrow, I can help.'

'Help? Help who?'

'Help you, Petra,' said Lara quietly. Lara didn't want to scare the woman and get thrown back out into the snow, but she needed information too.

'You were Viggo's best friend. The second in command in the kitchen, right?'

Petra gave a wary nod.

'And I assume you weren't offered the job of exec chef to replace Viggo, otherwise Kluven wouldn't be closing.'

The woman's head jerked back, as if Lara had struck her, so she quickly pressed on: 'You need to trust me Petra. I realise you have little reason to, but I promise I'm good at what I do and I'll look for the angles that the police won't necessarily see.'

'What's that supposed to mean?'

'Petra, you must realise that you'll be on the police suspects list?'

The woman looked stricken. The colour drained from her face and she sat down on the edge of the bed.

'Me?'

Lara knew she had to tread carefully, but she also needed Petra to understand her position.

'You had a close relationship with Viggo, you were in line to take over and – I'm not saying this is true, but the police will definitely be thinking this way – you could well have been angry that he was leaving so suddenly.'

Lara kept quiet, giving Petra a chance to process the idea – and hopefully to see that Lara was a potential ally.

'Viggo was my friend,' said Petra quietly. 'He brought me to Kluven. I would never do anything to hurt him.'

'Where did you meet Viggo?' said Lara gently. *Get them talking about themselves*: it was a vital piece of advice she'd been given in her days as a cub reporter and it still worked. Almost always, anyway.

'We met in Provence, at a restaurant. I'd been there a while when Viggo arrived.'

Lara smiled.

'I bet he made an impression.'

Petra nodded, a hint of a smile. Lara could almost picture it herself. Viggo walking in: handsome, cocky, full of life. He would have turned heads for sure – and Lara guessed he would certainly have turned Petra's.

'And were you close from the start?'

Petra raised her chin a little.

'In so far as anyone gets close to Viggo.'

'So you followed him to Sweden?'

Petra's eyes flashed and she gave a single shake of her head.

'We came together as a team. We were always a team.'

Lara nodded, but wondered if Viggo thought the same way.

'Were you aware of his plans to leave?'

Petra blinked at her, then looked down at her hands.

'No,' she said quietly. 'No, I didn't. But...'

'But what?' asked Lara, sitting forward.

'Well, Viggo could be erratic. That was part of his image, but there was some truth to it, especially lately.'

'Erratic how?'

Petra looked towards the window where snow was swirling around the light.

'It's hard to understand if you've only been here a few days, but half the year we only get a few hours of sunlight and even then it's gloomy. Some people find it hard to deal with, even the natives.'

'Seasonal affective disorder?' asked Lara.

She'd heard about people who got 'winter depression', but knew little about it. 'Viggo had that?'

Petra shrugged and pulled her towelling robe more tightly around herself as if she were feeling the cold.

'I don't know. I'd never noticed it before now, but this year, his mood changed as the weather turned and the days got shorter. He was more irrational than usual, would fly into a rage over the smallest thing. Pots were thrown across the floor, he shouted at staff for the smallest thing. Belittled them.'

'Kitchen life is intense though, isn't it?' said Lara. What she meant was, Petra had just described many high-profile chefs.

'That is the cliched image,' said Petra, tight-lipped. 'In fact, real chefs are super-calm.'

Lara's face must have betrayed her scepticism because Petra looked at her.

'Have you ever cooked steak?'

Lara sat back a little, defensive.

'A few times, yes.'

'Not easy to get the timing right, is it? Now imagine you have to coordinate that steak with a pot of steamed mussels and a souffle and a bowl of pasta perfectly cooked to al dente: four entirely different dishes plated and garnished and handed to the waiter at exactly the same time. Not just for one person but for an entire restaurant. And imagine that food not being standard food fayre but complex, world-class dishes. Being a chef is more like an air traffic controller than a cook.' 'And you're saying Viggo sometimes struggled to cope with all that?'

'Not always. Not before. But lately, Viggo was grouchy, irritable. He was in the kitchen less and less. I thought he was getting lazy, but perhaps he just couldn't take the pressure. Then a couple of weeks ago, he disappeared for three days.'

'Disappeared?' said Lara. Now this was news. 'Did he tell you where he'd been?'

'No. I asked, but he gave some vague reply. He said he was fine, but I could tell he wasn't. The next thing I know, Viggo's leaving.'

Lara took a step towards her.

'What do you think happened to Viggo, Petra?'

The woman looked down at her hands.

'I don't know.'

Yes you do, thought Lara.

'But who might have wanted to hurt him?'

'No one wanted to hurt him,' she said, looking up, her eyes bright.

'But you said he belittled people? Shouted at them?'

Petra gave a tight shake of her head.

'That doesn't mean to say that someone would kill him.

You don't know the kitchen team. Life up here is tough. We stick together. We're like family.'

Exactly, thought Lara. Families were full of rivalries and resentments. You only had to read the court reports of any local paper – or Shakespeare – to know how easily those emotions could boil over. But Lara could see that Petra had shut down, she wasn't going to get anything else from her. Thanking her, Lara turned back to the door and opened it, the snow billowing inside. 'You'd better lock this behind me,' she said, stepping into the storm. It was advice Lara would be following herself.

Chapter 16

Justin woke like he was falling off a cliff. He gasped, clutched at the covers, his feet kicking, every muscle in fight-or-flight mode. He twisted, rolling over to the edge of the bed, convinced he was going to be sick, but nothing came except a long groan and a thread of saliva. His stomach was cramped, vision flashing, but the overriding feeling was one of fear, the shuddering anxiety that comes with not knowing what was wrong. Something bad had happened, that much was clear, Justin just didn't know what. He looked around for Emily, but he was alone. Where was she? Another spasm in his stomach and Justin hauled himself up with the aid of the bedside cabinet, knocking over the lamp as he moved, see-sawing his way into the en-suite bathroom and locking the door. He sank down onto the edge of the claw-foot bath.

BANGBANGBANG!

The bathroom door vibrated with the knocks.

'Justin! What's going on in there?' Emily's voice. He wasn't surprised that his partner sounded concerned.

He leant over and flushed the toilet. 'Not feeling too good,' he groaned.

'Still?' Emily called impatiently from the other side of the door.

'I'm fine, fine. Just give me a minute,' he called. 'I'm going to freshen up.'

Justin was playing for time, trying to find some space to remember exactly what had scared him about the night before. He sat down again, clasping his shaking hands over scuffed knees. How had that happened? He didn't remember. There were scrapes on his knuckles too and a graze on the heel of his right hand. He touched the skin around his left eye. It was tender. Had someone punched him? It wouldn't be the first time, but still: shouldn't you remember something like that?

He bent towards the mirror to inspect the damage, then gasped. It wasn't his face that caught the attention, it was his shirt. It was the one he'd worn the night before. There were reddish-brown speckles down the front of it. Blood?

'Fuck,' he whispered, looking closer. It *was* blood.

And in a rush an image came to him: Viggo's angry face peering down at him. Viggo had grabbed him, there had been a tussle – a fight? But what about?

Justin couldn't remember any more.

He pulled the shirt off and screwed it up into a ball. He wrapped it up in a towel and kicked it into the corner of the room, making a mental note to dispose of it later. First he had to deal with Emily. Reluctantly, Justin unlocked the bathroom. She was standing in front of the window.

'Finally. You're up.'

'Don't give me grief, babe,' he said, perching on the sofa. 'I feel like shit. What time is it anyway?' It was dark outside the window.

'It's nine thirty,' she said, turning to face him. 'You haven't missed breakfast but you've missed all the drama.'

'Drama, what drama?'

'Viggo,' said Emily, those big green eyes wide.

Viggo? What did she know? Fragments of memory of the previous night felt just out of reach. All Justin could remember was running, running, running through the snow, then back in the cabin, drinking vodka, the roof spinning. And where had Emily been?

'What happened?' he croaked. He had to play the innocent, work out what she had seen. She certainly looked pale, concerned. Had Viggo reported him to the police for the drug use? For the fight?

'Viggo was attacked last night,' said Emily.

Oh crap. Despite the fug in his brain, Justin immediately began to think about getting onto his publicist, maybe even his lawyer. His heart jumped: would it come to that?

'Don't you remember that guy coming to the cabin to speak to us?' said Emily.

'When?'

'Around midnight.'

'I was dead to the world.'

Emily looked at him with astonishment.

'Justin, Viggo *is* dead.'

'*Dead*?'

Justin's hands gripped the arm of the sofa. If he didn't hold on, he was sure he'd fall down.

'What happened? How?'

'No one seems to know.'

Another flashback. Seeing Viggo in the forest. The scuffle over his stash. A punch. Blood. Blood on his shirt, red on white.

Panic gripped his chest but Justin forced himself to think. He knew he was fuck-up, but he still had a dream, things he still wanted to achieve. That was the reason he'd joined The Velvetines after Joystick had imploded. He had been so flattered at first when Gary and Steve had suggested forming a supergroup. Steve was the finest guitarist of his generation, no question – a twenty-first century Johnny Marr – and Gary was the master of post-Bowie image manipulation. Justin had imagined that with his song-writing thrown into the mix, they would do great things together. But The Velvetines had been a miserable experience from the start. His ideas for new music had been stamped out by Gary, who was convinced of his own genius, and in his heart of hearts, Justin had known what came out was sub-standard. In fact, it had been that first lacklustre gig that had put Justin on the path to where he was now, when Gary had offered him 'a little taste' to take the edge off of how he was feeling.

So, so stupid.

Deep down, Justin still believed that he could make good music once more. Every day he woke up, vowing to kick his addiction, reconnect with his old management team and start afresh. But even if he could do all that, no one was going to buy songs written by a murderer, however catchy they were.

Get a grip, his inner voice commanded. *Think, dammit.*

What happened in the snow last night? He closed his eyes, but all Justin could hear was Viggo's deep voice saying: 'I know, Justin. I *know*.'

He glanced back towards the bedroom door as a new horror hit him: was there blood on the sheets?

'Are you okay?' Emily was looking at him with concern now.

'Yes, I'm fine,' he replied too quickly.

He realised she was expressing sympathy about his friend's death.

'I can't believe it,' he whispered.

'Do you think it's still out there?' asked Emily, peering out of the frosted window.

'It?' he said.

'The bear, Justin. The bear they think killed Viggo.'

A bear. A bear had killed Viggo. The relief was almost as sweet as that first rush. He allowed himself to exhale, trying hard not to think about his poor friend being attacked by a wild animal.

'Apparently they sent a hunting team out into the forest last night,' said Emily. 'But what if it's still in the woods? What if it's stalking us?'

'I'm sure everything is under control,' said Justin. Clearly it wasn't, but he was at least beginning to feel he might be able to bluff his way through this. Emily sighed and gestured towards the luxurious cabin.

'All this lulls you into a false sense of security, doesn't it? The cashmere, the linens, the Wi-Fi. It makes you forget we're in the wild. But that's where we are. You know I saw a clip on YouTube once. It was a bear tearing open a car. His paw was like a super-charged can-opener, just to get at some peanut butter sandwiches.'

'Poor Viggo,' said Justin, not looking at her.

'It's weird though,' said Emily, looking back at him. 'I always thought bears hibernated in winter.'

'Do they?'

'My uncle lives in Montana. They go into their dens at this time of year and hardly come out. Not even to eat.'

'This is Sweden,' said Justin vaguely. 'Maybe it's different.'

He was beginning to sweat now, the headache behind his eyes growing like a hot coal. The familiar symptoms of withdrawal. He turned to go back to the bathroom, but Emily stepped out to head him off.

'Where were you last night, Justin?' she asked, head on one side.

'What do you mean?'

'After the meal, I came back to the cabin to look for you. You weren't here.'

He tried to remember the food poisoning story he'd spun to excuse himself from dinner. 'The cabin was so hot it made me feel even worse, so I went for a walk.'

Emily didn't look convinced.

'Well, you missed the Northern Lights.'

'I think I saw them. They were green, right?'

Emily shook her head, unamused.

'Justin, we came all this way for a romantic break. The Northern Lights were a magical moment and I had to watch them alone.'

He'd like to have seen the Northern Lights with his girlfriend too, but he had other things to worry about. His stomach was churning. Besides, he wasn't going to tell her that the real reason she didn't find him was because he was fighting with Viggo Widlund.

'I'm sorry,' he said with a weak smile. He meant it.

'No, I'm sorry too. Life's too short for arguments. I shouldn't give you a hard time. I know you must feel awful about Viggo.'

He nodded, but that wasn't it. Not really.

'I've let you down,' he said truthfully.

'Don't be silly,' she said, rubbing his back, her voice full of concern. 'It's not your fault.'

But of course it was. And if he kept on this path, he was going to lose her and Justin knew, even in the grip of his comedown, that the pain of losing Emily would be far worse than kicking any drug. The plain fact was that his life was a thousand times better with Emily in it. He knew he should tell her, throw himself on her mercy, ask for her help. And together they would build a new life together.

'Em, I need to...' he began, but Emily shook her head.

'Later,' she said. 'First we need to get you cleaned up. Why don't you have a shower?'

Justin's lip curled. The thought of getting under the hot water made his skin crawl.

'I could get in, scrub your back,' she said with a smile,

but he shook his head.

'Maybe later. I still feel rough.'

She looked disappointed. *You and me both,* thought Justin. If only the teenage him could see him now, turning down a shower with a supermodel.

'How about breakfast then?,' said Emily, 'Although we can't leave the cabin. They have to deliver it here.'

'Can't leave the cabin? Why not?'

'Not sure. When the guy came round last night to tell us about Viggo, he told us we have to stay put. If you ask me, they definitely haven't found that bear.'

'Yes, the bear,' he said, thinking about his fight with Viggo, suddenly getting a flash of the chef's face running with blood.

'I'm not hungry,' he said with a genuine wave of nausea. 'I don't think I could eat anything ever again.'

'It's a horrible thought, isn't it?' said Emily, lowering her voice. 'We ate the last thing Viggo ever cooked – and it made you ill. It's like an omen or something.'

'I think I'm going to be...'

Justin clamped a hand over his mouth and ran for the door. He yanked it open and puked into the snow.

'That bloody scallop,' he groaned, feeling like the manipulative scumbag he was. And wondering how far he'd have to walk before he found somewhere to hide his bloody shirt.

Chapter 17

Alex opened his eyes to the sound of tapping. *Tap, tap, tap.* Very soft like a distant dripping tap. He sat up and rubbed his eyes. He was still tired, but he knew he couldn't go back to sleep.

Next to him, Lara's bed was empty and by the looks of it, unslept in. Alex felt a vague sense of disappointment.

Yeah, and what were you expecting? He asked himself, rubbing his chin. When Lara had invited him to Kluven, he'd been excited. Excited to get out of the office, excited to go to Lapland and get in the mood for Christmas, excited to maybe see the Northern Lights, excited to spend some time with Lara. He'd tried not to dwell on the finer points of what the latter might entail – spending the night with his best friend in a luxury cabin.

He certainly hadn't imagined staying up all night, poring over the internet, looking for information about Swedish industrialists, chefs and bears, fuelled by coffee and a bottle of Akvavit from the mini-bar.

He'd lasted until 5am, when he'd finally gone for a 'lie-down', leaving Lara assembling a patchwork quilt of notes on the coffee table; suspects, motives and theories.

Clearly he'd gone out like a light, but he'd woken up still feeling groggy. He wandered into the living room finger-combing his hair; Lara was tapping quietly at her laptop on the sofa. He took a moment to watch her, hair pulled untidily back, a little frown of concentration on her face. He smiled to himself, knowing that Lara's naturally curious mind would rather be up solving a puzzle; sleep was for civilians.

'Hey,' he said, his voice gravelly. 'What's happening?'

She looked up, then turned back to the screen.

'The world's woken up to hear that a crazy chef has been savaged by a bear. Or a pack of wolves – one website even went with "trampled by a moose". No one's caught on about it being murder yet, but it's only a matter of time. I'm guessing that Theo told the staff the bear story and they all tweeted it as if it were true. Smart move by Kluven.'

Alex sat on the arm of a chair. 'Anything from Stella?'

Lara shook her head.

'Not yet, but she's on it. Stella reckons she'll have potted histories of each of the guests by the end of the day. I got a few names from the staff list, so she's working on that too.'

'Did you get any sleep?'

'A little,' she said, motioning towards the sofa. 'Enough.'

'I'll get you some coffee,' said Alex, getting up.

'It's fine. I'm good.'

Sometimes he wondered if Lara would ever need him for anything. She had always been so self-reliant, perhaps something to do with losing her parents so early, and it was one of the many things he admired about her. Even so, every now and then, he wished that Lara Stone would just accept his help, and let him show that he was there for her. But he wasn't going to hold his breath; Lara just wasn't the kind of girl who'd ever say, 'you complete me.'

Alex busied himself at the Nespresso machine on the

blond wood sideboard. Lara might not need her morning java, but he most certainly did.

'So what have you been doing while I was snoring?'

Lara pointed to the coffee table.

'I've been trying to build up a picture of everything we know and a timeline where we can, but we need a lot more information. That's why we need to get out and talk to as many people as we can before the police show up, try to create a map of where everyone was. You might have guessed we're not allowed to leave Kluven this morning.'

Alex wasn't surprised.

'What about our flights?'

Lara shrugged.

'I spoke to Theo this morning,' said Lara. 'We need to wait until the police get here and they're going to want to speak to everyone. Given there's only one flight out of Kiruna today, we're unlikely to make it, but Theo's team will make arrangements to reschedule.'

'I'd better call the office then,' said Alex, taking a sip of his coffee. 'I'm supposed to be back in work tomorrow.'

He sat down next to Lara so he could see her screen.

'So fill me in.'

'I've done basic searches on all the guests and the main players on the staff: Theo, Petra, Martin and Anna Svenson. All much as you'd expect so far, no red flags or previous offences.'

'Shame. A conviction for GBH might have saved us some time.'

Lara turned to face Alex.

'The one place we're light on detail is Viggo himself.'

'Really?' said Alex, surprised. 'Aren't there loads of interviews and features on Viggo?'

'Dozens, but they all repeat the same thing: mad Viking in the woods, blah, blah, blah.'

'Poor journalism,' said Alex with disapproval. 'That would never have happened on my watch.'

Lara grinned.

'Actually it did,' she said, pulling up a long piece from the *Chronicle* with the bold headline 'Viking Conquers'. Alex recognised it: the face-to-face with writer Lynda Brett they had run in the paper about six months ago.

'I remember that interview being pretty good,' said Alex defensively. Lynda Brett was the *Chronicle*'s top interviewer with a reputation for asking tough questions. He had personally poached her from *The Times* because she wrote with personality, which was a very rare thing in this day and age.

'Good writing, sure, but it was still a puff piece,' said Lara. 'It still followed the well-trodden path of Viggo Widlund as a crazy creative in the woods.'

Alex was going to object, but what she was saying was largely true. The Life & Style section of the paper had been re-launched the previous year with a more breezy lightweight approach. He could almost hear Darius, the *Chronicle*'s editor: 'It's a lifestyle product, Alex,' he'd said. 'It's meant to entertain not educate.' Consequently the interviews weren't exactly in-depth. Even so, Lynda Brett was a journo from the old school and Alex was pretty sure she would have done the appropriate legwork. At Alex's first job on a paper, the editor had taken him to one side and given him the secrets of interviewing: read everything ever written, decide what you'd like to know, then ask the questions. 'It's the last part that's difficult, lad,' he'd said, because the best questions were usually the ones the interviewee didn't want to answer.

Alex picked up his phone. 'I'll call Lynda. I'll bet she got a lot more stuff than went into the *Chronicle* piece. She wouldn't have been able to stop herself.'

Lara closed her laptop and reached for her gloves.

'In which case, I'll go for a walk. Give you some space.'

'You sure? The snow looks thick out there.'

'It stopped snowing about an hour ago. I could do with the fresh air anyway.'

Alex could see the truth of that: there were lilac semicircles under her eyes and he felt a tug of guilt. The whole point of this trip had been to have fun, to take some of the weight from Lara's shoulders, and yet here he was encouraging her to plunge straight back into an investigation.

'When you come back, how about we steal a couple of Ski-Doos?'

Lara looked up from tying her boots.

'Why?'

'Just for fun.'

'I'm not sure it's exactly the time, Alex,' she said. 'Viggo's dead and we're whooping it up doing donuts on snow machines.'

He supposed she had a point.

Alex followed her to the door and leant against the frame watching her go. No, it wasn't a conventional minibreak; diving headlong into an intense murder investigation wasn't exactly what they'd planned when they flew out to Sweden, but Alex couldn't deny that he was feeling a buzz of excitement. He certainly relished the chance to work side-by-side with Lara for once – they'd been colleagues for years, but journalists were lone wolves, they didn't usually collaborate. More than that, Alex was right at the centre of the action, which for a news man, was the absolute best place to be. Dangerous perhaps, but then who ever had any fun hiding behind a locked door? Alex picked up his phone, tapping out a message. It chirped to signifying an incoming message almost as soon as it had landed.

. . .

You want to know about Viggo? Thought you'd never ask. Talkback in twenty minutes? Lynda.

Alex's smile faded: twenty minutes. Just enough time to call Darius, the *Chronicle*'s editor, although it was never something he looked forward to. Everyone had someone in their office who sucked all the fun and energy out of everything; it was Alex's bad fortune that at the *Chronicle*, it was the editor-in-chief.

Steeling himself, Alex pressed 'call'.

'Darius, it's Alex. How are you?'

There was a grunt.

'I'd be better if my staff didn't call me at 9AM on my day off.'

Darius had recently bought a manor house in Oxfordshire, which he was in the process of renovating, which tended to make him even more grumpy.

'Just to let you know that I'm stuck in Sweden so I'm won't be back in the office tomorrow.'

'Sweden?'

Alex rubbed his forehead. *Of course* Darius wouldn't know where he was – or even which country he was in, despite the fact had made such a song and dance about Alex taking time off 'so close to Christmas'.

'Yes Sweden, I'm at Kluven. The restaurant.'

'I know it's a restaurant Alex. How the hell did you get in there?'

'Lara booked it months ago. Look, there's something of a situation here: the chef has been found dead.'

'The Viking guy is *dead*?'

That got his attention. It also confirmed Alex's suspicion that Darius had zero real interest in the news. Even on his days off, Alex checked the news feeds first thing in the morning – he would already know all about Viggo and the supposed animal attack. Alex could hear tapping in the background as Darius tried to catch up.

'Hold up: the MailOnline ran with this at 2am this morning?' he snapped. 'And you're right there? What the hell, Alex?'

Alex patiently explained his strategy to Darius, about cutting a deal with Martin Svenson for greater access. He could almost hear Darius thinking it through.

'Hmm... maybe we could follow the bear angle. Has this bear killed before? *Slasher Beast* could be a nice headline for us tomorrow. Late, but powerful.'

'It's not a bear, Darius,' said Alex. 'That's just a cover story by the resort. Viggo was murdered.'

'Murdered? Now, that's even better,' he said with more enthusiasm.

'Not for poor Viggo.'

'Are there any other interesting guests? Is Daniel Craig there? Bond in Peril, something like that? We'd have strong engagement with that.'

That was one thing you could say about Darius, he was never one to miss an angle, however unlikely. For a second Alex considered telling him about Justin Blake and his supermodel girlfriend, but he knew from experience it was always better to surprise Darius than disappoint him – and there was always a good chance the rock star would refuse to talk.

'Anyway, I should be back in on Monday, provided the police release the guests before tomorrow morning.'

'So you're literally trapped,' said Darius, clearly warming to the story. 'Stranded in an icy wilderness, alone with an axe murderer...'

'I'll see what I can do,' said Alex, keen to end the call.

'Wait,' said Darius. 'You're there with Lara?'

'Yes.'

'Look, I don't know what's going on between you two – don't want to know, frankly – but I do want to remind you that she is still a member of the *Chronicle* team and that means you need to be professional. At all times.'

Alex actually laughed.

'Darius, I've known Lara for twenty years. We're friends.'

'Right: friends. And are you in separate rooms?'

'Cabins.'

'Separate cabins then.'

'No. It's a twin.'

'Christ. Before we know it there's an HR situation. You do know her uncle owns the company? Just keep your hands to yourself, okay?'

'Darius,' said Alex, his irritation rising, but Darius had clearly moved on.

'Start thinking about the visuals on this one, Alex,' he said. 'Murdered chef, rabid bear, forbidden romance – I reckon we can get six-figures from Netflix for the rights on this one. The streamers are all over true crime at the moment, buying up a lot of content from the newspapers. This could be a real opportunity for us.'

'Darius, this isn't a rom-com, it's breaking news: the chef was actually murdered…' said Alex, then realised he was talking to himself: Darius had hung up.

Sighing, Alex pulled out his laptop and set it up on the desk in the bedroom, logging into the digital conference software Lynda had sent. He was immediately rewarded with a picture of Lynda sitting in front of a huge bookcase.

'Hey Lyn,' he said, waving awkwardly. Lynda Brett was a striking woman in her early seventies, with long grey hair and big chunky glasses. Lynda had been in newspapers since they were put together on hot type and Alex respected her – that too was a rare thing in newspapers these days.

'So you're live from Kluven,' said Lynda without preamble. 'Tragic about Viggo Widlund but it's about time you got out from behind the executive desk and started doing the work you're really good at. I was only telling my students the other day that your piece on the Janjaweed militia in Darfur was one of the most powerful things I've ever read.'

'I'm not back on the Foreign desk, Lyn, I'm on holiday.'

'Newspaper men are never on holiday,' said Lynda with a smile. 'Even when they're with a beautiful woman like Lara Stone.'

'How do you know I'm here with Lara?'

'I've been a journalist for fifty-two years. You expect me to have my ear to the ground, don't you?'

'We're just friends.'

Lynda held up a hand.

'As you say, Casanova. Anyway, I'm assuming this is a murder?'

Alex laughed; old school news instincts. Lynda looked like a slightly eccentric aunt but like Miss Marple, it was all misdirection: her mind was just as sharp as it had ever been.

'Have you got psychic skills as well as lightning shorthand?'

'You don't need to be psychic to know bears hibernate in the winter. Even with global warming, you're about 700 miles from the nearest polar bear.'

'You're right,' said Alex. 'I found the body; it looks like Viggo was stabbed to death.'

'Rough,' she said shaking her head. Alex smiled to himself. That was old school too: no concerned psychobabble about trauma or victimhood. One word of gruff support, then move on.

'So what do you need?' she asked.

'Anything you can tell me from your interview or the research, really. Anything that didn't make the piece?'

'All the interesting bits were cut out – obviously,' said Lynda with a hint of weariness. 'All your features editor wanted was some amusing colour – does this strange chef eat moose, does he chop steaks with an axe?'

'So what else did you get?'

'Actually, Viggo was very, very guarded, which was a surprise. He's been on TV, he's media savvy, yet he clammed up whenever I tried to get anything on his past.'

'I'm sure you didn't let that stop you.'

'Well, Viggo definitely had a tough upbringing, but not in the woods. That Viking wildman thing, it's mostly contrived. He grew up in Malmo. Viggo was from the poor side, suggestions of parental neglect. Certainly, his brother was killed by a member of a Swedish biker gang.'

'How come I've never heard that before?'

'Because the child you have on the features desk said she didn't want a dark tone. It might 'trigger' some readers.'

She held something up to the camera: it was a manila drop file, the kind they use in filing cabinets. 'All my research,' said Lynda riffling through it. 'It's mainly photocopies of old interviews, transcripts of a few phone calls I put in. But there's still some interesting loose ends poking out.'

'Really?' said Alex, sitting forward. 'Like what?'

'Like how Viggo ended up in Provence. As far as I can tell, he started cooking in Sydney, then bounced around Europe in various sketchy kitchens, before ending up in Paris.'

'So what else is in that file?' said Alex, pointing at the screen. 'I know you, Lynda. If there was something to find, you'll have found it.'

'Drugs,' she said.

'Drugs?'

Lynda took off her glasses and began to polish them.

'I got this from a chap who worked with him in Paris. The rumour is that the holes in Viggo's CV are covering up his drug habit. I mean, uppers and downers aren't that uncommon among chefs: cooks are pretty rock 'n' roll behind the scenes. They live in this urban nightlife world that's glamorous and seedy at the same time and when you add high pressure and an artistic temperament, it's no big surprise they get sucked in.'

'Just a rumour on the drugs though? No arrests?'

Lynda shook her head.

'Nothing concrete and I also think it was a long time ago. I spoke to a few insiders in the foodie world and the feeling was that Viggo had been in a dark place when he was in Paris, but left it all behind when he went to Provence. From that moment on, he was super-focused on making a name for himself as a chef.'

Alex nodded thoughtfully. It was interesting, but didn't help much. Of all the reasons Viggo could be meeting someone in the woodshed, scoring drugs was the least likely.

'Anything else?'

Lynda grinned. 'Another rumour, but this is a goodie.'

He waited.

'This one comes from another chef,' said Lynda. 'All this genius, all these incredible recipes?' She paused for dramatic effect. 'Not his.'

Alex frowned. 'So this chef is saying Viggo is not actually a great cook?'

'Oh, he's an awesome cook. Apparently he's a world-class technician, can make anything sing. But Viggo's myth is not based on his ability to make the perfect scrambled eggs, is it? It's the way he's dreamt up all these mad combinations of flavours – or not.'

'So you're saying someone else wrote the recipes?'

Lynda held up a finger.

'It's only a rumour, remember? But the scuttlebutt is that Viggo had plenty of vision, but lacked the imagination for those beautiful combinations and he was leaning on someone else to provide that magic.'

'Damn,' said Alex. If you were looking for a motive, that was a doozy. 'But how could you keep something like that quiet?'

'Not everyone wants to be in the limelight,' said Lynda with a shrug. 'You're into music, right? Look at Elton John – every one of those hits was co-written by Bernie Taupin all from the comfort of his ranch in California. I've met Bernie and he's never set foot on a stage, let alone worn diamond-studded glasses. He's just not that sort of man.'

Alex thought it was more like a group, maybe The Beatles. A load of talented egos jostling for attention, with Martin Svenson as the Brian Epstein figure, seeing the potential and the money in Viggo's brand.

'So who's Yoko Ono in all this?' he said. 'Who was breaking up the band?'

Lynda's smile faded.

'Well it's a little more serious than that, isn't it? If we're keeping up with the music metaphor, then it's Mark Chapman you're after, the guy who shot John Lennon.'

Alex pursed his lips.

'And he was crazy, right?'

'Right,' said Lynda. She jabbed a finger at the screen, 'So you watch yourself out there, Alex. And you look after Lara too, romance or no romance.'

Chapter 18

Lara walked down the steps to the lake and placed one tentative foot out on the ice. Johan, the driver who had brought them out to Kluven, had said the ice was almost a metre thick, enough to drive a school bus across, but even so she was nervous. The pond in the grounds of Lara's family estate in Oxfordshire often iced over in winter and she and her cousin Charlie had taken great pleasure in daring each other to edge out onto the ice, foot by foot, squealing if it cracked. In Lara's mind, ice was dangerous, possibly because she had seen too many movies where someone was trapped beneath the surface. Of course that was Hollywood, not real life, but Lara had never been able to get those scenes out of her mind, some poor doomed person banging helplessly on the underside of the ice.

'Don't be such a wuss,' she muttered, stepping onto the path, already cleared of last night's snow by some early-riser on the ground-staff. Clearly not everyone was forbidden to move about the estate, thank goodness.

Lara took a deep lungful of air, trying to force herself to think. She'd had very little sleep, having worked late into the night researching Viggo Widlund and piecing together a document on everything she knew so far about his death. She had finally crashed out, using the sofa as she hadn't wanted to disturb Alex. He had more energy than anyone she had ever met, but he still worked 100-hour weeks and after the horror show of the previous evening, he definitely deserved some rest. Alex had put a brave face on it, but Lara could see how shaken he had been finding Viggo's body. Lara hadn't liked it much herself. Seeing Viggo on the floor of the root cellar had raked up too many memories of her friend Sandrine. So beautiful, so full of life, Lara had been with Sandrine the night she died. If only she had stayed for another drink, if only Lara had insisted Sandrine come home with her; the past few months had been full of 'if onlys'.

She inhaled sharply, savouring the crisp, cold air as she carried on walking, trying not to think about cracking ice. Ever since Sandrine's death Lara had felt uncharacteristically brittle. Lara Stone was kick-ass, armour-plated, gung-ho. But not recently. Recently Lara had wanted to curl up under her quilt and not come out. She told herself that it was just the grieving process and that it would pass, but she still felt anxious and risk averse.

And yet here you are, walking on water, she thought, smiling to herself. Lara began to relax, heading towards a small wooden building ahead of her. She hadn't meant to come this way. When she had left Alex talking to Lynda Brett, Lara had intended to walk over to the restaurant to see about breakfast, but her attention had been caught by the sheer beauty of the view. And out here it really was beautiful, like standing inside a cloud, calm and eerily quiet. Hadn't Alex said something about snow being an amazing insulator during his 'Sweden Facts' lecture on the flight over? Perhaps the acres of white were absorbing what little noise there might be out there in the middle of nowhere.

She slowed as she approached the wooden hut, little more than an old-fashioned outhouse. Johan the driver had pointed it out the previous day: it was a rudimentary shelter for the ice-fishing hole Viggo had used to catch fish for the restaurant. Lara peeked inside: just a seat, a shelf with a small gas stove and various cooking and fishing implements hooked to the walls.

'*Hej.*'

Lara jumped as a man popped his head around the back of the shed. The man had sandy hair pulled back into a stubby pony-tail and what looked like a spear in one hand.

'Stuart Dell,' he said, putting out the other, 'I'm one of the chefs.'

'Lara Stone. One of the guests.'

'Exploring the grounds?' he asked in a thick Scottish accent.

'Something like that. I know we're supposed to stay in our cabins but I was going stir crazy.'

'Would some breakfast help? I can offer you coffee and a bacon roll.'

'Out here?'

Stuart smiled and reached inside the little building, coming out with a steel can with a wire handle. 'Hold that for a spell,' he said, walking a little way from the shed where there was a depression in the ice. Stuart lifted the spear and thrust it down into the hole with a wet 'thunk', then repeated the move, flakes of ice jumping in the air.

'This is an ice chisel,' he said over his shoulder. 'It's the simplest way to get to the lake – and to the fish.' After a few more stabs, Stuart had made a decent-sized hole and, taking the pan from Lara, filled it.

'Can't promise the coffee will be that good, but at least the water is pure.'

Returning to the shed, Stuart went inside and lit a small

two-ring gas stove, then took down a frying pan from a hook on the wall, setting it on the hob next to the water. Lara liked the simplicity of it all. Much as she had enjoyed the artistry and the complexity of the meal the previous night, there was something satisfying about a rustic fry-up. While Stuart expertly flipped the sizzling bacon, Lara examined the rack of hunting and fishing equipment at the back of the shed. Despite growing up on a country estate, Lara had little experience of the outdoorsy life, but she knew enough to recognise the hooked fishing lures, the gaffs for hauling the fish out, along with various tools for gutting and slicing the catch. Everything here was sharp and pointy and very capable of doing damage. Her attention was particularly drawn to the long, thin filleting knives with their wicked six-inch blades. Exactly the sort of thing which might be used to punch holes in an angry chef.

'There are a lot of weapons here,' she said.

Stuart looked up. 'Not weapons, Lara – tools. What's that phrase? 'Guns don't kill people, people do'? You can't hurt someone with a knife that stays in a drawer.'

'Good point.'

Stuart handed her the bacon roll and she took a bite. It was good. Just the right amount of crispy, sweet and salty.

'You could start a satellite restaurant out here.'

'Aye, I could,' smiled Stuart. 'Word has it that Theo wants to expand. Not that you'd get much passing traffic here, but that's what I like about it. I worked in Glasgow before I came here – anything's quiet after that.'

She took a sip of the coffee. Rich and dark: almost as good as the bacon.

'My compliments to the chef,' she said. 'This bacon is delicious.'

Stuart shrugged.

'Old sows,' he said. 'That's the secret.'

Lara had just taken another bite and almost choked. 'Old *what*?'

'Most pigs are slaughtered before they are a year old because it's more efficient: less feed, less chance of contracting a disease. But when it comes to bacon, the older the pig, the more tasty it is. And the oldest pigs are generally sows because they're kept for breeding.'

'Gosh,' said Lara, looking down at her roll. 'Is this the sort of thing you chat about in the kitchen?'

'Sorry, it's sort of my thing. I run the meat station. I'm le boucher, sometimes the rotisseur and le chef grillardin too – butcher, roasting and grilling. I also do fish and poultry sometimes. You've seen the meat locker in the grounds? I salt and cure the bacon in there. I could probably tell you the pig that roll came from.'

'Better not,' said Lara as she put the remains of the roll down. Attached to the little building's outside walls were simple benches covered with reindeer hides. They sat down and sipped their coffee, just enjoying the quiet and the solitude. After the tempest of the night before, it seemed all the more serene.

'You know this lake is half a mile long in the summer,' said Stuart. 'It's long and thin, like a loch.'

'Great spot.'

'It is. Me and Viggo spent a lot of time out here. We hunted together in the woods and fished in the lake. Once we caught a pike this big,' he said, spreading his arms out wide. Slowly Stuart's grin faded.

'I'll miss it. I'll miss him.'

'I'm sorry,' said Lara. 'It's tough.'

'Aye,' he said, looking away.

Lara kept quiet. They all had a lot to process after the night before. Lara knew what it was like to lose a friend, but this was an open wound for Stuart. It had to hurt.

'So how long have you worked here?'

'From the start,' said Stuart. 'Back then it was just me, Viggo and Petra. Viggo and Petra came up together from Provence, but Petra recommended me. She and Viggo flew to Glasgow to audition me – can you believe that?' He gave a rueful smile. 'Even now, I'm not sure I was their first choice, but it was flattering and I was game. Life in a kitchen is tough enough, but life in an Arctic kitchen? Not everyone could do that.'

Lara thought of Petra telling her something similar the night before.

'How do you cope? I mean, it's beautiful,' said Lara, gesturing to the white expanse in front of them. 'But it's a long way from Glasgow.'

'I'm used to life in the wild,' he shrugged. 'My dad was a gamekeeper for an estate in Sutherland, right at the northern tip of Scotland. Home was a stone crofter's cottage surrounded by 20,000 acres of moorland. Besides, I liked the Kluven team.'

He smiled wistfully and Lara knew what it was like to be part of a tight-knit working group. Until recently, Lara had run her own small department at the *Chronicle*; she didn't miss the pressure, but she definitely missed the camaraderie of the investigations team.

'Were they close? Viggo and Petra I mean?'

Stuart's smile dimmed a little.

'Sure,' he said quickly. 'Mostly.'

'Only mostly?'

Stuart shifted in his seat, suddenly defensive.

'Look, I'm not sure we're supposed to be talking about all this,' he said. 'The police are coming. And as you say, the guests and staff are supposed to be in their rooms.'

Lara knew she'd made a misstep somehow, but she needed to keep him talking whatever it took.

She turned to face him. 'I know you're hurting Stuart, believe me I do. My best friend was killed last summer, so I know you're not in the mood for talking to strangers – to anyone – right now. But for that same reason, I want to do whatever I can to find out who hurt Viggo. And it won't bring him back, but whoever did this shouldn't be allowed to get away with it, should they?'

Stuart twisted his mouth to the side, clearly struggling with it.

'Okay,' he said finally. 'What do you want to know?'

'A timeline,' said Lara decisively. 'Right now I don't know where anyone was last night. When did you last see Viggo?'

Stuart rubbed his chin wearily.

'About 10.50. He'd been very hands-on in the kitchen all night – he plated up the final course himself, then went out to say goodnight to the guests, but he didn't come back. It's kind of tradition to have a booze-up in the kitchen after last service, but he never showed so we just cracked on without him. Next thing we knew, Martin Svenson and Theo came to tell us he'd been found. Dead.'

Stuart out a long breath as if it had taken a lot out of him to tell the story; possibly it had, but Lara knew she had to press on.

'Did anyone else leave the kitchen around that time?'

Stuart hesitated.

'Pretty much everyone.'

'*Every*one?' said Lara in surprise.

'Look, it was the *last supper*. I was scrubbing my block while hitting the Scotch and singing football songs, I wasn't exactly paying attention, but I can tell you I left for a few minutes – I had a couple of bottles of champagne in my room, so I nipped out to get those. I remember Petra went to see Martin Svenson at some point and everyone else was in and out, making errands to the bins and maybe the meat locker.'

He pointed at Lara. 'If the question you're really asking is 'could any of staff have murdered Viggo?' then again the answer is "pretty much anyone".'

It wasn't exactly what Lara had been looking for, but at least it was honest.

'Was there anyone who...'

'Who might have wanted him dead?' Stuart laughed. 'A lot of people were pissed off last night and some were really upset. But not in that way. We're kitchen workers and restaurants are one of the most risky business ventures out there – what's the statistic, two out of three restaurants close within six months? – we're used to losing our jobs.'

'So no one was bothered that the place was closing?' said Lara incredulously.

Stuart shrugged.

'I'll miss the place, the people, sure, but look: I'm a skilled chef coming from one of the top kitchens in the world. I'll be fine, although I worry about some of the younger kids. Josh and Lucas – they're both quite new, general dogsbodies but keen. They're gutted. Working at Kluven was their big break.

Josh, particularly, was heartbroken. He idolised Viggo.'

'Is it definitely all over though? Couldn't Kluven re-open with a new chef?'

Stuart smiled to himself.

'I'd love Petra to be promoted. She's the most talented chef in the kitchen. I'd stay for her.'

He flushed a little as he said it and the penny dropped for Lara. Stuart's admiration for Petra was more than mutual respect. He *liked* her. Perhaps that was the real reason he'd come to Sweden in the first place.

'So what would you say Viggo's mood was like when he left the kitchen last night?'

'Good,' said Stuart. He paused. 'Which was strange because he'd been in such a weird mood for the past few weeks.'

'Weird how?'

Stuart looked away, clamming up again. Lara touched his arm.

'Petra told me,' she said gently. 'Viggo disappeared last week and no one knows where.'

Stuart sighed,

'Actually I do. He was at Kjell Norberg's farm. Kjell is one of Kluven's suppliers.'

This was new: Lara sat forward. 'Did Viggo tell you this?'

'No,' said Stuart, looking annoyed. After all, Viggo was supposed to be his friend.

'I only found this out about an hour ago. Kjell had heard about Viggo – word travels fast even in these parts and he called to give his condolences.'

He gave Lara a sideways glance.

'And Kjell told me something else too. He said a couple of weeks ago he found Viggo in a bothy on the outskirts of his land.'

Lara tried to join the dots.

'So that's where he was when he disappeared?'

Stuart took a slug of his coffee and nodded.

'What was he doing there?' asked Lara.

Stuart grimaced.

'Kjell didn't know, but he said he was in a bit of state, acting strangely, spending hours sitting by the river. Kjell was worried about him and I don't think anything fazed Kjell.'

'Didn't he have any idea what was wrong?'

'He said Viggo seemed frightened.'

'Frightened? What about?'

Stuart shrugged. 'I don't know.'

He ran a hand across his mouth nervously and looked back at Lara.

'I did have one thought. What if Viggo, you know – killed himself?'

It was a left-field suggestion. One that Lara hadn't even considered.

'Why do you say that?'

'We all know it wasn't a bear. I've been here five years and never seen one.'

'But you said he seemed happy last night.'

Stuart looked back at her.

'I read once that people who do commit suicide can seem happy before they do it, because they've found a way out of their problems.'

He turned to look at her.

'Viggo was like that. Like he'd made a decision.'

Lara looked out over the frozen lake, so calm and untouched, like no human had ever walked there. *Could* Viggo have killed himself? That was a question for Coulson, she supposed. And it was true that Viggo seemed to have made a decision that night. But to go where? And to escape from what?

Chapter 19

Theo bent to peer out of his office window. Nothing. The snow had finally stopped earlier that morning and the drive was clear – Johan the driver had taken the snowplough down to the road to make sure – but still there was no sign of the police. Not that Theo wanted them here, not really. In an ideal world, someone would wave a magic wand and make this whole mess disappear, but he knew that wasn't going to happen, not with Viggo's corpse still lying in the root cellar. So if the police had to come, he wanted them in and out as quickly and quietly as possible. Not that there was much hope of that either.

'Come away from that window,' said Kat irritably. 'They're not going to appear any faster just because you keep staring at the drive.'

'I know that,' said Theo, turning to face her. 'But until the police do get here, we have to keep the staff in their quarters and their guests in their cabins. It's hard enough as it is without the fact that everyone seems to know that Viggo was...' he lowered his voice. '*Attacked.*'

'You mean no one believes your stupid story about a bear?' she said with disdain. Kat seemed jittery; she certainly hadn't slept well; she'd been tossing and turning in the night, and when he'd woken that morning, she was gone and Kat hardly ever got up before him. Then again, Theo had had his own disturbed night. As a child, someone had once told him about the Mare – the thin, pale female spirit with long black hair and nails, who sat on people while they slept and turned their dreams into nightmares. His father had reassured him that scary, vivid dreams were just your brain processing something unsettling you had seen, but Theo had experienced real terror in his sleep. He'd seen blood, blades and maggots, heard the deafening cries of someone whose life was seeping out of them.

Theo felt his jaw clench. 'It's not a stupid story,' he said. 'It's still a possibility. We won't know anything for sure until the forensics people get here.'

Kat snorted, her arms folded tightly across her chest.

'Theo, we don't need forensics to know that some*one* killed Viggo. Not a bear. A human being. He was stabbed to death and whoever did it is still here on the compound.'

'Will you keep your voice down?' he hissed. 'The guests are jumpy enough as it is without you shrieking about murder.'

Kat shook her head, her mouth still in a tight line.

'The guests. It's always about them isn't it?'

'Of course it is – that's our business. To serve them.'

'Even if one of them killed Viggo?'

Theo sighed, and didn't even try to hide it. His wife was so negative these days. He remembered the first time he had met Kat at the Shelby Hotel in London, how the guests had all loved her big smile and sunny disposition; Theo had fallen for it too. On their first date, Theo had tried to impress Kat by booking a table at the Sark restaurant on the Southbank, but halfway to the entrance, Kat had taken his hand and pulled him into the mini-fairground next door.

They'd ridden the carousel and eaten candy floss and – he had to admit – laughed more than he'd laughed in years. But Kat barely even smiled these days; not at him, anyway.

And actually, now he thought about it, Kat's good humour had been fading over the past few months; perhaps it was the longer nights.

'It's amazing it hasn't happened before,' said Kat quietly. She was standing at the window, looking down towards the guest cabins. 'You're always banging on about community at Kluven, but the reality is we spend our lives surrounded by strangers. Every single day we open our life, our home to them – and they could be anybody.'

'That's the hotel industry, Kat. You can't vet the guests and only accept the nice ones.'

It was the first thing Theo had learned at hospitality school. People were the problem. Your hotel could be a sleek machine, but the guests were the grit that got into the gears and levers, sometimes making the whole thing judder to a halt. Guests getting sick, guests having sex in the lifts, guests stealing – not just towels and robes, but TVs and DVD players, even jewels from the lobby concession on one occasion. And that was without all the mad complaints about the food, the view and the weather – too hot, too cold, as if the staff had some celestial thermostat hidden beneath the front desk. In the real world, people could be utterly charming and wonderful company, but they could also be dreadful, and hotels had to deal with both kinds with equal aplomb.

'That's just the point,' she said, looking at him. 'If we can't choose the guests, it means we're vulnerable, especially as we're in the middle of nowhere.'

She was being melodramatic, overwrought, but she was right that dark things could still happen in beautiful places. Theo had seen plenty of them in his time. His career in hotel management had taken off quickly, zipping up the ladder of five-star resorts in Paris, Milan and London and that had brought him face to face with the best – and the worst – kind of people. Different hotels had different approaches, but they all agreed on one thing: deal with things swiftly and discreetly. Sexual assaults on the housekeeping staff, rooms gutted by fire caused by freebasing cocaine, a heart attack in the company of a hooker, it was all quietly wheeled out the back door, with tame cops and expensive lawyers deployed to draw a curtain over the crime, whatever it was. But murder? That was something else.

'We just have to keep an open mind at this stage. And I really don't think Viggo was stabbed to death by one of the guests.'

However much he suspected Kat was right, Theo would keep pushing the bear attack theory until the police could prove otherwise. It wasn't exactly reassuring to say there was a wild animal prowling the grounds, but when it came to reputation management – for Kluven, and for himself, it was the best option. His first mentor, the late great Georges Marsaud at the Plaza Soleil, had once said that the general manager was 'the spider at the centre of the web': he controlled every aspect, every thread, but the skill was knowing which part to give your attention to at any time. And right now for Theo and for Kluven, it was damage limitation. If it became known as the 'bloodbath hotel', then there was no future here – and Theo couldn't let that happen.

'And you're sure about that, are you?' said Kat. 'You're absolutely sure none of the guests could have killed Viggo?'

Theo narrowed his eyes. He had no idea why Kat seemed convinced that Viggo had been killed by *someone*, rather than something. It was making him nervous.

'What do you know?'

'Nothing.'

'Kat, if you have information about Viggo's death...'

She hesitated.

'I did see that guy Alex Ford sneaking off towards the woods,' she said.

'Alex Ford? When was this?'

'After we went out to watch the Northern Lights. He'd been asking a lot of questions about Kluven all day.'

'Kat, he's a journalist.'

'Yes and he found the body. And until a week ago, he wasn't even coming to Kluven. I checked, and the names on the booking were Lara Stone and Sandrine Legard.'

Theo didn't like the direction this was going in.

'Katherine, the press can be ruthless, but I doubt Mr Ford would kill someone just to make a headline.'

'You see?' she said, jabbing a finger at him. 'That's just typical of you – putting your precious guests ahead of people you're supposed to care about.'

'I'm not putting the guests first,' said Theo. He said it as evenly as he could but he could feel a hot temper rising in his chest. 'But Alex Ford is a newspaper editor. We don't want him writing some story about the time he was falsely accused of being a murderer. Let's just keep calm, get the police in and out of here as soon as possible, then we can think about the future.'

Theo stepped over to his wife, put his hands on her shoulders, trying to ignore the flinch as he touched her. 'We're all upset by this Kat,' he said soothingly. 'But we just need to get this over with as soon as possible.'

'And then what?'

'Then we take a view how to move forward.'

Theo said it casually, as if he had yet to consider the matter, but he already had a full, detailed plan in mind. Get the police out, have a brief mourning period, then bring in a new chef. And he had the ideal candidate: Petra Summers. It made perfect sense from a PR point of view. Petra was Viggo's prodigy, it would be like he was passing the baton to her. More importantly, Theo could control Petra. She was talented, sure, but she was calm. More importantly, if she had an ego, she kept it under control: exactly the kind of chef Theo needed in the kitchen.

'I think we need to go back to London.'

Theo looked at his wife in surprise.

'London?'

'It's home, Theo.'

Her home, not his – not that you would know it. Kat looked Swedish and she had made a concerted effort to smooth out her accent when she had begun in hospitality. He shouldn't have been so shocked, he supposed. Theo had always hoped his wife would come to love Sweden, but she hadn't.

'You really don't feel it, do you?' she asked.

'Feel what?'

'The claustrophobia, all these trees, the little cabins, the snowed-in roads. Don't you feel hemmed in?'

Unbidden, Theo thought of himself as a teenager, bent over a map of Sweden, his finger tracing the distance to foreign cities. As a young man, Theo had ached to get away from the village and the estate where there were too many trees with roots that tripped you. Then one day his father had taken him across the border to Tromso. A business meeting, some drug company selling their wares: 'an adventure', his father had said. The idea, Theo suspected, was to show his restless son just how hollow the big city was; how dirty, noisy and fast it was, where no one knew or cared what your name was. But – oh, Theo had loved it. And in particular he had loved the hotel, a warm church of glass and steel and smooth carpet beneath his boots. Where a hot chocolate might magically appear, then the empty cup disappear just as easily. Within a year he'd enrolled at Glion, the Harvard of hotel management, nestled in the hills above Montreux, learning how all those tricks were done. From there he'd worked in London, Milan, New York. And Kat was right: he'd felt free. But at some point you had to come home, didn't you? At some time you had to grow up.

'Remember when we met?' said Kat after another moment. 'You told me you got into hotel management to see the world. And yet here you are, back where you started, totally closed off, in a bloody ice cave.'

'I came back for my father, Kat,' he said defensively.

'Yes, I know you did. And I know what you gave up – what *we* gave up – to come here. You could have been GM of the Ritz by now.'

'I don't want to be General Manager of the Ritz...'

She took a breath. 'Your father's gone now, Theo. This mad loyalty to Kluven has got to end.'

'Mad loyalty?' he said, feeling a tightness in his throat.

'Viggo dying could be the best thing for everyone,' she said, pushing on.

Theo let out a nervous laugh.

'I hope you're not going to say that to the police,' he said.

'What? Why? Because I'm the only one who'll say what a bastard he was?'

Theo flinched. That was strong, even for her. Kat had never particularly seen eye-to-eye with Viggo. It was Kat's job to make sure the chef was available to the guests, while Viggo found it hard to disguise his disdain for the paying customers and their requests for ketchup and well-done steak. Viggo could be challenging, it was true, but there had been real anger in her words.

'Look, I don't think discussing Viggo's popularity is going to help,' said Theo, trying to calm the situation. 'We don't want the police looking for things that aren't there.'

'Why not? I haven't got anything to hide. Have you?'

Theo began to speak, but his words were drowned by a revving engine and the swoosh of tyres on snow. He turned to the window. A blue and yellow patrol car, and a dark grey Volvo, followed by a 'Polis'-marked van. They'd come in force: they were taking it seriously. *Was that a good thing?* Theo straightened his tie and smoothed down his jacket: he needed to look in charge. By the time he reached the main entrance, a tall woman in a neat blue parka was walking in flanked by a younger man in a navy blue suit. 'Kriminalinspektör Sonia Lindhart,' she said, not offering her hand. 'This is Sergeant Koln. You are Theo Mikaelsson?'

'Yes, yes I am, I hope your journey was not too...' he began, but clearly Lindhart wasn't here for small talk.

'The resort is locked down, I take it?'

'Yes, well, as much as it can be,' said Theo. 'All the staff are in their quarters apart from those needed to run the restaurant and I have asked the guests to stay in their cabins.'

Lindhart nodded, evidently satisfied. 'Very good. Do you have a list?'

Theo handed her a clipboard. He was ready for this. Prepared. 'All the guests with booking and contact information, plus a staff list with employment records and work permits where required.'

The inspector flipped through it, then handed it to her companion.

'Good,' she said. 'Now take us to the body.'

Chapter 20

Kriminalinspektör Sonia Lindhart was a bitch. That much Petra had decided. They had been sitting in the stuffy office for twenty minutes and all the woman did was repeat the same question again and again. Lindhart would ask her something, nod sceptically, then write cryptically in her notebook. Question, nod, write a note. Question, nod, question, question. Petra didn't have a lot of spare time, but she'd always liked the Scandi noir crime dramas where the detectives were quirky oddballs who wore Fair Isle jumpers. Instead Petra got Sonia Lindhart who wore a drab suit and had the personality to match – and her sidekick Sergeant Koln, a robot in a tie.

Petra knew she was letting her nerves get the better of her. The truth was Petra was becoming increasingly scared in this hot little room; she could feel beads of sweat collecting between her shoulder blades. Petra had always been a model employee, had never been hauled in front of a boss. Even at school she had barely had a cross word from a teacher. But this was the *police*. And they were investigating a murder.

Finally Lindhart sat back, tapping her pen on her notebook. *Tap, tap, tap.*

'We're just trying to establish a timeline here,' said Lindhart. 'Where everyone was and when.'

'I already told you...'

That nod again, a raised hand.

'Indulge me, Petra. So you say you left the kitchen around 10.40. Viggo was still there, correct?'

'That's right.'

'Why did you leave before the meal was finished?'

'Viggo was in charge, I didn't think I'd be missed.'

'Not missed? I thought you were second in command in the kitchen.' The detective lingered on the word 'second'.

Petra gave a thin smile.

'It was the last night of the season and it's one of the most skilled kitchens in the world. Everyone knew what they were doing.'

Lindhart made another note and Petra resisted the urge to crane her neck to see what the woman had written.

'So you went to see Martin Svenson?'

'That's right.'

'Why?'

Petra took a breath, and tried to steady herself. She'd been sitting by her bedroom window all morning, waiting for the police to arrive, going over and over in her head what she would say to them, the story she would tell.

'The announcement about Viggo leaving Kluven came out of the blue. The staff were worried. I wanted some clarification for everyone.'

'You felt as if you'd been left in the dark.'

'Yes,' said Petra, figuring that her tactic was to tell the truth as much as possible. At least, the bits that didn't incriminate her. Sonia looked at her notes again. Couldn't the woman keep anything in her head? Then again, this was

Kiruna in Northern Sweden. Just as Kluven struggled to keep staff in such a remote place, it was possible the Swedish police had a similar problem attracting the finest minds.

'But Martin Svenson said you spoke to him about taking Viggo's job?' asked Lindhart.

Petra had expected this: it was logical that the police would speak to Martin first.

'Yes, it was one of the things we talked about. As you point out, I'm Kluven's second in command.'

'And what did he say?'

'He told me it wasn't possible. They weren't going to recruit another head chef because he was going to close Kluven down. Apparently he and Viggo had an agreement that if either of them wanted out, they would shut Kluven.'

Lindhart nodded.

'And you spoke to Mr. Svenson for how long?'

'Maybe ten minutes.'

Lindhart met her eyes, then looked across at Sergeant Koln who was sitting next to her. He raised his eyebrows, then made a note of his own. *We'll be checking.*

'What else did you discuss?'

Petra took a slow breath; she needed to get this next part right.

'Martin assured me the staff would each receive a generous settlement. To be honest, he didn't seem in the mood to chat, he seemed a little... angry?'

'Angry?'

'Well, he was obviously upset that the restaurant was closing.'

Petra was pleased with how she had framed that; it had come out even better than she had practised. Martin Svenson clearly had no loyalties to her, so why shouldn't she shift suspicion towards him? If she had been Sonia Lindhart, Petra would certainly have been looking very hard at the restaurant's owner. He stood to lose the most from Viggo walking out.

'And then?'

'Then I went back to the staff quarters.'

'Straight back?'

No, not straight back. I met Viggo on the path to his cabin and yelled in his face.

'Yes. Straight back.'

Petra felt a thickness in her throat. Lying was new to her too.

'Did anyone see you go into the stables?'

'I... I don't think so,' she stuttered. Rehearsing this in her room, Petra had imagined she would sound confident and smooth. But now she was lying to the police.

'You don't think so?' asked Lindhart, emphasising the word 'think'. Petra pressed her lips together. She had been through this again and again in her mind. One of the benefits of having lived at Kluven so long was that Petra knew the place intimately. She knew all the suntraps – the courtyard behind the Ski-Doo storage barn, the little clearing near the lake. And she also knew the exact locations of the few security cameras on the complex, so she was confident that none of them would have picked her up on the path to Viggo's cabin.

But that was the cameras. What if a passer-by had seen her? A witness? Had they seen Petra spring at Viggo, claws bared? Was the detective about to reveal this crucial, damning piece of evidence?

'You didn't see Viggo at all in this time?' pressed Lindhart.

Under the table, Petra began picking at her nails, already short from her pre-emptive grooming, sure her anxiety was obvious to the detectives. Her heart was beating hard, her stomach churning, but she was frozen, unsure which way to jump. This was Petra's last chance to tell the truth – the real truth. But she couldn't.

'No,' said Petra, her voice hoarse. 'No, I didn't see Viggo.'

Petra assumed Lindhart was making one of her notes, but she didn't – couldn't – look up.

'How would you describe your relationship with Viggo?'

Petra took a careful breath, trying to calm herself. Stick to the facts, this was the easy stuff.

'We were colleagues,' she said. 'Friends.'

'Have long have you known him?'

'Eight years. We met at a restaurant in Provence and came here as a team.'

'So you were close?'

'I'd like to think so.'

'Romantically involved?'

Petra looked down again.

'No.'

There had been one time, early on. The two of them sitting on the floor in Petra's room, drinking cherry brandy wine, dreaming up new concepts and recipes, mapping out their glittering future together. Giggling, lips numb, she'd rested her head on Viggo's shoulder, the first rays of the morning falling across them. It had been the perfect moment, achingly romantic, utterly natural. All she had needed to do was turn two inches to the left and their lips would have met: fireworks, violins. But Petra hadn't turned, too scared to make the leap, waiting until Viggo's breathing had softened and deepened and then Petra had slept too. But when she had awoken, Viggo had gone.

'So you were just friends? Best buddies, as close as two people could be?'

'Yes.'

'And yet he didn't tell you he was leaving. That's curious isn't it?'

Petra looked away. As much as Petra hated Lindhart, the woman's instincts were right: she and Viggo *had* grown apart and in fact their confrontation outside Viggo's cabin was the first time they had spoken away from the kitchen in a long time. Although 'spoken' didn't really describe what had happened, did it? She curled her fingers, hiding the nails, nausea rising as she imagined Sergeant Koln grabbing her wrists and swabbing under the nails.

'What mood was Viggo in yesterday?'

Petra willed herself to calm down. Breathe in, breathe out. This was another chance to turn the focus elsewhere.

'He seemed in a good mood actually. If he was sad about Kluven closing, he didn't show it. He was certainly in a better mood than over the past few weeks. I'd been worried actually, especially after the disappearance.'

Sonia stopped writing. Her eyes were dark blue, narrow.

Speaking to the journalist Lara Stone the previous night had felt like an intrusion, but she had learnt one thing from it: people liked a story. She had seen the journalist's eyes light up when she had mentioned Viggo's missing hours.

'Disappearance? What disappearance?'

Petra didn't smile, but she was pleased that the great detective didn't know everything.

'Two weeks ago, Viggo just didn't come in. Which was fine, even if we only had the second-in-command in charge,' she said, unable to stop adding a note of sarcasm. 'But then he didn't come in the next day or the next.'

'He was gone for three days? Why?'

'Life in the kitchen is hard, inspector. Viggo was under a lot of pressure. Perhaps he just couldn't hack it.'

'And no one said anything?'

'Obviously I covered for him, but the guests were beginning to ask questions, yes.'

She tapped her pen again, thinking.

'So where was he?'

'I asked. He was vague. Meetings, or at least that's what he said.'

'You don't believe it?'

'I'm just telling you what Viggo told me. He said he'd left Kluven to sort some things out.'

'Where do you think he went?'

'As I said, I don't know.'

Sonia took a sip of her coffee. 'Who do you think attacked him?'

It was a blunt question out of the blue, no doubt meant to stun and surprise.

'I don't know why anyone would...' She looked down at her clipped nails, choked up. She took a ragged breath and tried to continue, but Lindhart stopped her with a shake of her head.

'You can go,' she said, waving a dismissive hand.

'What?'

'You can go.'

Petra gaped at her, then looked across at Koln. He shrugged.

'We'll be seeing you again.'

Unsettled by the sudden turn of events, Petra pushed her chair back, scraping the floor in her haste. As she closed it behind her, she heard laughter from inside the office. Petra stood in the corridor, trying to slow her breathing, clasping and unclasping her hands. She felt sick, shaky. Ashamed. *What have I done?* She thought as she walked blindly towards the kitchen, on autopilot, not sure where she was going or why. She had lied to the police. She had tried to implicate Martin. She had bad-mouthed Viggo, trashed his memory. Petra looked up and caught her reflection in the dark window by the back door. The woman looking back looked hollow-eyed, ghoulish. And something else: she looked guilty.

Chapter 21

Justin was lying curled on the edge of the bed trying to ignore his cramping stomach when Emily put her head around the door.

'Hey, do you fancy playing Scrabble?'

Justin tried not to groan. Emily had been in the living room for the past hour, watching some Christmas movie on Netflix and he had been hoping she'd stay there.

'I don't really like Scrabble.'

'That's not what you told me on our first date. You said your biggest ever word score was 3,200.'

He wanted to laugh, but everything hurt. Everything felt terrible. Everything felt hopeless.

'That bloody scallop has really floored me, Em.'

She tipped her head sympathetically.

'What you need is water, you need to rehydrate after vomiting. I'll go and get you some.'

'Thanks,' he said.

He felt both irritated that she wouldn't leave him alone and guilty at how kind she was being. Emily was nursing him through what she believed was simple food poisoning, when in fact he was going through drug withdrawal:

sweating, shivering with the occasional dash to the bathroom. And on every visit, his reflection in the mirror seemed to look worse, like a corpse slowly decomposing. Justin was about to call out to enquire about more painkillers when Emily came back into the room holding a waste bin.

'Justin, what's this?' she said.

Justin sat up suddenly, trying to read the expression on her face. Had she found the bloody shirt? No – she couldn't have. He'd ventured out of the cabin, grateful for the murky Arctic morning light, walked into the woods and buried it under the snow.

'Justin, what the hell is this?' she repeated, her voice, louder, firmer this time.

'What's what?'

She tipped the bin on the bedcover.

Dozens of squares of dark chocolate fell out and Justin let out a laugh of relief.

'Chocolate? God, for a moment there I thought you'd found my porn stash.'

'What's it all doing in the bin?' said Emily, her voice serious.

'Swedish chocolate, man – it's gross. Have you tasted it? I tried it last night. Almost vomited it up. Had to chuck the rest.'

She didn't look convinced. He didn't have his girlfriend down as the cynical sort. Back in LA, she jumped on every bandwagon going, crystals, nutritional 'dust' aimed at boosting your sex life, energy wands, out-there psychics; Justin was sceptical of it all, but Emily embraced it with enthusiasm. It seemed strange that she would now be so suspicious about chocolate.

'You launched into the mini-bar last night?' she said cautiously. 'I thought you had food poisoning.'

'I did,' he replied, trying to think on his feet. 'But I just wanted to get that slimy, fishy taste out of my mouth.'

Emily didn't smile. Her eyes were cold, was in a firm line.

'Be serious Jus. What's going on?'

What was he going to say? The truth? That he'd dumped the chocolates because he'd used their foil wrappers to smoke drugs? He'd no idea if Emily had connected the dots. He knew that she was street smart enough. As a model, she'd been to thousands of parties in her time, worked in a fast industry. But she was also a well-brought up girl from Houston.

'Look babe,' he said gently. 'I know I've been acting a bit weird, but don't start reading things into some silly pillow sweets.'

Emily's face softened and she sat down on the edge of the bed.

'Justin... why don't you tell me the truth?'

'Truth? That I've gone off Scrabble and don't like Swedish chocolate?'

'I *know*, Justin.'

He looked at her sharply, scattered images from the previous night flicking through his head.

'You know what?'

Emily lowered her voice as if they might be overheard.

'You're using, aren't you?'

He pushed away from her, up against the headboard.

'What? No!'

She grabbed his arm.

'Please Justin, I've been around musicians enough to know.' She shook her head, her voice faltering. Justin felt something give in his chest and he reached for her. Emily crying was his Achilles heel. Some rough, tough drug addict he was.

'Em, don't. I hate it when you cry.'

She nodded, used an elegant finger to stem the tears.

'Then maybe you should try being honest with me.'

He felt terrible, but he was suddenly sobering up. It was as if his body had recognised how much danger he was in.

'I can't stay if you won't talk to me,' she said after a moment.

Emily had never been anything but wonderful to him; patient, understanding and happy to put up with his self-indulgence. Justin just wanted to run off to the khazi to puke, but he knew he owed it to her to at least attempt some semblance of the truth.

'Okay...' he said slowly, then in a rush: 'So maybe I had a little smoke last night...'

'A little smoke. Using tin foil. You mean heroin.'

'It was stupid, childish. I've been under such pressure with the band. I just wanted to relax a bit.'

Emily pushed the heel of a hand into her eye, then fixed Justin with a serious look.

'Relax a bit? Justin, this is *heroin.*'

He looked away towards the window. He hated her using the word, it was dirty, shameful. And coming from Emily's mouth, it somehow made it real.

'God,' he gulped, pressing a hand to his face, to hide the tears he could feel coming. It was only his eyes watering, he told himself, maybe he was coming down with a cold or even the flu, but deep down he knew. Knew that it was out of control, that he was sliding into a dark hole he might never be able to claw his way out of. And here he was, treating the only person who could help him – the only one who *wanted* to help him – like dirt.

'I'm so sorry Em,' he said, his voice thick.

Emily was crying properly now.

'I can't believe I've been so stupid. How did I not know?'

'Because I'm a bloody addict. And addicts are the best liars in the world.'

'But I thought I knew the signs.'

He didn't want to ask how she knew. When they first met, he'd googled her. Wasn't that what everyone did? Rock stars were no different. He'd seen that Emily had been linked to several musicians before him, and at least one of them, Todd Stevenson, he knew was a user. But he hadn't wanted to probe her about whether the rumours of a relationship with Todd were true – he hadn't wanted to know the details about her previous love life. Who did?

Justin shook his head. 'Don't blame yourself, Emily. There's nothing more sneaky than a junkie. We make the Stasi look like amateurs.'

'But how the hell did you get those drugs into the country...' she replied. She held up a hand and then turned her head away from him. 'No, don't tell me, I don't want to know.'

It was just another reason to feel guilty, another example of the way he'd deceived her.

She stood up and walked across to the other side of the room.

'How long has this been going on?' she asked.

It sounded as if she were asking about an affair, but actually there was something in that. Being hooked on junk *was* like having an illicit lover, a third person in the relationship, someone who was blisteringly attractive who you knew was wholly bad for you, but still you couldn't keep away.

He didn't reply.

'*How* did it start?' she asked, her watery eyes wide. 'How did you let this happen to you?'

It was a question he'd asked himself a lot recently. Drugs were commonplace in the music industry. The truth was that touring was boring and repetitive. Listening to a drum soundcheck was enough to have anyone calling their dealer. Drugs took the edge off, made the days fly and helped you sleep after the spiralling high of a thousand girls screaming your name, or at least that's what musicians who took drugs told themselves. From the start, Justin hadn't really been bothered with any of it. He'd had the odd spliff in his early Joystick days, but it hadn't agreed with him, made him feel sick. He just didn't want to go down that road – until he did.

After Joystick had split, Justin had tried to enjoy his new found freedom – and money. But within a few months, he'd felt lost, sitting in one room of his house in the Hollywood Hills with the curtains drawn, eating take-out and binge-watching zombie movies, anything to block out the creeping sense that his career was over.

When Gary Banner had come along with his idea for a supergroup, Justin had grabbed it with both hands, until that first Velvetines session at a studio in downtown LA. Justin had bounced in clutching a demo of his ballads only to find Gary had already decided on the direction of the band: avant-garde electronica. Industrial drum machines and droning synths all complemented his vision of dystopian ennui; 'No one', he'd declared, 'wants bloody boy-meets-girl,' in the age of terror and social breakdown. Justin could have walked out of course, but he was already committed, the press releases sent, a tour booked. And when Gary offered him the magic powder which would take away all that doubt and shame, Justin had taken it.

'I joined The Velvetines because I wanted to feel the buzz again, that joy and magic I felt when we started Joystick. But it wasn't like that. Working with Gary was hollow, soulless. The new music felt flat. I started taking drugs because I wanted all those feelings to just go away.'

The music press had been enthusiastic, but Justin could see the faces of the fans in the front rows – and their smiles didn't reach their eyes. Justin had felt a fraud.

'It's over now. That was the last time. I promise,' he said.

'You can't promise that,' said Emily, shaking her head. 'You can't promise anything.'

He opened his mouth to object, then remembered he owed her the truth.

'No, you're right. I can't. But I can try. I can try for you.'

'For me. Is that what you want?'

'He sat forward, grasping her hand. 'You're the best thing that's ever happened to me.'

That at least was true. He'd met Emily a few weeks after Joystick had split. His buddy Rob from the record company had bullied him into coming over to his house for a party. 'Just a few mates, very low-key,' he'd reassured him.

Of course it had been a full-bore rave with DJs and fire-jugglers, an album launch for one of Rob's endless procession of one-hit wonders. But, hiding out in the gardens, Justin had bumped into Emily who had also been dodging the chaos. When she had smiled at Justin, it had been like the clouds had parted and he'd rushed home and written 'Best Day', a song Justin immediately knew was the way forward.

Meeting Emily had been like turning on a creative tap. It was one reason why he'd been so keen to join another band and had said yes to Gary's suggestion for a supergroup.

'Then why are you doing this, Justin? Aren't I enough?

'Listen Em, it's not you, it's me,' he said. 'The Velvetines is full-on. Honestly, we've hardly seen each other this year with you working...'

'So this is my fault?' she asked.

It wasn't Emily's fault, but she worked away from home most of the time, and in the past eighteen months he'd seen too much of Gary and his crowd of high-functioning addicts. Perhaps if he'd spent more time with her, devoted more time to their relationship then things might have been different.

'No, it's not your fault,' he whispered.

He stood up and walked towards her. Every joint ached, and his head was pounding, but he had to go to her.

'Why, Justin, why?' she said, another tear dripping down her lovely face.

Why? How could he explain it? It wasn't about the high, not really. As a teenager, Justin had seen the movie 'Drugstore Cowboy' where Matt Dillon had embodied heroin chic, robbing mid-west pharmacies in a stylish thrift store leather coat. Back then, the thought of actually taking heroin terrified Justin, but he had seen the movie again, more recently, and something other than the costumes had stood out. In his dreamy voiceover, Dillon's character had explained that the appeal of drugs wasn't about getting high, it was actually the opposite. Drug fiends, he said, had always had a pretty good idea how they were going to feel. And it was true. When you were on dope, you knew exactly how you were going to feel that day. No surprises, no spikes. None of those tiny paper cuts of everyday living – nothing could hurt you. Until it all did.

'I love you and I'm going to fix this,' he said taking her hand.

'Then you've got to start being honest with me,' she whispered. He swallowed hard. If he was going to keep her – and he couldn't stand losing her – Justin knew he had to start opening up.

'Justin, what is it?' she asked. Her voice had a tremor.

He was starting to sweat again and he felt his heart flutter – panic, anxiety.

You love her. Tell her. Be honest, no matter what, said a voice in his head.

'Viggo,' he said finally. 'I think I did something to Viggo last night. And I woke up with blood on my shirt.'

He expected her to look frightened, stricken, disgusted, instead she stood up straighter, her expression calm and composed.

'Tell me what happened.'

He shook his head.

'Justin, tell me.'

'I can't, Em! It's all a blur. Just... snapshots. All I know is that I got high, then Viggo was there yelling at me – or I was yelling at him – and there was some sort of... scuffle and then the next morning I had blood on me.'

He held up his hands. Showed her the scratches.

'I don't know what happened, but I'm worried I might have something to do with all this. I... I just don't know what.'

Emily nodded slowly, as if thinking it all through.

'Okay,' she said. 'But I know one thing.'

'What?'

'I know you didn't kill Viggo.'

'What? How?'

'You're many things Justin Blake, but you're not a killer. You're a poet and a singer and you've got the biggest heart of anyone I have ever known. Maybe you had a tussle with Viggo last night, but I know you wouldn't kill him.'

Justin felt a sob collect in his throat. Her words were more than he deserved.

Emily seized Justin's shoulders and looked him directly in the eye.

'Where did you go last night?"

He was crying now.

'I don't know. The trees,' he said pointing out of the window. Things were beginning to come back to him. A soft undergrowth, the black umbrella of trees, the light of a cabin in the distance.'

'Justin, did you go to the root cellar?'

He squeezed his eyes tightly, searching his memory. There was a building. It was Viggo's cabin. He could hear the chef's boots crunching across the snow as he came towards him.

'No, I didn't. I was in the forest,' he said.

Emily put her arms around him and he felt flooded with relief and love.

'I believe you,' she said.

She did. She believed *in* him..

Haltingly, he told her everything he could remember. How he'd faked the food poisoning, how he'd gone back to the cabin, then gone off to find somewhere quiet to smoke. He remembered darkness and snow and trees. Then something shook loose and he held up a finger.

'I remember... shouting. Coming from Viggo's cabin, yes I'm pretty sure. I was sitting under a tree and I could hear it.'

'Shouting? Viggo?'

'Two people.'

'What were they saying?'

He forced himself to think, but what he had heard didn't take any shape.

'Not sure. I couldn't really hear it. Maybe I couldn't understand it.'

'So the voices were speaking in Swedish?' said Emily quickly.

Justin shook his head. The memory was almost there, but just out of reach.

'Maybe Swedish, but it could've been Norwegian, Danish, any of those languages. In fact, remember we were given the tour of the kitchen and you spoke to that Scottish guy?'

'Stuart?'

'He had such a thick accent, it could even have been him...'

Emily clutched his hand urgently. 'We've got to tell someone, Justin. The police will want to talk to us soon.'

'No, Em. How can we? They'll want to know why I was there, why I can't remember more. I can't tell them about the gear. And they'll want to know how I got blood on my shirt.'

She grimaced, grasping the situation. Even when she was grimacing, Emily was beautiful.

'Okay, we'll sort it out. Stick together,' she decisively.

'Thank you,' he said simply.

'What for?'

'For loving me. God knows I don't deserve it.'

'Don't worry, you'll make it up to me,' she smiled. 'But first we've got to get our stories straight. We'll say we were here together. You came straight back after the meal – you were sick – I watched the Northern Lights, then came back and nursed you.'

He blinked at her, feeling tears coming.

'You'd say that?'

'Why not?' she said. 'Just one condition.'

'Anything.'

'Just say no, okay?'

'I can do that,' he said, forcing a smile.

He only hoped that he could.

Chapter 22

Kluven had become a crime scene. From the window by the back door, Theo could see that the forensics team had set up lights in the root cellar and were crawling about taking photographs and taking samples or whatever it was they did. They all seemed very high-tech and efficient beetling around in their hooded suits, but couldn't they just get it over with? How many samples of Viggo's blood did they need? At least the interviews with the staff and guests over here in the lodge seemed to be moving more quickly, but none of this was good for business.

'Sir?'

Theo turned as the young detective – Koln, was it? – came out of the interrogation room: the repurposed bookings office.

'I don't suppose we could have another refill of coffee in here?' said Sergeant Koln. Over the young man's shoulder, he could see Inspector Lindhart leading the chef Mr Namato out; presumably his interview was over.

'Coffee, yes, of course. I'll arrange for that immediately,' said Theo, pushing through the double doors into the kitchen. The catering operation had been officially closed down, but the police had allowed a skeleton staff to carry on to provide food and drink for everyone on the compound. Thankfully Michel the pastry chef was there.

'A large pot of coffee for the office, please Michel,' said Theo.

'Right away, monsieur.'

Theo nodded with satisfaction. Michel was old school in the sense that he did things without complaint and with pride. Not like some of the youngsters, thought Theo. They wouldn't say 'sir' if it choked them.

'Would they also like some pastries?'

Theo considered. Elaborate cakes weren't exactly in keeping with a murder investigation, were they? But then Theo had always believed that small things made a big difference.

'Yes, if you would Michel.'

Even if they were to suffer the indignation of a police investigation, this was still Kluven. Why should the interviewees be denied flaky pastry? Michel handed him a tray and Theo bumped out through the doors and down to the office.

'Härligt,' said Koln, his eyes wide. Theo smiled graciously; he didn't imagine a policeman often ate in starred restaurants and it was good to keep them on-side.

'Thank you for this. And thank you for making your office available to us,' he said.

'Oh, it's not my office,' said Theo. 'This room is used by the reservations team when we open the website for bookings, but... well, I don't think that will be happening this year. My office is through that grey door over there, should you need me. Now if you'll excuse me, I had better check on the guests.'

The policeman nodded gratefully, as if he was reassured by the idea. Theo retreated to his office and carefully closed the door. Yes, he was checking on the guests, but not in the way the policeman imagined. His mentor at The Shelby hotel had once told him that the skill of a general manager could be summed up as 'information, preparation' – you had to know who your guests were, what they expected from their stay, then arrange it in advance so that everything worked 'like magic'. The analogy was apt – in fact the legendary Fat Duck restaurant had once recruited illusionist Derren Brown to provide insights into the guests' desires, then literally served them up with their meal. Earlier that morning, Kat had complained that they were 'surrounded by strangers', but Theo begged to differ. He researched all of Kluven's important guests beforehand, found out their dietary requirements, how they liked their coffee, how soft they liked their pillows. In the age of social media, it was amazing how easy it was to dig those things up.

But all that was small-fry, amateur stuff. Now Theo had another source of information. He looked up at the air vent to the right of his desk and waited, his breath held. And there it was: muffled, but still perfectly audible. Inspector Lindhart was discussing Miles Namato's interview with Sergeant Koln.

'...Miles didn't like Viggo, did he...' he heard her say.

'...professional jealousy...' Koln answered.

'...Sure, but at least he was honest...'

Theo smiled. He had discovered this quirk of the building within a few weeks of Kluven's opening. He'd been at his desk when he'd heard noises. Feral noises. The sound of sex.

At first he'd thought he was mistaken; was it the wind or a TV playing somewhere? Then he had realised the air ducts above the bookings office ran down the corridor to his own. Something to do with the acoustics of the piping meant that when the vents were both open, Theo could hear every word spoken in the adjacent office.

That first discovery had ended up in a disciplinary procedure and the resignation of a kitchen porter and a waitress, but for Theo it had been very useful indeed. He looked down at his desk jotter, reviewing his notes from the morning's interviews. So far he had found out the following:

1. When Viggo had gone missing two weeks earlier, he'd gone to stay with Kjell Norberg and slept in his bothy.
2. Stuart Dell believed that Viggo was having a breakdown, backed up by Viggo's paranoid claims that he was being watched.
3. Alex Ford, under pressure from his newspaper to supply stories, had been trying to secure an exclusive interview with Viggo Widlund and had gone looking for him around the complex. That's when he had stumbled on the body.

And now, number 4: Miles Namato believed that Viggo had been a 'fraud'. Listening to the chef's interview, Theo had to say he agreed with Inspector Lindhart's assessment that Miles had detested Viggo, although Miles had refused to explain why he believed Viggo was deceiving them. It didn't matter to Theo: he was strangely enjoying the theatre of it. Kat had always been a fan of true crime podcasts and this investigation used a similar process: methodically assembling the facts which would reveal the killer's motives and, slowly, inevitably, their identity. It was thrilling to listen as each new revelation came, with the added frisson that it was live, happening only a few metres away from where he was sitting.

But Theo wasn't just here for the macabre entertainment. No, all of this information was vital now. Kluven's reputation was at stake here – perhaps even its future. It all depended on who the police believed had killed Viggo. Staff? Guest? Or in a surprise twist, would Viggo's shadowy watcher in the woods turn out to be the killer?

Theo chuckled to himself. *Don't get carried away.* As Inspector Lindhart kept reminding her sergeant, 'stick to the facts.' And surprisingly, the facts in Viggo's case were fairly clear. The chef had been killed in a narrow window of time between Viggo leaving the kitchen and Alex Ford discovering his body roughly thirty minutes later. All of the staff apart from Petra were 'probably' – Lindhart's word – in the kitchen at the assumed time of the murder, although two of the porters were certainly shuttling back and forth between the bins and the meat locker.

Martin and Anna Svenson had an alibi as they had been at home in their house up the hill: Petra Summers had confirmed to Lindhart she had seen them both there. Martin's house guest Kenneth Roscoe had spoken to them too, when he'd gone directly back to the house after the meal. Serena Roscoe had watched the Northern Lights near the Lodge, between 11pm and 11.15pm, as had a number of other guests, although no one was entirely sure who was there, as everyone's attention had been directed towards the heavens.

Each of the interviewees had been more than happy to speculate on who they thought might be the killer: Connie and Graham thought Dr. Green 'had a shifty look', while Miles the chef thought Lara Stone the reporter seemed 'a little too keen to point the finger at everyone else'.

More revealing had been the conversation between the police officers themselves. He'd been surprised that Alex Ford had been dismissed so quickly as a suspect. According to Sonia Lindhart, he was one of the most well-regarded journalists in the UK and his explanation that he'd gone looking for a scoop was believed. Most of the other guests were also discounted. Connie Edwards barely had five minutes with the officers, much to her evident disappointment, but Justin Blake, Patrick Green and Coulson Miller had yet to be interviewed. Stuart Dell's theory that Viggo had killed himself had been quickly rejected by one of the on-site forensics experts. Someone had killed Viggo Widlund, and Theo was pretty sure the police had their prime suspect – Petra Summers.

Kluven's sous chef had means, motive and opportunity and no one to provide an alibi. Plus Lindhart thought Petra was lying about 'almost everything'. Theo considered this both a blessing and a great shame. Petra was a hard worker and kept the kitchen in line when Viggo was away. Theo had always seen Petra as a strong candidate to one day replace the Viking Chef.

But if the police arrested Petra, it was, perhaps, the cleanest solution to this mess. The sous chef who had been driven to murder by a broken heart and thwarted ambition – people could easily see how it might happen. It was certainly a less awkward narrative than arresting a guest. Who would want to come to an isolated resort if they thought the guy in the next cabin might stab you through the heart? No – charging Petra was the best outcome, especially if they charged her quickly. It meant that Kluven could move on.

Theo turned to the window where he could see Miles Namato leaving the lodge. If he was quick he could catch up with him.

Grabbing his coat, Theo took the side-door and hurried down the path towards the cabins. Mid-afternoon and it was already as dark as a moose's behind; one of his father's more colourful phrases. To the people of the village, the doctor had been a very upright and proper man, but in private with Theo he would sometimes let in a little light. Sometimes. Not that there was much light now; at this time of year, it went from insipid grey late morning, through gloomy grey around noon, straight into 'mostly black' after lunch.

'Ski-iiit!'

Theo slipped on the icy path, pitching sideways and into a drift beneath a tree. Momentarily stunned, Theo lay in the snow facing towards the forest where dark bodies seemed lie in the gloom beneath the branches. *Just illusions*, he told himself. *Just his mind playing tricks.*

He squeezed his eyes closed but he saw it again. The same image that had haunted his sleep the previous night. His body lying on a cold floor, a ribbon of blood, the legs and arms at unnatural angles, like the twisted limbs of a tree.

It's your fault, whispered the wind shunting through the trees.

'I'm a good man,' he told himself, trying to catch his breathe. 'I'm a good man'.

Shakily Theo clambered to his feet. He brushed himself down and looked at the path to see what had tripped him up.

On any normal day, the paths around the estate would have been cleared long before the guests woke up; that illusion of seamlessness which was vital in any luxury resort: the grass perfectly green, the soil beds raked smooth, the waiters appearing at the perfect moment. But today wasn't seamless, was it? Most of the ground staff were locked down, cowering behind shutters. In the blink of an eye, Kluven seemed to have skewed sideways into some parallel universe where nothing worked, nothing made sense, even for him.

He turned a corner and saw Miles Namato standing on

the path. *Varje moln har en guldkant,* another of his father's sayings: 'Every cloud has a golden lining'. The Swedes always went one better. And if he played this right, it might still be a productive day for Theo.

'Hello?' he called. 'Mr Namato?'

Miles looked up, cupping the cigarette behind his back until he recognised Theo, then visibly relaxed.

'Ah. It's you,' he said, blowing smoke up into the grey sky. 'I know we're not supposed to be out unaccompanied, but we're not cattle, you can't keep us penned up like this.'

He looked at the general manager directly.

'Is anyone prepared to tell us what's going on yet?'

'This is a matter for the police now. If you would like me to arrange anything for you...'

'How about a transfer out of here?'

'I will, as soon as I can, Mr Namato.'

Theo let the man take another puff of his cigarette.

'Mr Namato,' he said. 'I have no desire to put you on the spot, but I had something I wanted to ask you.'

Miles looked at him through a haze of smoke, his thick black brows knitting together.

'Oh yeah? What?'

Theo smiled.

'I think we may be able to help each other.'

Miles let the cigarette drop to the floor and stubbed it out with the toe of his boot.

'Help each other?'

'More of a business opportunity,' said Theo, smoothly. He glanced at the cabin, thinking of Miles' jumpy wife inside. 'Can we walk?'

Miles looked at him, clearly wondering if it was a good idea to go strolling through the woods when there was a murderer on the loose. Theo held up his arms. 'You can frisk me if you like.' It was a weak joke, but Miles managed a snort.

'Okay, but make it quick,' he said, nodding back towards the lodge. 'I've done enough talking today. I was made to feel like a criminal back there.'

'We've all had to go through it,' said Theo as they began to follow the path towards the lake. It was true, Theo had been the second to be interviewed by Sonia Lindhart, straight after Martin Svenson. The detective had been polite but straight to the point: she wanted to know where had he been, who had he spoken to, if the root cellar had been locked. Theo had been so surprised by the deluge of questions, he had begun babbling and even now, an hour on, he wasn't sure exactly what he had said. *I have nothing to hide.* That's what Kat had said. But it wasn't true, was it? Everyone had something that kept them awake at night.

'So what do you want to talk about?' asked Miles.

'I'd like to present you with an opportunity. A very attractive opportunity, actually.'

Theo hadn't needed the air ducts to find out about Miles Namato; he'd already done the research on him. He was a classically trained chef who, like Viggo had worked in Sydney and Paris and now was head chef at the highly-respected IHG hotel in Tokyo, he was considered innovative and something of a maverick: a good thing in the culinary world. Theo took a quick breath, then launched into the pitch he had been rehearsing since the morning.

'What do you think about coming to work for Kluven?' he said, matter of factly.

'In what capacity?' said Miles, still looking suspicious.

Theo ploughed on.

'If Martin Svenson decides to keep Kluven open, there's obviously an opening for a head chef.'

'Isn't this a little in poor taste?' replied Miles, his face crinkling in surprise. 'I mean, your colleague is barely cold.'

'Sure, sure and it's terrible, heartbreaking for all of us,' said Theo quickly. 'But as you recognise, Mr. Namato, we still have a business to run. And, well, Kluven is much more than a restaurant. It's a community – a beautiful little village – and one that needs our support.'

He began talking about Skellstad, about the little stone bridge leading to the ancient market square, the Alpine-styled houses, the town hall where they held the Christmas celebrations and the warmth of the people who would do anything for each other.

'It's the polar opposite of the noise and colour of Tokyo, I know, but I'm sure you'll agree with me that Kluven is one of the most exciting restaurants in the world.'

As Theo watched Namato's face soften with interest he felt his own rush of excitement. The rational part of him knew that it was crazy to open negotiations with another chef so quickly. Kluven was remote, the conditions inhospitable for much of the year, but it was a plum job and Theo knew that by the end of the week, his inbox would be flooded with CVs and emails from some of the world's top chefs. But Theo also recognised that any recruitment could take a very long time, but time was something he didn't have if Martin Svenson was really thinking about closing Kluven. And Theo couldn't allow it to close. Not after everything he'd done.

That's why Theo's instincts told him that Miles Namato was a perfect replacement for Viggo. He had the skill and the reputation for creativity. An internet search had also told Theo that Miles was heavily into martial arts; he was known to use a Japanese katana in place of a carving knife and he had a love of headline-making soundbites. The image was practically ready-made. Manly, macho and a little crazy. Replace the Viking with the Samurai.

When he had finished, Miles stood there for a moment looking at Theo.

'I have to say I'm intrigued. And obviously, what's happened is a tragedy but...'

But you're crazy enough to do it, thought Theo.

'The next step would be a meeting with Martin Svenson,' added Theo. 'He has to make his final decision on whether to keep Kluven open, but I'm fairly sure that if we've found the right chef to carry on Viggo's legacy, he'll agree to it.'

'I'd want to do things my way, of course,' said Miles.

Theo held up a hand. How foolish of him to forget that chefs had such delicate egos.

'Of course. No one wants things to stay the same, however good they once were.'

Miles stepped forward, lowering his voice. 'Although perhaps we'd better keep this between ourselves just for now, hmm? Just for a few days.'

Theo knew what he meant: just until the police finished their investigations. Even if the Kluven offer had come posthumously, the timing might look suspicious given that Miles suddenly had something to gain from Viggo's death.

'No problem,' smiled Theo, putting out his hand. 'Just between us.'

Miles looked at the hand for a moment, perhaps sensing a whisper of a threat in Theo's words, then he shrugged and shook.

'Don't stay out too long, don't want to worry your wife,' said Theo. 'And there *are* bears in the forest.'

Theo turned back towards the main building, his wide grin hidden by the dark.

Chapter 23

Lara looked at the laptop screen, then out of the window. She didn't see anything in either case. The cabin's lights were reflecting off the window glass; too dark outside now to see anything beyond the snow piled up on the sill. The inbox on her computer screen, meanwhile, was sitting there stubbornly refusing to change. *No news ain't always good news.*

Lara knew Stella was working hard on the research back in London – Lara had been hassling her on the half-hour, every half-hour – but she hadn't yet turned up much. So far it seemed as if the guests and staff were exactly who they claimed, no serial killers hidden in the woodshed, no retired assassins roaming the staff quarters. And since the arrival of the police team, Lara and Alex's investigation been seriously curtailed. Sonia Lindhart had made plain her displeasure with Lara's 'meddling' during her own interview.

'This is not a game, Miss Stone,' the detective had said. Lara had been sorely tempted to respond that she was well aware of the fact, having needed to wipe Viggo Widlund's blood from the toes of her boots. Instead she had apologised, tried her best to look chastened and mumbled something about how she fully intended to 'leave it to the professionals'. Lara wanted the police to think they had given up because being put under house arrest would have put a full-stop on their investigation.

'Such as it is,' Lara sighed, crossing to the mini-bar fridge, pulling it open with a jangle of tiny bottles of spirits. She grimaced: no. Appealing as wine might be right now, it wasn't going to help her cause having a foggy head either.

'I'll have a beer if that's the fridge opening,' said Alex, leaning against the bedroom doorframe. He'd been in there talking to the *Chronicle*'s London office for the last half an hour. Occasionally she had heard his voice rise. Mostly he'd sounded exasperated.

'Who was that?' she asked, sorting through the drinks.

'Darius, and Paul on the news desk,' said Alex, wearily rubbing his face.

'Isn't Darius at the *manor*?' she said with a complicit smile.

'They patched him in. You know he springs to action when he thinks there's a sexy story. Paul on news says he's doing Zoom calls from the manor house on the hour. Needless to say Darius wants an exclusive for the Sunday edition from me by six o'clock.'

'Let me guess, he wants you to make a dramatic citizen's arrest after chasing the murderer by dog sled.'

'Something like that. I think he's seen too many Agatha Christie adaptations.'

'But are you going to file something?'

'I'll have to. So we'd better crack Viggo's murder before Sonia Lindhart,' he said with a weary laugh.

Lara could see how tired Alex was. He was clearly under pressure both from London and his own ridiculously lofty standards. The newsroom took its toll with a high percentage of burn-outs; just one of the reasons Lara had specialised in investigations. It was intense work, sure, but at least with slow-burn stories you were allowed to take your time. The glory days of 70s and 80s journalism were gone, where a reporter would be given three, four, even six months to research a story, but it was still a slower pace than the main newsdesk.

'You look like you need this,' said Lara, handing him a bottle of Swedish ale. Alex raised it in toast. 'Well, it's nearly Christmas.' At least Alex still had a sense of humour; as Deputy Editor he'd worked through the previous two Christmases. On one, he'd been working 'til midnight on Christmas Day and his festive dinner had been a pot noodle at his desk. Turkey flavour, obviously.

'So what are you up to this Christmas?' he said, dropping onto the sofa opposite Lara.

'I'm not sure yet.' She did at least have choices: a formal lunch at her Uncle and Aunt's Oxfordshire estate, where veiled comments would be made about her single status and lifestyle choices, or a meal for one on her little houseboat moored along the Thames. Neither particularly appealed.

'Why don't you come home with me?' said Alex. 'I'm going back to the Lakes for a couple of days. My dad was going to come down to London but he's put his back out. You know Terry would love to see you.'

Lara raised her eyebrows.

'Spend Christmas Day with you?'

'Well, it'll be more like spending it with my dad,' smiled Alex, 'You know how he likes to talk, especially when you're around. But The Setter pub does a lock-in on Christmas Eve and there's always a decent chance of snow.' He gestured towards the window with his bottle. 'Although possibly that's less of a novelty right now.'

It was tempting. Lara had been to the Fords' home

many times, a cosy stone cottage backing onto high meadows dotted with sheep. Her first time had been the week after she and Alex had graduated from their course at City University; they were supposed to go island-hopping in Greece, but Alex had been offered his first gig at the *Chronicle* and somehow he had convinced Lara that a weekend in Windermere would be an adequate substitute. She had loved it and climbing up to Angle Tarn with a rucksack full of sausage rolls had been the perfect end to their studies, but even then, there had been an undercurrent of *something* – an intimate, expectant energy, that told her that their platonic relationship might deepen into something else on the trip. In the event, it had rained non-stop, putting something of a damper on any sparks, but still, Lara wasn't sure that returning to Windermere was a good idea. Christmas was a time for loved ones and she didn't want to think too deeply about what it meant if she spent it with Alex. There was too much baggage, too many complications and right now Lara just wanted things to be simple. 'I'm guessing I'll be press-ganged into going to Aunt Olivia's family soiree this year,' she said. 'I've been avoiding it, but I think I've finally run out of excuses.'

Alex looked disappointed, but nodded as though he understood. He was well aware of her Aunt Olivia's persuasiveness.

'So what are you going to write for Darius?' said Lara, changing the subject.

'I don't know. But I need to get something,' he said, pushing himself up with a groan. 'I'd better go speak to Martin Svenson, see if I can trick a confession from him.'

'Do you really think Svenson might have done it?' she asked.

Alex shrugged. 'It's possible. Besides, it's what Darius thinks. And obviously that's all that matters.'

'What about trying Justin Blake again?'

Alex had been round to Blake's cabin twice that afternoon, but each time, the supermodel girlfriend had said he was sick in bed.

'I'll try his cabin again on the way back from Svenson's.'

'I can't believe you're actually putting your rock idol crush forward as a suspect,' said Lara with amusement. 'He won't be recording many albums if he's in Sweden's Belmarsh for the next twenty years.'

'Might inspire some heartfelt ballads,' grinned Alex, bending to pull on his heavy boots.

'Are you staying here?' he asked.

Lara cast a sour look towards the computer.

'Waiting for intel.'

Lara stood at the window watching Alex's silhouette disappear into the Arctic twilight. She hated him going out into the dark, taking risks just to get the scoop. She was exactly the same way of course, but it was different with someone you cared about. She had felt sick every time Alex had flown into some war zone: Kabul, Aleppo, Fallujah, but when you had the news in your blood, wild horses wouldn't keep you away.

As he faded from view, she wondered why the hell she had turned down his offer of spending Christmas together. It wasn't as if Lara relished the idea of going up to the Oxfordshire estate and playing happy families with the Averys. Alex could do with a fun end to his year too; he had been hit by Sandrine's death too and he'd seen his relationship with a serious girlfriend fall apart. *Fun.* Lara had an idea. She pulled on her coat and grabbed a torch, zipping her parka to the neck as she crunched down the path, heading up onto the approach road.

'Ski-Doos,' she muttered to herself. 'Where would I find the Ski-Doos?'

Earlier in the day, Alex had joked about stealing some snowmobiles and having fun, and Lara had poo-pooed the idea.

I used to be a laugh, she thought. *When did I become such a killjoy?* If she could find a friendly groundskeeper, that guy Johan perhaps, then maybe she could arrange for a trip on the snow-mobiles for the two of them the following morning; surely the police would have released them from their curfew by then?

Lara moved carefully up the drive: logically the Ski-Doos had to be kept near the road. She didn't remember seeing anything when they had arrived with Johan yesterday – damn, had it only been a day ago? – back then, Lara had been too excited to pay much attention to the out-buildings. To Lara's left was Martin Svenson's personal residence; it was the one part of the resort she hadn't had a proper look at before. Modernist and slick, it had black metal sidings and huge glass sections to make the most of the view down to the lake. Lit up now, it looked amazing, warm, welcoming. No hint of the terror and blood that had filled the root cellar a few hundred yards away.

Lara wondered what it was like for Martin Svenson to live out here, bringing people to your home, having them wandering around the grounds, peering in those glowing windows. She supposed that was why Lara hadn't seen very much of him: why would you mix with the customers? That's why he had staff like Kat and Theo.

There. Dead ahead, was what had to be a garage, a converted barn with a red snowplough parked to one side. Icicles hung from the eaves like jagged teeth, the silver cedar wood cladding frosted with white like an embroidered veil. And yes: poking out from the shed's double doors, Lara could see skis. Three Ski-Doos lined up like matchbox cars.

'Hello?' she called, 'Johan?'

Suddenly Lara felt foolish: of course there wasn't anyone here. What, did she expect a driver to be waiting in a freezing cold garage just in case a guest popped in, especially since the police had told them to stay in their cabins? Lara was just turning back towards the lodge when she heard something. She tilted her head, frowning. An owl perhaps? No. It might be dark, but it wasn't actually night yet.

She heard the noise again. It was louder now as she took a step inside the garage.

'Hello?' said Lara, her nerves jangling. She had dismissed the bear attack story as PR spin, but it would just be her luck to come face to face with the only grizzly awake in Northern Sweden. It was another moment before she realised that it was the sound of someone crying.

'Hello?' she called again. 'Who's there?' Running her torch beam along the doorframe, then into the garage, Lara's heart jumped she saw a figure perched on one of the snow mobiles.

'Petra?'

The woman's body language told its own story: arms crossed, head bowed, handkerchief scrunched in one fist.

'Oh. It's you,' said Petra, wiping her eyes. Lara approached slowly; she didn't want to scare the woman any more than she had already.

'What are you doing out here?' she asked.

Petra gestured towards the Ski-Doo beneath her.

'I was thinking of taking one of these, getting as far away from here as I can.'

'Funny,' said Lara quietly. 'I came here for something similar.'

She pointed to the snowmobile next to the one Petra was sitting on. 'Can I join you?

Petra shrugged. 'Sure.'

Lara awkwardly clambered into the saddle. It was cold, but it was better than standing in the snow.

'You were really going to steal a Ski-Doo?' said Petra.

'Borrow, not steal,' said Lara with a soft smile. 'I'm here with my friend Alex and, well, I've been a bit of a cow to him, so I thought zooming about in the snow might cheer him up.'

'You might get arrested too,' said Petra.

Lara grinned.

'That's the least of my worries. I think it's far more likely that I'd drive it straight into a tree.'

Petra tried for a smile, but clearly it was going to take more than Lara's lame jokes.

'What about you, Petra?

'Me?' said Petra, her voice catching.

'Why were you going to take a snow mobile?'

'Because the police clearly think I killed Viggo.'

'Did you?'

In the dark emptiness of the shed, it sounded blunt, brutal, but it was a question Lara needed to ask.

'No,' said Petra after a pause. 'But that doesn't matter, does it? The police need to find the killer so they'll keep going until they do – and I'm the most likely candidate, aren't I?'

Lara wanted to tell her no, to reassure the girl, but she couldn't. On paper, Petra should be top of Inspector Lindhart's list. They sat in silence for a while.

'Why are you mean to him?' said Petra finally. 'Your friend Alex? Is it because you like him?'

It was the first time anyone had asked her so directly. Not even Sandrine pushed her on the details of her relationship with Alex.

'Honestly? I'm not sure. Sometimes I try to push him away, because...' she struggled to find the right words. Petra had asked an honest question and Lara felt she deserved an honest answer. 'I think it's because he's the most important person in my life.'

Petra wiped her eyes.

'And we always hurt the people we love, right?' She looked up at Lara. 'Guess I shouldn't say that with the police so close, hey?'

Lara just waited for Petra to carry on talking.

'Viggo hurt me. He hurt me so much. By leaving, by closing the restaurant and by going back on his promises. I'm not sure it meant he loved me though,' she said glancing across. 'But I loved him Lara. And I would do anything – *anything* – to bring him back.'

Her eyes were glittering with tears again.

'Is that why you came to Kluven together?' asked Lara. 'Because you wanted to stay close to him?'

Petra looked down at her hands, rolling the handkerchief between her fingertips.

'Viggo needed me,' she said, more quietly.

Lara could feel the atmosphere change. There was something in the way Petra said it, like that was the key to this whole mystery. Lara sat forward, examining Petra's face.

'He needed you how?'

Petra sighed, like she was explaining something she'd been over again and again, but Lara was beginning to suspect this was the first time Petra had said it out loud.

'What makes a restaurant stand out is being the best,' she said. 'And Kluven is best at innovation. We combine flavour and texture in ways other chefs could only dream of. We are unique.'

And with that word, Lara felt something go 'click'. Her eyes widened as she realised what the woman was saying. During her time on the *Chronicle*, Lara regularly gave lectures to budding journalism students and one of the most common questions was 'what makes a good reporter'? Her answer was always the same: instinct, knowing when something was significant, knowing that what you heard was *right*. Lara looked at Petra, feeling the tingle of the scoop.

'You mean *you* are unique, don't you Petra? Viggo had to bring you with him because you *were* him.'

Petra looked away from her, shook her head. But Lara leant forward, pushing the point.

'You're the innovative one, aren't you? Not Viggo.'

Petra let out a long ragged breath. Then she nodded.

'Viggo is a brilliant technical chef, but he doesn't – didn't – have the instinct for flavour. Some people just have it.'

'And you do?'

'I suppose I always have,' said Petra. 'My mother tells me that when I was little, I'd follow my grandfather around his vegetable garden, just smelling the tomatoes. Then I'd pick out the ones to make a salad, tell him, what to put in it, peaches, pear, apples that I'd pick from the fruit bowl. He used to say it was uncanny how I'd always choose the sweetest, most flavoursome things he had.'

Lara smiled. 'That skill must have helped you as a chef.'

She shrugged.

'Maybe. What most people want in a kitchen is consistency. Someone who can poach halibut exactly the same way every time. No chef wants some commis showing off her versatility and neither do the guests. They want what they ordered from the menu.'

Petra smiled sadly, as if thinking of a cherished but long-gone memory.

'That was why Viggo and I became a team so quickly. We both wanted the same thing: to innovate. To do things differently.'

'But you said Viggo wasn't good at that.'

'No, but he was ambitious and he had the charisma to get us noticed. So we made a pact: I would create the menus, he would create the noise. And it worked, Viggo flew through the ranks.'

'But why didn't you just push yourself forward, Petra? You were the one with the talent.'

Petra gave an ironic laugh. 'Do you know how Viggo became head chef at La Ferme Mougins?'

Lara shook her head.

'When the vacancy came up, Matthau Chastain– he was the owner – he held an audition for the job. Pitch everyone against one another, survival of the fittest, that was his mindset.'

Lara frowned. 'But wasn't that the perfect chance for you to shine without Viggo?'

Petra shook her head.

'You don't know Matthau. He's a world-class misogynist, he wouldn't even consider me. 'Head Chefs are all men': that was all he would say on the subject. So I helped Viggo with his pitch.'

'Did he ask you to?'

'I offered.'

Lara nodded, wondering how many other women had sacrificed their dreams for the men they loved.

'I put salt with sour. I burnt the garlic, I added marshmallows to filet mignon,' said Petra, her eyes lighting up. 'All the things you shouldn't do. And Viggo executed it perfectly; that was the magic with us. Whatever I could imagine in my head, Viggo could put it on the plate.'

She laughed. 'And then he'd bullshit about it for hours.'

The smile faded from her face.

'Anyway, he got the job. And then Martin Svenson arrived.'

'Was Martin looking for a chef?'

'Not specifically, no, but Martin is a foodie, a restaurant nerd and Viggo was making waves, getting noticed. It's like a soccer player scoring goals, people come to watch. Martin was in the early stages of turning his Swedish vacation retreat into a farm-to-table place, but when he tried Viggo's food, he offered him exec chef of Kluven on the spot.'

'So you both came.'

She nodded.

'As I said, he needed me.'

'And what was in it for you?'

Petra looked down again, as if she was embarrassed.

'In Mougins we were friends, best friends. But Cannes was just down the road, Nice and Monaco not too far away, people and parties were everywhere. I thought if we came to Lapland, a remote place, and it was just the two of us, finally he'd see me, look at me... in the way I looked at him.'

'But he didn't?'

'No.'

Petra shook her head and gave a quiet sob.

'I loved him,' she whispered. 'I loved him so much. How could anyone think that I killed him.'

Lara touched her shoulder.

'I believe you, Petra.'

The other woman looked up in surprise.

'You do?'

Lara nodded. She hadn't known it until that moment, but it was true. She believed everything Petra had said to her and in particular Petra's insistence that she would never have harmed Viggo. Lara didn't have any hard evidence – what evidence could there be for that sort of thing? – but her instincts were tingling. Petra was head-over-heels and heartbroken all at the same time.

'I believe you because, well... I know people,' said Lara.

'It's the same thing as you with flavour I suppose, instinctive. I can usually tell when people are lying.'

Petra looked at her with hope.

'Will you help me?'

'As far as I can. I'm not a lawyer, but I am good at what I do. If you're telling the truth, I'll find the proof.'

'Then you'd better have this.'

Petra reached into the pocket of her jacket and handed Lara a leather journal. It was worn and old, held together with rubber bands, with frayed papers sticking out the side.

'What is this?'

'All my recipes, all our plans, the blueprints for what happened in the kitchen. There's some letters to Viggo, notes from him too. It's pretty much our relationship in written form, sad though that is.'

Lara frowned.

'So why don't you give it to the police? This could help you, show that you and Viggo were in it together from the start.'

'That only helps if you believe my story.'

Lara knew she was right. A clever lawyer would just say it was proof that Petra was bitter and resentful. In the wrong hands, the book would be like a confession.

'You can trust me.'

'It looks as though I'm going to have to.'

Lara put out her hand and they shook. It didn't mean much, but maybe it helped them both. A symbol of intent.

'Come on, we'd better get back to our cabins before we freeze to these machines.'

'But what do I say?' asked Petra as they walked out onto the drive. She sounded much younger than she was, more frightened than she looked.

'My advice for what it's worth: keep schtum,' replied Lara. 'If the police interview again, exercise your right to silence and just say 'no comment'. At least until you can get a lawyer here.'

'Won't I look more guilty?' asked Petra.

'If the police have already decided you're guilty, everything you say is just more evidence,' said Lara. 'It's up to them to prove you killed Viggo, not the other way around.'

'What are you going to do?'

Lara looked back towards the forest.

'I'm going to catch the real killer,' she said.

Chapter 24

Alex turned off his phone, put it in his pocket and turned his face up to the black sky. His editor had only been on the phone for five minutes, but it was enough to make Alex want to strangle him. Darius. *Bloody Darius.* Alex wanted to scream out exactly what he thought of his editor-in-chief and his unreasonable demands, but with an effort, he resisted. Right now, a howl in the night might cause panic and would certainly raise yet more questions from Kriminalinspektör Lindhart – and Alex had no desire to spend any more time in her company. Alex vented his frustration by kicking at a pile of snow, which only resulted in getting a wet sock.

'Get me an interview with the owner, Svenson or whatever his name is,' Darius had said, practically shouting into Alex's ear. 'Don't come back without it. I want tears, I want anger, I want his theory about who killed the Viking chef. Better still, I want a confession from him!'

Darius was arrogant, bombastic and demanding: not unusual characteristics among newspaper editors. The problem was Darius just didn't understand the news. He'd come up through the features side of journalism, landing the job as the editor of a men's lifestyle magazine, before moving to the big chair of the *Chronicle*. Darius was great at schmoozing advertisers and celebrities, he was a genius at bringing in commercial partnerships and yes, he cared about the front page splash. The problem was, he had no grasp of what was required to get them.

Alex looked up the path to Martin Svenson's house and blew out his cheeks. 'We need an exclusive for the Sunday edition,' muttered Alex in a mocking impression of his boss's voice. 'Show me what you're made of, Alex.'

He took a deep breath and as he gave a sharp knock on the Svenson's front door, he felt a flutter of anxiety in his belly. In his time Alex had hassled generals and warlords in places where journalists could be made to disappear. But that all felt a long time ago: as deputy editor at the *Chronicle*, Alex ran the team and the budgets; he hadn't really been in the field for years. Clearly Darius felt he needed a reality check. *Yeah, reality. That's just what I need.*

The door opened and a woman looked out. Pale, drawn, but poised and immaculately dressed in a way that only the very rich could truly pull off.

'Mrs Svenson?'

She nodded warily.

'I'm Alex Ford, one of the guests. Could I have a word with your husband? With both of you, in fact?'

'What about?'

Alex didn't answer. Anna Svenson gave a thin smile.

'Of course. Well, I suppose you'd better come in.'

Alex stamped his feet and stepped inside. The interior of the Svenson place was just as impressive as the outside: warm and sumptuous, the home of a couple who could afford the best of everything, which Alex supposed was a fair description. Stella had come through with her research on the Svensons: a long marriage but childless, he had diverse business interests, she had a successful interiors consultancy. Private, well-liked, no scandal prior to this. Bland, but extremely wealthy.

'Martin is in the kitchen,' said Anna, 'If you'd follow me.'

Alex wavered, wondering if he should take off his boots before stepping onto the herringbone wood tile: it was that kind of place. But then Anna Svenson didn't look as if she cared about the parquet. She didn't look as if she cared about much right now. She had a shawl pulled around her shoulders protectively. Understandable really, there was still a killer out there in the snow.

'Mr. Ford?' said Martin Svenson, looking up as they walked into the kitchen. He was sitting at a large island in the middle of the room, a large glass of wine in front of him.

'Has something happened?'

'No, no,' said Alex. 'But I wanted to ask you both a couple of questions if you don't mind.'

Martin glanced at Anna.

'Mind?' he said, standing. 'Yes actually. We are all in shock here and I think I have already made my position clear on how I wish to handle Viggo's...' he looked at Anna again. 'Well, the tragedy.'

Alex had expected this of course. No one wanted to talk to the press at a time like this.

'I understand all that, Mr. Svenson, but you must have seen that the news is out and the internet trolls are already hard at work spreading speculation and wild rumours. I really feel it's time you gave your side – Kluven's side – before some of these rumours become fact.'

He could see Svenson was about to object, but Martin Svenson was a canny businessman. He would grasp the tactical advantage of being able to control the way the story was told.

'Have you spoken to Inspector Lindhart?' he asked.

'Of course,' said Alex.

'And she had no objections to you talking to the witnesses.'

'No.'

No objections because they hadn't actually discussed it at all. In fact, Alex had spent his interview with the Inspector in defensive mode; Lindhart hadn't shied away from asking leading questions. 'What were you doing in the root cellar?' 'How did you know Viggo would be there?' 'Why was the blood all over your clothes?'

Alex had mostly kept his cool and told her exactly what had happened, as well as he could. Alex had noticed his hands shaking as he recounted it. Perhaps that was what had convinced Lindhart: maybe when you spoke to liars all day, the truth was easier to see. Either way, the detective had let him go, which was all he could ask at this stage.

'Mr Ford, last night, I thought we agreed that you would back off from this.'

'I said I wouldn't break the story before the police came. But the news is all over the media now. You say you've got a camera at Kluven's gates. Well, have you used it to see how many reporters are outside the compound?'

Alex was fairly sure the answer was 'none', given the difficulty of getting here, along with the fact that the gates were decorative: there was nothing to stop anyone just walking in, but the point was made.

Martin frowned and took a took a sip of wine.

'Alright,' he said reluctantly, as Alex turned on the dictation function on his phone. 'What do you want to know?'

'First, did the CCTV cameras pick up on anyone moving around the resort? Surely if we examined the footage we could get an idea of who was where?' But Martin was already shaking his head.

'I've already explained this to the police. Kluven is light on security, I'm afraid. Johan and the other drivers are ex-military, but as far as CCTV goes, there are only two working cameras, one on the gate, one on the main entrance.'

'That's it?'

'In five years we haven't had so much as a fork go missing. We didn't feel we needed intrusive security of that kind. This is a very safe part of the world. We couldn't predict a freak incident, a tragedy like this of course. One we are all still reeling from.'

His words were sliding back into bland corporate speak. Alex didn't blame him. Why say anything contentious, especially to a journalist?

Alex noticed Martin looked towards his wife. Anna was standing by the door, listening in. He turned his attention toward her.

'Could I ask if you saw anything last night, Mrs. Svenson? I understand you were here at home most of the evening?'

Anna came closer. She had the posture of a dancer and seemed to glide into the room on her bare feet.

'I went down to the lodge for pre-supper drinks, and then came straight back. We'd been entertaining our friends Kenneth and Serena for the past couple of days, so it was good to have some downtime, especially after the drama surrounding Viggo's resignation. Martin was working so I went to work on a mood board in my studio upstairs. I did come down for some headache tablets and went outside for some fresh air. That's when I saw Petra. She'd come here to see Martin. We had a brief chat. I came in and went back upstairs, although I could hear what was going on. Petra was highly emotional, screaming and ranting about how she deserved to replace Viggo as executive chef.'

'And you saw nobody else?'

'Only Serena and Kenneth.'

'Alright, alright,' said Martin holding up a hand.

'You've got some quotes, some background, now please, I think it's time you left.'

Alex didn't need to check his notes to know he had nothing. There was enough for five hundred words at most and even with a good picture, he knew it wasn't quite the splash that would satisfy Darius.

Alex needed to get them onside – and quickly.

'Can I go now?' asked Anna. She seemed even more pale than when she had answered the door.

'If you could give me one more minute of your time,' said Alex. 'I have an idea I'd like to suggest.'

Martin sighed.

'What idea?'

'Well, as you said a few minutes ago, this is a tragedy. Nothing can bring Viggo back, but how about you protect his legacy?'

'I'm listening,' replied Svenson.

'How about this,' said Alex thinking on his feet. 'Kluven launches a foundation for the training of new chefs. The Widlund Fund, the Viking Project, whatever. From my understanding Viggo had a tough upbringing. How about you find talented cooks, or young people interested in food and give them a leg-up out of poverty. Put them on a new track.'

'You mean like a scholarship in his honour,' said Martin cautiously.

'Exactly like that,' said Alex pointing in Martin's direction. That way you can acknowledge the tragedy, but you turn it into a positive – and actually, a more interesting story.'

He watched the Svensons think it over. It was, frankly, a wild suggestion off the top of his head and to do it, he imagined the Svensons would have to invest hundreds of thousands. But Martin was canny and Alex was fairly sure that if Kluven had a half-decent PR company they would be suggesting something similar.

'I think it's a good idea,' said Anna tucking her hair behind her ear, showing off a large pearl stud. 'It's good for Kluven and a wonderful tribute to Viggo. We could even set up a culinary school right here.'

'I don't know about that,' said Martin, 'But I agree, it's a smart idea.'

Martin looked over to his wife who nodded.

'I'll need to speak to my lawyers, our PR, but yes. I'd say we're interested.'

He paused.

'And where do you fit into this, Mr Ford? What's in it for you?'

'We'd want the exclusive story on it. We can help launch it with the help of a Swedish media partner. Plus a short interview with you for our newspaper tomorrow, and a couple of photos of you and Anna at Kluven.'

'And then are we finished?' said Anna, turning to Alex.

'We're finished.' He replied, putting his phone back into his pocket.

'I'll find a photo and send it to your cabin,' said Anna with a curt nod, before she left the room.

'Thank you, Mr. Svenson,' said Alex.

'You will be kind, hmm?' said Martin playing with the stem of his glass.

'I will,' said Alex. He was already turning to leave, but stopped and faced Martin once more. 'Completely off the record,' he said. 'But I'd value your insight in the murder. You are, after all, the man who knows more about Kluven than anyone else. If you had to say who killed Viggo...?'

Alex waited for a long moment, not sure Martin was going to answer.

'I think Petra Summers killed Viggo,' he said finally. 'It's what I told the police.'

'Why?' asked Alex. 'Why Petra, I mean?'

'I saw the look in her eye last night when she came to me begging for his job,' said Martin. 'I had to turn her down because of an agreement I had with Viggo. She walked out of the door, and the fury was pouring out of her. She loved him. He rejected her. And then she hated him.'

Svenson raised a hand.

'As far as murders go, it's the oldest reason in the book.'

Chapter 25

Petra wanted to scream. She covered her face with her hands and dug her fingertips into her temples, trying desperately to control her rising temper.

'I told you this an hour ago,' she said, glaring at Sonia Lindhart. 'I've told you this story a dozen times already. I left the kitchen, then went up to the house to see Martin Svenson.'

It felt to Petra as if she had been in this tiny office all day, but she supposed it had only been an hour since she and Lara Stone had walked back into the Lodge and Lindhart had immediately demanded another interview. And all that time Lindhart had been needling her, picking, picking, picking at everything she said, twisting it around, looking at it from a dozen angles, making her doubt everything she said. Lara Stone's policy of responding to her questions with 'no comment' had lasted about two minutes under Lindhart's constant pressure. God, Petra loathed her.

'And then?' asked the inspector. 'Where did you go after you'd spoken to Martin?'

'I went back to the stables.'

Petra felt her heart rate speed up as she said the words.

She'd made the choice in her first interview to say she went directly from the Svenson's back to her room, so she couldn't change her story now.

'Who saw you?'

'I don't know,' said Petra through gritted teeth. 'How can I know that? How can I know what someone else *saw*?'

'You can tell us who you saw,' said Lindhart.

'I didn't see anyone,' said Petra, her words clipped, precise. 'Everyone else must still have been in the kitchen.'

Lindhart nodded and made another of her infuriating notes. Petra was beginning to believe that the detective was simply keeping a tally of the times she had asked the same question. They must be up to six or seven times for each. Perhaps when she had asked all her questions a dozen times, she'd let Petra go. But Petra had a rising sense that that wasn't going to happen.

'So you didn't see anyone?' the detective asked again, this time putting her pen down.

'No,' said Petra, twisting her hands in her lap.

Lindhart took a sip of her coffee. It must have been cold by now, but the officer didn't seem to notice.

'Let's go back to when you left the kitchen...'

Petra felt as if she was banging her head against the wall. If she had felt anxious in her first interview, this was ten times worse because now Petra knew how high the stakes were. This wasn't just about getting caught in her lie about confronting Viggo outside his cabin, this was life or death. If she slipped up now, they might actually send her to prison.

Don't let her get to you, don't let her get to you.

'You left the kitchen at what time?'

'10.40 or thereabouts,' said Petra in a monotone. She knew for a fact that it was written down on Lindhart's notepad more than once.

'So you arrived at the Svensons' a few minutes later, is that correct?' Lindhart didn't wait for an answer. 'And Martin Svenson answered the door when you got to the house?'

'No,' sighed Petra. 'As I have said at least a dozen times, Martin's wife Anna was standing on the porch. I told her I wanted to speak to Martin. I followed her into the house.'

'Which was where Mr. Svenson rejected you.'

'Rejected me? Look, I told him I was ready to step to the head chef's job but he had some arrangement with Viggo.'

'That must have hurt.'

'It was disappointing, yes.'

'It must have felt like a slap on the face. All your ambitions gone.' Lindhart clicked her fingers in the air. 'Like that. You must have been angry.'

'There are other restaurants in the world, you know. It was hardly the end of my career.'

Lindhart didn't seem to be listening.

'And where did you go then?'

'I've *told* you a hundred times,' said Petra, her anger rising. 'I went back to the staff quarters.'

'Straight there?'

'Yes.'

'Are you sure?'

'YES!'

Lindhart picked up her pen again.

'That's strange, because I spoke to Josh Holmberg, one of the juniors in your kitchen. He said he heard someone shouting Viggo's name at around eleven o'clock. He said he went to see what was going on and saw you and Viggo arguing on the path to Mr Widlund's cabin.'

Petra wanted to run. She wanted to jump up, kick open the door and run and run and never stop. But instead this tiny office seemed to be getting smaller and smaller. Petra felt nauseous: she had walked straight into a trap. Now would probably be a great time to use Lara Stone's advice and refuse to answer.

'I saw Josh before I went to the Svenson's house,' she said trying to speak calmly. 'He was by the bins. He is possibly confused.'

Sonia flipped through her notebook as if she was enjoying the theatre of it all.

'Josh Holmberg said he saw you at around 10.40 when he was taking out the trash. At around 10.55pm he was returning food to the meat locker when he heard someone shouting Viggo's name. He went to look and saw you and Viggo arguing.'

Petra tried to picture it. What was Josh doing at the meat locker? Lucas was the other kitchen hand but had recently registered an interest in butchery to Stuart and so was assisting the meat station. If anyone was taking food back to the locker it should have been him.

'Petra?' prompted Lindhart. '*Did* you see Viggo after your visit to the Svensons' house.'

She could hardly breathe now.

'Yes,' she said, her voice gravelly.

'And why didn't you mention this before?'

'Because it wasn't relevant. We barely had a conversation.'

'But you did have a conversation, yes?'

'Yes, but it wasn't important!'

'No Petra,' said Lindhart, 'It's very important because it tells us that you are being very economical with the truth. It tells us you are leaving out significant details about your movements last night.'

'I didn't – I haven't!'

'Yes, Petra,' said Lindhart. 'You did and you have. Which makes me wonder what else you're leaving out? It makes me wonder if you've told me a single truth this whole time.'

'I am telling you the truth! I am!'

Lindhart sat back in her chair, examining Petra.

'What did you and Viggo argue about?'

Tears were beginning to flow now. She thought of Lara's kindness in the Ski-Doo shed and the advice she had given her. She thought of her father, the senior partner of a law firm who would know how to deal with this. Suddenly she wanted to see him. Her parents had never been to Kluven but right now she wanted her father by her side.

'No comment.'

She forced the words out, but Lindhart just kept going.

'You were so angry, weren't you Petra? Viggo hadn't told you he was leaving the restaurant. Hadn't told you that would mean it would close down. His partnership agreement with Mr Svenson meant that no one else could take the reins. But if Viggo died, that meant the dissolution of the agreement.'

'No comment,' she whispered again.

'He had scratch marks on his face. Did you inflict them?'

'No comment.'

'Petra, I've spend the past six hours building up a picture here, and I can see it now. You go to see Martin Svenson to ask for a promotion but are turned down. You're angry. Furious. Meanwhile Viggo leaves the kitchen to go to his cabin. He's returning back to the complex – Josh Holmberg said he was coming down the track, not going up it, and you see him. You argue, but it's cold. Viggo suggests finding shelter to talk and the root cellar, which is very private, is close by. Perhaps you even suggest going there in the hope of seducing him, and changing his mind. There's all sorts of implements in the root cellar. Pickling knives, hammers, blades. I think the conversation got out of hand and at some point you attacked Viggo. Your nails caused the wound on his cheek, but then you lashed out with something far more dangerous. I think you grabbed one of the pickling knives and stabbed him.'

'It's not true,' said Petra, weeping.

'Petra, forensics have been into your room. They found a nail clipping. It had flakes of blood on it. It's been sent to a lab and we're pretty sure it will be Viggo's blood.'

'I would never hurt him! I loved Viggo!'

Lindhart pointed at her.

'Now that *is* the truth, Petra. You did love Viggo, in fact I think you were deeply in love with him, but he didn't love you back, did he? He was going away, leaving you all alone. With nothing, no career, no position, no friends. He'd taken everything from you.'

Petra was crying now. 'No, no, no,' she sobbed.

Lindhart stood up.

'Petra Summers, I am arresting you on suspicion of the murder of Viggo Widlund. You have the right to remain silent, you have a right to legal counsel...'

Petra didn't hear anything else, her own sobs filling her ears. She barely felt Sergeant Koln putting the handcuffs on her and leading her out of the office. As she was pushed into the corridor and up towards Kluven's entrance, there was a shout from behind them: Lara Stone was running towards them.

'Inspector!' called Lara. 'Where are you taking her?'

'Miss Summers will be coming to the station.'

Petra pulled against Koln's grip.

'Lara, please, you have to help me,' she said, her panic rising.

'I will Petra, just stay strong.' Lara Stone turned to

Lindhart. 'Inspector, seriously, I don't think this is the person you're looking for.'

Lindhart's expression remained stony.

'Let's go,' she said turning to her colleague.

Outside, another officer had pulled up in an unmarked car. Koln opened the door and waited for Petra to get into it.

Petra twisted, turning back towards Lara.

'Lara! Please! Tell them I didn't do it!'

The sergeant placed his hand on Petra's head and gently but firmly pushed her into the car, closing the door with an ominous click. Petra pressed her face against the window.

'LARA!' she screamed, but the police car was already moving.

Petra turned in her seat, watching Lara standing on the Kluven steps, helpless. And then Petra was on her own. Utterly on her own.

Chapter 26

In the dark of the bedroom, only Alex's face was illuminated by the glowing screen of his computer. Lara could make out the shape of his hunched shoulders and hear his fingers frantically tapping, trying to get everything down. Petra's dramatic arrest had only happened an hour ago, but the scene was a ready-made headline for his story and Alex was racing to file it for the front page of the *Chronicle on Sunday*.

'Viking Chef's lover arrested after knife attack'. 'Swedish police catch Kluven bloodbath killer': Lara could actually picture Darius sitting next to Ollie, the Chronicle's art director, suggesting ever more sensational, click-baiting headlines for the late edition. Darius might even be smiling for once.

By contrast, Alex's expression was one of grim concentration, with no hint of the excitement he must be feeling. It was a hot story and Alex was right there on the spot; of course, he'd be carried along by the adrenaline of it all, but the trouble was those little black letters were indelible. When he pressed the return key and sent the file flying off to London, the story would be permanent.

Petra might be innocent, but her name would be tarnished forever, a question mark of doubt hanging over her name whether she was convicted or not. That was the thing about news. It could create heroes, but it could also ruin your life.

'Nearly done?' said Lara, leaning against the doorframe.

'Almost,' he said glancing up. Alex was wearing black-rimmed glasses Lara had never seen before.

'Quick work even for you,' she said.

Alex stopped typing.

'What's up?'

Lara looked at him for a moment.

'Petra didn't do it.'

He took off the glasses and laid them on the desk.

'Lar, we've been through this. The police must have been pretty sure Petra did it if they are detaining her and allowing the rest of the guests to leave.'

Lindhart had announced they could go home on the next flight the following day.

'And it does all fit,' continued Alex. 'Petra was resentful, rejected. Viggo owed his career to her, but then he turns around and says "see ya". It's enough to send anyone over the edge.'

Lara couldn't deny the logic, and she could see that Petra was the obvious suspect, but it still felt wrong to her. A journalist had to trust her instincts and right now, Lara's instincts were telling her that Petra was innocent. Either way, Alex could see that Lara wasn't going to let it go.

'Okay,' he said. 'Perhaps Petra didn't plan to kill Viggo, but good people can still do bad things in the heat of the moment, even if it was a terrible mistake.'

Lara took a step into the room.

'Alex, you should have heard her when we were sitting on those Ski-Doos; either Petra's an Oscar-worthy actress or she was telling the truth. And given she's a world-class chef, I think the chances of her being both are slim.'

'Maybe, but Martin Svenson told me they have forensic evidence.'

'They *think* they have forensic evidence,' corrected Lara. 'The samples won't even have arrived at the lab yet. Nothing will have been tested, cross-referenced, verified. It's not proof yet.'

Alex rubbed his face.

'You don't want me to file this story do you?'

No Alex, I don't, she thought, but she knew she couldn't say that. Not outright.

'I want you to file the right story,' she said carefully.

Alex puffed his cheeks out and glanced across at his laptop. She could see he was torn. He was the deputy editor of a top newspaper and they'd already surrendered the scoop about Viggo's death to the 'net. He wouldn't want to lose this too.

'Do you trust me?' said Lara, walking across and sitting on the edge of the bed.

'Of course I trust you,' he said with a hint of exasperation. 'But I've already told Darius there's been an arrest. Even if I don't file the story, someone else will write it.'

'You can stall them. Just until we're sure. I know you want to get this out ASAP, but what if the police have arrested the wrong person?'

She let the question hang in the air. Getting there first was one thing, but getting it wrong? That was always bad. Alex was a company man, part of the *Chronicle's* senior management team, and that made for a delicate high-wire act, balancing the need for reader-grabbing headlines with a reporter's thirst for the truth. She watched him struggle with it.

'I can hold off for maybe another hour,' he said finally,

looking at his watch. 'I'll call them now and say they'll have something by eight o'clock. But then I'm sending them the story.'

He leant forward in his chair, rubbing a hand across his chin. As a student, Lara had covered her pin-board with postcards of French movie stars and right now, Alex would have fit right alongside them. He looked like a man out of time, an adventurer or a poet captured in monochrome by Cartier-Bresson or Robert Doisneau. He'd look good smoking a Gitane, she thought.

'Alright, if not Petra, then who?' asked Alex and Lara resisted the urge to hug him. Despite having just spent an hour carefully laying out the evidence to support the case for Petra being the killer, Alex was still prepared to consider that she might be innocent. Not that Lara had any hard evidence to back that argument beyond her 'gut feeling' and she knew that basing a newspaper story on feelings was understandably unpopular with editors who might have to go to court to justify it.

'I don't know,' she said honestly. 'But everyone has a secret.'

'Not me,' said Alex. He said it with such uncomplicated simplicity that under normal circumstances Lara would have laughed. Instead, she felt a swell in her chest and pressed a hand against her lips. Alex immediately picked up on the change in her mood.

'Hey, what's wrong?' he asked.

The letter, thought Lara immediately. No surprise that Viggo Widlund's killing had dredged up memories of Sandrine's murder, but that wasn't the only thing tugging at Lara's heart.

'That night we filed Sandrine's story,' she said. She'd been debating whether to tell him for weeks but there had never been the right moment. 'Do you remember?'

'Of course,' said Alex. 'We went for a drink at The Mermaid.'

Lara nodded. She could still feel the tangle of emotions as she had walked home along the Thames. They'd found out who had killed Sandrine and were about to bring them to justice, but it still wouldn't bring her friend back.

'When I got home, there was a letter in my mailbox.'

Alex was frowning now.

'A letter? From whom?'

'That's it,' said Lara. 'I don't know. But it said, "Your mother is dead. Your father is alive." That's all.'

Lara had been eleven when her parents had died in a boating accident in Croatia. Lara had been staying with her grandparents while her parents had gone on their annual sailing trip. There had been an explosion, possibly the fuel tank, possibly a stove, no one really knew, even after a diving crew went out to the Balkans to investigate. In the end, it didn't really matter because the one important fact was that David and Ramona Avery were dead. And that was how it had remained for over twenty-five years. Almost, anyway. There had always been whispers, poisonous rumours that David Avery had killed his beautiful but difficult wife and then set fire to the boat – the lack of any evidence was merely proof of a cover-up by the powerful Avery family. It was a horrible, hurtful slur that Lara had always carried with her – and now this anonymous note had opened the wound all over again.

'Was the letter typed?' asked Alex. 'Do you still have it?'

'It was hand-written, no stamp. And yes, I still have it back at the houseboat.'

Alex nodded thoughtfully.

'And you haven't had anything like it since?'

Lara shook her head.

'It sounds like a postage version of an internet troll,' said

Alex with a frown. 'Some people just get off on sending malicious messages. Your family is wealthy, well-known, the history of your parents' death is out there. And it's not difficult to find out someone's address.'

This was exactly what Lara had tried to tell herself. The *Chronicle's* music editor had once been sent a box of doggy-doo after giving someone a one-star review and the theatre critic had received more poison pen letters than he'd had lunches at Joe Allen's. Lara herself probably had more enemies than them all, having exposed dozens of corrupt businessmen and politicians in her time at the investigations team. Alex was right too: the foul rumours about her parents weren't exactly a secret in spite of the efforts of her Uncle Nicholas. A few years before, *Tatler* had devoted an entire page to the story in a special on 'High Society Scandals'. Olivia had been outraged and Nicholas had mobilised his lawyers, to little real effect. After all, you can't libel the dead.

'You're right, of course you are,' said Lara. 'That's why I haven't mentioned it before. But it sits there in my brain, Alex, refusing to fade. And when I stop to think about it, I can't help but wonder, 'What if... what if it's true?'

Alex came and sat down next to her and put his arm around her shoulders.

'Lara, whoever sent the letter, that's what they want you to think. They want to upset you, unsettle you. They're getting off on making you feel bad.'

'Well it's worked,' said Lara. Why pretend to him? She would have been made of steel if she hadn't harboured even a tiny hope that it was true, however impossible that might be.

'I thought I'd at least mention it to Nicholas at Christmas,' she said. 'Dad was his brother after all – maybe he'll have some ideas about who sent it.'

Alex nodded. 'You should do that.'

Lara wasn't sure she actually would bring it up: Nicholas Avery wasn't the warmest of men and he'd always had a fractious relationship with Lara's father, but it did give Lara an excuse for not having taken Alex up on his offer of Christmas in the Lake District. That was something at least.

'Sorry,' she said, standing up quickly. 'We're getting side-tracked here.'

'No, Lar, this is important to you,' said Alex, reaching for her. He took her hand but she stepped back away from him.

'It will wait,' she said, shaking her head. 'If you're going to file that story in an hour, then we need to concentrate on one thing at a time.'

She beckoned him through to the living room where her notes were still arranged on the coffee table, each potential suspect getting their own page of pros and cons. Alex was still lingering at the door, still thinking. She knew she shouldn't have brought the letter up, should have known it would distract him.

'Let's go through all this one more time,' she said, sitting down next to the papers, trying to shift her thoughts back to Viggo Widlund's death.

'Let's start with Martin Svenson,' she said, tapping a note. 'We know he's a foodie and a restaurant nerd: Kluven will be the jewel in his crown.'

'Sure, but it won't make much money,' said Alex, stepping into the room. 'I doubt it will ruin him to close the restaurant.'

Lara had thought of that.

'Agreed, Martin's a successful businessman, but he's not really known outside Sweden. Kluven, meanwhile, is internationally famous. Don't discount bruised male pride and loss of status. That's a powerful motive, especially among alphas.'

Alex went across to the fridge and took out two beers.

'Let's talk about Justin Blake some more,' he said, as he walked back.

'So much for hero-worship,' said Lara with a smile.

Alex shrugged. 'At dinner, Emily said Justin and Viggo knew each other. That's why they're here. Justin wanted to come, Kluven had a cancellation so Viggo invited them.'

'But it doesn't necessarily mean there was a problem between them. And Justin has an alibi, doesn't he?'

'Food poisoning,' said Alex. 'But given the circumstances, that could be considered very convenient. Besides, no one saw him actually go into his cabin.'

Lara pulled a face: the real truth was all the guests had equally shaky alibis. Lara remembered her friend DCI Ian Fox telling her that most alibis were like that: 'I was watching TV', 'I was asleep at home'. It was when the alibis had a hint of the Agatha Christie about them – 'my watch stopped and I went into a shop to ask the time' – that was when you started to suspect.

'So what about Stuart Dell?' said Alex, moving onto Lara's next note. 'He told you that he left the kitchen to go and get a bottle of champagne from his digs. Could he have got to Viggo then?'

'I'm not sure the timings fit,' said Lara. 'He said that was ten thirty-ish – too early – and the rest of the staff could probably confirm it. But I'm sure he has a crush on Petra.'

'Doesn't that give him more of a motive, like he's angry on her behalf?'

'But I don't think he'd let her go to jail in his place.'

Alex gave a cynical smile. 'You're a romantic, Stone. So what else have we got?'

'Theo,' said Lara. 'Remember I saw him with his coat on

when you called me from the root cellar? He could well have been coming back from there. The snow would have covered his tracks – literally.'

Lara knew it was pure speculation; she desperately needed more information and Stella still hadn't got back to her with profiles of the suspects. It was a tall order, of course. A deep dive search like that could take days, but time was something she just didn't have. Reading her thoughts, Alex looked at his watch.

'One hour, Lar.'

'Alex, this isn't *Bake Off*.'

'I mean it,' he said sternly, his voice suddenly in 'boss mode'. 'This is all so thin. If we haven't got anything else, I'm filing the Petra story at eight o'clock.'

'I hear you,' she said, but Lara could feel the excitement growing. She was glad to be back in the saddle of an investigation that meant something. Sandrine's death had put Lara into a professional slump. She'd quit the *Chronicle*, taking on a freelance 'at-large' role instead. She'd worked hard to try to forget her grief, but the stories she'd worked on, a financial scandal at a local council, and an insider-trading controversy at a minor bank, hadn't felt especially important or worthwhile. But clearing Petra's name, if she wasn't guilty of killing Viggo, that was something else. Lara hadn't been able to save Sandrine, but she was damned if she would let an innocent woman go to jail. She walked to the door and picked up her boots.

'Where are you going?' frowned Alex.

'Next door to speak to Coulson. Remember what Doctor Green said in the bar last night, that the doer was full of rage and that Coulson would have more insight into it? We need to find the person who hated Viggo with a passion.'

Alex crossed to the window and looked out at the snow.

'I should go instead,' he said. 'It's dark out there.'

'No, you stay here and pester Stella,' said Lara, reaching for her coat. 'She might respond to her Editor.'

There was a squeak as Alex wiped the condensation off the glass. 'Well you'd better take your swimming costume,' he said. 'I think they're in the hot tub.'

Lara ran into the bedroom to change, then pulled on her coat and put up the hood. She grinned at herself in the mirror: puffed-up body and bare legs. 'I look like Snoopy's friend Woodstock,' she muttered out loud.

She was trying to make light of it because the truth was she wasn't wild about going out in the dark, but she was buoyed by the thought that Alex still believed in her, so she pulled on her boots and clumped to the door feeling slightly ridiculous.

'Wish me luck,' she said, her hand on the door. 'There's a good chance I'll freeze solid before I'm halfway there.'

'I'll run over with the kettle if that happens,' said Alex.

'By the way, I never asked: why were you at the Ski-Doos with Petra?'

Lara opened the door, letting in a flurry of snow. 'I was going to try and steal one,' she said.

'Steal one? Why? I thought you said that...'

She shook her head, cutting him off.

'For us,' she said and stepped out into the snow before he could see her blush.

Chapter 27

Theo knew he shouldn't be in Kat's office. And he knew he shouldn't be sitting at her desk. But most of all, he knew Kat would go ballistic if she caught him hacking into her computer. That was why Theo had waited until he knew she would be busy, arranging supper for the guests, before he used his pass-key to slip inside. And it was why he had neglected to switch on the overhead strip-lights, using a single desk lamp for his low-level espionage. Theo looked over his shoulder, then quickly tapped in Kat's password. 'P-I-N-A-C-O-L-A-D-A'. Kat thought it was an uncrackable code, but it was her favourite tipple on nights out – and she used the same code on virtually every device, including their widescreen TV at home. It would have been weird if Theo *didn't* know Kat's password.

And anyway, it wasn't technically spying, not really. As general manager, Theo needed to know everything about Kluven, the staff and its guests. Still, Kat would be furious if she found him here. So he needed to be quick, in and out.

Happily, Kat's computer was easy to navigate. Everything was in clearly labelled folders, her diary synced with the staff's: by necessity she needed to know Viggo's movements and the food orders, she had to know where to find house-keeping, maintenance and security, plus anything that might make the guests' visit easier.

And that was why Theo was here. Miles Namato.

The chef had indicated he was open to the idea of taking over from Viggo in the executive role and the more Theo thought about it, the more he felt Miles would be perfect. But – and it was a big 'but' – Theo knew precious little about Miles. For a resort manager, intelligence was everything and the vacuum of data around Miles troubled him. For a chef of Miles' status, there had been very few interviews in the foodie press and those he could find online concentrated on the food. Theo wanted to know about the man, specifically he wanted to know if there were any red flags. Theo's experience with Viggo had taught him that while words like 'mercurial' and 'passionate' looked good on a press release, they could turn into a management nightmare. And even on the most basic level, personal circumstances could have an impact on a business. Viggo was a single man with no family tying him to the area; in hindsight the surprise was that Chef Widlund had stayed in Kluven so long.

'Okay Kat,' Theo murmured, clicking onto her emails. 'Let's see what you know about Mr. Namato.'

It was part of Kat's job as Guest Relations Manager to know everything about their clients from food allergies to how soft or hard they liked their pillows, anything to make their stay as seamless as possible. The first thing Theo wanted to know was Namato's marital status. Via the office vents, Theo had heard Miles refer to his female companion Nami Falk as his 'partner' rather than 'wife'. Nothing was guaranteed of course, but a married chef would probably be more stable than one in a more casual relationship.

Kat would have known this information off the top of

her head, but he didn't want to ask her directly, didn't want to alert her to his new plans for Kluven. Not yet. After her remark earlier that day, "You could have been in charge of the Ritz by now," Theo suspected that she would use Viggo's death as an excuse to leave Kluven, and he didn't want to get into that argument again.

Theo scrolled through, careful not to click on anything that might flag up that he'd been looking at Kat's emails. He simply wanted to know about Miles' marital status, then he'd be gone. In and out. *Like a spy,* he thought, smiling.

Most of her messages were mundane: adjustments to the driver schedules, alerts from the airlines, requests from guests regarding a desire to avoid feather pillows, or emails from strict Vegans who wanted 'no contact' with fur products.

'Why would a vegan come to Kluven?' he muttered, his finger still on the mouse. It was like going to a zoo and complaining it was full of animals. Then again, he realised the compromises people would make for status, for the exclusive badge of honour that came with a trip to Kluven.

Theo kept scrolling but there didn't seem to be anything about Miles or Nami in Kat's inbox: Nami Falk was the name on her passport – but plenty of women kept their name after marrying.

Theo clicked on Kat's 'sent' folder, eyes searching for any sent to Miles Namato. Theo knew Kat was excellent at her job and she often got into a personal dialogue with guests. 'So wonderful to welcome you here next week, please let me know if there's anything I can do to make your stay more comfortable'. At this level, the guests expected a little fawning.

Then Theo stopped, his finger poised over the mouse. There was a message sent to an official-looking email address: G.Adderley@HaddonAllin.org.

Theo checked that the office door was still closed and clicked on the message.

Re. re. Your divorce proceedings.

Dear Mr. Allin,

Thank you for your note, I will read the attached and get back to you ASAP.

Kind regards,

Katherine Mikelson.

Theo couldn't breathe. Divorce proceedings? Hands shaking, Theo scrolled to the original message below the 'sent' text highlighted in a different colour.

Dear Mrs. Mikelson, further to our telephone conversation of the 14th, should you wish to proceed with a legal solution, I would like to outline the partnership's terms of engagement...

The words swam before his eyes. Divorce. It made no sense. Why would she even consider such a thing? Hadn't he always given her exactly what she wanted in life? What more could he do? His heart hammering, Theo read down to the end of the message.

Further, should you wish to instruct us in the matter of the assault, we would be more than happy to help you out in that regard.

What assault? Theo curled his hands into fists, seized with the unfamiliar sense of being in the dark. Information was his strength, the core of his self. Theo Mikelson always knew where everyone was, what they were doing and what they wanted, but right now, he felt out of control, nothing made sense. He rubbed his hands over his eyes. *Calm yourself. Focus.* He'd got through worse than this. For one moment, his mind flashed onto the body, his body. The arm extended at that odd angle, almost pointing in accusation. *No, not my fault.* Theo let out a long breath. He'd handled that and he'd handle this too.

His hands went back to Kat's keyboard. All he needed was information. And he was going to get it: one way or another.

Chapter 28

Dr. Green was drunk. His cheeks were flushed and he was a little unsteady on his feet as he peered at Lara through a crack in the door.

'Lara,' said the doctor with difficulty. 'How lovely to see you.'

The last three words ran together like hissing steam: Lara could see the doctor was holding a large glass of what looked like expensive Scotch.

'Are you okay Patrick?'

He waved his glass vaguely.

'Yes, yes, fine.' He didn't look fine, but then Lara could hardly blame him. It had been an unusual couple of days.

'I wondered if I could speak to Coulson?'

Dr. Green narrowed his eyes as if it was taking real effort to think about how to answer.

'Round the back,' he said. 'Hot tub.'

He closed the door.

'Charming,' she whispered, making her way around the little covered walkway to the left of the cabin.

The hot tub was made of wooden slats, like the sawn-off end of a huge barrel. It was surrounded by decking in a similar wood and clearly heated by a black metal boiler with a tall chimney happily puffing white smoke. Coulson was alone, his head resting back against the side of the tub, his arms floating lazily at his sides.

'If you've come to plead his case, I'm not interested,' he said without opening his eyes.

'I wouldn't dream of it,' said Lara. 'What happens in Kluven, stays in Kluven, right?'

Coulson chuckled and looked up.

'May I join you?' she asked, unzipping her coat.

'I thought you'd never ask.'

Lara was glad she had brought a bathing suit on the trip. In her mind, she would be chinking champagne flutes with a handsome man with a jawline not dissimilar to Alex Ford's, but a hot tub in the snow was still a hot tub in the snow.

'Woof,' she said, dipping a leg in. 'They weren't joking about the "hot", were they?'

'It's lovely once you're in.'

Brisk wind blowing over the lip of the tub encouraged her inside and she slid down into the water, settling opposite Coulson.

'So you and Patrick have had words?'

Coulson raised an eyebrow.

'You Brits and your understatement. Yes, but it's... it's a bigger thing,' he sighed. 'He's freaking out about the corpse, sure, but it's more about our relationship,' he said, framing the word with finger quotes.

'Is everything okay?'

Lara didn't need to be a shrink to know that Coulson was upset.

'I want to get married, he doesn't, because he's a fifty-seven-year-old man who still cares about what his conservative eighty-something parents think. That straitjacket of his upbringing still makes him feel guilty about being gay and I'm not sure he'll ever truly allow himself to accept who he is. At least not whilst his parents are still alive.'

He sighed and sat up straighter, giving Lara a good view of his toned upper body.

'Sucks being a shrink sometimes, I suppose?'

He smiled sadly.

'Much harder to do it on yourself, yes. And sometimes knowing how his mind works... ticks me off.'

'Look, for what it's worth, I think real love's a rare thing. If you've found the right person, then you've won the lottery. You've got to do whatever it takes to make it work.'

'You old romantic.'

'That's twice someone has said that to me in the past hour. Truth is, I'm a bit of a cynic.'

'Well don't be. You're much too young for that.'

He paused and smiled back at her.

'I'm guessing you didn't come out here just to peek at my hot bod, right?'

She laughed.

'Not entirely no.'

'You want the shrink's perspective, right?'

'I want to know what sort of person could stab Viggo like that.'

'Ah, that's easy: any kind,' said Coulson. 'Doesn't help you much, but it's the truth. We're all animals and under the surface, we've all got teeth and claws.'

Lara wasn't convinced. 'We get angry, sure, but to kill?'

'Lara. A mild-mannered soccer mom could kill a home-invader if she was protecting her kids.'

'But that would be self-defence?'

'That mom still killed him though. Look, we don't know what happened between Petra and Viggo in that root cellar and who was the aggressor. I'm sure when the police are done we'll know soon enough.'

Aggressor. As Coulson said it, Lara realised she had never even considered the possibility. In her mind, someone had lured Viggo to the out-building, then brutally stabbed him as a reaction to Viggo's dramatic announcement. But what if Viggo had been the one who had set up the meeting? What if the 'doer' had used the knife in defence, as a way to escape? In that case, the reason wouldn't matter, would it? Viggo would be just as dead and the killer would be just as keen to hide their guilt. Clearly Coulson read some of this in Lara's face.

'That's the problem, isn't it?' he said. 'Right now, we don't know why Viggo was stabbed. We only know that he was stabbed.'

She paused to think, feeling the bubbles pop around her body. 'Okay, so what could make that happen? What makes someone kill?'

'Jealousy, frustration, fear, any of the negative emotions. But also the so-called "good" ones: loyalty or empathy, for example, in the case of assisted suicide. Love being the most powerful, of course. We will do anything for love. Good and bad.'

Lara nodded, thinking.

'What about obsession?'

'Yes, that too. But why obsession in particular?'

She glanced beyond the balcony into the dark fringe of trees surrounding the compound.

'Apparently, Viggo thought he was being watched. In the weeks leading up to his death, he was quite jumpy. His colleague in the kitchen wondered if he was having a breakdown, but what if he was actually being followed?'

'A stalker, you mean?'

Lara nodded. 'What would the profile be? Who might we be looking for?'

Coulson raised a black brow. 'You'd need a specialist for this – there are half a dozen different kinds of stalker and sub-divisions within those. There's intimacy-seekers, resentful stalkers, predators. But usually stalkers are someone people know, often someone they've had a relationship with – a spurned partner who refuses to believe they've been rejected for example.'

'Anyone else?'

'What makes it even more complicated is that the stalker may be latching onto the victim because they were rejected by someone else – even years before – and in their minds, they are recreating the original relationship with this new "host" if you like. Remember that Viggo was famous, which adds another layer. Reduce someone to a poster on the wall, then the crazies can make them represent whatever they like.'

'Crazies?'

Coulson leant forward, his voice a whisper.

'Shrinks aren't allowed to use the word, but I do like busting taboos.'

Lara smiled as she thought it through.

'You could also be looking at a Mark Chapman kind of situation.'

'The guy who shot Lennon?'

Lara had been thinking about it ever since Alex had mentioned the tragedy after his chat with Lynda Brett.

'No one really knows why Chapman killed Lennon. For notoriety, perhaps. But there's one theory that he was angry with Lennon because of his "Bigger than Jesus" remarks, so if Viggo was becoming similarly disenchanted with Kluven, a stalker might see it as a betrayal of some kind.'

Lara frowned.

'But does any of this sound like Petra?'

'I didn't speak to her, but Lara, we've all heard the whispers today. The sous chef was in love with Viggo. If he rejected her on multiple levels, personally, professionally, that was a motive for a killing, even if she wasn't obsessed with him. Patrick told me about Viggo's injuries. If you want my opinion, it was a crime of passion.'

'But what if it wasn't, Coulson. What if Viggo was being stalked?'

'Then it means they're still here,' said Coulson, his easy-going expression suddenly vanishing.

Lara looked beyond him into the woods.

'Shall we go inside? I think the water's starting to go cold.'

Chapter 29

Alex walked across the room to the coffee machine. He'd lost count of how many cups he'd had that day, but he had to stay alert. He glanced at his watch. Seven fifteen and yet it felt like the middle of the night. He made some mental calculations. The first edition went to the presses at 10pm, which meant getting it through the subs, editors and legal before that. There was still time to file the story on Petra's arrest but it was getting tight. And tight was the word for how he was feeling: Alex had never felt so hemmed in. He had barely been in this cabin for two days, but it felt like weeks. It was one of the secrets of the Arctic: it was effectively a desert, snow for countless miles in every direction, but nowhere to go even if you could move through it. The sand metaphor was strong too: stray a few steps from the path and you'd sink up to your waist. And if you blocked that single road between Kluven and Kiruna everyone was trapped – unless you had access to Santa's sleigh of course.

He added sugar to his espresso and knocked it back in one: a technique he'd learned in Sarajevo from a local guide who'd lived through the city's three-year siege. 'Good for the nerves,' he'd said.

Walking back to the window, Alex strained to see Lara, but the snow was falling again. Alex could admit he was worried about her. If Lara was right and Petra was innocent, then that meant the killer was still out there.

'No secrets,' he whispered, shaking his head.

Alex hadn't exactly been honest when he'd said that to Lara. In the context of a murder investigation, he supposed it was a small thing, but he'd promised his father he would bring Lara up for Christmas this year. Ever since Alex's mother had died, Terry Ford had been on the slide. He'd closed his newsagent business – 'too much bother' – and stopped going to the pub. His father was a proud man, so he'd never ask for help, but Alex knew he was struggling. And Terry had always adored Lara, came to life when she was around. And it was how Alex felt too.

Since the summer, the idea of being *together* with Lara, together as a couple, had taken root and bloomed. *Why not?* a voice in his head had reasoned. In the early days, when they had been students at City University together, he'd been secretly in love with her. The feelings had faded when they had clearly not been reciprocated and Alex had moved on to more straight-forward relationships. But now, in his late thirties, there was part of Alex that recognised he was simply happier whenever he was with Lara. And if that was the case, surely he owed it to himself to at least try and be together. Surely the promise of finding the love of his life was worth the risk of losing her friendship. That was the real reason he had come to Kluven, to share a cabin, relax and have fun, in a remote winter wonderland, away from the pressures of everyday life. To see if they could be a couple – and to see if she felt the same.

'Better call Stella then,' he said out loud, keen to divert

his thoughts away from Lara, reminding himself that they were in the middle of a murder investigation, not a romantic mini-break. He went back to his laptop and fired up his video call software.

'Hey Alex, I was about to call Lara,' said Stella, as her camera phone picture appeared on the screen. 'Glad to see you're still in one piece.' Behind Stella, Alex could see the chaotic mess of her flat. It was a strange relief to see someone familiar sitting in an urban setting. No snow, no rabid bears, no secrets. None he knew about, anyway.

'Still alive so far,' said Alex. 'No promises how the rest of the day's going to go, though.'

Alex liked Stella Harris. Ever since Nicholas Avery had merged Lara's investigations department with the *Chronicle's* news team, Stella had been a rising star. She was dogged and hard-working, happy to do the most menial task, which was more than could be said about some of the new recruits, who expected to be interviewing Tom Cruise from day one. Plus Stella was unfailingly positive, which you definitely couldn't say about most journalists of any vintage.

'I heard from Darius that the police have arrested the sous chef,' she said with a frown. 'Am I too late with this research?'

Alex shook his head. 'We're not entirely sure we agree with the detective.'

Stella broke into a grin.

'Honestly, you two. It's typical you go to Kluven on the weekend the chef gets murdered, then you discover a conspiracy.'

'Not quite a conspiracy. Anyway, believe me, I would love to have come on a quieter weekend.'

'Really?' asked Stella surprised, then looked away. 'Sorry, none of my business.'

Alex smiled to himself, then felt it fade. He was excited,

yes: how often were you this close to the centre of a story – Alex had even found the body. But at the same time it was a tragedy, not an amusement created for adrenaline-loving journalists.

He remembered all too clearly the horrific aftermath of the Bataclan terrorist attack in Paris. Alex had been dispatched to the city to report on the story, and had experienced a similar mixture of shock and sadness, empathy and energy. That night had been more visceral than he'd care to repeat; he'd seen things he could never forget. Alex could admit there was a buzz about being there on the front edge of things, reporting it back to a breathless and appalled world. But that buzz faded and what you were left with were things that haunted your dreams.

'Okay, let me give you an update,' said Alex, quickly filling in the events of the last few hours: Petra's claim that she had been behind Viggo's recipes, her dramatic arrest and Lara's strong sense that Petra had been falsely accused.

'But why? She had means, motive and opportunity,' said Stella. 'Although so did you, Alex.'

'Me?'

'You found the body, which means you had Viggo on his own, you said the shed was full of potential weapons, knives and such. And motive – Lara says you are very picky about how your steak's done.'

Stella was joking, but there was another unspoken detail here: Alex had secretly been relieved when Petra had been charged because it meant he was off the hook. Motive aside, Stella was right that he ticked a lot of boxes and he had been genuinely afraid that Inspector Lindhart might decide he was a viable suspect. Alex knew he was innocent, but it wouldn't be the first time a miscarriage of justice had occurred. He'd come to Kluven for fun and possibly romance, a prison sentence was definitely not what he had in mind.

'Well, you'll have to take my word for it that I didn't do it,' said Alex gruffly. 'So let's move onto who might have.'

Stella nodded eagerly, clearly keen to skate over her evident faux pas.

'Okay, with the large caveat that there's an awful lot here that could be entirely innocent...' Stella shuffled a sheaf of papers theatrically and Alex suppressed a stab of irritation. He hadn't been lying when he said he wanted to file the Petra story by eight o'clock and he was aware how quickly the clock was ticking.

'Let's start with the least likely candidates: Connie and Graham. From the Manchester suburbs, she's recently retired from a travel agency, he owns a storage company. The twist is that they're not married.'

'Not married? So how come they told us they were celebrating their golden wedding anniversary?'

'They are, sort of. Apparently Connie and Graham were

childhood sweethearts.'

'So they're having an affair?'

'Seems so. And they've told their other halves they're on a Saga holiday.'

Alex raised his eyebrows: the torrid lives we lead. It would certainly explain why Connie and Graham had kept the details of their lives quiet. Didn't give them much of a motive though. Stella carried on running down the guest list.

'Dr. Patrick Green and Coulson Daniels. He's a plastic surgeon, he's a shrink. Doc Green is successful, but there have been rumours of malpractice suits.'

'Dodgy operations?'

'Yeah, and there's just the hint that Doc Green has a drinking problem.'

She carried on shuffling through her notes.

'Miles Namato – talented, ambitious chef. American/Japanese heritage. Martial arts expert. Recently recruited a publicist for personal branding and PR, which could be a coincidence or not. Apparently briefed them that he wants a media profile like Gordon Ramsey, Marcus Wareing and Viggo Widlund. Justin Blake, you probably know about. Rumours of drug addiction, which hold water if you compare recent photos of him with some taken three years ago.'

'Lynda Brett said Viggo had substance abuse issues too,' said Alex. 'And it seems he and Justin knew each other. What about Kenneth and Serena? I met them. Didn't really warm to them much.'

'Kenneth is one of Martin Svenson's business partners,' said Stella. 'He's English, although has a Swedish mother. Met Martin at Cambridge. Martin bought Kenneth's tech company a decade ago, then put Kenneth on the board of Martin's holding company. Serena's the standard wannabe society wife.'

'So potentially Kenneth and Serena's money could be tied up in Kluven?' asked Alex.

'Not the restaurant itself. Kluven is privately owned by the Svensons.'

'So what about Martin himself?' asked Alex. 'He's the most obvious suspect after Petra.'

Stella pulled a face.

'The most obvious suspect, but the biggest mystery too. You know when you're researching someone and it feels as though someone has been through before you and swept away the footprints? It's like that.'

Alex nodded. It wasn't unusual among high-fliers.

While some people like Elon Musk and Richard Branson made a big deal about being businessmen, revelling in their profits and their relative placings on the Rich Lists, many billionaires actively avoided the limelight, paying specialist PR firms and lawyers to keep their activities under the radar.

'Professional whitewash, you think?'

'He's certainly whiter than white on the face of it. And super-connected at a high level. Martin is even friends with the Swedish premier, who's been to Kluven more than once. But I spoke to Neil on the City Desk. He called his opposite number on Sweden's biggest paper *The Inquirer* and there are rumours that the Svenson empire is in trouble. Over-exposure in the Far East markets, whatever that means.'

'So potentially Martin's got financial problems.'

'Looks that way, but I'd need more time to find out for sure.'

Stella shuffled through her papers again, momentarily losing her thread. Alex guessed Lara had been right: Stella was trying harder because Alex was, indirectly at least, her boss.

'The wife is more transparent,' continued Stella. 'Anna Svenson used to be an editor on one of the decor magazines. Twenty years ago, in her late thirties, she married Martin and moved into interior design. She does a limited number of high-end projects a year, but recently has registered a bunch of trademarks.'

'Planning to expand?'

'That was my thought. And it links in with Theo Mikelson, the general manager. If you ask me, you need to be looking closely at him. Theo's local to the area and on a personal crusade to put this part of Sweden on the map. Prefers to recruit locals and apparently has been planning a major expansion of Kluven. There's talk locally of tripling the capacity and adding husky tours and the like.'

Alex saw the logic: if Viggo suddenly bailed, it could nix the idea of his dream resort – more than enough motive.

'What about the rest of the staff?'

'No obvious red flags,' said Stella. 'Although it might be worth mentioning Stuart Dell. He's from Scotland, son of a gamekeeper, competed at national level for various shooting events before he turned to cooking. Brother had a spell in prison for GBH, but apparently Stuart's a straight-up bloke.'

'So why mention him?'

'Because Stuart is like the third Musketeer; he was at Kluven from the start. If anyone knows Viggo's secrets, it's him.'

Alex nodded: Stella had good instincts, but he had to say he was disappointed. There were interesting angles there, but no smoking gun and certainly not enough to make him change his mind – or his story – about Petra.

'Well, thanks, Stella, you've been brilliant as usual.'

He looked at his watch: it was getting close to his deadline now and despite his misgivings about over-ruling Lara, Alex was already feeling the rush that came with filing a breaking news story. Okay, both Lara and Stella had sown seeds of doubt on Petra as Viggo's killer, but he felt no qualms about reporting her arrest – and was excited to be reporting the news from the ground again. There had been many times recently when Alex had doubted the wisdom of staying in a slowly dying industry like print news, and in the summer he'd been sorely tempted to jump ship onto his friend Dom's digital media start-up, but it was times like these which reminded him that the job still could set his pulse racing.

Stella sipped something from a mug, then held up a

hand. 'Hey, before you go boss. One other name you should be aware of. Josh Holmberg.'

Alex looked back at the screen.

'Who's he?'

'Kitchen hand. He's low down on the Kluven totem-pole but I did look into him and it seems that Josh Holmberg is actually over-qualified to be a dishwasher. Born in Stockholm, but he graduated from the Paris Cordon Bleu last year. He's talented and got a job as a commis chef straight out of the Institute in a one-starred restaurant here in London. He didn't last long – got kicked out. "Unhealthy behaviour" towards the maitre d' apparently.'

That got Alex's attention.

'Unhealthy?'

'*Obsessive* was actually the word they used. Like a stalker was my impression.'

'Stalker?'

Alex looked towards the door, suddenly seized by the feeling that he shouldn't have let Lara go off to speak to Coulson on her own. Viggo had talked about being watched, about seeing things in the woods. What if it hadn't just been paranoia? And what if the killer was still in the resort? Then everyone was in danger, but particularly anyone asking awkward questions.

'Thanks Stella, got to go,' said Alex, jumping up and reaching for his parka.

'Hey, what's up?' Stella called, but Alex was already running for the door. Outside, it was fully dark and the snow was falling again. Alex dashed down the steps and out onto the path, slipping and regaining his footing, coat flying behind him as he ran. Turning left onto the path leading to the next cabin, a dark shape loomed up in front of him.

'Alex?' said Lara, pulling her hood back. 'What's going on?'

Relief stopped him in his tracks.

'Are you okay?'

Lara's brows knitted together.

'Of course, I'm fine. Has something happened?'

Embarrassed now, Alex looked beyond her towards the Lodge, then back into the darkness of the forest.

'The stalker,' he said, panting. 'The watcher in the wood? I think he's real.'

Chapter 30

Justin was dozing on the bed, trying to ignore the cramp in his stomach when Emily walked into the bedroom.

'I'm going to the lodge,' she said, pulling on her parka. 'I'm going stir crazy, plus I'm starving. Do you want anything?'

Justin shook his head. The very thought of food made his throat close in rebellion. His head was splitting, his temperature was swinging between fever and chills and his skin felt like it had been grated. Justin felt if he didn't keep an iron grip he might actually shake himself apart.

But as Emily bent to kiss his damp forehead, Justin noticed the dark shadows beneath her eyes. She had been nursing him all day; no wonder she was tired.

'You look beat, babe,' he said, his voice still croaky.

'I am,' she sighed. 'Do you know I spent 240 days away from home this year? It's been go-go-go since New Year.'

Justin frowned.

'So how come we came here? You had a gap in your schedule, why didn't we just crash at home?'

Emily laughed.

'Because you wanted to come to Kluven, Jus,' she said,

'You've been talking about it for ages. It was too good an opportunity to miss.'

Justin felt his heart give a little jump. Even though she was wrung out from jetting all over the globe for modelling gigs, Emily had still been happy to schlep all the way to Northern Sweden simply because he wanted to come. No word of complaint, in fact Justin hadn't the slightest suspicion Emily was anything less than enthusiastic about this jaunt. He really didn't deserve her.

'Maybe I'll see if they have some chicken noodle soup,' said Emily, zipping her coat. 'That's supposed to be good when you're sick, isn't it?'

He watched her go, feeling a mixture of love and apprehension. He'd once read that life was the sum of your choices. Leaving university six months into his course had been a choice. Not a very sensible one perhaps: he knew he'd upset his parents and that he was putting all his eggs in one basket. But concentrating wholeheartedly on the music, on the band, had worked out: a good choice.

But then there were the bad choices. Quitting Joystick, firing his manager. All of them seemed clear cut decisions at the time; the band was holding him back, his manager saw him as a cash cow, but in hindsight he'd had his head stuck firmly where the sun don't shine. Then there was the choice of joining the Velvetines – done for all the right reasons but Justin had allowed himself to ignore all the red flags. And yes, that first hit of heroin. That had been a choice too.

But so had Emily; maybe his best choice. He'd chosen to talk to her at that party in the Hollywood Hills, chosen to call her the next day, to keep calling. Justin knew he needed to keeping making choices like that. And that was why he felt the worry; Justin wasn't entirely sure he was up to the task.

'You can do this', he whispered to himself. He pushed

himself upright. 'You *can*'. Stumbling into the bathroom, he opened the cabinet and shook two painkillers out into his hand – bought legitimately in Heathrow, not in some nightclub khazi – and swallowed them with a swig of Gaviscon: he couldn't stand anything more substantial in his stomach right now. But he had to get through it because he couldn't contemplate losing Emily. *Just do it*, he thought, crossing to the Scrabble board, still set up on a low table in front of the fire. Justin had lied to Emily when he'd said he didn't like Scrabble anymore. Board games were a tie to his childhood. Justin's dad had been a crossword buff, so games involving words and strategy had been an opportunity to bond with his bright-but-aimless son – and there was still something comforting about being governed by strict rules when his world seemed entirely lawless and chaotic. Still, his hands were shaking as he picked the letter tiles from the little black bag to set up the board. He desperately wanted it to be a surprise, so Justin tried not to notice how grating the clacking sound of the plastic squares was. Be a brave soldier, he told himself. That was his mother's saying when he was sick as a child.

When Emily walked back into the cabin, Justin had rearranged the cushions and had even lit a candle.

'This is nice,' she said appreciatively. Emily held up a small grey crate filled with enamel pots from the kitchen.

'Now we can have a hot Swedish picnic.'

'Sounds saucy,' said Justin.

'Actually it is. Look at this stew,' she said, lifting the lid from one of the containers. 'I know you don't feel like eating much but this will be good for you.'

Despite himself, despite the headache and the chills and the nausea, he found himself smiling at the absurdity of it all: the supermodel and the rock star talking about stew. For a moment he wasn't sure he'd ever been happier.

'A few people were having supper over in the lodge,' said Emily, fastening her long glossy hair into a ponytail and getting to work serving up the food. 'Connie and Graham, they're funny. The chef and his partner – what's her name, Nami? Oh and I saw Alex, that English guy I was sitting next to last night. You know he wants to talk to you.'

'What about?'

'Not sure. He's a journalist though, editor at one of British nationals. Imagine he's poking around the Viggo story.'

Justin swallowed.

'Why does he want to talk to me?'

He was beset by that now familiar spiralling feeling, of being out of control, like he'd woken up and realised he was still in the dream.

Seeing Justin's discomfort, Emily came over and put her arms around him.

'Relax, hon. The sous chef has been arrested, remember? It's over.'

She was right, of course. Justin had been petrified by his police interview, paranoid that they would produce a witness who had seen him with Viggo in the woods. Justin had convinced himself that the voices he'd heard coming from the chef's cabin the previous night had been his imagination, a hallucination brought on by the drugs. But what if someone else had been at Viggo's house? What if he or she had seen Viggo find Justin underneath that huge Nordmann fir.

But in the event, his concerns about the police interview had been premature. Sergeant Koln had grinned in the background while the Inspector asked a few polite questions about food poisoning, then Koln had grilled him for fifteen minutes about the second Joystick album. Apparently, he had seen them in Stockholm and Oslo on the *Born*

To Drive tour. Justin knew he'd been lucky and never wanted to feel so on edge again.

But what was the point of getting a death-row reprieve if you sat around moping? Right now Justin needed to start enjoying his charmed life.

'So, how about we have that game of Scrabble?' he said.

Emily gave him a sideways look.

'I thought you hated Scrabble.'

'Nope. Love it. Board games are the new rock'n'roll. Ozzy's a big fan of jigsaws, you know.'

Taking a drink each, they sat down at the board. 'Now remind me,' said Emily, reaching for the little black pouch. 'How many letters do you start with?'

'Seven,' said Justin, with a waver in his voice.

'Right, I'll...' She stopped talking and let out a little gasp as she looked down at her tile rack. There were already letters arranged across it. Justin knew what they read because he'd put them there.

M-A-R-R-Y M-E

'Justin,' she said softly, 'Do you mean it?'

'More than anything,' he said. 'I know I'm probably not the best option in the world right now, but I promise that if you'll have me, I'll do everything to set things right.'

Emily's eyes were sparkling in the firelight.

'Justin, these are the best seven tiles I've ever had.'

He swallowed with a click: there didn't seem to be any moisture in his throat.

'So what do you say?'

Emily took two tiles from her rack, then searched for

another one from the black bag, before placing them on the board.

Y-E-S

'Yes?' asked Justin.

'Yes,' said Emily. He came around the table and took her in his arms and for one long minute, Justin felt entirely at peace. His friend Doyley, the famous singer-songwriter who'd had his own well-documented rollercoaster ride in the music industry, had once told him how, after a similar descent into his own personal hell, he had found a way out. He had moved to a crofter's cottage on a tuft of windswept headland in Connemara, grown a beard and did cold turkey the hard way, with nothing but strong Irish tea to help him. But, he told Justin, he'd also written the best tunes of his life. Right now, for the first time, Justin felt something like that was possible, and it was what he wanted to do too. Except he wanted Emily to be there in the windswept cottage with him.

'Come away with me,' he said.

Emily laughed. 'Where?'

'I don't know, somewhere remote – even more remote than this. I just want to sit in a shack with you and my guitar, and write songs about being in love. Is that crazy?'

'It sounds wonderful,' said Emily. 'But first, we've got to get all this poison out of your system.'

After the mad high of the proposal, Justin could already feel he was beginning to crash. The shivers and the fever were coming back, the restless limbs, the tapping fingers. And the skin that felt like bugs were crawling just beneath.

‘I think you should go to the spa,’ said Emily.

‘Babe, I think I need more than a quick dip in the hot tub.’

‘Haven’t you ever heard of a sweat lodge? In Native American culture they use them to purify the body, mind and spirit.’

Justin thought it sounded like a load of hippy codswallop, the sort of thing they went mad for in California, but he recognised now probably wasn’t the time to voice that opinion.

‘How do you know all this?’ he asked.

‘An old boyfriend,’ said Emily. ‘Apparently sweat lodges are brilliant for flushing all the toxins from your system super quick.’

Justin didn’t want to hear about her old flames and their heroic struggles to kick the junk. And neither did he relish the idea of subjecting his fragile body to a Swedish sweat box. His hands began to shake at the very thought of it.

Emily looked into his eyes.

‘Give it a try?’ she said. ‘For me?’

Justin thought it sounded like hell on earth, but he smiled.

‘For you. I’ll do anything for you,’ he replied, and he meant it.

Chapter 31

When Lara and Alex walked into the Kluven kitchen,

Stuart Dell was chopping meat. He looked up briefly, then turned and swung his cleaver, impaling it with a disconcerting 'thunk'.

'If it's food you're after,' he said over his shoulder, 'call room service.'

'No Stuart, we need your help,' said Lara walking across. Stuart dropped the cleaver with a clatter and began wiping his hands on an already-stained towel.

'Help? And why should I help you? You said you were going to find who killed Viggo – and now my other friend has gone too.'

Lara could hardly blame him; ever since they had arrived, Stuart's world had turned upside down. Boss dead, job gone and all of the expected end-of-season festivities replaced with fear and suspicion.

'I understand how you feel Stuart, but I did try to help Petra.'

'Did you?' he said, taking a step towards her. 'Well you didn't do a very good job, did you?'

'Whoa, whoa,' said Alex, slipping between them, hands raised. 'Lara did her best, okay?'

Lara flashed him a grateful look. 'Look, Stuart, none of us believe Petra killed Viggo, so don't you think we should try to do something about it?'

'Ach, what can we do? She's in a cell in Kiruna by now.'

'We can find the real killer, Stuart.'

The chef looked at her sceptically. 'What, by following his bloody footprints?'

Lara could understand why he was acting this way. How would she feel if Alex was carted off by the police, protesting his innocence, begging for help? It was something Lara had seen depressingly often in her line of work – the aftermath of events, the pain of people left behind. It was bad enough when parents or partners were railing against injustice, but it could sometimes be worse to watch someone crushed as they realised everything they thought they knew about someone was wrong.

'Look, we need to find Josh,' said Alex. 'Do you know where he is?' He was already over his self-imposed deadline and it was beginning to show. Lara raised her eyebrows at him meaningfully: *wait*. Stuart gave a cynical laugh and shook his head in disbelief. 'Josh?' he said. 'That's your best idea? That kid is scared of his own shadow.'

'Sure, but we think he might have seen something important,' said Alex, more diplomatically. 'He might not even know he saw it.'

Lara saw hope creep into Stuart's expression, then just as quickly fade.

'I haven't seen him. Maybe he's gone,' he said. Alex and Lara exchanged panicked expressions.

'When?' asked Alex urgently 'When did he leave?'

'As soon as that police inspector told us we were free to go, I guess. I haven't seen him around the complex since.'

'Doesn't he have things to do here in the kitchen?'

'Not really. Our contracts end today and we're on skeleton staff until the guests all leave. We usually have an end of season shindig, but given the circumstances, you can imagine not everyone is in the party spirit. It's not just Viggo. It's Petra. She was popular.'

Lara looked at Alex anxiously.

'But has Josh actually left the resort?'

Stuart shrugged.

'He won't have gone far. Theo had laid on a coach to get us to Kiruna for the flight and train down south, but that's not until tomorrow. There's a bar in the nearby village he might have gone to.'

'So he'll be in the staff quarters?'

Lara was already backing towards the door.

'Probably. He's sharing with that Lucas, the Escuelerie?'

He put his hand in his pocket.

'Take my key card, it'll get you into the building. It's the old stables block. Their room is on the first floor. Studio 6, I think.'

He looked into Lara's eyes as he handed it over.

'You find who did this, for Petra – but for Viggo too. He wasn't perfect, but he...' Stuart's gruff voice caught. 'He was my pal.'

Lara squeezed his arm and nodded. 'We will.'

They reversed their route through the kitchen exit and along the path towards the former stables.

'Escuelerie?' asked Lara, as they jogged through the still-falling snow.

'Fancy name for dishwasher,' said Alex.

At the old building, Lara led the way inside. 'Petra's room was down there,' she said, pointing towards the far side.

'I saw the stairs towards the back.'

They turned right into a large hallway, which Lara supposed would have been where the carriages would have been stored and was, from the looks of it, a communal socialising area for the staff.

'Lara,' said Alex quietly, nodding towards the far end.

Dominating that side of the common room was a pool table and bending over it, apparently playing against himself was a young blond lad, gangly and awkward.

'Are you Lucas?' called Alex.

The boy hefted the cue in what he probably imagined was a menacing manner. 'Who wants to know?' he said with a prominent Irish accent.

'I'm Alex and this is Lara. We're...' he stopped as Lara raised a hand and pointed to a cardboard box sitting on a chair next to the pool table. 'Are you friend of Petra's, Lucas?' said Lara, looking into the box.

Feigning indifference, the blond bent over the table and lined up a shot. 'No, why?' he said, sinking a red with practised ease.

'I was just wondering why you had her things,' said Lara. The box was filled with cooking utensils, a packet of green tea and a crumpled apron. Lara lifted out a worn mug and held it up.

'Hey, leave that alone,' said Lucas. 'That's not yours.'

'It's not yours either, is it? I recognise it: Petra was using it when I was in her room yesterday.'

Lucas looked stricken. 'I was just helping out. Got all her stuff from the kitchen and in here; left the mug in the sink. I was going to put it in her room, but it's all sealed up with that police tape.'

The boy eyed them suspiciously.

'Are you with the police?'

'No, we're friends of Petra's too,' said Alex. 'Stuart sent us over. He said you could tell us where to find Josh.'

Lucas did that same 'what would you want with Josh?' look as Stuart. Clearly, Josh wasn't high in the Kluven pecking order.

'He's not here,' said Lucas, looking back down at the table.

'Do you know where he is?'

'Dunno. He ran off. He's probably in the woods.'

He bounced the white ball off a cushion, sinking a yellow with a satisfying 'clump'.

'Why?' asked Lara.

'Because that's what he does, he's always lurking about the grounds somewhere.'

'No, I mean why did he run off?'

Lucas curled his lip.

'We had a fight.'

'A fight? What about?'

The boy's expression turned surly and defensive. 'Who did you say you were again?'

Lara could sympathise. Lucas was young – probably barely twenty. No doubt he'd been interviewed by the police that day and asked lots of leading questions about Petra, a woman he obviously liked. The poor kid had just come here to learn how to cook. It took gumption to come to this part of the world for your career, especially when you were so young. No doubt he'd come for an adventure, an experience he would remember for the rest of his life, and somehow it had turned into a nightmare.

Alex stepped forward. 'We're trying to help Petra, Lucas,' he said. 'Just like you. And no, you don't have to talk to us, but if you do, it could help get her out of trouble.'

As he spoke, Lara was reminded that Alex ran an entire unruly newsroom and he did it with tact and authority. He had a gift for getting people to do things they'd rather not. She had often been on the receiving end of it herself.

'Look, I know this is asking a lot, Lucas,' Alex continued, 'But could we wait for Josh in your room?'

The younger man looked nervous.

'What d'you want to speak with *him* for?'

'We think he might have seen something.'

Lucas' eyes widened. 'About Viggo? Like, who killed him?'

'Maybe,' said Lara. She watched the boy consider getting involved, then saw him shake his head.

'Nah, man...' he began, but before he could finish, Alex pulled out his wallet. Ever the newspaper man, he produced 500 Krona and held it in two fingers. Lucas' eyes followed it like a snake. Clearly they weren't paying the junior staff enough.

'All we want to do is talk to Josh,' said Alex. 'And it would really help if we could wait in your room.'

Lucas' hand shot out and took the note, eyes flicked right and left, then muttered 'this way'. They walked through the common room to the stairs and Lucas led the way up.

'So what was the fight about?' asked Alex as they walked.

'Difference of opinion,' shrugged Lucas. 'Josh loved Viggo you know? Idolised him. So when the police took Petra, Josh said some pretty bad things about her. Petra's been pretty cool to me and I told him so. I told him what I thought of him.'

'Which is what?'

'He's a bloody weirdo. I shouldn't have said it, but he is.'

'Weird how?'

'Always hanging about watching people. Gives me the creeps.'

Lucas opened a grey door at the far end of a narrow

corridor. 'Here,' he said. 'I'd rather not share, but the layout means we get our own privacy. That's Josh's part.'

The room was a twin, but the space was L-shaped, neat and Nordic, like an Ikea show-flat, except it had the smell of teenage boys – the tang of sweat and unwashed clothes. It reminded Lara of her boarding school dorm, with added *Hygge* styling.

'Tell me about him,' asked Alex, casually wandering into Josh's area and opening a drawer. 'Did you get on before the fight?'

Classic Alex, thought Lara. Get the subject talking about themselves to distract from what you're really after: a search of the room. Lucas certainly didn't seem to notice.

'He was okay I suppose,' he said. 'At first I thought he was just shy. Felt a bit sorry for him to be honest. He doesn't seem to have much family or friends. None he talks about anyway.'

'You said Josh was a big fan of Viggo's, right?'

'Huge,' said Lucas without a moment's hesitation. 'Thought the sun shone out of Viggo's... you know,' said Lucas, blushing slightly as he glanced at Lara. 'That was the one thing he wouldn't shut up about. 'Viggo did this', or 'Viggo said that.'

Alex was poking around on Josh's narrow desk.

'So you two don't hang out between work?'

'Not really.' He put his hands up. 'Look, I don't know anything. I sleep here. He sleeps there – that's it. He keeps to himself messing about on his computer mostly.'

Computer? Thought Lara glancing around. She couldn't see one on Josh's desk or next to his bed.

'Where is it?' she asked. 'Do you know where he keeps it?'

As Alex opened a wardrobe, Lucas moved across

waving his hands. 'Hey, hey, I just said you could wait here, I didn't say you could mess about with Josh's stuff.'

But Alex had already pulled a battered laptop from a shelf and put it on the end of the bed.

'Is this it?' he said, quickly flipping it open.

'Yeah,' said Lucas, trying to get past Lara to grab the computer. 'But that's his personal things, man. This wasn't the deal.'

Lara turned to face him.

'Look, we appreciate you're trying to protect your roommate,' she said, 'But we're here to try and help Petra. We think Josh might know something about Viggo's death...'

Lucas stopped, his pale face looking even more drained.

'Wait, you think Josh might be involved somehow?'

Lara knew she had to tread carefully here. Josh was a kid. Was probably innocent, so she didn't want to directly accuse him of anything.

'No, I never said that.'

'Lucas, this is for Petra,' said Alex. 'We need to know what Josh has seen.'

This was part of the job that Lara hated: the invasion of people's privacy. What Alex was about to do – search through Josh's computer – was wrong. Dead wrong. As an investigative journalist, you could convince yourself about the ethics of research if it was in pursuit of the truth, to stop an innocent person from going to jail, or even to save a life, but there were still rules, laws and lines in the sand and they were about to cross one.

Lucas didn't move. He looked hesitant, conflicted, torn between doing the right thing and potentially getting into trouble.

'There's another computer,' he said finally. 'One that he hides.'

Lara knew she'd been told something significant.

'Where is it, Lucas?'

'He thinks I can't see him stashing it away. But I can, in the mirror,' he said nodding towards the small sink by the window.

'Show us,' said Alex quietly.

Lucas hesitated again, then went to Josh's side of the room. Alex followed him and Lara hung back for a moment, watching them in the mirror as Lucas got down on his haunches and took something from under Josh's mattress.

'Here,' said Lucas handing it to Alex.

'I always wondered what it was for. Figured he used it to, you know, download porn or something.'

He glanced back at Lara, blushing again.

'But if you think it's important, maybe you should look at it.'

Alex perched on the end of the bed and opened it. It was a very old machine, not password protected. He clicked on the cloud storage icon, which took him to a grid of images that Alex began to go through one by one.

Lara sat next to him to take a look.

On the screen was a close-up picture of Viggo, apparently bending over a steaming pan.

'So?' said Lara, confused.

Then Alex clicked on the 'next picture' arrow: a shot of Viggo tasting something from a spoon. Then the next, a picture of Viggo opening an oven, the heat making him turn his face away. And the next and the next, all photographs of the chef in the kitchen.

'There are hundreds of pictures,' said Alex, clicking faster. 'Right through the day.' Pictures of Viggo chopping, Viggo frying, Viggo bent over a plate, a look of concentration on his face. Viggo laughing, pushing his long hair back, Viggo changing into his whites. But then the photos changed. The bright strip lights of the Kluven kitchen replaced by the snowy darkness, Viggo's silhouette moving from the grounds, then more blurred shots taken through a window.

Lara leaned forward, fascinated despite herself. When she felt breath on her ear, she turned her head and saw Lucas peering over their shoulders.

'That looks like Viggo's cabin,' he said pointing at one of the pictures. 'I've been there a few times on errands.'

'See how the quality of the pictures have changed,' said Alex, almost to himself. 'I'd guess the kitchen shots are taken with one of those spycams that look like a button. These were taken on a camera phone: look at the shape.'

Whatever camera Josh had used, they were evidently taken from behind trees, the pictures framed by spruce branches. He hadn't wanted to be seen, that was for sure.

'I told you Josh was always in the woods,' muttered Lucas.

Lara watched, mesmerised as Alex clicked onto pictures of Viggo inside his cabin. Viggo sitting on his sofa, at his desk. Viggo sleeping, which somehow seemed more creepy than the others.

'Looks like he was peering in through the window for this bedroom shot,' noted Alex, tapping the screen. 'Some of the other pictures might have used other kinds of spy camera technology.'

Lara nodded. She knew a little about this from Paul, a techie she sometimes asked to help out on a story. Once the realms of Bond movies, spyware was now relatively simple to obtain and install. Tiny pinhole cameras could be inserted into pens or key fobs, light-bulbs or alarm clocks. Twenty-first century tech was a snooper's paradise.

'Did you know about this?' said Lara, looking at Lucas.

'What? No way,' he said, moving back to his side of the room, as if that would distance him from the crime.

'I had no idea he was doing any of that,' he said, quickly becoming agitated. 'I told you we don't really talk. I'm more friends with Oscar, you know the new commis? I only really see Josh at night. Besides, his computer was hidden, wasn't it? How am I supposed to know?'

'But you said he was always messing about with the computer – do you think Josh has been stalking Viggo for a while?' asked Lara.

'Stalking?' Lucas practically squealed the word. His eyes grew wide. 'Do you really think Josh had something to do with... Viggo?'

Alex stood up and started pacing the room. 'No, no,' he said soothingly. Clearly that was the logical conclusion, but they didn't want the poor lad in hysterics.

Lara picked up Josh's computer from the bed, where he'd left it.

'We need to call Sonia Lindhart and tell her about this.'

'Have you got her number?'

'No, but it won't be hard to find. I'm sure Theo or Martin have it or we can just call the station directly.'

That was the moment the door opened and a dark-haired young man stepped inside.

'Josh,' said Lucas unnecessarily.

'What the hell are you doing?' he asked.

Lara saw his eyes dart to the computer in her hands but it was a split-second too late. As he snatched it from her grasp, there was a moment when they all seemed frozen, like a theme park pirate ship pausing at the top of its swing. Then Josh turned and ran and disappeared through the door.

Chapter 32

'What the hell are you doing?'

Theo had been so preoccupied; he hadn't heard Kat open the door.

He was still sitting at his wife's desk, hunched over her computer, scrolling through her private things. It had been quite compulsive for Theo. Once he'd found one email about divorce proceedings, he'd wanted to delve deeper into Kat's secret life, and had been ploughing through her gmail account when he'd been caught red-handed. In that split second Theo knew there were two ways to play this. Outrage or indignation at what he had discovered, but his anger was simmering, not quite ready to boil over.

'You ask what I'm doing?' He pushed his chair back, his voice low and measured. 'I should ask the same question to you.'

'What do you mean?'

Theo could feel every muscle in his face stiffen.

'You don't you think I deserve to know that my wife has begun divorce proceedings against me?'

Kat's eyes widened.

'You... you shouldn't have been reading that.'

Theo lent against the office wall, still trying to process it all. His legs didn't feel particularly stable. He felt as if he might even throw up.

'That's why you're going to Stockholm isn't it? Not for some Christmas shopping,' he spat, imagining her in a fashionable office in the capital, conniving with some man in a fancy suit.

'I just spoke to them to find out where I stand.'

At least she didn't try to deny it.

'Where you stand? Right here, next to me is where you should stand. Or at least that's what I thought was going to happen when we got married.'

Kat coughed out a laugh.

'Really? Is that what you really think? I'm some sort of eighteenth-century possession, a good little woman who should be seen and not heard?'

'We're partners, Kat. Husband and wife. You have a problem, we should talk about it.'

'We have talked about it, Theo. We've talked and talked and you never seem able to hear.'

'Hear what?'

'That I'm miserable here,' she shouted, gesturing angrily around the office. 'That I loathe this place, that I'm desperate to get away.'

He could hear the bitterness in her voice, clipped, angry resentment.

'But why? This place is important, it's where we belong.'

She shook her head in a cold and cynical gesture. 'Where you belong, perhaps. Not me – not us. Living in Northern Sweden was your dream, not mine. I came with you, to support you, because you wanted to spend time with your sick father, but he's been gone for over two years, Theo. It's time to move on.'

'Do you not feel any responsibility for the work we do here? Do you think life is all about shopping and going out?'

He'd admired that once about his wife. When they'd first got together, back in London, he'd marvelled at the size of her circle of friends and her energy – she could go out five nights a week after her shift at the hotel and never seem tired. But now it seemed so shallow, frivolous and immature.

Kat glared at him. 'Don't pretend you do all this out of the goodness of your heart,' she scoffed. 'You do it because you feel guilty.'

'Guilty?'

'You do this for yourself, Theo!' she snapped. 'You want to be the big man around the village to ease your guilty bloody conscience.'

'What guilty conscience? I just want to continue my father's good work and be a pillar of the community,' he said, hating the way his voice was wavering.

'Bullshit Theo,' said Kat. 'I know.'

Theo thought he had stopped breathing. He felt himself press his body against the wall as if he were trying to get away from her words.

'You know what?'

'Your dirty little secret,' she said with a hint of triumph. 'Oh, you're so pious about your father and his memory and how you want to carry the torch, being the stalwart supporter of the village. And all that back-slapping at his funeral... "Oh Theo, you were so good to him",' she mocked, '"So attentive".'

'I did my best for my father.'

'Did you? Perhaps if you were there at his house, as you were supposed to be that day, things might have been different.'

Theo squeezed his eyes closed. He could see it again.

That image. His father's body on the floor. Broken and lifeless because he had got there too late.

Theo felt his mouth go dry.

'I did go to his house.'

'Eventually,' said Kat. 'You were supposed to spend the day with him. You left here at nine in the morning. But you went to Kiruna first for a meeting. An off-the-record chat with Eventyr, the hotel group, about starting your own resort in Norway. So much for your loyalty to Kluven and to the village.'

His head was spinning. He had no idea how she knew but everything she was saying was true. Theo hadn't been able to resist when the hotelier Lars Eventyr had been passing through the area to visit the nearby ice-hotel and had called Theo up for a chat. Lars was looking for someone to head up a similar venture near Tromso and he thought that Theo was just the man to lead it. Theo had thought it would only be a quick coffee and with the journey time to and from Kiruna, he could be in Skellstad by noon, but by the time he was back at his father's house in the village, it was past two o'clock and the old man was dead on the cold stone floor at the foot of the stairs.

'That's not true,' he replied, but his voice was little more than a whisper.

'It is true. I know you went to Kiruna because you left your scarf at the restaurant where you met Lars. His assistant called Kluven to arrange for its return, so I knew where you'd been. I never said anything at the time because I knew how upset you were about your father's death. But now, honestly I'm sick of your justification to stay here.'

He saw the triumphant twinkle in her eyes and his stomach went tight. Theo felt like he'd been mauled by a bear. How could she be so... cruel? What had he done to deserve that? He'd just tried to be a good husband, to make a better life for her and the people who lived in the area.

'Don't pretend to take the moral high ground,' he hissed. 'Tell me why you really want a divorce, Kat. You talk about moving on but that isn't it: you've found someone else, haven't you?'

He knew he was lashing out, but he was only saying a fear out loud. Deep down, he knew it wasn't just Kluven his wife was tired of, it was him. He'd seen the signs, but had tried to ignore them, pass them off as Kat's attentiveness with the guests. But he'd seen her making eyes with the more attractive male visitors to Kluven for months, if not years. The previous evening she'd been all over Alex Ford, taking him on 'the Grand Tour'.

'You flirt with any half good-looking man that comes through here. He doesn't even have to be good looking if he's rich.'

'What? You're crazy!'

'Am I? I know what good customer service is and it isn't batting your eyelids at anyone in trousers.'

'How dare you,' she spat. 'You're just as bad as he was.'

She stopped herself.

'He?' said Theo quietly.

Kat looked away. She knew that she had just said something she shouldn't have.

'Viggo,' he said quietly, a penny dropping.

It was all making sense. Lately he had felt her simmering dislike towards their executive chef. He'd assumed that she just didn't like the man, but Kat hadn't always been so hostile whenever Viggo's name was mentioned.

'You were screwing him, weren't you?'

'Viggo? No!' she said, recoiling back.

Her mouth was pulled into a tight line and he saw it all right there in her expression. Shame. Hatred. Rejection.

'What happened Kat? Did he end it?

'There was nothing to end,' she screamed.

'Just. Tell. Me.'

'I never had sex with Viggo Widlund. But he wanted to have sex with me.'

'What do you mean?'

It was a few more seconds before she spoke.

'Every season I'd pray that you'd be offered another job so we could get out of here,' she said, a tear slipping down her cheek. 'But you showed no sign of wanting to leave or even recognising that I was so unhappy. Instead all you started to talk about was Kluven's expansion. How it would create *opportunities* for the village. I knew you'd never leave here of your own accord, so I took matters into my own hands.' The tears were streaming down her face now, her words thickening. 'A couple of months ago I went to see Viggo at his cabin. Begged him to find a replacement for you, so we could be let go. I told him that our marriage wouldn't make it if we stayed in Lapland.'

She let out a bitter laugh.

'He said if my relationship was in trouble he could provide a little pick-me-up. He tried to kiss me and put his hands on me. I said no, but he didn't stop. Told me that I wanted it. That I wanted him.'

'Did you?'

'No!' she screamed. 'I hated him, especially after that. And you know what? I'm glad he's dead.'

Theo's heart was pounding hard. Everything was slotting together like the jigsaw puzzles his father has loved.

'Kat, tell me it wasn't you... Tell me you didn't kill Viggo.'

Her sobs started to soften.

'No, I didn't kill him.' she stammered.

'Do you think anyone is going to believe you after what you've just said?'

'I didn't kill Viggo,' she said, clenching her fist until her knuckles turned white. 'Petra Summers killed him. She's been arrested.'

'But not charged,' said Theo, slicing a hand through the air. 'Not yet. Sonia Lindhart told me to call her straight away if I had any new information.'

The expression on Kat's flushed face froze.

'You would do that? To me? I'm your wife,' said Kat, her eyes widening with fear.

'My wife?' he scoffed. 'I thought you wanted a divorce?'

Theo took a step towards her, his confidence slowly returning. Another rule in the General Manager's playbook. Deal with all problems as quickly and efficiently as you can.

Kat was shaking her head.

'I didn't do it, Theo. I swear.'

Theo was trying to think it all through, trying to place everyone's movement around the complex the night before. 'Yesterday. After the supper, you took everyone out to see the Northern Lights. I went out to look for you, to watch the light show with you. But I couldn't see you anywhere.'

'I was in the lodge.'

'Were you? Maybe that's for Sonia Lindhart to find out.'

'Theo, what are you saying?'

'I'm a loyal man, Katherine. You might think otherwise, but I am devoted to the people and things I support. I also expect loyalty in return. You don't want me to tell the Kiruna police what I know, then I would like something from you.'

'Something from me?' she said, her voice cracking. 'What?'

'Stay with me at Kiruna. Help me build it, expand it so it reaches its potential.'

She looked at him with an incredulous expression. 'No one is going to want to come here anymore. The bloodbath resort.'

'You're wrong,' he said. 'Within six months everyone will have forgotten all about what happened here last night. Another hot chef, more hype and publicity, and people will barely even remember Viggo's name. That reservation line will be ringing off the hook again, I promise you.'

'Did you not hear me, Theo? I'm leaving.'

He willed himself to power on with his plan. Moving forward, Theo knew he would hate seeing Kat flirt with future guests, despised the idea that she might want sex with some of them. But at least now he knew where he stood with her. Their cabin had two bedrooms, and if she wanted to move into the spare one, he wouldn't stop her.

'Kluven needs you, Katherine. If you leave, if you turn your back on us then I'm afraid I'll have to tell Lindhart that Viggo Widlund propositioned you, assaulted you, angered you... Any half-decent detective can see it's a very strong motive.'

'This is blackmail.'

He stood back, folding his arms, feeling himself recover his control. All was beginning to feel right in his world once more.

'I say we should just think of it as a business deal,' he said, and turned and left the room.

Chapter 33

Alex sprinted down the corridor, his footsteps loud on the old wooden floorboards. Reaching the stairs, he slipped, missing the first step and clattering down the next few, scraping his shin in a flower of pain. Cursing, Alex hauled himself up and limped through the common room to the wide open front door.

'Dammit,' he said, squinting at the white expanse in front of him. Josh had gone. The snow was falling harder now and it took Alex a moment to get his bearings. There: to his right, a skid where Josh had burst out of the stables, then the slight indent of footsteps running north towards the drive. Was Josh planning on stealing a snowmobile too? *The irony*, thought Alex as he set off in pursuit. It was hard going through the snow, which was clinging to his boots with every step, plus the path was getting slippy with the new fall. And then suddenly, Josh's footprints just disappeared.

'What the hell?' he muttered. Bending closer to the path, Alex retraced his steps and now could see what had happened: Josh had run towards the road, then veered off the path towards the woods.

'Sneaky,' said Alex, plunging into the deeper snow. It was up to his knees and like wading through wet cement. He felt his boots were filling with melting snow, which he then imagined would refreeze along with his toes. Just then, he saw movement up ahead – a shower of white as a pine branch was nudged.

There you are, thought Alex, picking up his pace, feeling his heart pumping and his thighs burning. Alex made one last push, his breath echoing in his ears. He kept as fit as he could, but Josh was twenty years younger and had a head-start.

'Josh!' Alex shouted, making a last desperate lunge, throwing himself forward in a rugby tackle, pulling the boy down in a tangle of limbs, a cloud of snow puffing up as they fell. Alex clambered to his feet, twisting Josh's arm behind him, but he felt almost no resistance from the boy. His head was hanging down and he was weeping into his chest.

'I didn't do anything,' he cried. 'I really didn't.'

'So why run?' panted Alex.

'Because I knew no one would understand.'

You've got that right, thought Alex. Just then Lara ran across, scooping up the laptop Josh had dropped, dusting it off.

'That's mine,' said Josh miserably. 'It's *mine.*'

Alex wasn't a psychologist, but he guessed Josh meant it literally. That the computer, the photos and therefore the connection to Viggo were actually part of him. In his mind, it was like they were looking at his private thoughts.

'Let's take him to the Lodge,' she said.

'Why can't you just let me go?' wailed Josh as Alex steered him in that direction. 'I didn't do it.'

'Didn't do what, Josh?' asked Lara.

'I didn't kill Viggo,' he sobbed. 'I know that's what

you're thinking, but I didn't. I would never... I couldn't. He was a great man.'

Perhaps, thought Alex, but it didn't look good for him. It was easy to see how an obsession of that level could tip over into dangerous fury if the subject of your fixation let you down. Which was exactly what Viggo had done. Alex looked at Josh, slumped and beaten in front of him in the snow. He was what, twenty? Thin, bad skin, living a twilight existence; he looked sad, not dangerous.

'Why, Josh?' he asked. 'Why take all those photos?'

The boy muttered something into his chest.

Lara leaned closer. 'What did you say?'

He looked up.

'Because he was amazing.'

They had reached the main entrance to the Lodge now and suddenly Josh began to struggle.

'No, please!' he wailed. 'You have to believe me, I didn't kill Viggo. They'll send me to prison and I didn't *do* anything.'

Lara looked up at Alex.

'Who did then?'

'Petra?' he said it almost as a question.

'Are you saying Petra because that's what the police told you,' asked Lara, 'Or because you really think it?'

Josh twisted to look at her.

'Do you know Petra lied to the police about going to see Viggo that night?'

Lara nodded. 'She told me she saw him. That she met him on the track to his cabin.'

'Did she tell you she attacked him?' said Josh. 'I saw it. She really went for him like this,' he said, swiping at the air with his free hand, fingers curled like a claw.

'So you think Petra is the killer?' asked Lara.

To Alex's surprise, Josh shook his head and gave a heavy sigh.

'Who then?'

Josh didn't reply but in the low light Alex could see that his pale face had coloured.

Josh began to struggle again. Alex held him until he realised the boy was trying to get at something in his pocket. Reasonably confident he could catch the boy if he bolted into the building, Alex let him go. Josh reached into his jacket and pulled out a phone, and held it up, his cold, red fingers trembling. 'This will prove I didn't kill Viggo.'

'How?'

'I can show you who Viggo's been meeting in the root cellar.'

Alex swallowed, feeling a jolt of excitement. Did he really know? What a scoop this would be.

'Josh, show me.'

Josh sat up in the snow and Alex watched warily as Josh bent over the phone, quickly flipping through apps, then handed it to Alex. But there wasn't a picture of the root cellar on the screen; instead it was another shot of Viggo's cabin. As Lara looked over his shoulder, Alex swiped through a sequence of pictures looking through the cabin window: no one inside.

'Keep going,' said Josh. His breathing was still heavy. There was a trail of saliva on his lip. More shots of another window from the outside, then looking through the glass. Viggo's bed, the sheets rumpled. A pale leg, then Viggo from behind, naked and sweaty.

'Jeez,' said Alex as he clicked onto another snap: Viggo entwined with another body. Alex flipped to the next photo and immediately looked up at Lara. Her mouth was open.

'I don't believe it,' she breathed.

'He's not going to like this,' said Alex.

'No,' she said. 'No, he's not.'

Alex looked back at the photo of Viggo Widlund lying in bed with a woman. A woman they could all easily recognise. It was Anna Svenson.

Chapter 34

Gary was, predictably, furious. 'You stupid junkie loser!' he yelled. 'I let you into my band out of the goodness of my heart and this is how you repay me?'

Justin turned down the volume on his phone. He didn't want the people in the next cabin to hear it.

'Gary, you asked me to be part of The Velvetines because you thought it would raise your profile.'

'Profile?' he laughed. 'You think I need you, you cheeky sod? Ask around: I'm the biggest name in rock. This is the gig of a lifetime and you want *out?*'

Justin coughed out a laugh.

'What's funny?' snapped Gary at the other end of the line. 'You think that's funny? People would crawl over hot coals to be in a band with me.'

Yeah, well I'm crawling over hot coals to get out, thought Justin, smiling to himself.

'Look Gary, I'm sorry but it's over. For me at least. Tell Steve I'll miss him.'

'Steve? Who cares about that waste of space?' shouted Gary. 'What about *me*?'

Even with the volume turned down, Justin had to hold

the phone away from his ear. 'Oh no, mate,' he called out. 'You're breaking up. Sorry, I'm in Sweden, in the middle of nowhere here.' He rubbed the microphone on his T-shirt to make it sound like static. 'Speak to you in a few weeks, yeah?'

He pressed the red 'end call' button and laughed out loud.

The door of the bedroom door opened a little and he saw Emily's face peering through.

'You've done it?'

'Just like that,' he grinned, waggled the phone. 'Rock history happening right here, live and direct from Kluven.'

Emily threw her arms around his neck and kissed him hard.

'I'm so proud of you,' she said in a rush.

'You might not be so proud when I'm signing on the dole.'

The enormity of what he had just done was sinking in.

'Em, it feels bloody brilliant,' he said stepping back. 'I just feel lighter.'

It was true. For the past year he'd felt as if a dark cloud was hanging over his head. He'd dismissed it as a side-effect of his drug use, but now he had ditched The Velvetines from his life he was definitely feeling better, despite the withdrawal symptoms.

'What are you going to do now?'

'I'm going phone Dec and then the rest of the band.'

'The band?'

'Joystick. I think we should get back together.'

He was definitely feeling a jangle of excitement now. A nervous anticipation and thrill that he felt back in those very early days when he had first put Joystick together. Only now could he appreciate how fun and carefree they were. Justin, Doug, Jeff and Neil – a gang of four, driven by ambition, fuelled by cheap beer from the union. They'd all met at a gig during Freshers Week, discovered they were all obsessed with music, each one of them had a secret dream to play Wembley. They'd worked so hard: every single night, they'd piled into Neil's student house after lectures and jammed, wrote songs and found their sound. Looking back, it had been the best time of his life, when everything was possible, every night was an adventure. They were all in it together. If someone had told him they'd end it all over money and writing credits, Justin would never have believed them.

But the truth was, Justin missed his old bandmates. He missed the fun they had and the simplicity of it being just about music and friendship, not money, record sales and Grammy awards.

'There's time for all that, babes,' said Emily, slipping on her parka. 'First we got to go and listen to some whale music.'

'Do we have to?'

He still wasn't sure about the sweat lodge idea. Emily wasn't a medical expert. Just as life seemed to have turned a corner, it would be just his luck for the sweat lodge to make him pass out.

'Come on. Let's at least try it,' pressed Emily.

His hands were still shaking. He wasn't sure if it was the adrenaline racing around his blood stream after his phone call with Gary or whether this detox would be more difficult than he thought. But a brisk walk in the cold might be what he needed. His body was going through a hot phase, and he could do with cooling down. At least before he warmed up again in the sauna.

Emily and Justin walked hand-in-hand all the way to the spa. His skin felt clammy but he enjoyed the sensation of togetherness, feeling his palm in hers, the sense that he was no longer alone, with no way out.

Both of them had been to plenty of nice places before but they both agreed that Kluven's thermal suite was impressive. A low-rise, cedar-clad building with a shimmering steaming pool surrounded by black slate, outside there were also three barrel-shaped hot tubs in the snow that were bubbling like cauldrons.

'In or out?' he said.

'In, I think. It's the sauna we're looking for.'

He hesitated on the doorstep until Emily stepped inside and the tranquil sound of tubular bells tinkled. Music had always been Justin's balm – and now it was working its trick again.

'Separate changing rooms? I thought we were in Sweden,' he grinned.

'See you the other side, lover,' smiled Emily coquettishly.

Justin couldn't stop smiling. He wasn't just Emily's lover. Not anymore. He was engaged. He knew that Emily would want to indulge in the engagement period – several of his mates had got married in the past couple of years, and that was what they all said about their partners – they all loved being a bride-to-be. But if it were up to Justin, they would get married straight away. If there was a local priest in the Kluven area who could officiate, he would do it that weekend.

Or imagine Father Christmas marrying them! Now that would be cool. He felt sure that Theo the General Manager could sort it out for them if he asked nicely.

He poked around the changing room, genuinely interested in Kluven's thermal suite. Justin had been to hundreds of luxury hotels in his time, but you'd never find him in the spa. He didn't get the appeal of strangers touching him. The one time he had been persuaded to go, he'd forgotten to give the therapist a gratuity and found to his horror, a story in *The Sun*, the following week about "Cheapskate Justin" – the tight rock star who refuses to tip. He hadn't been to a spa since.

But this was nice, he decided, clocking a drinks trolley laden with jugs of infused waters, a huge basket of high-end beauty products and a rack of fluffy white towels that looked like a bundle of clouds.

Justin frowned. He'd brought his swimming trunks but was that how they did things in this part of the world? He remembered the time when Joystick had been on tour in Helsinki and Neil had gone to try out the sauna. He'd actually got told off for keeping his swimmers on and not going in totally nude.

He peeled off his jeans and jumper and crossed the room to a bank of lockers near the hair-drying station. He opened one, took out the waffled bathrobe, hung it up on a peg, then rolled up his clothes and stored them away.

'Trunks or no trunks?' he muttered to himself.

He turned when he heard the soft pad of footsteps.

Emily had come into the changing rooms wearing just a tiny white bikini.

'Wow,' he grinned, throwing his boots into the locker.

'Are you coming or not?'

'I was just debating to go full-on naked or not.'

'You should be nude,' said Emily more seriously. 'Remember why we're here. Clothes will only inhibit the process.'

'I'm not sure, Em,' he said, reaching for the robe. Justin felt faintly ridiculous standing in Kluven's changing room without a stitch of clothing.

'Didn't you say there's a journalist here? The last thing I

need is getting snapped by him and being a naked centrefold for Christmas.'

'Maybe we should speak to him,' she said with more humour. 'You know, announce our news.'

'You want to do that?' smiled Justin putting his arms into the white waffle sleeves. He still had to pinch himself that Emily, the bikini-clad goddess in front of him, had said yes. Not only that – she wanted to tell the world.

'Why not? They can run the story. At least after I've posted it on Instagram.'

'Let's do it then,' he grinned. 'Let's go public.'

Despite his good mood, he was still going to bring his trunks into the sauna – just in case.

He'd brought a pair of Vilebrequins with him on the trip. Emily had bought them for him in Milan when she'd been on a job for Italian *Vogue*. They had yellow bananas on them; happy shorts, she called them. Justin felt sure that Emily had imagined the first time he'd wear them would be on a beach in Maui or poolside at some exotic Four Seasons, not trying to detox heroin in a remote sauna in Lapland, yards from where his friend had been murdered. Still, they would preserve his modesty, whatever the circumstances.

As he shoved the shorts into the pocket of the robe, he felt resistance. Something was already in there.

'What's this?' muttered Justin. He threw his trunks onto the bench and reached into the pocket, pulling out one phone, then another. They were identical. The cheap kind you could buy in a bubble-pack in convenience stores. Justin instantly recognised them as the kind used by drug dealers to keep their communications with customers untraceable.

'Phones?' frowned Emily.

'Disposable ones. Either that or someone's on an extreme budget, which doesn't sound likely at Kluven.'

'Still, someone will be missing them,' said Emily. 'We should probably hand them in to Guest Relations. What's the front of house manager called? Kat?'

'Should I do it now?' asked Justin looking at them.

'They can wait,' said Emily with a half-smile. 'I want to get you hot and sweaty.'

Justin pushed the phones into opposite pockets of his robe.

'Hot and sweaty you say?' letting Emily lead him into the sauna.

Chapter 35

'What exactly are we going to say to her anyway?' said Alex as he and Lara left their cabin to go to the Svenson house. 'Hi Anna, I understand you've been having a torrid affair with the murdered chef?'

Lara gave a grim smile.

'That's possibly a little direct, but that is about the size of it, yes. I guess we let the pictures do the talking.'

Lara felt for Josh's phone in her pocket, needing reassurance that it was still there. It felt warm: she and Alex had spent the last twenty minutes going through every photo on Josh's mobile, looking for more evidence of Anna and Viggo's affair, but also hoping for clues to the chef's movements on his final day. They had been disappointed: it appeared as though Josh had ceased his obsessive photography the moment Viggo had made his announcement. Of course they had asked Josh why and the boy had simply begun to weep again. 'Heartbroken', 'betrayed', 'shell-shocked': that was how Josh had described his feelings between sobs and Lara had little doubt he was telling the truth – about that part at least. However, their search of the phone had revealed many more pictures of Anna Svenson meeting Viggo at his cabin, talking closely in the woods or, chillingly, sneaking into the root cellar together. The pictures of Viggo and Anna went back five or six months to the height of summer. It was remarkable that no one else had spotted Viggo and Anna's illicit relationship before. Lara had found one other thing curious too: the whole mood of the affair. There were no passionate embraces and precious few smiles when Viggo and Anna met. It had looked like a relationship that was already grinding to a halt rather than in the heady eye of a storm. Perhaps that was the key to its secrecy. That it was restrained and they hadn't taken risks.

'I'm going to try Sonia Lindhart again,' she said scrolling to contacts. Alex had got the inspector's direct line from Theo Mikelson. Apparently, the general manager hadn't been overjoyed to hand it over but Alex had given him the right assurances, or perhaps a veiled threat.

Still, the number didn't seem very direct to Lara. She'd tried it twice and each time had got through to a man who sounded suspiciously junior. He had claimed that Lindhart was unavailable but he would pass on the message.

'Pratar du engelstar? Ja?' Another junior officer. Possibly the same person as before, asking if she was speaking English.

'Yes, my name is Lara Stone. I'm a guest at the Kluven resort. I need to speak to Inspector Sonia Lindhart as a matter of urgency.'

Lara sighed as she was given the same response as before. She left her number and rang off.

'Urgent?' asked Alex as they traversed up the path towards the Svenson's.

'I thought you'd got a story to file.'

He didn't deny it.

The Svenson house loomed up ahead.

'Someone's on the move,' said Lara. Ahead of them, parked on the drive in front of the Svenson house, were two of the Kluven Land Rovers.

'Kenneth and Serena are going back to London,' said Alex. 'Theo told me that Martin has made his private jet available to them. How the other half lives, eh?'

Lara increased her pace. If Kenneth and Serena could simply fly away, that meant Anna and Martin could just as easily disappear.

Lara walked over to the cars and peered inside.

'Someone is definitely ready to leave,' she said, looking at the luggage inside.

'Maybe someone has arrived,' replied Alex.

'Guests?' Lara wasn't sure the Svensons would have more visitors after everything that had happened.

'I thought Martin and Anna threw a party at the end of the season.'

'Surely not tonight?'

Still, Alex had a point. The conversation they needed to have with Martin was not going to be an easy one and it needed to be done in private, not in front of his friends. She looked up at the house and pointed.

'Look,' she said. 'Lights coming from the back. Let's see if Martin and Anna have got company.'

Lara skirted around the building, and Alex followed close behind.

They kept a discreet distance from the house as they went around the back. Through one of the glowing windows Lara could see what looked like a library and in the warm golden light, she could see Anna and Martin standing with Kenneth and Serena, each holding a glass. Presumably toasting a 'bon voyage'.

She stood back into the dark shadow of a fir tree and beckoned Alex to do the same. Her eyes scanned the house

– top to bottom, left to right. It was two storeys high, with a balcony that ran across the entire width of the top floor, with a flight of stairs running down to ground level.

'Seen the fire escape?' said Alex.

Lara nodded. She knew they were both thinking the same thing.

'Let's run through what we know again,' she said, keeping her voice low.

'Petra went up to the Svenson house at around 10.45pm and saw Anna standing on the front porch. According to Petra, Anna went back into the house and she followed her. Petra saw Anna go upstairs, so she assumed that Mrs Svenson was in the house at the time of Viggo's death, giving her an alibi.'

Alex nodded towards the top floor of the Svenson's grand home.

'But Anna could easily have left the house via the fire escape. The house is so big, she could have done it unnoticed.'

'Yes, she could,' agreed Lara. 'The snow was heavy during the night. It's thick on the ground today but yesterday, around eleven o'clock, it wasn't that bad. The storm hadn't kicked in so the snow was just a few inches deep. It would have been relatively easy to walk on so Anna could have stayed near the tree-line and taken a discreet route to the root cellar.'

'And who would have seen her in the pitch black anyway?' agreed Alex.

He exhaled and the air mushroomed in front of his lips in the dark sky – white on black.

'Look Lar, it's eight o'clock. I'm going to have to get back, call the office."

'And say what?' she said, turning to glare at him. 'Alex, we are *this close* to working out what has gone on here.'

'I know. But I still need to file a story, so can we quit shivering in the dark and go and speak to Martin Svenson?'

She knew he was right, a voice in her head telling her that they were just procrastinating.

'Let's do this,' she said, touching Alex on the sleeve.

As they walked back round to the front of the house, being careful to stay out of view through the plate glass windows, she wondered how much they should tell Martin. If Anna had killed Viggo in a fit of rage or if Martin knew about the affair and confronted Viggo, they were hardly going to admit it.

Lara checked her phone to see if Lindhart or Sergeant Koln had called her back. Lara was desperate to speak to one of them, knowing that the police really needed to be involved here. How Anna reacted to the photos, what she said, even her body language, it all might be important when it came to making an arrest.

They were almost at the front steps when Lara heard a loud cough from above.

'What *on earth* do you think you are you doing?'

Lara looked up: Martin Svenson was on the porch looking down at them.

'Is this an example of the British gutter press in action? Will you be going through our rubbish bins later?'

'I'm sorry, Mr. Svenson, but we need to talk to you.'

Martin looked unimpressed. He looked at Lara and then Alex. 'Well, the feeling is not mutual. We have guests. Can you please return to the Lodge? This is actually private property.'

Lara realised that this was their moment – they had Svenson alone.

'Martin, we have information that we think might be relevant,' said Alex. He began to climb the stairs, but

Martin blocked the way, both hands held out in a clear 'stop' gesture.

'Relevant to what?'

'Viggo's death,' said Lara.

'No, Miss Stone. Whatever you were about to say, the answer is "no".' I simply don't have time for this. The police have the situation under control. As you know, an arrest has been made. If you go back to the lodge, Kat will arrange your transfer to the airport tomorrow. Beyond that, I have nothing to say to you.'

'Martin, your wife was having an affair with Viggo.'

There. There was no easy way to say it, so she just said the words.

Lara pulled out Josh's phone containing his pictures of Viggo and Anna.

'You don't have to talk or even listen,' she said, climbing the steps. 'But I really think you are going to want to see what's on here.'

Martin didn't react.

'Mr. Svenson?' said Alex behind her. 'Did you know Anna was in a sexual relationship with Viggo?'

'How dare you come to my resort, my home and make these accusations.'

Lara noticed that he hadn't looked down at the phone.

The night seemed to press in around them; even the sound of her voice seemed muffled by the new dusting of snow.

'We thought you should know,' said Alex. He was on the porch now, level with Svenson. Lara took one final step to join him.

Martin shook his head. 'You know nothing about our lives, Mr Ford. My wife was not having an affair. Not with Viggo Widlund or anyone else.'

'The pictures on this phone say otherwise,' pressed Alex.

'Martin, we've told the police,' said Lara.

She watched Svenson, saw his Adam's apple move up and then down. She wished she had given the desk sergeant at Kiruna Station more information on what they had discovered. That she'd given scant detail made her feel vulnerable and exposed.

Without saying another word, Martin picked up his own phone and made a call. 'Kenneth? Would you come out here for a moment? I'm on the porch.'

They waited as Kenneth Roscoe walked out and closed the front door behind him. He was holding a glass of Scotch and wasn't wearing a coat. He looked at Lara and Alex with surprise, but didn't comment. Martin placed a hand on Kenneth's shoulder.

'Could you tell our journalist friends here what you told Inspector Lindhart during your police interview, specifically regarding our movements last night.'

Kenneth looked bemused, but shrugged.

'I told the Inspector that I came back to the house straight from the meal, arriving here at around 10.55pm. You and Anna were both here. Martin was in his office. Anna was in her studio where I went to chat to her.' He turned to Lara. 'Apart from Martin leaving when Theo Mikaelsson called to tell Martin that Viggo was dead, we were all here together.'

Lara had a sinking feeling in her stomach.

'What about your wife?'

'Serena stayed to watch the Northern Lights so she arrived back at the house a little later than me. But once we were here, I don't think any of us could have left without being seen.'

Martin gave a thin smile to Kenneth, who dutifully nodded and went back inside.

'Satisfied?' asked Martin.

'Not at all,' said Lara, holding up Josh's phone. 'The fact remains that we have evidence of...'

'Evidence?' snapped Martin. 'Then take your so-called evidence to the police. Inspector Lindhart seemed very happy with our alibis. Moreover, she seemed entirely convinced that poor Petra was the protagonist. But be my guest in wasting police time.'

Alex stepped forward.

'And what if we printed our photos in the *Chronicle*, Mr. Svenson?'

Martin barked out a laugh.

'I think we all know how hollow a threat that is, Mr. Ford. I know that the *Chronicle* has been to the Royal Courts of Justice for one libel trial this year. I doubt your superiors will want to go through the time and expense of another one.'

'I can assure you it is not a threat,' began Alex, but Lara put a hand on his arm. She looked up at Martin.

'Alex, let's go,' said Lara, turning to leave, pulling Alex with her. 'Mr Svenson, you've been very helpful.'

'Good night Miss Stone, Mr Ford,' said Martin. Then he turned and walked back into the house.

'What the hell was that?' hissed Alex as they walked back to the drive, but Lara just shook her head wearily. She knew that Svenson was right about legal proceedings. The bruising libel trial he'd mentioned was about one of her stories and when the *Chronicle* was found guilty of defamation, it had directly led to Nicholas Avery, her uncle and Chairman of the company shutting down her department.

And Martin was right: they couldn't run the pictures from Josh's phone. A judge would immediately rule that

Viggo and Anna could expect privacy inside Viggo's cabin: it was a private matter.

'"*You've been very helpful?*"' said Alex.

'I was being sarcastic,' she said.

Alex looked back at the house, then down at his watch and sighed.

'So that's it, isn't it?' he said. 'We're out of time.'

'Not necessarily,' said Lara. 'I think Martin already knew about Anna: no reaction at all when we told him, did you see that? So the question is how long he knew.'

Alex shook his head.

'It doesn't matter.'

'But it does,' said Lara urgently. 'If he found out last night, maybe he killed Viggo.'

'Trouble is, it's only a theory, we can't prove a thing,' said Alex gesturing back towards the Svenson house. 'You heard them: they're all giving each other alibis.'

'We need to talk to Anna,' said Lara, but Alex just snorted.

'Good luck with that. Aside from the fact that Martin would probably have one of his drivers put us in a headlock if we went anywhere near his wife, do you seriously expect her to tell a couple of journalists she'd been screwing the chef?'

Lara shook her head. She knew he was right of course, but she hated his defeatist tone.

'We can't give up, Alex.'

He gave her a thin smile.

'It's not giving up, Lar. It's accepting the reality of the situation.'

'Which is what, exactly?'

'Viggo is dead and the police have arrested Petra in connection with his murder. That's it. That's all we have.'

'But Petra didn't do it, Alex.'

He threw up his hands in a gesture of frustration. 'Perhaps not, but I'm a newspaper editor, Lara.'

'*Deputy* editor,' she said. It was childish, but it was either that or scream. Alex looked at her evenly.

'We have zero evidence that anyone else was involved in Viggo's murder. Lots of doubt, lots of loose ends, but *nothing* we could actually print. All I can do is report about Petra's arrest. And that's what I'm going to do.'

Lara stepped in front of him.

'Please, Alex. No.'

'What do you expect me to do, Lara? Run a headline saying "Police Arrest Wrong Woman: Holidaying Journo has alternative theory in stabbing story"?'

'It would be honest at least.'

She saw that one hit its mark. Alex narrowed his eyes.

'No Lara, I'm the one being honest here. Honest about what's actually happening.'

'And what about the truth, Alex?' she shouted.

Lara turned and began to walk back towards the Lodge. The snow was falling again, the sky fully dark.

'You might have given up on it, but I'm not going to stop until I can prove what's happened.'

She heard him calling her name, but she didn't look back and soon she couldn't hear him at all.

Chapter 36

Alex pressed 'send'. He watched as the little drawing of an envelope whooshed across the screen and disappeared. So that was it: the story about Petra's arrest was out there. In a few short hours, the front page of the *Chronicle* would be rolling off the presses and the narrative would be set. Alex let out a long breath and massaged the back of his neck.

'Sorry, Lara,' he whispered. Alex could admit he'd been angry after their argument and for about three hot seconds, he had wanted to show her exactly who was in charge. He almost laughed at that: as if anyone could ever be in charge of Lara Stone. And of course he sympathised with Lara's position that this story might change the course of Petra's life, but Lara knew as well as he did, that was just how the news worked. It was a journalist's job to relate the facts, not to decide who was worthy of help. Ultimately it was up to the readers – and later, the jury, he supposed – to read a dispassionate account of what had happened, then decide whether they agreed with Sonia Lindhart's assessment that Petra had killed Viggo.

In reality, Alex wasn't sure of Petra's guilt. Even in the

middle of his bad-tempered exchange with Lara, Alex had his doubts: anyone would after having seen those photos of Anna Svenson and speaking to Martin with his stonewalling tactics. There was clearly much more to this story than they had managed to unearth in the few short hours they'd had allotted to them but again, that was the nature of the news too. You reported on how things looked *right now* – and if things changed tomorrow, you reported on that too – but as a writer on a daily newspaper, you rarely had the luxury of seeing the big picture. The full story could only be assembled much later, after a dispassionate study of all the evidence from every angle. That was a job for a historian, not a reporter and right here, right now, it was Alex's job to tell the world about Petra's arrest. Nothing else.

He closed his laptop. He knew damn well that Lara would not agree. When he'd come back to file his story, Lara had stomped off back towards the bar to look through more of Josh's photos with the parting remark that she wasn't going to stop looking for the truth, even if Alex had. He hated disappointing her, but he didn't see what choice they had; time had simply run out. Of course, time was the real problem. Alex and Lara came from two different disciplines. Lara's investigations were like a legal argument, carefully constructed and unpicked over a long period, every scrap of evidence assessed, every box ticked. Alex was all about the headline: 'Chef Killer Caught'. The detail came later, if at all.

He walked into the living room and opened the fridge: *damn.* No beer left and he definitely wasn't in the mood for spirits. He was sure he could still pick up the phone and have someone run over with a refill, but Alex guessed the staff felt as beaten down as he did right now. Besides, he could do with getting out of this cabin. Luxurious though it was, he was getting sick of Kluven and was looking forward to going back to London, back to work where things made sense. He pulled on his coat and crunched out down the path toward the main building. He'd seen Emily the model gathering a picnic from the kitchen earlier, perhaps he could do the same for Lara, a peace offering of sandwiches and hot chocolate. He smiled grimly. *Some chance.* But it was still worth a try.

'Hey, Alex!'

He turned to see Justin and Emily coming his way, their paths converging. They were walking arm-in-arm and grinning like a pair of cats in a bathtub full of cream. Even from ten paces it was obvious, a marked change from the worried, watchful expressions everyone had been wearing for the past day.

'What's going on with you two?'

He watched Emily glance towards Justin, raising her eyebrows as if asking a question.

Justin nodded. 'Sure, why not?'

Alex laughed, their smiles were infectious.

'Come on – what *is* it?'

Emily entwined her fingers with Justin's and raised them up.

'We're engaged!' she squealed.

'What? Wow – that's amazing! Congratulations, guys!'

He thrust out a hand and slightly startled, Justin shook it.

'Thanks man,' he said, slightly sheepish. 'You're the first one we've told.'

'You do know I'm a reporter?'

He'd avoided the issue at dinner the previous night. He hadn't wanted Emily to think he had an agenda. But they looked so happy, he felt he owed it to them to tell them the truth.

'We know you're a journalist. That's why we're telling you.'

Alex grinned.

'Well, I'm still honoured.'

Justin looked at Emily with a look of melting love.

'Em's pretty special and I just didn't want to let her get away, you know? You can quote me on that.'

Alex nodded, and found his thoughts drifting to Lara, presumably hunched over a drink in the bar, plotting her next move. She was special too. But Alex kept letting her get away.

Then Alex had another thought: perhaps here was a solution, even if it was a temporary one. Alex knew his editor-in-chief inside out and Darius would drop the Viggo splash in a heartbeat if he thought an exclusive about a celebrity engagement would sell more copies. News was a funny thing – it was fluid, constantly moving and the readers really didn't differentiate on subject matter, they just wanted something to talk about. A political scandal, a house fire or a royal baby, it was all gossip.

'So this is like a world exclusive?'

Emily laughed.

'At least give me a chance to tell my mum, but then I want to shout it from the rooftops.'

'Just make sure you say I'm the luckiest man in the world,' grinned Justin.

Despite his gloom, Alex couldn't help but be buoyed by the happy couple in front of them. He felt a pang of envy as he watched Justin hold up Emily's hand and kiss it. The bloke looked like shit, but he'd written some of the best songs of the past decade and a woman so beautiful she looked like an alien was clearly hopelessly in love with him. As Rod Stewart once said, some guys had all the luck.

Alex looked away awkwardly as the couple started

kissing again. He felt as though he was intruding, which of course he was.

'So where are you going now?' he said quickly. 'To the bar for some champagne?'

'Actually we're going to the office.'

Emily held up a pair of mobile phones. 'We just found these in the spa. Think they must belong to a guest. Not yours are they?'

'No,' said Alex frowning. 'Can I see?'

Emily handed them over. Cheap, but functional, they were the kind of cellphones which would just make calls and send text messages, but nothing else. They certainly seemed incongruous in the luxury of Kluven. Alex checked the back: not even a camera. Odd. And two phones. One on its own you could put down to a cleaner having mislaid, but two?

'You found them together?' he asked.

'Both in the pocket of a robe,' said Justin. 'We were just going to hand them in to the guest relations lady.'

Alex turned the first one on and scrolled to the contacts.

'There's only one number stored in the phone,' he said.

'Presumably the other phone?' said Justin. Alex nodded and handed it to him. 'You turn that one on, we'll test it out. I'm going to look at the texts.'

The burner phone was slow and clunky compared to Alex's smartphone, but he found his way to the messages section and opened one sent the day before.

I really have to see you. You can't leave.

Immediately Alex felt his heart jump, his instincts tingling. He clicked onto the next message.

Please, I need to talk – just talk. This still can be good for us.

He looked up at Justin who was still clicking at the buttons on the other phone. Alex turned back to the message log on his: five more messages from the previous day.

Why aren't you replying? I know you're there.
I'm not going to be ignored.
Do you want me to tell him? I will – you know I will.

'Holy shit,' said Justin. Alex looked up. He and Emily were both peering at the little screen on the other phone. 'I think this is Viggo's phone,' he said, eyes wide. 'It has to be: look.'

He held it up so Alex could read the message.

I'm sorry. It's over.

Heart beating fast now, Alex stood next to Emily as Justin clicked onto the last message sent:

Leave me alone Anna.

'Anna?' said Justin. 'Who's Anna?'

Instead of answering, Alex turned back to the phone in his hand and opened the last message, sent at 10.48pm the previous night. It read:

I have to see you.
NOW, Viggo.
Meet me in the root cellar.

Chapter 37

At least the bar was empty. Lara took a sip of her brandy and rubbed her eyes, trying to focus on the screen in front of her. Lara wasn't a big drinker, she never had been: it always led to trouble. In her teens, contraband alcohol had almost got her expelled from boarding school. In her twenties, Lara had thought wine spritzers gave her Dutch courage but really, all they did was help set her up with unsuitable men. And now, in her thirties, booze just dulled her senses and gave her a hangover that lasted far past the weekend. But after her argument with Alex, Lara had needed something. Fuming at his narrow-mindedness, she had stomped back to the Lodge and set herself up at the bar, poring over the pictures from Josh's secret computer, hoping to see something, anything, that might deflect the police's interest from Petra and onto Anna Svenson. Lara had to admit there wasn't much. The only thing Josh's surveillance had revealed was that Anna and Viggo had been conducting an affair, nothing more. It was mildly scandalous, she supposed, but here in Sweden, possibly not even that. It certainly wasn't illegal. And as a motive, Lara knew that Sonia Lindhart would see Petra's unrequited passion for Viggo as a much more likely trigger for violence.

Lara had sent a dozen emails to Stella requesting information about Anna Svenson, particularly the trademarks she had registered, but Lara's hopes weren't high in that area either. Expanding your design business wasn't against the law either.

Lara shook her head and pushed the brandy away. Another bad choice to end a year of wrong turns, humiliation and heartbreak. Perhaps she was simply in the wrong business. Journalism hadn't been a choice exactly, it was more like going into the family business. And she had been good at it, won awards and travelled the world; she couldn't deny it had been fun, but perhaps there was somewhere else where she could make a difference, or at least not feel as if she was banging her head against a brick wall half the time. Teaching or research, perhaps?

She closed her laptop with a sigh. No, it was Alex. Her argument with him out there in the snow had got to her. She was never angry at Alex, but tonight she felt as if he had let her down. Why couldn't he have waited another hour? Why was his bloody deadline so important? She'd always felt they were both on the same page, but today Lara had felt him pulling away.

Couldn't he have filed the story a bit later even if it meant running it in the second edition. She looked at her watch. Probably not, Alex was a company man.

'Lara!'

She heard running footsteps to her left, but didn't look up.

'Lara, please,' said Alex, panting. 'You really need to see this.'

She glanced across and could see he was holding up a phone, but she had no interest in looking properly. What was it? His front page exclusive on the *Chronicle* website? *Well, congratulations.*

Alex leant across the bar, thrusting a cheap mobile in front of her.

'Read it,' he said urgently. 'It's important.'

Reluctantly, Lara looked at the screen.

Meet me in the root cellar

The breath froze in her throat as she snatched the phone from Alex's hand.

'What is this?' she gasped. 'Where did you get it?'

He waved another identical phone at her.

'Both hidden in the spa. They are Anna's and Viggo's, no question. There's a full exchange about meeting last night.'

Lara slid off her stool, her pulse racing. She looked up at Alex, eyes wide. This wasn't just a twenty euro phone, it was a smoking gun. With a sudden whoop, Lara threw her arms around Alex and squeezed.

'Alex Ford, you're a bloody marvel!'

She stepped back, feeling herself blush.

'Does this mean I'm forgiven?' he asked with a grin.

'Not quite, but it's a start.'

Alex quickly filled her in on meeting Justin and Emily. As he spoke, Lara was already thinking it all through.

'The problem still remains that Anna Svenson has an alibi,' she said. 'Petra saw Anna at the house at around 10.47 and Kenneth Roscoe swears he was with her straight after the meal from around 10.55. So how could she have met and killed Viggo in the root cellar? There just wasn't the time to do it.'

Alex grimaced, shaking his head. 'You've met Martin's friends. They could all be covering for each other. Martin even denied that Anna was having an affair when the evidence was right in his face. People lie, Lara.'

'Yes, they do,' said a voice.

They both turned: Serena Roscoe was standing there, chin raised, poised and elegant. Lara took her in: she wore leather riding boots that weren't made for the Arctic, the scarf was cashmere and her parka had probably cost more than her motorbike. But the main detail Lara picked up on was that Serena's eyes were glittering, red-rimmed. And Lara didn't think it was from the cold.

'Who lied Serena?' she asked gently.

'Kenneth,' she said after a moment. 'Kenneth lied.'

'Your husband?' said Alex.

She nodded. 'For now.'

Lara leant across the bar and, taking a clean glass, poured Serena a brandy. The woman took a swallow, grunted, then took another.

'What did Kenneth lie about, Serena?'

Serena took a deep breath.

'He lied about where he was last night. And where Anna was too.'

They waited as the woman composed herself.

'Kenneth's story is that he went straight back to Martin's house after dinner and spent time chatting to Anna in her studio between 10.55pm and 11.20. But I don't think he did.'

Lara glanced at Alex.

'Why not?'

Serena hesitated, then bit down on her lip.

'Kenneth has a bad back and Martin suggested he try

out the hot tubs, apparently they have hydrotherapy jets? Anyway, there wasn't time before dinner, so

Kenneth took his swimming trunks down when we went to the dining room. He was going to pop into the spa on the way back.'

Lara nodded. She remembered him saying something about that at dinner and had left straight after the petit fours.

'You didn't go with him?'

Serena shook her head.

'After coffee, I went to speak to Kat about our transfer to the airport. Then the Northern Lights appeared so I hung around the Lodge to watch them. I think I got back to Martin's house at 11.25.'

'Was Kenneth there?'

She nodded.

'He said his back was feeling better so he'd skipped the spa and gone straight back to the house.'

'But you don't believe him? Why?'

Serena reached for the brandy with shaking hands and took another sip.

'I found his swimming trunks in the bathroom. They were damp. I think he did go to the spa.'

Lara felt her excitement grow. If Kenneth had lied about going to the spa – and they could prove it – then it seemed very likely he had also lied about seeing Anna at the house.

'How do we know Kenneth got back to the house at 10.55.'

'Anna vouched for him.'

'So they gave each other alibis,' said Lara.

'Did you tell this to the police?' asked Alex.

Serena gave a tight shake of the head.

'I wanted to keep my interview as short and uncomplicated as possible. I didn't think it was particularly significant. Besides, Kenneth is my husband.'

She took another sip of brandy.

'But then I heard you talking on the balcony earlier. I heard you say that Anna and Viggo were having an affair, and so...I wanted to tell you what I know.'

Lara knew she had a very delicate question to ask.

'Why would Kenneth lie? If he did go to the spa, why say he went back to the house and give Anna an alibi?'

Serena gave a cold laugh.

'I know what you're thinking. Rich people. They all cover for one another to protect their interests. Well, it's actually less complicated than that.'

She paused.

'Martin was well over forty when he got married. We didn't think it would ever happen, we'd even given up on setting him up with friends. And then he met Anna and he was smitten. Everyone was enchanted by her. Some more than others,' she added tartly.

'Kenneth, of course, thought she was wonderful. I'll never forget the look on my husband's face at the wedding when Martin and Anna were at the altar.'

Serena looked down at her hands, touching her engagement ring with one finger.

'He looked crushed. I knew then that Kenneth was in love with Anna. Martin always asks why it's taken us so long to come to Kluven, but the truth is, I've been making our excuses from the day it opened. I wanted to keep my husband as far away from her as possible.'

Alex sat forward, checking that the bar was empty before he spoke.

'Serena, what do you think happened last night? Do you think Anna killed Viggo?'

The woman pulled her scarf tighter around her throat and stood up.

'I don't know. But I know my husband lied and I know he did it to protect her.'

She raised her chin.

'I'm glad we've spoken. I couldn't have it on my conscience letting an innocent woman go to jail – and letting a guilty one get away with it.'

'You know the police are going to want to hear this too.' Lara thought of the suitcases she had seen in the back of the Kluven Land Rovers. 'Will you stay to speak to them?'

'Oh, I think I've seen enough of this place,' said Serena, and she turned to hurry out of the bar.

'Serena,' called Lara. 'Where's Anna now?'

'I saw her ten minutes ago,' replied the woman, not looking back. 'I think she was heading towards the spa.'

Lara looked at Alex and they spoke at the same time: 'She's looking for the phones.'

* * *

It wasn't far from the Kluven bar to the spa building, but first Lara needed to make a call. She clicked it to speaker-phone so Alex could hear as they walked.

'Is that the Kiruna Police Station?' she said, as the line connected. 'This is Lara Stone at the Kluven resort. I need to get an urgent message to Inspector Sonia Lindhart.'

There was a pause.

'But the Inspector is in a....'

'I don't care where she is,' snapped Lara, cutting the operator off. 'You find Sonia. You tell her that Anna Svenson met Viggo Widlund in the root cellar last night. Tell her that we have photos and phone messages to prove it.'

There was a loud click, then a buzz.

'Miss Stone?' It was a second before she realized she was talking to Sonia Lindhart. 'You have information for us?'

Lara couldn't get the words out fast enough. She told Sonia about Josh's pictures, about the burner phones and the text messages and how Kenneth Roscoe had almost certainly given Anna a fake alibi.

'The Svensons have their private jet fuelled and ready to go at Kiruna airport,' said Lara, still walking towards the spa as rapidly as she could. 'Apparently it's for their friends the Roscoes, but I think Martin and Anna are going to board it too.'

There was the shortest of pauses, then Lindhart spoke again.

'I'll send officers to the airport,' she said, with crisp efficiency. 'And I'll leave for Kluven immediately. We have a helicopter. I'll check the weather conditions. If we can fly, I'll be there in twenty minutes. Meanwhile, do what you can to keep Anna at Kluven, Ms. Stone.'

Lara pocketed the phone and broke into a trot, the snow puffing up in clouds around her feet. 'We need to keep Anna on the compound,' she called to Alex, jogging at her side.

'We could let the air out of her tyres,' said Alex flashing her a smile. Lara looked up at the sky; snowflakes were drifting gently down, nothing like the storm of the previous night but Lara knew nothing about helicopter aerodynamics. Perhaps even the slightest flurry could ground a chopper. Otherwise it would take Lindhart at least an hour to come by road and she doubted Anna Svenson would hang around waiting to be arrested, especially if Serena told her husband what she had just said to them in the bar.

Lara clattered down the spa stairs and pushed through

the glass doors: the foyer was empty, deserted. Concealed blue lights behind the reception desk made the place look even more eerie.

'Where did Justin find the phones?' she whispered. If Anna was here, they didn't want to make her bolt.

'Men's changing rooms,' Alex replied. They slipped through a doorway to the left: empty, although every locker door was open and a pile of white robes were strewn across the floor. It was the same story in the ladies dressing room, evidence of a frantic search, but no Anna. Lara pointed towards a corridor at the back, a sign directing them towards the sauna and pool. They walked as quietly as they could past the steam rooms, dark and unoccupied, then through an archway. The humidity hit Lara as they stepped into the pool area. It was a strange sensation after the dry cold of the past thirty six hours. The water in front of them shimmered turquoise and gold, tastefully lit from below, reflecting across glass walls on three sides. During the summer days, Lara supposed the view would be glorious – a seamless transition from indoor to outdoor with the spa garden beyond. But tonight, with the dark Arctic night on the other side of the glass, it was as if they were sealed inside a black box. And there at the far side, pulling towels from a huge laundry basket, was Anna Svenson.

'Looking for something?'

Anna whirled at Lara's voice. Her face was as pale as the moon, pink spots of anger at the centre of each cheek.

Lara was immediately reminded of the description Josh had given of Petra clawing at Viggo: Anna looked like she might spring at them too. Alex must have noticed it as well, as he walked around the pool towards her, patting the air in a calming manner with one hand, a burner phone still held in the other.

'We know what happened Anna,' he said, stepping

closer. 'We know you met Viggo in the root cellar last night. We know you've been having an...'

'You know NOTHING!' yelled Anna. She leapt forward, trying to snatch the phone from Alex's grasp. Alex jerked backwards, his wet boot squeaking as he slipped on a tile. Anna backed up into the far corner, teeth bared like a cornered animal.

'The police are on their way, Anna,' said Lara, trying to calm the situation. 'We have proof. We have proof of everything.'

'Proof?' sneered Anna. 'You think you know it all, don't you?'

'We know you loved Viggo,' said Lara, softening her voice.

'Love?' laughed Anna. 'You think I loved Viggo?'

Lara frowned.

'You argued, you attacked him,' she said, imagining what had happened in the root cellar. 'Why? What was it all about?'

'This!' shouted Anna, gesturing towards the pool, then out beyond the windows to where they could just see the silhouette of the Svenson house. 'I had a perfect life here. I had Martin who would do anything for me, I had my beautiful home, and I had Viggo for...' Anna snorted to herself. 'For stimulation.'

Seeming to weary, Anna sat down on dark wood bench.

'I had everything I'd ever wanted. And then he took it all away. He took away my life. He took away my future.'

Lara watched Anna's hand tighten into a fist. Her cool demeanour had completely gone and had been replaced by white-hot fury.

'I've spent years building my reputation as a designer. Viggo had always said I should use Kluven as a springboard for a whole interiors empire. Fabrics, ceramics, furniture, design commissions. Kluven was the centrepiece of it all, my calling card, my brand statement. And then he turned around and ruined the whole thing.'

'Why?' asked Lara. 'Why did he want to leave?'

'He said he'd had enough,' spat Anna. '*Enough*? Can you believe that? How could you ever have enough of Kluven?

Lara nodded. 'It's special, that's for sure.'

'Special,' Anna let out a laugh. 'It's *perfect*. I have honed every last detail. People always talk about the food at Kluven, but it's the *place*. I created it all,' said Anna, looking at Lara, 'Me, not Viggo, not Martin. Me.'

'Did he tell you he was leaving before the announcement?'

'No,' said Anna darkly. 'No, he didn't. And he didn't tell me about that pathetic agreement he had with Martin either. Neither of them did. Who would agree to something so childish?'

'Couldn't you change Martin's mind?'

She gave a bitter laugh.

'You don't know my husband. He said he was sick of Kluven, said we were moving back to Stockholm full-time. No discussion.'

'So you arranged to meet Viggo in the root cellar,' prompted Lara. She wanted to keep Anna talking, but she was also fascinated to hear the answer. Finally, here was the key to the puzzle they had been searching for.

'I wanted to convince him to stay, but his mind was made up. He was a selfish bastard. Only ever thought about himself.'

'Anna, we think Viggo was burnt out. Had mental health issues. That's why he wanted to leave.'

'Burnt out?'

She frowned so heavily, her eyes almost disappeared.

'Anna, what happened?'

She was crying now, her rage dissolving into regret.

'We argued. I just lashed out. I grabbed the nearest thing; it wasn't even a big knife. I didn't think it could do so much damage....'

Anna raised her hand, like she was seeing the blade still held there.

'It went right into his chest. All the way in. It was like someone had cut his strings; he just...dropped. I didn't know what to do.'

'But you took his phone,' said Lara.

Anna's eyes met Lara's and she was glad of Alex's silent presence at her side.

'Yes, I took it,' she said. I took his phone and the knife. You'd do the same.'

Would I? Wondered Lara. She supposed no one really knew the answer to that.

'So you came here to wash off the blood?'

Anna nodded.

'It was the nearest place. I didn't think anyone would be here. I threw the knife down a drain but I still had the phones when I heard a noise. I stashed them in a robe but then I saw Kenneth. He was in the shower about to go in the hot tub. I told him there had been an accident. He believed me. I was shaking. He told me to get back to the house. He'd return too so he could vouch for me and I could vouch for him. We went into the house the same way I'd come out. Through the fire escape. We agreed we'd say we were talking upstairs in my studio.'

'So he helped you cover it up,' said Alex, joining the dots.

'Because he's in love with you,' said Lara.

'Because he is my friend,' said Anna in a monotone. 'Isn't that enough?'

'Where was Martin all this time?'

Anna gave a snort.

'He left the house too after Petra had left. I saw him.'

'Where did he go?'

'We'd argued that evening. I was upset that Viggo was leaving,' she said, shaking her head as if she was disgusted by her own weakness. 'He guessed something was going on between us. I suppose he went to Viggo's cabin, no doubt to tell him what he thought of him.'

'What the hell is going on here?'

The booming voice echoed around the room, making them all flinch. Martin was standing in the doorway, hands on his hips.

'Anna, tell me,' he commanded. 'What's going on?'

Lara watched as Anna folded her arms tightly across her chest.

'They know,' she said, almost a whisper, 'They know everything. They have my phone.'

Martin shook his head and strode towards her down the other side of the pool.

'They know nothing, Anna. And they have nothing. So it means nothing.'

'Martin, they know about me and Viggo.'

'So what about you and Viggo,' he said flatly.

'Don't you care?' she asked, her face twisted in pain. Lara knew that Anna had felt betrayed by one man. She doubted she could stand being rejected by another.

'I do care,' said Martin, taking his wife's hand. 'You know I care. I care about you a great deal.'

They stood there for a moment, looking into each other's eyes, then Martin switched his gaze to Lara and Alex.

'Don't try to leave,' he said, pulling a plastic card from his pocket and waving it over a panel.

'No!' shouted Lara, realising far too late what was happening. In the darkness, the glass door had looked like it was part of the wall; they just hadn't seen it. A protective arm around Anna's waist, Martin stepped outside and closed the door behind him with a click. Alex was already running, but they were on the wrong side of the pool. Reaching the door, he slammed his hands uselessly against the glass, but it was locked.

'The front,' shouted Lara, running the length of the pool and down the corridor. Sprinting through the spa foyer, she rattled the entrance doors, but they too were locked.

'Damn it,' she hissed, crossing back to the reception desk and snatching up the telephone just as Alex arrived. Running a finger down the speed-dial buttons, Lara jabbed the one marked 'Manager's office'.

'It's ringing,' she said to Alex. Once, twice, then a click and Theo's voice came on the line. *You have reached the office of the general manager...*

Lara slammed the receiver back down in the cradle.

'Hold on,' said Alex, pulling out his wallet, 'I've got an idea.'

Chapter 38

Kat yanked the drawer open and grabbed an armful of clothes, tossing them into the open suitcase on the bed.

'Kat, please,' said Theo from the doorway of their bedroom. 'I made a mistake.'

'A mistake?' snapped Kat, crossing to the wardrobe and pulling dresses from the hangers. 'You tried to blackmail me, Theo.'

She stopped and turned, raising a finger. 'No, it's worse than that. You accused me of *murder*.'

Theo had seen his wife angry before – Kat was a passionate woman – but this was a new level of fury. And he could hardly blame her. Theo's ultimatum hadn't gone at all the way he'd planned. Theo didn't seriously think that Kat had killed Viggo, but everything was leverage and so he'd offered Kat a devil's pact: stay here at Kluven and help Theo with his ambitions to expand or he would tell Sonia Lindhart everything about Kat and Viggo, the assault and her hostility towards him. If he'd expected a tearful confession and meek acquiescence, he was sadly disappointed. Kat had screamed profanities, swept a tray of glasses onto the kitchen floor. Then she had stormed back here and started to pack.

'Listen to me, Kat. I was confused.'

'You've been confused for a long, long time Theo,' she said as she tipped a forest of beauty products into the case, then slammed it shut, zipping it all around.

'Ever since your father died, you've believed that this stupid bloody resort was more important than me, it was more important than our marriage and now it appears as though you think this place is more important than life itself.' She glared at him. 'You'd actually have me sent to prison for this snowy shithole?'

Theo bristled at the description, but knew he had to try to make her understand.

'You're right, I have had my priorities upside down. But I wanted – I needed - to make a success of Kluven.'

She dropped the suitcase on the floor with a thud.

'Success at any cost?'

Theo closed his eyes and nodded, suddenly deeply ashamed.

'I suppose so. Yes.'

Kat looked at him, hands on her hips.

'Tell me why, Theo. Tell me why you'd sell out your own wife just to build some stupid husky trails next to a lake.'

He shook his head, looked away. His heart was hammering, his mouth dry. He put up his hands, as if to ward it all off, backing towards the door, but Kat grabbed his wrist.

'Tell me!' she shouted.

Theo yanked his arm away.

'Because I let my father down, okay?' he yelled back. 'Because I let him die alone! I should have been there for him, but I was selfish. I was off chasing more money, more success, more status.' To his shame, Theo began to cry, his words only coming in sobs. 'My dad...I think he came looking for me,' he stuttered, his voice husky. 'That's when he fell down the stairs. If I hadn't gone to Kiruna to meet Lars Eventyr, it wouldn't have happened.'

Theo looked up. Kat had stopped packing. 'Theo, it was an accident,' she said, all the anger disappearing from her expression. 'A terrible, tragic accident. And you have to start forgiving yourself.'

'I can't,' he replied.

'You can and you will.'

She handed him a tissue, then stepped back.

'You know why I fell in love with you Theo?' she said with a sigh. 'Because you were strong. You were in control, like Captain Kirk on the Bridge of the Enterprise.'

He looked at her, then barked out a laugh.

'Kirk?'

'Exactly like that. You were utterly unflappable, you knew everyone's names, you knew their *kids'* names, you ran a dozen schedules and spreadsheets in your head. And you know what else? You were fun.'

'Fun?'

'The end of season blow-out in the kitchen? You started that, do you remember? And that first year, you bought everyone toboggans and we all slid down onto the lake.'

Theo nodded, wiping his nose. Yes, it had been good when they'd first arrived. How had it all gone so wrong?

He reached out and touched Kat's hand. 'I'm sorry,' he said. 'I wish I'd...'

Just then, her phone started ringing, loud and insistent from the depths of her pocket.

'Hello? Kat Mikael...hey, slow down...'

Theo frowned. He could hear someone shouting into the receiver.

'Alex, wait, I can't do anything right now,' said Kat and

Theo felt his heart drop. Of course. She was going to go back to London with Alex Ford, the handsome editor. Theo had seen them flirting, but he hadn't guessed that it had gone this far.

'Theo,' said Kat, thrusting her phone towards him. 'He wants you...'

He looked at her, completely bewildered.

'Hello?' said Theo, putting the device to his ear.

'Theo, it's Alex Ford,' said a voice. 'We're locked in the spa.'

'The spa? But how...?'

'That's not important right now. What I need to know is can you close the gates? Lock them.'

There was something about his voice that made Theo click into professional mode. 'It's possible. The gates are automatic, yes and there is a master switch, but I'd need to be at the Lodge. Right now, I'm in my cabin. Alex what's wrong?'

Theo's eyes opened wide as Alex quickly explained. 'Anna Svenson killed Viggo?' he said, looking up at Kat.

'Yes, and I think she's about to flee Kluven. Martin too. We need to stop them. The police are on their way but we can't let them leave for the airport.'

'But...'

'Now, Theo. Now. And can someone let us out?'

He was stunned for a moment then glanced up at Kat.

'I got it, Anna's the killer,' said Kat quickly. 'And she's making a break for it, right?'

'He wants us to lockdown Kluven.'

'What are you bloody waiting for?'

His mind was reeling. This was a worst case scenario situation and a potential death blow for Kluven. Reputation management was one thing, but no amount of spin would get past the owner murdering the chef in cold blood. Kat evidently read all this on his face because she grasped him by the shoulders and looked into Theo's eyes.

'Do the right thing, Theo,' she said. 'And do it now.'

He blinked at her, then nodded decisively.

'Okay,' he said, suddenly all business. 'Mr. Ford and Ms. Stone are locked in the spa. Run down and let them out. Try calling Inspector Lindhart on the way. If that doesn't work, call the airport and get Hilde in the tower, extension 453. Tell her to hold Martin's plane and remind her she owes me for last summer. She'll know what you mean.'

He ran for the door, then stopped and ran back, kissing Kat on the mouth. 'I'm sorry for everything I've done and said. For how I've made you feel. Never doubt that I've always loved you.'

He sprinted out of the cabin, through their little garden and onto the snow-covered drive. He paused, looking back up to the Svenson house. Alex Ford had said Martin and Anna had left the spa a few minutes ago and he'd felt sure they were running for the Land Rovers parked outside the main house. If that was the case, they'd be at Kluven's gates at any moment.

Theo could hear the faint sound of a car engine heading his way.

'*Javla*,' muttered Theo. There was no time to run down to the main gates to close them by hand. The lodge was also a five-minute walk away.

The nearest building to his cabin was the Ski-Doo shed. Theo ran for it, his shoes slipping as he reached the open door and swung inside. There was a box attached to the wall and he scrabbled in his pocket for his keyring. 'Come on, come on,' he muttered, finding the right key to open it, then grabbing the red fob and running out again.

He saw the flash of a green Land Rover through a gap in

the trees. Thirty seconds away, if that. Theo jumped up into the cab of the snow plough parked outside the shed and fumbled the key into the ignition. It immediately coughed to life, the big diesel engine roaring. It had always been one of Theo's priorities, keeping the vehicles maintained in tip-top condition: if you couldn't clear the roads, you couldn't bring in guests. Theo slammed his foot down on the accelerator and was rewarded with a great roar.

He turned his head and saw car headlights coming down the drive. The snow plough's wheels span, slipped, then bit into the snow – and then all at once, it jumped forward, shooting across to the drive. The snow plough had a V6 engine and as long as it wasn't actually pushing drifts out of the way, it ran pretty fast. Theo drove it down towards the gates, stopping at the thinnest part of the track; it was flanked on both sides by giant Spruce trees making it impossible for anything to pass. Theo stood on the brakes, jerking the plough to a halt so the giant machine blocked the road, just as the Land Rover entered the last curve.

Theo's breath was fast, anxious and fear gripped his belly. Martin Svenson would be furious. He had no idea how angry he might be - for all Theo knew, he might have hunting rifles in the car.

Overhead there was another noise. The whoop-whoop of something in the sky. He looked up, just catching sight of the source as it swooped over trees: a helicopter, 'POLIS' written on the side.

Theo jumped out of the cabin and started to run, the keys to the snow plough deep in his pocket.

Svenson's 4x4 had stopped a hundred yards behind the snow plough and Martin got out of the car.

Theo could hear his deep baritone rip through the still night air.

'What the hell are you doing? Get out of the way! I'm the boss here, not you.'

Not anymore, thought Theo as he ran towards the helicopter. He knew, right then, that Kluven was over. The funny thing was, he suddenly didn't mind. What he felt was relief. Kat had seen it all along, of course. Theo had poured all his emotion into the resort as a way of blocking out his grief and guilt and he'd done it with such single-minded obsessiveness that there had been no room for anything else. No fun, no relationship. No life.

Another Kluven Land Rover was coming down the drive. It stopped and two figures jumped out. Theo squinted in the low light but recognised Lara Stone and Alex Ford and as the car's cabin illuminated, he saw his wife, Kat, sitting at the wheel.

The journalists were out of breath as they approached him, the noise from the descending helicopter huge, whipping snow and pine needles into the air.

'Is the gate secured?' shouted Alex.

'Nothing is getting past that snow plough,' said Theo.

He could see Kat grinning at him through the windscreen.

The helicopter touched down in the widest part of the track and Lindhart and Koln jumped out then ran towards them, crouching under the still-spinning blades.

Sergeant Koln kept running towards Martin and Anna's car.

'He'll deal with them,' said Sonia Lindhart as Theo, Alex and Lara gathered. 'Now how about we go inside and you can tell me everything from the beginning.'

Chapter 39

'Fancy going to the party then?' asked Lara, coming out of the bathroom, where she'd applied a slash of red lipstick. If they'd been invited on a rock and roll night out, she figured she should at least make some effort.

'One second,' said Alex, tapping furiously at his laptop.

Lara glanced over his shoulder, where Alex was just adding the by-line to his story about Anna Svenson's arrest.

Restaurant owner confesses to celebrity chef death. Words by Lara Stone and Alex Ford.

She touched his arm, flattered.

'Why have you put my name first? I didn't write it. Switch it around,' she said, as Alex pressed send.

He turned to look at her.

'I got the words down on the page, but without you, this would have been a very different story,' said Alex with a slow smile.

He stood up and ran his fingers through his dark hair, his only concession to grooming and getting ready. How different from the previous night they looked, when Lara had been trussed up in her tight velvet dress and Alex had worn a suit. But this felt more like them. More relaxed. More real.

Justin and Emily's cabin was the furthest from theirs, on the fringe of the forest, but still Lara could hear music as soon as she stepped out into the snow.

No one had been in the mood to party, but when Emily had suggested drinks at their cabin to celebrate their engagement, it had been agreed that it sounded like a nice pick-me up.

Connie Edwards opened the door. She was wearing another sequined top and was holding a martini glass.

'Come in, come in. It's the heroes of the hour.'

Alex gave a bashful grin.

'Team effort, Connie. We couldn't have done it without Justin or Theo.'

The two men were chatting to their left, and both of them looked up when Alex said their names.

'You better not have put me in your story,' smiled Justin.

Alex clapped a hand on the singer's shoulder.

'You might have been mentioned but it was all flattering. And Theo here was the Superman of the piece.'

The General Manager looked flustered.

'It's possibly overstating my contribution,' he said, taking off his glasses and wiping them with a cocktail napkin.

Lara went to get a drink, accepting compliments from the other guests about her pursuit of the story. Miles and Nami were here, locked in conversation with Michel the pastry chef, who apparently had whipped up a quick celebration cake for the happy couple. Patrick and Coulson seemed to have forgotten their earlier argument and were laughing together on the sofa. Kat had sat down with Theo. Every now and then, she would take his hand or they would share a private joke. She recognized some of the waitresses too, who were chatting with other members of the Kluven staff. They seemed happy, giddy. It appeared that the excitement of being at an intimate celebrity party made up for the shock of Kluven's co-owner being arrested for manslaughter.

Across the room Lara saw Alex talking animatedly with Justin Blake as if they were old friends. He caught her eye, then smiled and winked. She'd tease him later, but she knew he was enjoying himself. She felt certain that he'd secure his exclusive interview with Justin, even an invite to the wedding, before the night was out. He couldn't help himself.

She watched him get his phone out of his pocket, no doubt to tap Justin and Emily's details into his contacts, but then her own phone vibrated.

She read the incoming text.

'You look knackered, Stone. Want to leave?'

'Charmer,' she typed back. 'Anyway, can't leave. You're in your element.'

'Let's just go.'

The cabin door opened and everyone seemed to stop what they were doing as Petra Summers and Stuart Dell walked into the party.

Theo led a cheer. Petra put up a modest hand for them to stop. Lara was surprised when the sous chef made a direct bee-line for her.

'Lara. I just wanted to come and say thank you. If it wasn't for you, I'd be....well, I don't want to think about it.'

Lara gave her a big squeeze.

'Are you okay?'

'I'm just so relieved. Sonia Lindhart authorised my release as soon as they picked up Anna. Stuart came to collect me from the station.'

'He's a good friend,' said Lara with a knowing grin.

'He is,' said Petra blushing. 'He's invited me to Scotland for Christmas.'

'Are you going to go?'

'I'm not sure.'

'Come on, what's stopping you?'

'Well, I want to go. But I'm just a bit worried that...'

She trailed off.

'What?' Lara knew that Petra was in an almost identical position to herself and she was keen to hear someone else justify their decisions.

'I'm just worried that something might happen between us.'

'Don't you *want* it to happen?'

'I guess I'm just afraid of crossing that line in the sand. Stuart's my mate. If something romantic happens with him, that's it, isn't it? It won't be a Highland fling, it will be the real deal.'

'Isn't that what everyone wants?'

'But where's the romance in ending up with your best friend?'

'I think it's the most romantic thing in the world,' said Lara, not even thinking about it. 'You don't have to spend years developing intimacy and trust because it's already there. They've seen you vulnerable, at your worst. Your friendship means you've worked out you *like* each other, which I think is what makes love, real love, last.'

Petra nodded as if she was taking in every single word.

'I think I'm going to go,' she whispered. 'I'm going to spend Christmas in Scotland.'

Someone had given her a drink. Petra took a sip and then looked back at Lara.

'What really happened with Anna and Viggo?'

'They were having an affair,' said Lara. 'They met in the root cellar to talk and Anna just lashed out. She had everything she wanted at Kluven. Love from Martin. Sex from Viggo. Glory from her design talent. If the resort closed, she thought her life was over. She didn't realise it would just take on a new shape.'

'Well, it will now,' said Petra.

'Yes it will,' she said, imagining the elegant blonde in a cold cell in Kiruna.

Theo, Kat and the rest of the Kluven staff all seemed to gather around Petra at once and Lara drifted away from the group. All the talk of friends and going away for Christmas had made her want to talk to Alex.

'Justin, have you seen Alex?'

'He's gone back to your cabin. I think he's waiting for you.'

Lara gave the musician a peck on the cheek.

'Congratulations on your engagement, again. And thanks for everything. If you hadn't found the phones, the wrong woman could have gone to jail.'

'Good job I went to the spa then.'

He looked embarrassed as he said it, but Lara didn't probe.

She stood outside on Justin's porch and looked up at the black sky peppered with dots of white light. There were great night skies in the Lake District. The first time she had gone to stay with Alex, they'd climbed up the hill behind his village after an evening at the pub and had seen a shooting star.

'Just say yes,' she told herself. 'Spend Christmas with your friend. And if something happens....'

It will be the most romantic thing in the world, said a voice in her head.

She thrust her hands into her pockets and ran to their cabin, the music from the party fading as she went.

She was glad she'd gone to raise a glass to Justin and

Emily. She felt as if she had made some new friends that weekend, and she was so pleased to have seen Petra. But right now, she just wanted to be with Alex.

He'd written the story about Anna Svenson sensitively. She had no doubt that Darius would instruct the editors and headline writers to 'sex it up', but Alex's piece had been restrained, nuanced. It had acknowledged that it was a tragedy, a crime of passion, a momentary lapse of judgement that, perhaps, could have happened to anyone.

She opened the door of their cabin and went inside.

'Alex?'

Silence.

There was bottle of champagne on the table and two glasses but no Alex. She went through to the bedroom and he was lying on the bed, fully-dressed but fast asleep. She tip-toed towards him and stroked his hand. He stirred but then fell back into his exhausted slumber.

He was tired. So was she. Whatever they had planned to do that evening, whatever they were going to talk about, it could wait. He wasn't going anywhere and neither was she. And she turned off the bedroom light.

Thanks for reading!

If you enjoyed The Last Supper, why not join Tasmina's VIP Book Club for news on releases, giveaways and events? www.tasminaperry.com/joinbookclub

And have you read the other books in the Lara Stone series?

The Yacht Party

What happens onboard, stays onboard...

Investigative reporter Lara Stone is heartbroken when her friend Sandrine is found dead, but Lara doesn't believe it was an accident. Sandrine's death seems linked to the murder of Jonathon Meyer, a secretive financier famous for hosting glittering networking parties on his Monte Carlo yacht Pandora.

What secrets are hidden onboard Meyer's yacht? What deals were brokered that were worth killing for? And can Lara get to the truth before she herself becomes just another inconvenient guest at the party?

The Yacht Party takes you from London's high society

to Paris, via Monaco and the Caribbean in this glamorous escapist mystery.

You can find the Yacht Party here.

Also in the Lara Stone series from Tasmina Perry:

The Ivy

When investigative reporter Lara Stone goes to visit her best friend Alex in Los Angeles, she books a beach house in Malibu for them to stay in. The Malibu House is gorgeous, but it also has a glittering history. And it has secrets.

Once the home of celebrated singer-songwriter Quince Wilson, the house is notorious as the place he died in a tragic accident almost fifty years earlier. Quince is almost forgotten now but the secrets of the house still linger. And as Lara digs deeper into the singer's star-studded career and torrid love life, she begins to suspect that his death was no accident - and that someone is copying the killer.

You can find The Ivy here.

AND you might also enjoy the latest glamorous stand-alone from Tasmina Perry:

Seven Nights in Paris

Zoe and her new husband Mike head to Paris for their honeymoon. But the happiest day of Zoe's life turns sour when her husband vanishes into thin air within hours of arriving at their luxury hotel. At first no one takes Zoe's claims that her husband is missing seriously. The police, the embassy and hotel security all think the groom simply got cold feet and has walked out on their marriage. After all, theirs was a whirlwind romance – perhaps he just had second thoughts. But Zoe can't believe that Mike would just leave her, and as the hours pass, her concerns grow.

Alone in Paris, Zoe turns to the one person she thinks could help – her ex-boyfriend Lucas, a Parisian-based photographer who knows the darker side of the city better than anyone.

Lucas quickly discovers that Zoe doesn't know her new husband as well as she thinks she does and that Mike has a hidden agenda that has put his life in danger.

Set over the course of a week in the City of Lights, Seven Nights in Paris is an exhilarating romantic suspense story about secrets, love and the things we do in the pursuit of money.

You can find Seven Nights in Paris here.

www.tasminaperry.com

About the Author

Tasmina Perry is a million-copy international bestseller.

She is a former lawyer and award-winning journalist. She was editing the UK edition of *InStyle* magazine when her debut novel Daddy's Girls became a *Sunday Times* top ten bestseller. She has since written fifteen novels, been published in twenty-one countries and sold over two million copies worldwide. She lives in London with her husband and son.

Also available from Tasmina Perry:

Daddy's Girls
Gold Diggers
Guilty Pleasures
Original Sin
Kiss Heaven Goodbye
Private Lives
Perfect Strangers
The Proposal
Deep Blue Sea
The Last Kiss Goodbye
The House on Sunset Lake
The Pool House
Friend of the Family
The Singles Table
The Yacht Party

Printed in Great Britain
by Amazon

47307247R00209